A BETTER WAY TO DIE

With love and thanks to Roz Kaveney, Marcus Rowland, John Scalzi, Jared Shurin and Michael Damian Thomas.

The author dedicates this collection to
Mrs. Skipper.

A BETTER WAY TO DIE

THE COLLECTED SHORT STORIES

PAUL CORNELL

NewCon Press
England

First edition, published in the UK August 2015
by NewCon Press

NCP83 Hardback
NCP84 Paperback

10 9 8 7 6 5 4 3 2 1

ISBN: 978-1-907069-83-3 (hardback)
978-1-907069-84-0 (paperback)

Cover art by Ben Baldwin
Cover design by Andy Bigwood

Minimal editorial interference by Ian Whates
Interior layout by Storm Constantine

The Hardback printed in the UK by Berforts Information Press

Contents

Introduction

To begin, Paul Cornell is, possibly, the nicest man in the entire genre of science fiction and fantasy.

And you say, well, come on, now, how difficult is *that?* Science fiction and fantasy is a genre populated with terrible people! Awful people, to the last! Including you, John Scalzi! You are especially irritating!

And you'd not be (entirely) wrong about that.

But even *without* grading on the generous curve that one should employ with science fiction and fantasy authors, regrettable lot that we are, Paul Cornell is, simply, a very nice man.

Let's talk for a minute about what 'nice' means.

'Nice' is often the word you use when you can't be bothered to think of something better to say about something you were indifferent to but not discomfited by. How was lunch? It was nice. Did you see Cynthia's new beau? Well, he seemed nice. The day not too warm, not too cold, and you have yet to be attacked by angry bees? What a nice day!

'Nice' means 'all right," with just a hint -- an undertone, if you will – of being slightly more pleasant than not.

But that's not what I mean when I speak of Paul Cornell, and when I say he's nice.

Here's what I mean, when I say Paul Cornell is nice.

I mean to say that he is gracious, in situations where I know others, including myself, would have given into the temptation to be somewhat less so.

I mean to say that he is kind, in a manner which is unmannered and without the need to call attention to itself.

I mean to say that he is principled, and keeps to his principles, unfashionable as they may occasionally appear to others.

I mean to say that he is warm, not in a striving "we're all lads" way, but in a way that makes you feel like he's genuinely happy that you are in his presence.

And I mean to say he is a decent human being – another word undervalued, isn't it, "decent" – in the way he treats others and in the way that he asks for others to be treated.

That is what is encompassed in the word *'nice,'* as it applies to Paul Cornell. It is not to say Paul is a pushover, or is artificially pleasant, or is incapable of a sharp, absolutely delicious wit. He's not, he's not, and oh my, watch out, you. 'Nice' doesn't mean masking the fact you're human. It means striving to be a good one.

And so, to repeat: Paul Cornell is, possibly, the nicest man in the entire genre of science fiction and fantasy.

All the things that make him nice – the graciousness, and kindness, the principle and warmth and decency, the gestalt of Paul's world view – are part of the fuel for his fiction.

Along with, it must be noted, an imagination that positively delights in the mash-up of the weird and the well-known, the pop culture and edge cases, the universal emotion and the strangeness in the universe. An imagination that skates to the very edge of "likely unhinged" and does a shotgun spin where the ice is especially thin.

It's the two things in balance that makes Paul's stories so readable, so accessible and, yes, so much fun. Paul's imagination takes you out to deep waters (literally in the case of at least one of the stories here), and Paul's empathy – his niceness – lets you know it's okay to dive in and explore.

This is not to say that Paul's *stories* are always safe or can be relied on for a pleasantly happy ending. That's not the case, and anyway it's not nice to write bland stories where everything is comfortable and nothing is ever at risk. It is to say that who Paul is, imagination and niceness both, combine to make him an excellent storyteller. They make him someone you can trust to tell you a tale worth reading.

You have several here in this book. Get to them.

Paul Cornell is possibly the nicest person in the entire genre of science fiction and fantasy. Lucky you, dear reader. Lucky you, indeed.

Yours,
John Scalzi

P.S. to Paul: Dear Paul, I have just told everyone that you are a very nice man. Please do not get caught strangling live kittens on national television, or some other such thing. It will be awkward for us both. Thanks in advance – JS

The Deer Stalker

From the Journal of Dr. John H. Watson:

I write as best I can, in this darkness, illuminated only by a grating to the street. Holmes has disappeared, lost of his own accord. I have done my best to follow his example, if not his person. I could not leave London, but I feel sure that he has. I think I know where he has gone. It is best, at this point, if we are not together.

I sit alone in a wine cellar, the second level of a coal cellar beneath a building which has been sold but into which a tenant has not yet moved. It is the kind of abode found by beggars. But it is a situation that I have mentioned nowhere in my writings, and which therefore I hope may remain unknown to those that seek me.

I hear some of the noises of London life continuing above me and outside. Things are perhaps more quiet than they should be. The inhabitants are wary, hungry for news, aware of the attacks on myself and on my friend, and anticipating another outrage, while understanding the nature of the raids. I am gambling the lives of all those folk that no assault will find me here. None of these buildings could hope to withstand the weapons these bandits have at their command.

Holmes will surprise the pirates. They will not find him, he will find them, as he has done so many times before, and this time he will not fall into their trap. I know his methods. I have faith in them and in him.

I must embark upon my account, fragmentary as it is, for the sake of history. Let others... I pray, let Holmes, if you are reading this, dear friend... make sense of it.

I do not know where it began. But I shall begin it with Mrs. Hudson having her fit.

I had entered 221B to no greeting from Billy or from Holmes' housekeeper, the door being surprisingly open, and had made my way to the kitchen upon hearing a noise.

Holmes had his fingers in Mrs. Hudson's mouth as she thrashed to and fro. His form was pressed up against hers in the corner of the room. She made noises like an animal, and was spitting blood, both his and her own.

I quickly took her from him, and assured him there was no possibility of her swallowing her tongue. I placed her in a more secure posture on the floor in order to check her vital signs.

"It is intolerable," Holmes muttered, absently holding his white, bitten hand. "When she entered this state I had no knowledge of what to do, I could only guess. What good could I have been to her? Tell me, have I even injured her?"

I was about to reply in the negative when a thin sound escaped the lips of the pathetic woman. "They're through," she said. "They are here."

I paid her no heed, taking her words to be the meaningless spasms of the organ of thought in crisis. "I shall send a message to St. Luke's, and I will make sure there is a bed for her at once."

"'They are here.' What can she mean?" asked Holmes, rhetorically, his face still a portrait of compassion. "Nothing for us, but perhaps everything for her."

That, I am sure, was the point. The point where Holmes, and the world, started to be wrong.

The next few days were busy for me, both looking after my own practice, going home to my... no, to one of the poor women that I have, in the course of these narratives, referred to as "my wife" but who the world would doubtless refer to as... I shall use the word and rely on your tact, old friend, as I slowly realised during our acquaintance I must always have relied on it in this matter... 'a dollymop'. Yes, there, it is out. I shall not drag her name into print. I do not wish to make a character out of her. Let them make of that not what they will but what I make of it, which is that I loved her... But I must not divert myself. I also spent time seeing that Mrs. Hudson got the best treatment available to her.

Holmes I saw little of. I assumed, by the cries of the newspaper sellers, that his thoughts would be taken with the latest outrage they described, a new series of murders committed in a style quite similar to those that had baffled the police in the latter months of 1888. At that time, Holmes had kept his distance, thinking in a brown study but never leaping to his feet with the quarry in his sights. I, and others of my profession and acquaintance, convinced the killer was a medical man, or a man of science, awaited such a move most hopefully, but it had never come.

Perhaps it was that these squalid, meaningless murders, were unworthy of Holmes, the creations of pathology rather than the superior intellects he was used to matching wits with. Indeed, this time the killer was being bolder than ever: seen running from the scenes of his crimes, heard laughing, noted by many observers as being dressed like a gentleman. It was as if he had decided to live up to the inflated accounts of himself that were the lifeblood of the penny dreadfuls. And such arrogance in the face of the law would, all thought now, surely lead to arrest sooner or later. It was astonishing that the police had not caught him already, leading me to think that there was perhaps another dimension to this man and his deeds, a dimension that would be a matter for my friend's intellect.

It was with this in mind, eager to discover Holmes' thoughts on this matter, that I returned to his rooms a week or so after Mrs. Hudson's visitation.

My finger was on the bell when something made me turn.

Perhaps there had been a sound. If there was, I cannot recall hearing it.

There was only darkness against darkness in the building overlooking my friend's rooms, on the other side of Baker Street. But by one particular window, the shape of that darkness had changed.

I give myself credit for my actions now. I looked back to the door and pressed the bell, for all the world as if I had only been breathing deep of the late November air. I waited, my senses stirred to a pitch of battle, as Billy opened the door and bade me enter, and even waited a moment as he closed the door behind me.

Then without shedding my coat and hat I ran up the stairs to my friend's room that faced onto the street, ran like the devil was on my heels!

The light of the lamp was on. I could hear Billy crying out behind me.

I burst into the room. "Holmes!" I shouted.

The shot came through the open window. It blew the stuffing out of the pillow that stood atop the hatstand.

I threw myself to the floor and bellowed as Billy opened the door. "Stay there, boy!"

But the boy entered the room, breathing not only from his run but from the emotional faith that my friend inspires in all those who know his methods. "Mr. Holmes' complements, sir," he said. "And could you be joining him on the top floor of the house opposite. The door is open."

I was later to discover that the round that had passed through the window had flattened itself against the hardwood of one of Holmes' bookshelves barely an inch from my ear. And the intuition of that fact followed me down the stairs and into the street. I took a moment to catch my breath before venturing into the second rate townhouse opposite.

I found Holmes standing at the window of what looked like it had once been a library, or a study similar to his own. Beside him lay a rifle of extraordinary construction: it was a slim beast, with sights the memory of which even now confounds me.

"Good Lord, Holmes," I said. "What has happened here? Was I the target, or –?"

"No, Watson. It was I. I had become aware of certain trends within the underworld, a movement of Cubans through the docks, Italians, Bolsheviks... So I contrived a trap, as I did once before. However... somehow our assassin has contrived to elude me. And I am at a loss to explain how."

He listened with interest to my account of being shot at.

"A second assassin, in one of the other houses, while the promise of a first lured me here. The aim from this window covers the street. See, it is impossible to fire successfully through my window from here."

"So I was their target?"

"If you truly were, old friend, I suspect you would be dead. No, this is a feint, a poke in the ribs. And from someone who knows of our history, eh? You have mentioned the incident I referred to in your accounts, have you not?"

I allowed that I had.

Holmes directed me to examine the weapon.

I must confess I flinched at the sudden closeness those extraordinary sights provided. "Holmes, this rifle, I have never seen the like."

"No," said Holmes, his eyes locked on the distance. "Neither have

I."

I stayed with him over the next two days as he paced and thought and looked through endless books, comparing every part of the rifle to his indices of weapons and their manufacture.

"I see its heritage," he said at one point, "in the weapons I observe today. As one who is skilled in such things may look at the weather and say what conditions will be a day or a year hence."

"Holmes, what do you mean?"

"It is a 6.5mm military carbine, probably of Italian manufacture, but I do not know if I may class those inferences as facts, for facts are occurrences, and... come, you will see." He beckoned me over to his microscope, and bade me look into it. I brought into focus a tiny part of the firing mechanism that had been imprinted with a name: Mannlicher –" Carcano, and a date –"

Once more, I leapt back from a sight. "Holmes, this must be a misdirection, a mirage designed to throw off your aim. It makes me think of –""

"Myself also, Watson, but he is dead. And even he could not alter the world to his whim. That date is real." He walked back to the sideboard, and began to stuff his pipe.

That night I stayed with the woman I have previously mentioned. She was a typist, who made a poor living which I was pleased to supplement on an exclusive and voluntary basis.

I felt appropriate guilt, obviously, but in the early hours of that morning it was as if guilt had reared up out of my sleep and found me out.

I was suddenly awake, and a terrible sound was shaking the building from top to bottom, as if a train were passing. I could hear cries from other abodes within. I went to the window. There were lights up in the sky! I crossed myself. My darling was at my side then. I told her to dress, that we would make our way at speed to –" I was about to say to 221B, and hang all decency, or... I do not know, perhaps I was more prudent and said we would find my consulting rooms.

A dark shape was suddenly between me and the light. It moved towards me - Someone was outside! The window shattered.

My narrative breaks here. I do not recall the rifle butt clubbing me to the ground. I was told of it.

I am sure, however, that I heard the struggle and the two shots that made it cease.

Strange hands slapped my face. I called aloud for my darling. I opened my eyes.

I was sitting beside a dark figure. He had the eyes of the devil. With him sat other figures. It took me a moment to realise that I could understand them, and that they knew my name and were speaking to me. They were shouting over the same great noise that I had heard above the building where warmth and love had lived so distantly now.

I turned to find my darling. And saw that we were high above the city. I had never seen the like. I have never ascended in a balloon. The lights! The sombre mass of parliament! The great darkness of the river!

But I had no joy in that sight then. I was out of control, yelling threats and insults. They were telling me she was dead! That they had shot her! The villains, oh the villains!

They had enough of me then. They took me to the back of their craft, opened a door that seemed too small to be a door for men, and threw me inside.

A match was struck, and Holmes was looking at me from a bare wooden bench. He showed small signs of violence on his person.

"Watson, so they have you also! I thought I had tracked them down, but they were prepared for me, they sprang a trap! Imagine that! What is your condition? You must bear up, old fellow, we are attacked!"

It took me a moment to answer him. "I shall bear up with the intent of fighting," I finally whispered, keeping the passion from my voice as best I could.

He must have understood about her, about the loss of her, from everything about me. It is hard to have secrets from such a man, and at that moment I had none from anyone.

"Good fellow," he said gently. "I have had much to observe, perhaps too much, and I have come to some conclusions. They are raiders, a small party, though their arms belie it. They do not come to conquer, but to plunder, and I believe their plunder is, uniquely, us!"

At that point my narrative breaks again, into unconsciousness, and I can only suppose I have my friend to thank that there was not an end to it.

I woke once more inside what I immediately recognized as a military tent. Holmes had opened a bottle of smelling salts under my nose.

"We are somewhere in Surrey," he whispered. "A clearing in the woods near a small town. I should think it is Dorking, I have seen a spire which may well be St. Martin's. There is but one tent, and I have counted four of these pirates, including two ladies, one of whom is a child. But do not be fooled. They are armed to an extent I have never seen."

The ragged group who stood around us parted, as one entered who was obviously their commanding officer. He was thin, with very short dark hair, presented in a stark parting. He stood like a soldier, but any scientist would have declared that his face was that of a criminal. He carried the rifle I had last seen in Holmes' study, the very one, I was certain. Though the weapons his fellows had with them made it look simple.

"Lee Oswald," he said, his voice high and reedy, "you, Mr. Holmes and you, Dr. Watson, I'm your best friend. I'm here to set you free."

I gathered that he did not mean he was going to release us.

Holmes stood to face him. "You imagine you have us at a disadvantage, sir, but perhaps I know rather more about you than you imagine. You have spent some time in Russia. You are happily married to a woman of foreign descent, and were apprenticed to a carpenter."

Oswald laughed. "Close, but not quite right. I guess you've heard something in my accent, which is kind of a mongrel's bark. Got a lot of disappointment in it, while you sound like you own the world. Where you're wrong is, you've seen something about my hands. I just like playing with the skin with my knife a little, just toughening it up. Just the way I am. Doesn't mean anything. Not a lot about me does anymore."

On a handful of occasions I have seen my friend confounded. Rarely have I seen him so lost as he was in that moment.

"Perhaps you would be good enough to inform us of your purpose?"

"As I said, we're here to free you. Like me and the other guys have been freed. That's Vlad over there, the Count, some days he likes us to call him Dracula."

"Dracula is a fictional character, he is not real," said Holmes.

"And these are Calamity Jane and Alice."

So I recognised three of this group. Calamity Jane was the female scout, the hero of Goose Creek Camp, just a few years ago. Here she looked most strange, with blonde ringlets and a cavalry hat. She carried a vast cannon that would have looked obscene in any hands, let alone those of a lady. And little Alice... was this the Alice from the fiction of Lewis Carroll? The mean face and heavy armament of the small child spoke of a vast distance from the quaintness of that work.

"Interesting," said Holmes. "I believe you are not heavily armed delusionals. So what are you?"

"Where's his deer stalker?" Oswald had rudely turned to interrogate the others. "We've got his violin, his pipe, his magnifying glass..." I noted that he counted these objects onto a table from a bag. "Didn't he have it with him when you sprang the trap?"

"He was as you see him now," said Dracula, in an extraordinary accent.

Holmes stared at them. "Are you referring to a hat? I do own one, but of what relevance –?"

"We have a list of what makes you yourself, Mr. Holmes. We're going to need the hat. We've successfully targeted Professor Moriarty, and you should see him now, the big changes now he's been freed..."

"What?" I blurted. "You confirm, I take it, that he lives?"

"Yeah. And what's happened to him, it's so obvious. I didn't realise until I'd caught him with the device. The top hat and the opera cape, that's what did it. It took a struggle to get him into them, but it really paid off."

"Are you seriously suggesting, sir," said Holmes, "that the content of one's character is determined by the hat on one's head? The deer stalker is worn only by someone in the countryside who wishes to go out in the rain."

"You know that expression – never let the facts get in the way of a good story"? Well you just did that, mister. Not your fault. It's the times you live in. The times everybody lived in until I came along. I guess maybe that's why they chose me. To be the guy that does the freeing. The inventors of this little doohickey, I mean. It zaps you, kind of exposes you to all the random stuff out there, frees you, like I said. What comes out the other side... It ain't what you'd call random, you can see a method in the madness, but us guys who got zapped... It's stuff we'd never have thought of for ourselves." He went over to a table and picked up a strange-looking weapon, a bulky silver barrel with sights and a trigger mechanism.

"I got experimented on in jail, right after they faked my death. The Decontextualisation Corps, they called themselves. They looked the part: white coats and pipes, or Germans with fuzzy hair. They didn't tell me much, just that I was going off into some other world. Or rather worlds. That I was going to be cut out of history and made into something bigger, something that would run and run. Now I've always got this rifle with me, yeah, this one here that I used to make you interested, to make you come after us. It always comes back to me. And I'm always kind of skinny, but you should see how the rest changes! Some days I wake up a Commie, some days I'm from outer space, hey, some days I'm even innocent!"

"Good Lord, Holmes," I whispered.

"Hey, I love that! Do that again! That's you all over!" laughed Oswald. "And that part's gonna stay, boy, the big details do. But the rest: one zap with the device and you're anything to anybody. That's my mission. I scout around fiction, zapping people, making them like me: easy to understand, what anyone wants them to be. That's the way my bosses like it, who knows why? Another world to conquer, I guess. I have to pick who I do it to, though. Some of them just won't take. You know, the average man in the street? You can't take the man out of the street, you can't take the street out of the man. But don't worry, Mr. Holmes: you're the centre of this world. Nobody remembers much about this place apart from you. From here, it's you, Watson, Moriarty, and who cares about the rest? We're the lucky ones who get to be all the different versions of ourselves. Every idea of us that anyone's ever come up with. For instance, you'll be stupid while Watson is intelligent –'"

"Watson is intelligent."

"Sure, sometimes that's fashionable. Then it's gone again. Sometimes you'll be queer, because being a bachelor is kind of odd."

Holmes' face was a picture.

"You will meet creatures from space, you will be American, Canadian, German, travel through time to meet Sigmund Freud, be two dogs in costume, robots, cartoons, computer doohickeys come to life. You'll always be kind of eccentric –"

"I am not eccentric!"

"Cut off from this world of yours, I'd say you are. A guy in a deer stalker. That's what people remember. That's why we need it. To zap you properly. I love doing this stuff. The guys here love it too, now I've zapped them and set them free."

"We've come out of the rabbit hole," said Alice.

"Why be vun when you can be two, two, or three, three different people?" laughed the Count, suddenly affable.

"So," summed up Oswald, "we're gonna keep Holmes here until we can get a hold of that hat. Alice, you can go find a milliner tomorrow. But Dr. Watson," he hefted the machine in my direction. "You can join us right now."

I braced myself to move. I swear I would have attacked him, weak as I was. But there came a sudden dislocation of events, as often I have experienced in war. Everything happened at once, that's what writers such as I say at this point. Holmes would point out that that was simply incorrect.

There were shouts, and shots, and explosions, and a sudden ripping noise.

A cavalry sabre through fabric.

A carbine was shoved through the gap and fired.

It missed Oswald, who was already firing, his brigands with him.

A horse burst into the tent, its flanks flaring with blood and flesh as the guns that fired too fast blasted it apart. But on its back was a Dragoon, firing back even as he fell, and behind him was another and another.

I have since learnt that they had left barracks and galloped through the streets of Dorking, forming up through shouted orders and the calls of onlookers in windows. There had been a great charge of them, straight at this encampment in the woods, the moonlight off their sabres matching the stark white lights that Oswald's pirates had erected.

I have heard that eight in ten of them were cut down, by devices launched on the perimeter of the camp.

The tent collapsed, and something caught me on the side of the head once more.

I saw Holmes look at me with concern, his face had an expression of decision on it. And then I saw nothing more.

I woke in the Dragoon barracks.

They had surprised Oswald's men enough to force a swift retreat. Their craft had taken them off, but had not been tracked as well by astonished observers as it had in its flight to Dorking.

I knew I had to leave. I took a train to London, having wired ahead to some friends in the major hospitals. When I got there I received word that what I feared was so, that my darling was indeed gone, the victim of two bullets when she tried to prevent them manhandling me out of the window.

I visited her home and saw what was left. And then I knew not what to do. Holmes, I was sure, had left me to save me. He was Oswald's main quarry. Surely he would attempt to take the brigands somewhere out of the city, where the pursuit would be a contest between them and him and not cost innocent lives?

He might subtly suggest to them a place where he might be found, somewhere featured in my writings, and then turn the tables.

I could not return home, or go to my practice, to places where they would know to find me. I could not stay in the streets I had often described. I was sure, with the inventions they had to hand, that they could find me there too.

So I found my abandoned place of darkness, broke in, and sat to think and, now, to write. And there is where my account fails me, and time catches up with words. I hope that you will read this, old friend. I hope that your place in our world, the necessity of you, will be affirmed by this account, rather than undermined. I fear that I have written of you once again. But I have written of the real Sherlock Holmes, not the chimera that Oswald imagines him to be. I have done my best to make my subjectivity into an object that will survive me. And I have sent it to an audience that I love. I am certain that your battle with these forces will be worthy of you.

I wait to see what, by the grace of God, will save us.

Here the Journal of Dr. John H. Watson ends.

Holmes comes into view in the crosshairs of the sights of the device. He stands looking intently over the grassy knolls of the Great Grimpen Mire, across from the shooter, oblivious.

He wears an Inverness cape and a deer stalker, and in his mouth is clutched a briar pipe. In his hand he holds a magnifying glass.

Perhaps the perfection of the sight is what makes Oswald hesitate. His finger is on the trigger.

He hesitates.

His men are spread out along the route they thought Holmes would have to take. They are all lone gunmen now, the helicopter left back at the hall.

He hears and feels something land in the dip behind him.

He turns, not in time.

Professor Moriarty is upon him, silently, a long medical blade in his hand. He wears his opera cape. His top hat is on his head.

His gleaming eyes and wild grin shove themselves into Oswald's face. One huge, brutishly intelligent hand throws the technology aside. "Thank you," he tells Oswald, "for setting me free."

Oswald sees the blade enter him. There is no pain for such a long moment.

Not until Moriarty's hand jerks it expertly: back and to the left.

The Deer Stalker' came about because I'd got to know the people who ran the BBC Cult website, an attempt by the Corporation to engage with what they then regarded as the interesting but small audience who were open to the fantastic. BBC Cult were closely associated with my Doctor Who animation 'The Scream of the Shalka'. Their Sherlock Holmes season came relatively late in the site's life, five new stories, including entries by Kim Newman and Christopher Fowler, produced in association with BBC 7 (the name at the time of BBC Radio's archive channel), presented online with artwork (in my case by D'Israeli, who I'd worked with on XTNCT for the 2000AD Megazine). They were also read as audio books by Hannah Gordon and Andrew Sachs. My intention was to explore Sherlock Holmes as a useful case study in the fundamental differences between literary creations, no matter how layered over time and real people. I've returned to this character and theme, unconsciously raiding this story quite a lot, it turns out, in the third Shadow Police novel, which I've just delivered to Tor.

Michael Laurits is:
DROWNING

– Please Help!

That was the Lief status update Cal Tech Professor Laurits' 311 friends were startled to see around ten thirty EST one Saturday night last October.

The genial, soft-spoken Laurits, who looked more like a country rock star than the Nobel laureate he was, was a polymath with friends in fields ranging from social engineering to Federal military intelligence. Maybe a third of the 311 of those he kept in touch with via Lief knew vaguely where he was at that moment: on a trimaran in Japan's Inland Sea, attaching biological shepherding systems to whale sharks, part of a vacation project to manage and systemise the Sea's ecology under the auspices of Nagoya Penguin Torii.

None of them knew that at that very second, Michael Laurits, his feet caught in a weighted line, his craft a fiery husk, was already thirty feet underwater, dropping like a stone, with no chance of regaining the surface.

Laurits had joked that he spent far too much time in Lief. "He'd get applications ideas and work them up right in front of us. People doing other things in the same touchspace would start yelling at him to stop waving his hands around," says Ryoumi Nofke, one of Laurits' closest friends on the faculty. Nofke, voluntarily autistic in pursuit of her own thesis on Sub Planck Metaphysics, and with three suspended marriages backed up as a result, perks up only at the mention of Laurits' current situation. "Oh yeah, he's Aut now. People say they're not sure. That he's exactly the same as he was. They're wrong."

Fortunately for Laurits, Nofke's words, like those of any voluntary Aut, are inadmissible in a court of law. Exactly how wrong the people who think that Laurits is still Laurits are, is currently the subject of legal action.

Laurits was inside the cabin of his vessel, the Torii Gate, when he heard 'a thumping sound' from overhead. He reached the deck at the same moment that a rocket propelled grenade, fired from a nearby launch, landed on it. Laurits puts his (possible) survival down to the fact that the grenade bounced, right past him, through the open cabin door.

The explosion sent Laurits flying into the ocean. He landed amongst his equipment, became tangled in the lines, and fell into the depths.

The attacking vessel was a patrol boat associated with the Atheist organisation Ground State Sanity. The Sanists are regarded as terrorists by the Japanese prefectural authorities, and are engaged in what, subject to a UN vote, is likely to be defined as a Minor War with rival Atheist organisation Obvious Caution Sanity. The difference of opinion between the two factions concerns whether or not the undisputed appearance of a divine being would be reason enough to re-think their post theist principles. Ground State say yes. Obvious Caution's point of view, as outlined in their manifesto, is more complex, but boils down to the question being immaterial.

The Torii Gate had ventured into what the Ground State Sanists had decreed were their current personal territorial waters. The Shinto designs on its stern may have been seen as provocation.

I was able to talk, within Lief, ironically enough, to an unidentified but code genuine individual from Ground State. "It's always sad when an individual is 'killed'", she said (inverted commas subject's own), "but it's important to say he's not Damned. He'll be back after the Singularity and doubtless form part of the Academy."

"It's interesting," says Laurits' wife, Amy, the shaking of her hand on her teacup showing exactly where she's put her mental resources in the last six months, "that they don't even seem to note the possibility that the afterlife they claim to be seeking is already here."

Laurits can be thankful that the extreme opinions of my Ground State contact are also unlikely to convince a jury.

Of the many ironies in this case, the greatest is surely that Laurits' own researches in the field of chaos management mean he might have been expected to see this coming. His memes have been successfully applied in weather forecasting, city planning, and mobile war prevention within the Federal Government. "The world," he once said, in the introduction to a book by fellow Nobel Laureate Dally Ah Pascoe, "is fixable. Chaotic systems can be predicted over large scales, exactly as one predicts the large scale results of extra-physical activity under the Planck Length observation limit. In Hampshire hurricanes hardly ever happen. Like consciousness hardly ever happens outside of a vast memory storage system. But, though we still can't begin to imagine how, when you've got enough memory, consciousness can and does happen."

Those words, to coin a phrase, may come back to haunt Laurits.

As he dropped into the darkness, Laurits, involuntarily he insists, started shifting his sight, hearing and skin senses into Lief, as anyone would when playing game or collaborating on a project. "It felt like a reflex, like ducking under cover," he says, "the most natural thing in the world. In reality, I was trying to breathe water, I was facing certain death. In Lief, I didn't have to be aware of that. That was all I had in my head."

"He was always a fatalist," says Amy Laurits. "He was never happy being happy. He always expected that he'd have to pay a price, that something terrible would happen."

Within seconds, a number of his friends had joined Laurits in Lief, and were asking if his status update was literally true. Several of them, all of whom now decline to be named, started yelling that, as per Lief law, if Laurits was in physical jeopardy, he should immediately leave Lief and become conscious.

"They were, in effect, telling me to follow the rules and die," says Laurits.

But one of that crowd had a more constructive plan in mind. He took on board Laurits' garbled package of fastword and understood that he had seconds to act. He took a connector block from the vast memory array at the University of Burma in York and attached it directly to Laurits' Lief page.

If Laurits' life has been saved, it's because he was fortunate enough to befriend one of the few people with the access and imagination to take that action: David Savident of Carbon Futures.

Savident, a neat, conservatively dressed man with the salty turn of phrase of a self-made entrepreneur, had made his fortune through carbon balancing bacteria, then sold on that business and invested heavily in one of the assets his former area of expertise had also caused to bloom: the vast memory tanks that are required to metacalculate chaotic systems.

"Mike was dying," he says, "and there were all these tossers standing around waving their neon arms and talking about ethics. I thought 'bugger that, we've all wondered about this, this is the only chance we're ever going to get for an ethical experiment, let's do it. And save my mate in the process'."

Savident told Laurits to transfer all his sensory processes into the vast array. He was contacting hundreds of his own engineers and pulling them a bigger and bigger work space around Laurits, elbowing out concerned friends in a way which others there that day remember as being rude, 'predatory' as one said, but which Savident insists was all about rushing to help his friend.

Within a minute, Savident had created vast capacity connections which allowed whole transport of processes from the parietal and temporal lobes of Laurits' brain. His aim was to try and move everything that could be defined and isolated: memory; sensory systems; a series of discrete brain state snapshots.

But instead, before Savident could start the terrible task of picking what could be saved from the archive of his friend's mind, desperately hoping to reconstruct something resembling a person from the pieces, if we're to believe Laurits and his many advocates –

The entirity of Michael Laurits made the journey all at once.

"I don't know how I did it," says Laurits. "Lief is hooked into your kinesthetic sense, your central idea of where your body is; that's how it works. It was as simple as moving my hand. I desperately wanted to be in some other place than my body, and then I was suddenly aware that there was such a place, that the... tunnel... was big enough to go down." (Laurits equates this moment with Savident providing a big enough connection and big enough memory space at the other end.) "So I went."

The mystery of that process will surely be a central argument in the forthcoming court action brought by Sona, the owners of Lief.

"We were initially pleased that Lief had been made use of so positively in what looked like a humanitarian act and a scientific breakthrough," says Kay Lorton, a legal spokesperson for the company. "But the more our people looked into it, the more we began to suspect that Mr. Savident hadn't transferred Mr. Laurits' mental state into the memory array, but had simply created a copy. A barely functioning copy, that is, without many of those attributes which we would regard as indicative of self-awareness. Exactly the same as the ghosts that pop up in memory tanks from time to time, and then generally cease to be detectable, or, as some would have it, move into other universes. As Mr. Laurits himself noted in his work, intelligence arises out of sheer memory. The only difference is that this intelligence wishes to interact with the world, because it mistakenly believes itself to be Mr. Laurits."

The reason these matters of philosophy have ended up before a court of law is that Sona are seeking to recover damages from the stress the connection to the memory tank is putting on Lief. They claim that work activity has slowed 32%. Any regular user will tell you that the difference is palpable.

Furthermore, they claim that Savident's action was tantamount to industrial espionage, since he's a major shareholder in rival workspace company Transgress. They seek a legal ruling concerning their stated desire: to erase the Lief page that now represents Michael Laurits, through which he senses and communicates.

"That," says Amy Laurits, "would be murder."

Savident is contesting the legal action, stating that every action he took was allowed under Lief law. Sona had accepted connections to vast memory arrays in the past, without slowing their systems.

"The difference is," says Laurits, "that I'm in here now. Whatever a person is, here I am. I take up some processing space. Sorry."

Savident has employed teams of engineers from Odashu and Google to develop a new interface, hoping to transfer Laurits' complete mental processes, if that's what they are, from Lief to the new workspace. But since nobody knows exactly what happened in the moments when

Laurits willed himself into his familiar escape from reality, replicating the event is proving a difficult task.

Laurits himself is helping with the research. "It's a problem in manipulating chaotic systems," he said. "We have to try and move the package of who I am without understanding or being able to measure or predict what's inside the package."

In a high-profile step to popularise their point of view, Sona has hired time on the cameras mounted on the underside of Federal global warming control mirrors in an effort to find Laurits' body. They seek to prove that Laurits' claim that he still sometimes has hazy sensory input from the cadaver, particularly while asleep, that he is, in effect, one person who can move between two bodies, is nonsense.

The corpse, subject to predation and tidal drift, should lie on the seabed some sixty metres beneath the site of the attack. But so far it hasn't been found.

Laurits' family and friends are convinced that the person they meet several times a day in Lief is Michael. Though a few of them share Nofke's impression that he's been changed somewhat by the transition. But how much of a change would be needed to convince a jury that what Amy Laurits speaks to, holds in her arms, has even, as she deliberately and precisely tells me, made love to, isn't a man, but a copy of one?

Certainly, talking to Laurits feels like talking to a person. He passes the Turing Test. But then, so have many programmes and devices in the last twenty years, including Lief's own personified help systems.

"I continue," he says, showing me some of the art he makes when nobody's visiting, which can't be often, considering the pilgrimages made to him by everyone from the Dalai Lama to the King of Brazil. "I'm the sum of my surroundings, and something else that's still quite mysterious, just as I've always been. I always expected that something terrible would happen, a revenge for all my prosperity and silliness and presumptuousness. And then it did. But then I discovered that even so, it was all going to be okay."

I'm a great fan of editor Jonathan Strahan (one of those people who's been nominated for a Hugo Award so many times people often wrongly assume he's won one), and was delighted to be able to pitch 'Michael Laurits is: DROWNING' at him, in 2009, for the second of his Eclipse series of original anthologies. I'm always interested in what new media does to story, and the way that magazines (specifically Wired) started to stack pieces of journalism at the turn of the century: emotional lead; interesting titbits; hard detail to follow if you were still interested. I'm also fascinated by the grey areas in science and technology, the points where we're obviously missing something, artificial intelligence being one topic about which we're still not sure if we know anything. Part of the original project of science fiction seems to me to have been a faith in scientism. We would go to the moon, then on to Mars, then to the stars, and to doubt that was treachery. I feel much more at home in the New Wave of the 1970s, who stole the toolbox of science fiction and added the spanner of doubt. Said spanner is still left out of a lot of SF toolboxes. Those are defective, and should be returned to the maker.

Global Collider Generation: an Idyll

1:

When he first met Li Clarke Communication, lead writer of the Conceptual Design Report, Jerry Cornelius was standing on the back of an elephant that only took commands in French, using a flamethrower on what had been a Hmong poppy field.

The opiate smoke and the screaming masses had been entertaining him only slightly.

A military helicopter had landed, and out she'd stepped, a joyful smile on her face as she'd descended onto the ashes.

"The Short War for Circumferential Survey Completion is over," she told him. "The Laotians have capitulated, and enthusiastically embraced particle physics."

This was back when the Global Muon Collider was still just an idea that required a ring of clear ground around the world.

Back when it was still possible to think, as the Laotian politburo had, that the conclusions of the Circumferential Survey could be ignored by a country that had declared itself neutral in Cold War 2.

Jerry had switched off the flamethrower and sighed.

He increasingly felt that he was doing wild stuff in the name of things that were not, in themselves, all that wild.

"Our universe may be nothing more than a thin sheet flapping about in a higher multiverse. This kind of idea, if correct, would be akin to the Copernican revolution in our understanding of the cosmos." – Rob Appleby, Accelerator physicist at CERN, Geneva and the Cockcroft Institute, UK.

2:

Forty years later, Li Clarke Communication was posing for the news crews, letting her pride show. She had adopted a heroic worker's pose, in a fabulous silver/grey dress, the design of which illustrated the design of the Global Muon Collider itself. The dress was not a *metaphor* for the GMC, for in the People's Republic, such metaphors were illegal. Rather, it was a lesson about what was inside the four metre wide concrete arc she was pointing at, the characters printed on the fabric clearly indicating it as such.

She was standing on one of the concrete bulwarks that she had ordered set into the seabed, the GMC behind her, the skyscraper lights of the Chilean town of Concepcion shining through the sea mist behind them both. In the time lapse movie of this section being built, those lights had grown higher as Concepcion became a boomtown.

Exactly where her finger was pointing: the last section of the concrete casing was being lowered into place by one of the giant marine cranes that were normally used to construct thermal vent power stations and carbon sinks. The arc of the GMC vanished into the sea mist to the north behind it.

"The twin fabrics of this dress," she said, the microphone implanted in her mouth clearly projecting her words to the media crews in their boats and helicopters, "illustrate the cryostat, the central container of the GMC, inside which run the two beam pipes, each containing a vacuum. Beside these runs the cryoline," she indicated the silver thread down the left of her dress, "the liquid helium distribution system. Here we are looking at –" she'd rehearsed this to sound blind to the double meaning, indicating the arc of the GMC with a nod, "one of the *curves*," she didn't look at the faces of any of the media she could see, through the displays projected onto her eyes. "Where the dipole magnets accelerate the beam. Rather than..." she ran her fingernail down her ribcage, as if absent-mindedly drawing a line in the air, "the straight stretches, where the GMC does not intimately follow the arc of the Earth's surface. That's where we place experiments."

The collision of seemingly accidental metaphor and politics, of science and glamour, would set them talking all over again. She'd carefully arranged what she'd said so that, picked apart, not all the fragments made sense in any one interpretation. Except the purely literal.

Li loved her job. It kept her young. Literally. All the higher ranking Cold Warriors in the People's Republic were now functionally immortal. Because that way the same people would always be in power, the balance between nations would always remain stable, and there would be no actual war or terrorism or rebellion, except when the major powers needed to let off a little steam. That was how her country did it. The others had their own checks and balances against radical change.

She'd often wondered if Cold War 2 had something to do with the discoveries of previous Colliders. They had shown that what were once called particles were actually the varying oscillations of sheets. Each fluttering appeared as a different particle, and these particles *had* to appear not just in the four directions familiar to human beings, but also in others, imperceptible, wrapped up inside what we knew. Gravity, the everyday business of the universe holding itself together, might only be possible because of micromanagement inside that fine, unseen, network.

The notion that we were fundamentally *missing the whole story*, that we *couldn't see everything that was real*, had slowly penetrated the public consciousness.

We were all falling in a void, asking urgent questions.

Hence a search for stability. Hence Cold War 2.

But still, one journalist the other day, had looked at the GMC, going from horizon to horizon, and told her that it proved the world was round.

She lowered her finger, and moved into her next heroic worker pose, spreading her left hand to indicate the bulk of the tube behind her. She was grateful as always that the world media was no longer in the hands of random individuals, but was once again, in its different ways, civilized and part of the body politic. There would be no stupid questions as she was coming to the big climax.

"We are here," she said, "at this important point on the way to GMC First Turn, *because* of Cold War. Cold War is the natural state of mankind. It is the only practical form of global government in which prosperity, scientific advance and human happiness are maximised. Our partners in Cold War do not necessarily share these views: that's the point. Cold War is the only state in which anyone gets anything *done*. It's better for the minds of children, also. Human beings are prey animals, used to being hunted. We have evolved to anticipate death. Better to anticipate a *practical* ending, such as nuclear conflict, that can be easily understood, always imminent, but we all hope never actually arriving, than the many vague and mystical 'ends of all things' that people start to imagine, start to actually *work towards*, in conditions other than Cold War. The creation of the GMC has taken on the resources, and the human urges, that had previously been spent on war. It demonstrates that, in Cold War, opposing ideologies can cooperate to create great things. But this cooperative effort does not mean we should strive to end Cold War, and bring chaos upon ourselves once more. The GMC is not a metaphor for the possibilities of human cooperation. The GMC *defies* metaphor."

She gently lowered her hand, her head turned towards the future, her face expressing the continuing hope she felt in her changeless old heart.

"What is the use of knowing things like protons, electron? this information is utterly use less, half of science is. just made of educated guesses and testable hypothesis, that have been some what proven. Why sit here pondering the origin of the universe? were will it get us? closer to the answer? what is the answer? the satisfaction of knowing? when will it end? what happens happens i guess?........but hey i'm just some kid in 9th grade who wants to become a dentist some day' – Derek D of San Antonio, Readers Comments, news.com.au, September 11th 2008.

3:

Jerry also hadn't aged a day in these forty years. Neither had anyone he knew. Well, not anyone fashionable. It was a bit off-putting. He supposed it was down to some spinoff from pure research, something that had happened to him when he was stoned. But he couldn't pin down what. He felt like a national treasure, sometimes, the Queen Mum of Ladbroke Grove. Certainly, Cold War 2 had put some life back into him. Being alive against such a background seemed to be *his* natural state, whatever people said about the planet.

Maybe that was why he was still angry. Because he was still alive.

He watched Li's speech on a black and white television held in the hands of a Yi pedlar on the street in Kunming, the 'city of Eternal Spring', in the Yunnan province of the People's Republic. The pedlar had a boy in the crowd, demanding monies, ideally Tourist Euros, for the privilege of watching. Even though the real show, the Global Muon Collider itself, ran through the city. Shouting sweaty people doing business, shunting around him in both directions, threatened to overwhelm the sound, making his feet slip on the oily cobbles.

The sheer PR of the GMC effort was something to behold, he thought. Some tiny technological news item of such extreme importance, every day. It was like Apollo all over again. Global politics was once more the conflict between Apollo and Dionysus (which had also been, Jerry remembered, how Stephen Fry had once described *Star Trek*). It had ceased to be, as it had become between the Cold Wars, the conflict between Apollo and Starbucks.

Jerry, more of a Dionysian, was wearing a nice black frock coat, with a Ted collar. Retro, but the right sort of retro. Not the sort of coat that implied he was nostalgic for impossible notions of the future like Artificial Intelligence or Indistinguishable Virtual Reality. Beneath the coat he wore a black blouse that had been his dear old mum's. He was in Kunming on GMC business, working for the Americans. A few minutes ago he'd wandered into the Yuantong Si and shot a monk in the back of the neck with his needle gun. The backlash from that would help... Well, he almost remembered what the CIA man had said.

His thoughts snapped back to the television. Li had just said something incredible. That bit about the GMC defying metaphor. Did she really believe that? The Collider was an attractor for metaphor, a sump for it! Colliders always had been. He'd found himself reading, watching and listening to – separately! – the archive material from when the GMC's ancestor, the Large Hadron Collider, had gone online. Metaphors aplenty. The twin beams of life and death, colliding to produce, err, love, probably. That had been his favourite. Because it was so pitifully camp in the face of something real. Almost none of the authors involved had understood the physics. They'd turned the Collider into what they wanted it to be a symbol of, and written about that instead.

Jerry put a hand to his forehead. He would have to do his best to use metaphor wherever he went. This century was getting him down. He let go of the television, and started shoving his way through the crowd, willing himself to getting around to stuff like hiding out and leaving the area in disguise.

"These theories have been tested to the extent of measuring the distance from the earth to the moon to the precision of a human hair, and are still incomplete."

– Rob Appleby.

4:

Eighteen months later, Li marched through the main hall of Wonderland, in Arica, Colombia. The media followed, as always. They were recording the sights and sounds of the new rainforest that could be seen through the observation walls, water cascading down the transparency, the cries of nature echoing everywhere.

She was enjoying, as always, the ghostly sensations that the huge EM fields here conjured in her brain. It was the closest thing to a numinous experience she could ever expect. And it was one created by science and the people! It felt like that here because of the magnets, forty Tesla Japanese quadropole monsters, the biggest ever manufactured. The sensations would get even more intense when the magnets were cycled up to maximum, after the beams had been injected into the ring.

"This is one of the four places, around the world, where the beams can be focused and made to collide," she said. "These magnets do that. The establishment we call Wonderland was designed to examine the quark gluon plasma that's created when heavy ions, instead of the lighter muons, are collided. That plasma is like the first moments of the Big Bang. It gives us an insight into the moment of creation. It's one of the many other jobs that the Collider will have, besides probing the world of the very small and very energetic."

There was just over a year to go now until the First Turn, when the beam would complete a circuit of the GMC for the first time. "You could say all this began," she said, "in 2015, when resonances in the scattering of W and Z particles in collision at the Large Hadron Collider in Geneva indicated that there was indeed a new level of reality to be glimpsed. That, as had been theorised, those 'fundamental' 'particles' were made of 'smaller' 'particles'." She made all the inverted commas in mid-air, because she knew it looked funny to have someone so serious doing that, and because she enjoyed it.

"Do you think there's any end to that process?" one of the reporters asked. "Or do you think it's like Russian doll inside Russian doll?"

She winced inwardly at the use of the simile. European reporters often put things to her like that deliberately, to see if they'd get a reaction. "We don't know. But the end point is the Planck Length, the pixel of the universe as it's been called... by some Europeans –" which got a laugh – "the length under which measurement, and thus science, is impossible."

The thought of that had lodged in the popular imagination too. It had given the public another mental image: the grainy nature of reality, the possibility that all their experiences were just a... picture. That some pure, ungrained, free-flowing existence beyond their experience was more real.

This was, of course, a feeling humanity had always had, but the quest for the Last Length seemed to confirm it. This new angst wasn't so much salved by Cold War 2 as distracted by it. The prospect of total war, that missiles and germs could one day fall like sparrows, gave people something else to worry about.

"Will we ever get to see that?"

"The GMC takes us five levels of magnitude closer than the LHC did."

"But?"

"But there are still many decimal points to go."

"View Poll Results: *Will the activation of the Large Hadron Collider have terrible terrible consequences?* Yes: 50.00% No: 50.00% Voters: 12. You may not vote on this poll." – **www.geezersphoenix.com**

5:

In that eighteen months, Jerry had fled only as far as Xining, at the edge of the Qinghai-Tibet Plateau. He'd hitched on the supply trains that ran alongside the GMC. Multinational flags were everywhere, including the one bearing a Chinese ideogram best translated as Annoyed Detente Cooperation. That was usually referred to as the Second Force of Progress. The First Force of Progress was Annoyed Detente *Competition.* That ideogram was painted all over the NASA and RKA ships involved in the space race to Mars.

Jerry was annoyed himself, and the Official Heroin in his bloodstream wasn't helping. Oddly. He felt oppressed by the symbols passing by. Huge thermal buffers had been sunk into the ground for miles around, designed to warp and weft under earthquake conditions. They were a carbon sink too, the Long Solving of Global Warming being another one of those ADCOP things, because none of the sides had found a way to weaponise it.

Almost every aspect of life was now about a limited choice of ideologies. As the ice caps had vanished, so politics had frozen again. Maybe because people had gotten a long hard look at the chaos of the alternative.

That was the heart of his problem. He was a freelancer by nature, but couldn't find an employer that wasn't some vast block of cant.

When he got out of China, he decided, he was going to do something about that.

"The last machine we made of this scale was sensitive to the orbit of the moon. Lord knows how sensitive this one will be." – Rob Appleby.

6:

Six months later, and Li was looking at America. She was on the walkway that ran along the top of the tunnel as it passed from the ocean onto the dry land of Nova Scotia. She was in her uniform now, alone, comfortable, checking radiation levels. The sea spray was pleasant on her face. To the west there lay the United States, missing the path of the GMC by just a few miles. The US government had argued and argued about it, in the end only putting in a cursory amount of funding, just enough to say they cared about world peace. Li felt sorry for President Van Lent. As a representative democracy, the USA had to yield to all sorts of conflicting impulses. The trouble was, they had initially thrown their weight behind the notion of a neutrino study project, instead of the GMC. The Super Nu would have run East to West across the continental USA, Route 66 for neutrinos, bringing attention and funds to the flyover states. But that project had collapsed in senatorial wrangling, chiefly because it would have been much more expensive than running the GMC around the world. And perhaps because it looked just a tad selfish.

She was here to supervise the Muon Cooling Experiments at a Canadian laboratory purpose-built on this cold coast. Necessary for the GMC to proceed. Forever causing problems.

She wondered what had happened to Jerry Cornelius. He had been one of her favourite employees. He seemed to take genuine joy in what he did. She'd been fascinated by how old world he was, but that was where their relationship had floundered. He had that British disgust for hope. That 'joy' was always laughing in the face of something.

Every now and then it occurred to her that Collider science was like Marxist synthesis. Clashes between political systems created not just one Revolution, but harmonics, resonances that backed up and went forward across time, creating places of understanding, different Revolutions. And we gradually make our way towards –

What?

Some indefinable truth. What lies underneath everything. Unseeable by any system.

She liked the feeling of *that* joy.

"<!– if the lhc actually destroys the Earth & this page isn't yet updated please email **mike@frantic.org** to receive a full refund –>" – **http://www.hasthelargehadroncolliderdestroyedtheworldyet.com /atom.xml**

7:

It had taken six months, but Jerry had escaped from China. He was now in the middle of nowhere, several hundred miles away from a town called Moron. He was still following the path of the GMC. But this had stopped being an escape route, and started being the focus of a plan.

Mongolian tundra stretched in all directions, the distant bustle of wind broken by the concrete tunnel he walked beside. In some parts of the world it would doubtless have attracted graffiti. Here it was already home to the black moss, the nests of birds, and small animals hiding in the shade.

He was lugging the explosives in a black sack on his back, like some demented Santa. He'd stolen them from one of the construction sites, a dozen miles down the track. He'd attached the first load, with a radio detonator, to the underside of the GMC several miles back. He doubted it would be seen in this empty place. He was hoping to be able to steal some transport before he got to the next bomb attachment point.

Everyone in the world, he thought, was now on one side of the GMC or the other.

Jerry liked to be in-between.

He had no idea why he was doing this.

That was the whole point.

He was just an agent of history. Or against stagnation. Or

something.

"Time for a proton in this accelerator runs seven thousand four hundred and sixty one times slower than it does for the physicists in the control room. No one can intuitively understand that." – Rob Appleby.

8:

Four months later, Li led the grand ambassadors of the great powers off the bus and into the RF building. With just over two months left before First Turn, she was visiting all the major facilities in such company. The drive had been pleasant. The meadows of the 'Warming Islands' of Greenland got more lush with every visit. The building itself was a mile long, surrounding the GMC tunnel. It had grass growing over the roof and birds nesting everywhere. Here were the Radio Frequency cavities that accelerated the beams every time they went around the world.

"Ladies, gentlemen," she said, standing in the great jade hall that shone with polish, "imagine the future." She had to speak up over the low ohm ohm of the klystrons that produced the ever-changing electrical field that pushed the muons along when they passed this point. The locals enjoyed tuning in to the sound on amateur radio sets. There had been music made of it, but Li felt ideologically afraid of that, and hadn't taken pains to hear any. "I can't, because I have no idea what the fruits of pure research might be. But I'd like to hear what you think might result from an inquiry into the nature of the universe."

The Europeans talked philosophy. Someone brought up Kant. The Russians talked about prosperity, about new technology. The Americans decided that the most important thing was the peace process, bringing people together. The Chinese delegation politely stayed silent, assuming that their view should also be hers.

Li listened to all that hope and felt almost ecstatic.

"CALL YOUR SENATOR, YOUR PASTOR, YOUR IMAN, YOUR BISHOP, YOUR PRIEST, EMAIL, CALL , SCREAM , BESEECH THEM TO STOP THIS MONSTER OF CERN. MICHAEL SAVAGE, RUSH LIMBAUGH, SHAWN HANNITY, LARRY KING , MR PRESIDENT, BARAK OBAMA, JOHN MCAIN, OPRA WINFREY, YAHOO, GOOGLE, NEWSPAPERS, CNN, FOX,

CNBC, WHY IS THIS OMNIPITANT THREAT , THIS WORLD ENDING CATASTROPHY NOT TAKING PRESIDENT OVER ALL OTHER NEWS?"

– Comment by Dr. Brown on UniverseToday.com.

9:

In that four months, Jerry had got as far as Siberia. Near the town of Tura, to be precise, in Krasnoyarsk Krai, on the confluence of the Kochechum and Lower Tunguska rivers. Mud and insects and endless trees. The GMC looked good running through all that, with the low sun behind. There was something about it that spoke of Christmas. Or the Soviet Union. Or something. Up ahead stood one of the electronics galleries, a concrete bunker that sprang off from the tunnel.

He decided that now was the best time. He had been looking for something more meaningful, like doing it the moment before First Turn, but that might suggest a point to his actions. The last bomb was only a mile back. The blast would wreck big enough sections of tunnel that it would take months to repair them. Maybe it would change the thinking of the global Cold War 2 community, create ripples that would change the world.

Or maybe not.

Still, he would have made his No Point.

He took the radio detonator from his pocket. He'd hacked into a communications satellite that stood far enough above the distance he'd travelled to rebroadcast his message to all his bombs at once.

No audience. No need for a big moment.

He pressed the detonator.

Nothing happened.

Except that suddenly he heard engines a mile behind him. Coming after him.

Jerry didn't break his stride. He doubled it.

"Every civilization needs its creation myth. This is ours." – Rob Appleby.

10:

Two months later, they met in the Arctic, outside the Samson detector. The detector stood, black, as big as a cathedral, not reflecting the harsh night of the plain of rock. The black moss was the only thing that grew.

The night was clear and the aurora blasted overhead, and you could almost hear the radiation.

Samson was actually a pile of different detectors, containers of gas and liquid Argon, silicon semiconductors for particles to slam into, trackers to see where things went, calorimeters to see how hard. It had to be huge, like its sister at the Antarctic, to catch everything that flew from the collisions, and flew so fast.

Right now it was only looking at cosmic rays, only collecting particles that rained down from above. From vast and distant explosions that had happened across the galaxy, even from outside it, back in time to the start, the fireworks of the unfurling of the saddle-shaped flag that was the universe. Streaking into the atmosphere at random, they regularly produced more energy than the GMC did.

Those particles had such an effect on civilisation, thought Li. A tumour here. A mutation there. They were a force that killed great men and started new waves of evolution, accelerating things no matter which theory of history you followed.

Jerry stood like a burnt black stick against the darkness all around. He glowed with malice, charisma, an ugly grin.

She had come alone to meet him. Although such weapons were trained on this spot that she could have him reduced to wasted carbon with a gesture.

"One week to go now," she said. "Why did you even try to do it, Jerry?"

He nodded at the GMC. "Why did you try to do *this*?"

"Because relativistic particles, when accelerated, find it hard to turn corners."

He grinned. White on black. "You know, I might be on your side next time."

"Stranger things have happened."

"Anything *can* happen. Only it never bloody *does*." He produced his needle gun and brought it up to aim at her head –

Only to find she'd produced her own.

Oh yeah, they were manufactured now. Made in China.

They fired at the same moment.

And for a moment Jerry was sure that the two needles, sparkling in the bright dark night had hit each other, point to point, and that that energy, having nowhere else to go, had forced new particles into being yet again.

But neither of them could be sure where their shots went.

So Li fired again and Jerry fell.

Only a century later, they built the Grand Solar Collider.

It ran in free fall outside the orbit of Neptune, around all the inhabited moons and stations and worlds that then were federated and at another time might be at war, and it shaped lives and gave life, in general, another Holy purpose.

It would take humanity five decimal points closer to the Planck Length.

It would make other discoveries, of which we cannot know from where we are, even here in fiction.

It spoke of where everyone had been, and where everyone would go next.

On the way to something imaginable.

http://www.youtube.com/watch?v=j50ZssEojtM

Mr. Cornelius appears by kind permission of Michael Moorcock, who'd like to indicate that that's the only way he should appear.

Michael Moorcock has discovered, to his annoyance, that many people these days assume his character Jerry Cornelius to be 'open source', free to anyone who wants to use him. That's not the case. Moorcock's only condition when I asked if I could use Jerry was that I should vehemently point that out. Moorcock's Cornelius books blew my mind when I was too young to understand them. I recall sitting in my Dad's insurance office in the 1970s, in the violent little town of Calne in Wiltshire, reading his 'novelisation' of The Great Rock 'n Roll Swindle while surrounded by skinheads, who were presumably there to check their accident cover. Moorcock, for me, is up there with Christopher Priest and Terrance Dicks, the holy trinity of my childhood. As an adult, I felt similarly about Geoff Ryman until he took me for a walk outside an Eastercon, deliberately talking me down from being starstruck, as humble an act as one can imagine. (Then we went on the quiz show Only Connect together with Liz Williams and demonstrated our collective feet of clay.) It was Geoff who asked me to contribute to When it Changed (Comma Press, 2009), an anthology pairing up writers with scientists (mine being Dr. Rob Appleby, a high energy particle physicist). I decided that if I was going to be steering so close to the original project of science-y SF, I wanted Jerry Cornelius and his broken narratives and broken consensus at my side

Secret Identity

Jim Ashton heard the magic explosion. So could all of Mantos. He tried to look surprised. He put down his pint, spun around, looking out across the canal. Pretending he didn't know what that was.

"Look at Lois Lane," said Hugh, sitting beside him. He, typically, hadn't flinched at the noise.

"What?" Jim turned back from the window, annoyed at his grin.

"Is Chris really going to come out of the loo and sit back down here? Come on. It's all right. If anyone can keep a secret, this lot can."

"You reckon? And," he quickly added, "I don't know what you're on about."

Hugh lowered his voice. "Chris is the Manchester Guardian. Everyone knows they're the same bloke."

Jim found himself wearing a sad smile as the sound of another explosion echoed over the water. "Do they?"

The Guardian caught the second of the Top Hat's magic spikes a nanosecond after he'd thrown it, clenched his fist, and dumped the energy into the atomic void in his palm. This magic villain really could do anything: change time and space. The first throw had caught him off guard, spun him round in a whiplash of colours. But now he was closing on his opponent, flashing through the air towards him as their enhanced senses calculated the impact –

He had a second to see the shocked expression on the Top Hat's face –

He was there faster.

His senses were better.

He deflected the bolt intended for his head up into the sky. He wouldn't let it hit Canal Street.

Enough of this! He broke through the Top Hat's magical shields with one punch.

He grabbed the magician by the collar, and slapped the hat off his head.

It went spiralling down into the lights of the bars and restaurants along the canal.

The Top Hat tried to say something, his hands flailing, his expression demanding mercy now he was powerless. He knew where the Guardian would send him. His eyes reflected the moon.

The Guardian grabbed him with both hands and spun three times, until he was at maximum magical velocity –

He released the magician. Straight at the moon.

The Top Hat blazed a sudden bright line into the stratosphere. A reverse meteor. Faster than escape velocity.

He'd hit the lunar surface in about three days.

Without his hat to grant the wishes that gave him his powers, this time it might actually take him a while to escape.

The Guardian glanced down and used his magical vision to find the hat. A group of students had grabbed it, were laughing about it, trying it on. Gay lads from the Uni, a couple of fag hags with them. They'd been queuing outside one of the bars, while watching the battle. As Mancunians had always watched the magic 'hero fights' in their skies, treating them like the weather.

The group of straight sightseers in front of them had also been watching, but now they'd gone back to arguing with the doormen. That bar had a door policy of quizzing people who wanted to get in, trying to enforce gays only.

The Guardian didn't understand how people could be like that.

With a thought and a rainbow blur, he was there.

He took the hat from the kid who was holding it. "Dangerous magic. Would you please let me deal with that, sir?"

"Sure, sorry." The kids were beaming at him. "Bloody hell, it's you!"

"It is!"

"He'll tell you!" one of the girls from the party by the door called out. "We're mates of his!" She gestured over her shoulder at the party of grinning straight lads with her. "Tell him we're all very very gay!"

The kid who'd given the Guardian the hat looked at him with a twinkle in his eye. Go on!

The Guardian turned to Tall Ben, who was the one who stood at the door of this place on busy nights now, asking the embarrassing questions, with a hefty bouncer on either side of him. Ben met his gaze. The Guardian had never liked Ben, even before Ben had licence to not just tell people they weren't gay, but that they weren't gay *enough*.

The Guardian gestured to the girl and her boozed-up mates. "You've humiliated them enough."

"No, mate, I've just started. That lot just want to have a look at what they'll never have. They want to point and laugh."

The Guardian frowned the frown of a man impatient with debate.

Ben's clothes were suddenly ruffled by a blur of air. And there was the concussive noise of the door opening and closing too fast to see –

And the group of kids had vanished inside.

And the Guardian was back, his hands behind his back, whistling nonchalantly.

The kids from the Uni tried to hide that they were laughing.

Ben looked at the bouncers, and they tiredly headed inside to find the straight boys. "Guardian, or should I say Chris Rackham –"

The Guardian found himself taking a step towards the man, provoked despite himself. "I am not –"

"Oh, right, it's different when it's *you* being pointed at. Whatever. You do that again and you're barred. Whatever you're calling yourself." And he let the party from the Uni in, just to show he was on the side of good.

The Guardian stood sizing the man up, feeling lost in a way which didn't suit the costume he wore.

It was then he heard the noise.

The applause his magic hearing had picked up came from the tower of the old Refuge Assurance building.

It was the sound, across the city, of one woman clapping.

"Well done! Bravo!" She had placed her ivory staff to jut out from a ledge on the tower, and was standing on it like a gymnast, one foot in front of the other. She was wearing her long white coat and mask, her form-fitting white costume under it, black hair tumbling down her back. Very red lipstick and nails. Her voice was upper class, unashamed, committed.

The Guardian grasped all this in one magic glance.

And then he was standing in the air in front of her, his arms folded, aware of every car and individual in the street below, every face looking out of every hotel room window. Aware of them in a distant way. Much more aware of her.

"Bravo," she said. "Well handled, there."

The White Candle was a thief who stole art, mostly from gay men's' houses (probably more because of her area of operations than anything else) through magical means. She imagined herself to be doing nothing particularly wrong. The Guardian disagreed. They'd crossed paths three times before. She'd somehow avoided capture every time.

"This is daring," he said. "Even for you."

"I couldn't help but applaud your part in that little confrontation," she said. "I can tell, you see. With my magic gaydar."

"What?"

"Whatever that rainbow costume of yours says... you're one of *us*, darling."

The Guardian raised an eyebrow and stepped forward to confront her.

Jim woke up at the sound of the curtain being pushed back, the familiar slide of the window closing in the spare room. The soft concussion of air that marked the change.

Chris went to the bathroom, then came into the bedroom. He looked thinner than ever. Jim was sure he'd dropped half a stone in the last three weeks. Ever since this nonsense had started. It was all the Mighty Sphinx's fault. If he hadn't come out as really being that tiny librarian, maybe nobody would have started linking Chris, a man with a runner's physique, with the insanely muscled Guardian.

The shape of their face was different, even, because of the muscles. But if you had the thought in your head, and you got a good look... and of course the Guardian would never wear a mask...

Chris was still wearing his suit, because they'd gone for a pint after work, before that bloke with the hat had popped up again. He took off the jacket and plonked it on the hanger, tried to smooth out the creases.

"How did it go?"

"Bang, zoom, to the moon. As bloody usual. I got the hat this time." He held it up, and put it down on the side table.

"That's what people were saying. It sounds like you were hard on Ben."

"Yeah. 'Spose I was. Couldn't help it."

"I see why that place does it. I'd feel the same if a bunch of twats came in and started taking the piss."

"Me too." Chris had finished undressing, and now he got into bed. "I kind of agree with it, even. I was chosen to be the Guardian by the Coven because I'm all about... well, letting people be who they are. But the Guardian takes that right up to eleven. He's very focussed. More –"

"Straightforward."

"Yeah."

"I mean, he doesn't really *do* complexity."

"Right."

Jim let himself lie with his head on Chris' chest, as always. But it didn't feel good now. He wanted to get to the point. "So then what did you do? After Tall Ben? I was kind of thinking you'd be here when I got back." Benefit of the doubt. He wasn't going to be the jealous one. The thought crossed his mind that he was being cruel anyway, that it would have been easier on Chris to yell at him. "Did summat else happen?"

"Kind of."

"What?"

A long silence. Oh God. Jim found himself controlling his breathing. It's just time, just move on through time, get to the tough bit, you're strong enough to deal, you know you are.

"White Candle –"

Jim closed his eyes. "Again."

The Guardian had stepped on to the roof, and moved carefully closer to her. He could smell her perfume. It was trying to intoxicate him, to suggest all kinds of drama and exoticism about her, to mentally take him to the bedroom mirror where she put it on –

He stopped himself. Yes, it was indeed just perfume.

What was wrong with him? He couldn't sense any magic making him look into her face, making him concentrate on her eyes and mouth, making him consider how soft her hair was. Making his eyes glimpse her breasts and the shape of her pelvis.

There was no such magic coming from her. There hadn't been the last time they'd met either.

He knew what was wrong with him.

And it was very wrong.

He knew everything was simple, when you took away the evasions and lies that made life complicated.

But he was not what he was supposed to be.

He felt like punching her into the next building, for making him feel like this.

But that would be wrong too.

"How about you don't run away, for once?" he asked. "How about you really take me on?"

"I could say the same." Her voice was upper class, brittle. He could imagine the noises she'd make. He killed the thought.

And she'd suddenly laughed and thrown herself off the building.

He sped after her.

She danced across the rooftops, throwing glamours and dazzles and feints expertly behind her, some of which he walked through, some of which he had to smash aside, some of which he had to suddenly duck because otherwise they'd have had him.

A clever pattern of harmlessness then punch, varying always, uncertainly deadly.

He ducked ducked ducked, chose a moment when she'd stopping throwing and had to leap, was in mid-air –

And flashed past her.

He pulled the air carpet from under her and heard the fragments of the levitation spell fall singing into the void over Oxford Road.

Crowds were rushing on to the pavement from the Cornerhouse bar and the BBC and the hotels –

He caught her before she hit the ground.

She lay there in the crook of his arm, curled like a pussycat, au unperturbed smile on her big mouth. "If I've done something wrong," she said, "then you should punish me."

And then she kissed him.

And he let her.

"Oh, stop, stop right there!" Jim was sitting up, the quilt pulled defensively around him. "Did she really say that? I mean, that's the sort of thing you like, is it? Or are these your smutty fantasies?"

"Not *mine* –"

"Bollocks! If it's not *you*, how come I recognised you, three years back? That's why we're together, remember, because I saw through your clever disguise of a pair of glasses!"

"But –"

"You're saying *he's* not *you*. Even though he looks just like you in a Charles Atlas Before and After. How come you remember everything he does, then? How come you can do a little bit of detective work as you, and then change into him and –?"

"I don't know! I've got different... opinions to him –"

"If you act different when you're him, maybe that's just 'cos you with muscles knows he can finally get the *girl*, while mild mannered you has to settle for –"

"Because the gays are *so* much less about the body beautiful than girls are!"

"Well tell me then! Tell me how you in a costume and muscles is different to you now, to the extent where it's okay if –"

"I didn't *say* it was *okay!* Even *he* doesn't think it's okay!"

"You don't normally say you and him. Up until now it was all I saved him and I fought that villain!"

"Because I was proud of it up until now!" And that was a bellow.

Jim found himself silent in the face of that.

He didn't want to lose himself by matching that anger. He didn't want to lose... this.

That was why this was so terrible.

But damn it, he needed something. Something to balance this huge gaping harm that, in that calm, laid back voice of his, Chris had just...

"Beer," he said. "Now."

They went into the kitchen and sat down with a beer each and didn't say anything until they'd each thrown it back and got another.

Chris tried again. Carefully. "It's... like some sort of... drug."

"The power, you mean?"

"No. I mean... all the muscles –"

"What? Being macho means you go straight? My own research would seem to indicate –"

"I *mean* maybe there's summat chemical that goes with these *particular* muscles! They're not just my arms pumped up, they... replace my arms. When I change."

"Your eyes are the same. Your teeth and hair are the same. Well, maybe your teeth are straighter. And it seems that's not the only thing."

"They only *look* the same. The eyes can do all the magic stuff. The teeth and hair are *bulletproof.* Until now, I always thought it was the same brain in here, but –"

"Oh, what? You're saying being gay... or not being gay... is a *brain* thing?"

"Well... since *everything* about a person is a 'brain thing' -"

"I mean, not a mind thing, but something to do with the physical... brain! You're saying being gay is about your glands, a pituitary condition! So, you're the same mind, the same bloke, but when that mind is in the Guardian's body, with a healthy pituitary gland, all thoughts of faggotry –"

"I didn't say anything like that!"

"Well, good, because I have never heard anything so homophobic in my life."

"Whether it is or not, it might just be *true*, like."

"Well even if it is, how does this scientific explanation help?"

"This *magical* explanation. If you want science heroes –"

"I want London, I know. I wonder if their queero, queer hero, see what I did there? I wonder if he has these problems? Shall we call the Ravenphone and ask?"

"You said homophobic," said Chris suddenly. "Oh. What if that's deliberate?"

"I'm not past you shagging a woman on the roof of the Arndale Centre, so don't talk like we're into post match analysis now."

"No listen, I change into the Guardian by saying a magic word. We know the spell was created back in the Eighteenth Century. What if whoever started this put in... design limitations?"

"Oh, right. Because good magic is about natural things, noble things, heroic things, and not a bunch of fags like us, and that this is just you reverting to that –"

"Oh don't be..."

"What? My boyfriend tells me that, for the first time in -?"

"Ever. I've never fancied women. I started looking at blokes when I was nine. Everything I do as the Guardian, when I look back on it, feels like a dream I had. In this particular dream, it's like I was... eating something I'd normally hate, like broccoli, only in the dream I'm really enjoying it."

"I don't want to hear about whatever it was you ate. I'm thinking of packing my bags. I really am. Because we can't go on like this, Chris. This hurts too bloody much." He got up and walked around the kitchen a bit. And managed, after a swig of beer and a deep breath, to get to the point. "All right. When you're him... do you still fancy me?"

Chris closed his eyes. A very long silence. To the point where Jim was about to interrupt by thumping him –

"No. No, I don't think he does."

Jim was about to... He didn't know what he was about to do, but Chris got up and stopped him doing it. Put his hands to his face.

"I didn't know that, okay? Not until just that second, when I thought about it. Because in all this time I've only been him for a few minutes here and there, saving people and fighting villains and stuff –"

"And you haven't really had much time for dating?"

'Listen to me! *I* still fancy you! I *love* you –!"

Jim couldn't answer.

"I don't want to do anything to hurt you –"

"Chris, everyone will have seen. And everyone already bloody knows you're him! What happens the next time you become him, and she turns up? Because I suppose you let her go –"

"She slipped out of his... out of my clutches –"

"What happens?"

"Well, he's a very moral person. He doesn't want to see you hurt either. He just... can't be anything he's not. He doesn't do shades of grey."

"So he'll try to be... not faithful, 'cos he doesn't want me, but... celibate..."

"And eventually... he'll fail." There was such quiet loss in his voice as he said it.

"So what you're saying is, you're going to turn into him next time, *knowing* that sooner or later you're going to be unfaithful to me."

Chris was silent. Looking away.

"It's like you... get drunk on a regular basis, and every time you say it's not *me* who's doing this woman, it's not *me* who's driving this car –"

"You're right. You're right!" Chris threw his arms in the air, admitting defeat.

He slumped against the wall and looked out of the window into the night.

Then he looked back at him. And now he'd decided. "Okay. So I'll stop."

"What? "

"I'll stop being him. I'll pass the magic word onto someone else."

Jim felt suddenly more loved than he'd ever been in his life. And more guilty. At the same time. He rubbed his fist into his brow. "You'd really do that?"

"Yeah." And the look on his face said he meant it.

"Okay. Great. Do that."

Chris nodded, started moving, decisive as always. "I'll call the Coven, tell them to get the ceremony ready and start searching for someone worthy —"

Jim grabbed his arm. "Don't."

They sat back down together, looking at each other, silent.

"I love you," Chris said again. Meaning that he really would do this.

"And I love you." They snogged for a bit. Found great relief in holding each other, knowing they were going to stay together. "But Chris, are you sure about this? It's not just us, is it? You're very good at being the Manchester Guardian. Any new guy... It'd take him ages to get it together. It took you ages, didn't it? And in the meantime, who knows what'd happen? Who knows who'd come after Canal Street? Especially with all this publicity. It'd be a hell of a risk for you to do this now."

"None of that is more important than me and you. And besides, what choice do we have?"

Jim didn't know.

They went back to Canal Street the next night. Putting on a brave front.

It wasn't quite like that Welsh village where they'd flounced through the door of a pub and then, under the influence of a lounge bar of stares, marched to the bar like navvies.

But it was close.

Everyone was looking at Chris. Betrayed.

Jim wanted to say to them that the very same night their representative hero had been with a woman, he'd also saved the whole street from a villain who'd never cared what damage he did to the people and property who suffered in his endless vendetta against Chris.

And it wasn't as if this lot had unreservedly loved the Guardian lately, was it?

They went into Mantos. Jim thought for a moment that the barman wasn't going to serve them, but he finally did. So this was what it had come down to, feeling that old nervousness about whether or not people were looking, in one of their own bars, in their own street.

They found Hugh and sat with him. After a moment of awkwardness, offset by the sheer theatricality of how he played that awkwardness, he let them. "So," he said, "Chris. How *was* last night?"

"The Guardian," Jim found himself suddenly saying, "never *said* he was gay. He looks like he is, with all the rainbow flag stuff, but he never said it. Isn't it enough that he protects our lot?" He raised his voice, so that everyone looking could hear. "What, were any of you lot hoping to shag him?"

He would have gone on. But Chris put his hand on his and stopped him with a look.

He might have said something else anyway –

But from outside there came the sound of magic power crackling through the air.

Chris looked like he might make an effort and stay put.

But Jim gave him a shove. Go on.

Chris didn't bother with trying to be stealthy this time. He just got up, without a look at anyone else in the bar, and headed out the door.

Jim could feel people leaning over, craning to look out the door, hoping to see the change.

"Don't wait up for him, like," someone said.

Jim closed his eyes and felt pride rather than pain. He was making a sacrifice. And he absolutely knew that Chris was too.

Chris walked out to the water's edge, aware of everyone on Canal Street looking at him. Waiting to see if he was going to change. And probably then shag a woman immediately.

He looked up into the air, and there he was. Jumping Jack. He was stepping from sparkling magic disc to sparkling magic disc, throwing lightning randomly down into the streets, calling the Guardian out.

Not the murderous sort, this one. The fun kind of magic villain that Mancunians most enjoyed. His lightning just gave you a bit of a jolt.

Lives were not at stake. Not this time.

He didn't have to change if he didn't want to.

But where would he draw the line? He'd vowed to meet every

threat to this little community, vowed to stop every single affront, nasty or sporting equally, as the Guardian.

The Guardian would do his absolute best to not be seduced. He'd probably succeed, now he'd realised his true nature and wasn't being taken by surprise by a secret shame. That innocence of his was shored up now, prepared.

But that meant that his other half shouldn't be his whole self. That he should deny an aspect of what he was. And wasn't that what he was all about defending?

Chris kept watching Jumping Jack as his silhouette sailed past the moon.

And then an intense expression came over his face.

And he started to run in the direction of the house he shared with Jim.

That night, all of Canal Street looked up from their pints to hear a very solid impact of magic villain with water, and a subsequent yelling as magic lightning shorted out in contact with said water. And lots of huffing and puffing as said magic villain was dragged up onto the side of the canal and sent packing.

And then there was a long wait after the battle was obviously over, and Jim Ashton felt everyone looking at him, with pity and contempt.

Across the city, a pair of handcuffs closed onto the wrists of a surprised White Candle, who'd been only just about to leave her own bedroom window. "I can get out of these in seconds," she said, "unless you don't want me to."

"I *don't* want you to," said the Guardian, gently landing her on the pavement in front of a waiting van from the Manchester Constabulary's Magic Division, "and so you'll find, those being solid silver, that you can't."

"That was almost a joke. That's unlike you."

"Well, making jokes is one of the things I'm looking forward to doing a little more."

She tutted at him as she stepped into the van, like she was stepping into a limo. "And I thought we'd shared something important!"

"We did," he said. "Which gave me intimate knowledge of you. Enough to follow your perfume home." He took her aside from the police officer in the back of the van for a moment. "Once you've served your time, hey, I'd really like to take you out to dinner."

She looked boggled at him.

He gave her a wink and hopped out of the van.

He watched it drive away with slight regret in his new heart.

Late that night, Chris Rackham showed up at the door of that bar down the street that had Tall Ben standing there judging people.

"Astonishingly brave of you to even try," he said. "But no. Of course not. We all know about your alter ego."

Jim arrived and joined him. They stood there, holding hands. Together.

"It doesn't matter," said Ben. "What matters is what you're *really* like, Chris. When you're not lying to us."

The Guardian landed beside them.

Tall Ben looked between them. "Oh very clever," he said. "Magic trick, is it?"

"It's the truth," said Chris. "And we're going to go in now." And he led Jim into the bar.

Tall Ben considered for a moment and then didn't stop them. "Well then," he said to the Guardian. "Do you want in and all?"

"No," said the magic hero. "I came to let you know you can still call on me for help. I'm straight. But I'm still the protector of this area, and everyone in it."

Ben sized him up for a moment, and then nodded. "I 'spose it'll have to do."

The Guardian raised an eyebrow at him. And flew off into the night.

"What's the Guardian going to *do* all day?" said Jim, when they got home.

"Explore space, he says." Chris took the top hat from the kitchen table, where he'd left it after using it the other night, and hid the hat in the bottom of the wardrobe. "And get a girlfriend, I should think. He's all excited. He says it's like being alive for the first time. He says he always wanted not to change back, but thought it'd be oppressing me to even ask."

"Won't the Top Hat be able to reverse the spell, if he ever gets back from the moon?"

"I 'spose that'll be summat else for him and the Guardian to fight about. And if he puts us back together, I'll just beat him again and use the hat to split us apart again."

Jim brushed his teeth and got into bed, and relaxed, properly relaxed, for the first time in ages, as Chris lay against him. "And you aren't going to resent me for this?" he said. "Long term, I mean. Not being able to fly anymore and that?"

"It was always like a dream," said Chris, pulling him into an embrace. "And we all get to fly in our dreams. This way I get to be myself, all the time."

And from outside they heard the sound of magic explosions.

And they smiled.

Russell T. Davies, one of several mentors I owe so much to, once showed me around Canal Street, Manchester's gay quarter. It's really more of a sixteenth, but a lot of culture can be packed into a handful of buildings. I lived in Manchester at some of the most extreme times of my life, when it was the city of glamourous violence. I still love it, and think it's a much more obvious place for super heroics than London. Lou Anders is someone I've known since he was pitching ideas to Star Trek: Voyager and wanted us to work together to bring back Doctor Who. He's since done everything in the prose business from Hugo-winning editor to bestselling author. He remains splendidly enthusiastic and a dead ringer for the original Hood from Thunderbirds. When he asked me to write a super hero story for his anthology Masked (Gallery, 2010), my thoughts went to the original Captain Marvel, a character who transformed between a civilian life as a small boy and an adult super hero form, with, seemingly, an adult mind. (Alan Moore found the logic behind this in his Marvelman comics.) I wondered if a transforming hero might feel differently about all sorts of things in his two incarnations and if nature or nurture might play a part in that, and my thoughts turned to how apt it would be to see someone flying over Canal Street.

The Occurrence at Slocombe Priory

It was in the year 19– that Prof. Regulus took it upon himself to visit certain relatives he had in the country, mostly for the purpose of impressing upon them his new credentials as occupant of the Sebun Chair at Keble. They had taken to sending him chatty postcards, and on the arrival of each one he would turn to his companions at high table and remark that said relatives seemed entirely unaware of the sort of man they were addressing.

So it was with a certain energy that, upon the going down of his students (and if there was anything Regulus liked it was his students going down, though from the air of his fellow academics whenever he expressed that opinion, it was either not one widely shared or he was somehow missing something), Regulus journeyed that summer to the county of S–. He spent time in the bookshops of W– before he caught his connection, and selected several volumes, bought mostly for their bindings, the value of which was clearly quite unknown to the bookshop owners in question.

Unfortunately, when he arrived at the station in C– S–, he found no transport to meet him.

"Why, that is typical," he thought. "Still, it is only two miles. And it is a splendid summer day" (for it was, at that point). "I shall walk."

Regulus set off. But after a while he became convinced that he had already walked more than the two miles anticipated. The fields went on, empty. He was looked down upon by distant hills. The road went on. And there had been no traffic. Which began to strike him as odd.

So it was with some relief, and a jolt of annoyance at his own silliness for starting to worry when before there had been only an open road and a lovely day, that Regulus found a colourful conveyance coming up behind him. Why, it was some sort of van! Now, what was done in these circumstances? He remembered, and stuck out his thumb, for just a moment, before he realised how vulgar and pleading he looked, and turned the movement into an awkward sort of motion, half wave, half declamatory gesture, as though he were indicating to the van the beauty of the countryside beyond.

Thankfully, the vehicle came to a halt anyway. It really was most oddly decorated, with swirls of colour as might be painted by someone suffering an opiate vision. There was an insignia on the side, perhaps that of a company of players.

"'Mystery Machine'," read Regulus. Well! *Ad augusta per angusta!* And *absit omen* for that matter!

A youth looked out from the van. He might have been taken for a solid sort of the kind who won Blues, but for a cravat that gave him an altogether more worrying air. But his greeting was pleasant enough, and Regulus consented to his offer of transport.

Inside the van as it pulled away, Regulus was confronted with a young lady who was attired entirely inappropriately for anything of which a confirmed bachelor might conceive. He looked the other way, only to find himself seated beside another such. But this one at least was not so troubling, dressed as she was for far colder weather.

Regulus cautiously observed her vast socks and enormous pullover and asked if she was being taken for a hike. The young lady replied that she wasn't sure she'd heard him correctly, and expressed considerable relief when he repeated himself. She introduced herself as V– and her companions as D– and F–.

There came a sound from the rear of the vehicle, and Regulus was startled once again, this time at the sight of what he assumed to be a vagrant, dressed in a long smock of a light green colour. The man was introduced only as S–, a description with which Regulus could only concur. With him sat the most enormous dog the startled academician had ever seen. What could it be? Perhaps a Great Dane? No, for surely no such creature ever had such extraordinary features! S– opined that Regulus looked as if he had seen a ghost, at which the dog went into frightful conniptions, grabbing hold of his master and making noises both terrified and terrifying, until the peasant calmed the beast with some sort of foodstuff taken from a small and dirty bag.

Regulus turned quickly to face the front, and hoped they would reach the address he had given with all due dispatch.

However, it was not to be. After scarcely ten minutes' progress, the van's engine began to make peculiar noises, and F–, at the wheel, announced that some sort of problem with the mechanism had manifested.

They came to a halt in front of a building that, while having some features of architectural interest, offered a forbidding aspect. Rooks flew unseasonably from high windows, which gazed down long and cold. And could it be that it was getting dark already? A sign named the place as Slocombe Priory. Which, the travellers opined, as they left their vehicle, was the strangest name for an old dark house that they had ever heard.

Regulus felt that perhaps the best course of action would be to hasten away, but at that very moment, the door of the structure opened, and two shadowy figures could be apprehended within.

The dog very nearly repeated its earlier performance, but D–, her hands imperiously on her hips, called to the figures, asking if perhaps they could offer shelter and succour until aid arrived in the morning.

And so it was to be.

The two inhabitants of Slocombe Priory turned out to be very different in character. One of them, a Mr. Ambrose Angel, was surely the most agreeable, affable chap Regulus had ever encountered. His pleasant countenance and courtly manner immediately made the Professor and his new travelling companions, if they could be described as such, feel welcome. Which came as a great relief.

His assistant as caretaker, however, a Mr. Sidney Snarley, was as curt and rude as his superior was kind, and made no secret of his desire that no strangers should stay under this roof this evening. His wishes were, thankfully, ignored.

And yet, as Regulus took his bags into the house which loomed so massively over him, he wondered if perhaps he *was* thankful.

An hour or so later, Regulus locked the door of a piquant yet dilapidated little bedroom that had several features of interest, and attempted to sleep.

And he might have. Had he not been disturbed by certain noises.

Why, they were natural sounds, surely? They must be coming from the direction of what could only be the kitchen.

Regulus could have stayed in his bed. But he was an historian, an academic, and he had been born in the county of Y–, and now his loins were girded by rest and hospitality he felt himself the equal of whatever task might be before him. He was not one to be frightened by trifles! He went to the door and listened.

Yes, there it was again!

He took a breath, unlocked his door, and left his room.

He followed the sounds to the kitchen. Yes, there was definitely something happening within. Lights and noise came from under the door, a thunderous noise, impossible, as if plates and cooking utensils were being thrown around by some tremendous storm!

Even now, Regulus paused. Even now he could have retreated from that threshold. But finally he shook his head. He could not walk away now. He could open this door. Yes, what was he, a child, some don of Cambridge? He must see!

He flung open the door.

In later years, Regulus would only rarely speak of what he saw in that kitchen. The details remained consistent across his accounts. The enormous dog and his emaciated peasant master were the only inhabitants of the room. They both had their mouths open in the attitude of one who is eager to consume food.

But the mouths!

The sheer gaping vastness of those orifices! The impossible proportions of the spread they had set before them! The posture, like that of some huge tropical snake poised to strike!

Not just that of the dog, but also of his master.

Regulus slammed the door and, before his senses deserted him, he ran.

He ran and ran, until he was sure he could hear absurd music in his ears, that he was running past the same small section of wall, over and over!

He finally fell. He sought solace in the reality of the wall. But what was this? Had his senses deserted him, or was the part of the wall he was resting on of a slightly different colour –?

The wall gave behind him!

He found himself spinning, as if on a carousel, once, twice, and then into a different corridor!

He looked left and right, but could find no relief in any direction, so once more he ran.

In his panic, he managed to stumble half way up the main flight of stairs, which were not without architectural interest, but his attention was not upon their construction now, for his feet were all at once slipping beneath him, indeed, as, faster and faster, he tried to regain his footing, faster and faster the loose carpet flew past under them!

And coming at him thus, down the stairs, was a figure! A figure as startled and stumbling as himself!

The carpet at last exhausted itself, and at the same moment the figure loomed right straight before him!

Regulus fell, and as he fell, he grabbed, wildly, he grabbed –!

He did not want to know what he grabbed, what the looming figure might be was all the same to him, for he could still see the mouths, the jaws!

But oh, what was this?

Helping Regulus to his feet was but a man, a man in some sort of strange costume, as might be the thing at an undergraduate hop. The costume had been complete with a man, which the man had been wearing, until Regulus' desperately gripping fingers had pulled it from him.

And beneath it, oh blessed relief, thanks upon thanks, it was the beneficent Mr. Angel!

"Ah," said Angel. And then, "Why, Regulus, you look as if you have seen a –"

"Do not say it," said Regulus.

He inquired urgently of the man as to whether, despite all that had earlier been said and the arrangements made, he might be away that same night, before he had further sight of... he did not describe what he had seen... his fellow guests.

To his surprise, Angel readily agreed, and, having changed with surprising speed, back into his usual attire, drove the Professor to his final address, where his country friends were surprised to see him, and not at all offended to be woken in the middle of the night. They had missed him at the station, and were sorry.

Regulus realised, after he had waved a rather too hearty goodnight to his previous host, that he had not thought to ask his saviour about his strange attire, or to mention the inadequate manner in which he had secured his stair carpet, nor the features of (frankly too much) architectural interest which chequered his home.

When the man had shaken his hand on the step, he had offered a strange thanks, that because of Regulus he might now have a chance of 'getting away' with designs of which Regulus had no knowledge. He expressed opinions concerning the young people and the monsters they brought with them with which Regulus could only concur. 'Meddling', to be sure, was the least that could be said of them!

He asked Regulus never to return to Slocombe Priory. And Regulus heartily agreed.

He took to his bed in the home of his country friends, in a small room neatly arrayed with a simple eiderdown, and decided, on the edge of sleep, to pass the whole thing off as him having been, for perhaps the first time in his life, in the midst of something which would probably continue adequately without his participation. A thing, in fact, which might have happened many times before, and would happen many times again.

And with that, he slept.

But in his later years, Regulus never would walk a road alone. He was never the first to set foot within a kitchen. And he was never seen to consume a sandwich.

I'm a huge fan of M.R. James, down to his tics and habits and archness. I think you can feel the smile in his work, even (or especially) at its most chilling. This is, after all, the man who wrote one of his most frightening stories to be read aloud at a Boy Scout Jamboree. I'm glad StarShip Sofa Stories, vol 3 (StarShip Sofa, 2011) picked this story up, after it was turned down by a well known editor who'd never seen... the other thing this pastiches, and so took it all entirely seriously.

The Sensible Folly

Faringdon didn't have many other follies nearby that it could talk to.

There had always been Carfax Conduit over at Radley, but all that ornate thing ever went on about was how much it missed being in Oxford, where it had once stood, supplying water to the city. Being *useful*, it said.

At the time, Faringdon had found the notion of a folly that wanted to be useful a bit silly. The whole point of follies, Faringdon had been told from its earliest days, was not to have a point. That was something the other follies were very stern about. But it had put up with Carfax Conduit's tutting, because at least it was conversation, and because Faringdon had also been raised to be a kind folly.

Faringdon had only been around since 1935. Which sounds a long time to us little temporary things, but to the older landscape features it was as if Faringdon had appeared just a moment ago. Faringdon was the last folly to be built in Britain, and from the moment the ribbon had been cut and little temporary things had started to walk around inside it, the other follies had made sure it knew that. The Lansdowne Monument, on the Cherhill Downs, for instance, had been forever telling Faringdon important things it didn't need to know, such as how to make the right creaks and groans to get the little temporary things to start fixing one's cracks. It wasn't even as if Lansdowne itself was that old: its ribbon had only been cut in 1845. Lansdowne said that it might once have had a point, but had taken care to forget it almost immediately. Faringdon thought then that all that was probably why it went on so much, because the other follies had provided just such unwanted advice when it started out, and now it wanted to do so too. Barrington Park insisted that it was a Gothick Temple, which, it said proudly, was nothing real at all, and was only from the 18th Century. Siddington Round Tower was actually Victorian, but looked and acted Medieval, and boasted never to have had a useful thought in its life.

The newer features of interest nearby, beneath the notice of most follies, hadn't been much more exciting as potential friends. To the north stood a great chimney, Smokey Joe, which didn't often say anything, but would sometimes make long, rumbling sighs. The cooling towers of Didcot power station whispered only to each other, still not quite at home in the landscape, glad they hadn't come here alone. The phone towers at Wooton Under Edge and Stockenchurch, the TV mast at Beckley, and the radio tower at Sparsholt Downs sang all the time, millions of precise operatic doodles, songs of the little temporary things, the sheer amount of which made Faringdon give up listening. And the wind turbines to the west panted with their effort: wup wup wup.

But there had always been one thing in the Vale of the White Horse that made everything else feel young. So much so that the landscape was named after it. The White Horse at Uffington only woke occasionally. The last time had been when the wind turbines had just started their panting, and it had blinked awake to the new noise, its wild lines suddenly, like lightning, at the centre of what every folly and feature heard and thought. It had spoken serious words then, about how the chasms it lay beside were a sign of how everything changed, at the pace of the thoughts of a landscape, beyond the thinking of the little temporary things. About how the vale had once been under ice, and could be so again. About how the world needed saving.

And then it had gone back to sleep, and the little temporary things hadn't heard or noticed, and the follies had considered for a time, and then talked on.

The little temporary things that took to the sky, that made lines up there far too quickly, used Smokey Joe as a landmark and whizzed around it, in a way that had made Faringdon ache with wishing. Because, ever since it had been created, there had been something that Faringdon had missed. Faringdon had water underneath it, a great reservoir, and it liked the feel of that. And it had earth, of course, the hill it had been placed on top of, because the little temporary things thought such hills needed follies. And it had fire, every year, as the little temporary things built bonfires and splashed coloured light everywhere, and the tiniest ones stood around Faringdon's feet, waving fire in their hands. Which Faringdon liked very much.

But what it didn't have, back then, what it missed, was air.

Faringdon was almost concealed by trees. It could not be seen from a long distance as other follies were. It had not been able to look out over a landscape and have that landscape say hello, as thousands of the little temporary things looked up at it.

Sometimes Faringdon had felt hidden. Shunned. As if it had done something wrong.

It had never believed that this was what its creator had intended. Follies found the little temporary things hard to understand as a rule, but they felt different about the ones who had cut their ribbons and brought them into the world. Faringdon's creator had been special even by those standards, as Faringdon had come to realise from how other follies talked about those that had built them. Even the creator's friends had been different enough for any folly to notice. The creator's visitors had included one with a huge moustache, who'd said he wanted to paint Faringdon, but never had. He had once called out to Faringdon to watch him, which had startled Faringdon, as the little temporary things tended not to talk to landscape features. So much so that when it does happen, a folly immediately pays attention to whatever little temporary thing has seen fit to say. The one with the moustache, it turned out, standing as he was in the little town at the foot of the hill, wanted Faringdon as an audience. He'd put on a huge brass helmet, and had marched across the market place of the little town, in a diving suit, with enormous weights on his feet, making motions like he was pushing his way through water. It was brilliantly *pointless*. Faringdon remembered that guest of his creator as if he'd been a folly himself. *He* hadn't been little or temporary.

In its memories, Faringdon could still see the creator himself, in his long coat with a dove he'd dyed pink sitting on his left shoulder, at the moment of the folly's creation, grinning as the ribbon fell away, the big gold scissors in his hands. He'd said some words to a small crowd, and then had hugged Faringdon, and whispered that he was sorry about the saplings all around, that would soon become trees and cut off the folly from the sky. He had had to compromise, he said. Faringdon could tell from his voice that he'd hated to do that. Perhaps that was why Faringdon was the last of its kind. Because as more and more of the little temporary things filled up their world, they had to make more and more compromises. Especially, if the white horse was to be believed, if they all might have less room in the future.

After the trees had grown, Faringdon had still just about been able to see over the tops of them. And, having consulted with those who'd made follies of old, the creator had left four clear avenues, so it could see the horizon. If it hadn't been able to, the folly might well have gone mad, like the ruins whose frightening cries could be heard across the Vale at night. The trouble, always the trouble, had been that there was something between it and the bulk of the sky. That it had felt as if there wasn't the connection here that there should have been.

Then, one year, at the time when the world swung into more darkness than light, one of the little temporary things had started to do something new inside Faringdon's tower. He brought that temporary form of earth called glass, and the part of earth called metal, and the fire called electricity. He put his hands together inside Faringdon. And a moment later –

An expression of light had shot out of Faringdon, reaching out towards the horizon. And just as Faringdon was feeling the first slow yell of delight, the light turned, and reached out in another direction, and another, and another.

Faringdon had exulted in the darkness. For the first time, it was talking to the landscape! And the landscape was talking back, it could feel it: all the little temporary things moving along their lines on the ground, seeing the light ahead and thinking they were coming home, or missing home, or wondering.

But Faringdon, having been so excited, had despaired when the world had swung again, and the little temporary thing had moved his hands apart, and the connection stopped. But a folly moment later, as the world swung back, there he was again, and he'd brought a new light, a different one! And then that was good for a while and then gone for a while.

It had kept happening. Every time there was more dark than light, Faringdon would gain a light inside, and speak across the Vale.

At first, this had made Faringdon proud of being new. Now it could talk to its landscape better than anything older could.

But soon the folly had realised that the light made the older follies even less likely to respect it. Faringdon now had even more *newness* about it. There was, Lansdowne said, something rather too flashy about it. When Faringdon had protested, the others had taken this as proof that Faringdon had now become less than a folly. Obviously the little temporary things needed the light for something. Faringdon had stopped being pointless and become a mere *building*, something there for the *use* of the little temporary things. Barrington became a little terse with it. Siddington stopped speaking to it entirely.

Faringdon had regretted then that it had ever thought of Carfax Conduit as silly, and had made sure to talk more with it. They both needed the company.

So the next time the little temporary thing with the earth and fire came to see it, Faringdon wasn't looking forward to having the light again. Now the light would make it feel different and vulnerable.

The man had put his earth and fire together as always, but then, after his work was done but before he made the light shine out, he'd sat down, and he actually *spoke* to Faringdon. The first little temporary thing to do so since the time of the creator. He'd said to Faringdon that it was now a member of something called the General Lighthouse Authority. Faringdon had wanted to ask what a lighthouse was, but while it was allowed for the little temporary things, on the rare occasions when they did, to speak to follies, it was unheard of for follies to speak back. But still, the little temporary thing answered the question without being prompted. He said that lighthouses were useful buildings that stood by water and warned little temporary things of harm.

Faringdon had despaired again at those words. A *building! Useful!*

But then it had heard, in the way it did, with words carried by association, rather than by sound, strange calls in the distance. It had started to hear them more clearly: strong, confident hails from all around the horizon. From far away. From those with sideways beams of light that reached out the same way its own did. It could see them, in imagination, the imagination of a folly, which could reach out to encompass the whole country like a map.

It had realised: these must be the voices of lighthouses.

And they were welcoming Faringdon to their number. But there was something else. They sounded friendly. But Faringdon had suddenly realised... they were laughing.

'You're useless as a lighthouse, of course,' the little temporary thing had said then, with a smile on his face. 'So it's all completely pointless. But it's great fun. It's what a folly's for, really.'

And with that he'd made the light happen again. So Faringdon could start to laugh excitedly back to his new friends.

After that, Faringdon never again felt as if it had done something wrong. And it also stopped feeling that being so young was a bad thing. From its new friends near water, it learned many things about how much space and time the little temporary things had left in their world, and so it encouraged the wind turbines in their work. And that made it realise that, though it had been looked down on for being a building, it wasn't looking down on buildings now. Not Carfax Conduit, or the wind turbines going wup wup wup, or even Siddington Round Tower, which was actually, though it tried to deny it, being made into a house. Faringdon Folly was earth connected to the air, and it was young and old at once.

But above all, it was content that it was meaningfully pointless.

Which, it thought, would have made its creator, and the man with the moustache, proud.

My wife and I spent many happy years in Faringdon in Oxfordshire. It's a small town with a big arty heart, a hub of music, a breeding ground for new bands. It also boasts the last folly built in Britain, a tower on a hill commissioned by the 14th Lord Berners (1883-1950). An eccentric himself, his Lordship was once, the story goes, visited by Salvador Dali, who walked across Faringdon Market Place in full deep sea diving armour. (The details of this story seem to have vanished from the internet. If anyone knows on what day that happened, please let me know, so it can be commemorated annually.) In 2011 I was asked by the Folly Tower Trust to write a story to be sold in booklet form to benefit their finances, and I was only too glad to oblige. The booklet also contains an essay on local history and a guide to the many nearby landscape features mentioned in the story. You can still buy a copy of this rarest item from my back catalogue at: http://www.faringdonfolly.org.uk/folly-shop.html.

More

(Wild Cards)

I didn't mean for any of this to happen. Let me make that clear right from the start. It all happened *to* me. And I'm glad it did. In the end. But there were points there where it all got a bit choppy.

Honestly, it seems you can get arrested for just about *anything* in this city. Even involuntary public nudity. When I'd just been going about my business, walking down the street, and suddenly there I was, *au naturel*. I had to spell the word 'involuntary' out to the arresting officer, who was about twelve. He looked at what he'd written and said "oh" like he'd just realised what an oaf he was being, and then said he'd "been a little distracted". Then he and his fat, laughing partner hauled me off downtown for, basically, the crime of being in the theatrical profession.

The involuntariness of the offence ought to make a difference, I feel. The police finally told me that my sudden nakedness in the street had resulted from my being the victim of some perving ace called 'The Stripper'. And that time I can only assume they were right, because, just for once, I didn't feel like it was the fault of my own special talent. It's a shame I didn't have time to realise what was going on and give him a taste of his own medicine. I was finally released without much in the way of apology, despite being the victim rather than the perpetrator. Maybe I just *look* guilty? Maybe I protested too much.

And then there was that business with that valuable necklace that was in, and then suddenly out of, that shop window. Just as I was admiring it. The same officer appeared at the scene of the crime: the twelve year old. He remembered my face, made the connection, and acted like he was the great detective, until various wiser heads started pointing out that I'd initially stood there gawking at the jewellery that had appeared in my hands, that I had started waving to the jeweller and pointing at it, and that involuntary nudity was hardly the best preparation for a stealthy jewel heist. Once more, I told the truth, and let them draw their own conclusions, the wrongness of which, this time, I felt guilty about not in the slightest. They assumed it was because of someone else's power. And that must have been true this time. Sort of.

After I was told I was free to go, the twelve year old followed up his police brutality with an invitation to go on a date with him. Presumably because he felt that, having already seen the goodies, he felt he was some way into the process already. Needless to say I declined, quite vocally. Aren't there rules against that sort of thing? I was on my way to what turned out to be a disastrously failed audition for a dog food commercial. Following my public humiliation, I couldn't quite summon up the confidence to assert that my little Jack Russell had become supercharged with health. I think if I were American I'd be suing someone as we speak.

So that's the summary of my previous encounters with the law. Before I get to what I'm about to recount, that is. Which is all sorts of legal hoo hah. So far, at least, I haven't had to call my mum and ask her to send over bail money.

But those are old wounds, and I have quite a lot of new ones to get to. So. Right. Sorry. Anyway –

Hello. My name is Abigail Baker.

I am a serious actor.

I'm also basically a serious person. If you're looking for a coquettish sense of humour, or, it turns out, delirious enthusiasm about dog food, I am not your go to girl. One of my tattoos even says 'serious person' in Korean. Or at least the tattooist said it did. If I get laughed at by the staff and customers of one more Korean restaurant, I swear I'm going to get that laser thing done.

Sorry. Anyway –

During what I'm about to relate, all of this... havoc – that I did not seek or cause, I really can't emphasise that enough – I suppose I was being even more serious than usual, because I was doing my damnedest to get into character for a role that I'd been understudying. That of Anabeth Grey in *Grey Hearts*. Everyone knows the story. She falls in love with a secret joker. On their wedding night, he uncovers his secret, that he is, well, not quite as other men, let us say, but rather more... insecty. In disgusted horror, she kills him. She manages to cover up the crime, but, echoes of Lady Macbeth, his ichor is on her hands, and she keeps making slips that could give her away. Until, on her next wedding night, to a humane and tolerant man, her guilt, or perhaps something more solid, bursts from her and flies off into the night, forever damned.

She is not a bundle of laughs.

I work in the theatre. Guilty as charged. To be specific, I worked in *a* theatre, the Bowery Repertory, the lovely Old Rep. Though it hasn't run real rep for decades. I was, and thank God still am just about, on a work placement, which was initially just over the summer, but ran into my new term, at the New York School of Performing Arts. Yes, like in that movie, which I still haven't seen, and people still mention all the time, weirdly enough. The School's great, but it was the placement I was after, and thanks to what I gather were some gentle words to the School from the theatre owner, Mr. Dutton, I'd been able to hang onto it. I don't know if you can tell by the accent, because when I go back home they all think I've turned into, I don't know, Popeye, but I'm not from round here. I'm British. From deepest rural Dorset. Though I'm the sort of British person who, I suppose, regretfully, would rather stare at the old country with some horror from a safe distance from over this side of the Atlantic than actually trudge through it every day. I suspect however that, emotionally, I've become a bit *more* British, now I'm seen against a different background. Perhaps sort of pretend British. *Billy Idol* British. I'm sure Quentin Crisp, for example, was *capable* of the occasional use of 'guy' or 'truck' when across the pond, but as soon as he pitches his tent here, it's all English muffins and having his toast done on one side, neither of which I'd even *heard* of before I got here –

Sorry. Anyway –

I came here for Broadway. Okay, so there's the West End in London, and that's great, wouldn't kick a job there out of bed for farting, but it isn't Broadway.

And neither is the Bowery, I know. But at least it's on the right continent.

I mostly did odd jobs for the Rep. I worked in the office, I refilled the water cooler, I emptied the wastebaskets. But that was awesome. Because I was emptying the wastebaskets *in a theatre*. And during the production of *Grey Hearts* I also helped out during set building, got shown the ropes, literally, by the stage manager, Jan, and got to watch Alfre use the lighting and sound decks, using all those arms of his. I'd been up in the rafters with the riggers, who were... just a bit too spidery for me, actually. Sorry. I'd actually *been* prompter, which is a highly skilled task I'll have you know, for a couple of matinees, with Klaus looking over my shoulder. With that eye on the end of his finger. Which did rather freak me out.

All of this was solid gold for me. The fulfilment of my dreams. Almost since I was old enough to think of what I wanted to be when I grew up (when I was five I wanted to make chocolate biscuits and that would have been a damn sight easier as a life's ambition, let me tell you) I've wanted to act professionally.

I mean I've wanted to act. Professionally.

So, when Eliza Baumgarten, the lovely Liz, went down with chicken pox, I was ever so slightly delighted. Liz had been understudying for Anabeth Grey, watching Shauna Montgomery's performance, matching her tic for tic as it were, having learnt the lines, ready to step in. Shauna, of course, is her from *Accident!* on Fox, taking about a hundredth of her normal pay check, keeping the theatre alive with a short run as a favour to Mr Dutton, who, a few years back, put her joker son through exactly the sort of on the job experience I'd gone through. But she's also a proper trooper: full of stories; respects the craft; nothing but kindness for non-combatants, seems to love jokers, really really *nice*.

Which made it all the more awful when that enormous light fell on her.

Thank God I wasn't up there at the time. Because I do seem to get blamed for things. Usually things that, as I may have mentioned, I did not do.

The chicken pox was nothing to do with me, either. I mean, how could it have been?

Sorry. Am I starting to sound guilty because I keep protesting? I mean, because I doth protest too much? I suppose I may still be a tiny bit in character, then, after all these months, because I really did have nothing to do with –

Sorry. Anyway –

I was, however, the (unwitting) beneficiary of said accident. Because with Shauna in the hospital having bits of stage picked out of her and her ankles reconstructed, and Liz looking like Jackson Pollock was her beautician, the Rep were suddenly desperate for someone, preferably someone Nat, to play Anabeth. As in that very night. Because a full house had been sold, the show must go on, as Shauna had said before they put the oxygen mask on, and the hole in the stage was very easily repaired.

"I can do it," I said, stepping forward, perhaps a bit too hastily, but I got the feeling every other female actor in the building was about to do the same, and Kevin as well, who's a bit slight with those bendy bones of his, and could have got the frock on. We'd all been brought up on those MGM musicals with sudden dance routines about how nice it would be to be in sudden dance routines, and we all always rather hoped for something like this to happen, and, well –

I suppose I was the one young enough and foolish enough to get the dream out of my mouth first.

I suppose I didn't exactly *say* it. I bellowed my availability.

"I've memorised the part," I lied, and chucked a few random lines at them, that I recalled from the prompting.

"You're a child," said James Clark Brotherton, who's been called the finest joker actor of his generation, despite, or perhaps because of, his ability to look entirely Nat, and who was playing Nick Grey, the unfortunate victim, a role so made for him he's done it on three continents. He's rather more British than I am, but is from Chicago, so what does that say? "Anabeth is –"

"A much younger woman than her husband," I said, "trying too hard, out of her depth even before she learns who he really is. Or at least she will be, just the once, tonight. And possibly for the matinee tomorrow."

Vita, the director, made a sudden squeal with those throat pouches of hers, and she pointed at me like I'd got the answer in charades, and everyone looked at her like she was mad, but then she rushed over and hugged me. And I tried to hug her back. At a slight distance. And one press release about Shauna urging between grating breaths that the role be recast from within the company and me being her personal choice later (gosh, she *is* a trooper) –

I was *in*!

So.

I had a day to learn the part.

I went back to the office, and leaned on the door, and tried to stop myself shaking.

I took a look at the script. To tell you the truth, I was surprisingly undaunted. At the time. It's not the width of Anabeth Grey that actors find alarming, it's the quality. She's on and off and sitting at tables which could have scripts glued to them and spends quite a bit of time actually *looking at her palms*, for goodness sake, and I do have very tiny writing.

It was my big chance. And I was so not going to blow it.

I sat there in the big wicker chair writing notes in the margins of the script, and Vita kept everyone out of the office, and I let Buffo the cat leap up onto my lap and was completely oblivious to anything –

Until I started to wonder if Buffo was putting on weight.

As in, putting on weight in that second. Having got suddenly heavier.

I looked down. And saw that it wasn't just Buffo sitting there now. But two of her. Exactly the same. Looking at each other with startled cat expressions that were half "hey that's another cat, I must defend my territory" and half "who is that charming stranger?"

And then, suddenly, there were four of them.

I realised that Buffo was touching my bare arms.

I leapt up, and all four of them went flying... but they stayed being four and ran into the corners of the room, alternating between hissing at each other and looking intrigued.

Not that I couldn't tell which was the original. She was the one who was displaying a full range of startled cat expressions, while the other three were looking more absent, less *real*, somehow.

I stood there. I knew what this was. And it was absolutely not what I needed right now. Not with curtain up on my big night a mere ten hours away.

But I could fix it. And I had to. As quickly as poss.

I dropped the script and ran out of the office. Out of the theatre. Into the smelly alley behind it. And I should mention how brilliant and somehow surprising it always is to walk out onto a New York street, too hot in summer, too cold in winter, and right now, in the first week of October, just right and bright with promise. To live in this city is like you're living in the roots of the most tremendous magic forest, but made by people, really *for* people. With breath coming from under the street and music echoing around every corner and the trees in the park gold, and everyone talking to each other very loudly all the time. And *you* can find sleep if you want to, but the city will always be here ready for you.

None of that was in my head at that instant, though. But I put it here because it really should have been. Because of the magic of what was going to happen next.

I stood in the alley and looked up at the buildings.

I'd never even thought about what sort of place the Old Rep might back onto, what sort of room might share a wall with the theatre office. Whenever I call Mum, she has another *Daily Mail* scare story about what happens in 'Jokertown'. She's not keen on me being here. But I didn't give a stuff about who or what our neighbours might be. Or I tried not to. I often failed, actually. I still looked twice at jokers I passed in the street, I still found myself moving into different cars on the subway when something that looked, frankly, like a monster out of a fairy tale, got on and sat down with its newspaper. And I hated myself for it. Mr. Dutton was an entrepreneur in the joker community. He employed lots of jokers. And he'd been willing to take me when all the other theatres had turned me down. I kept telling myself that the theatrical community has always been a haven for those who are different, for those who needed to hide, be they gay people, transvestites, Gypsies, Jews –

Or... me. I suppose. Sorry. Should have mentioned that. Probably rather obvious now. I think maybe that was the last thing I had to get past, me being proud of –

Sorry. Anyway –

I worked out which was the building in question, and saw that it was a nondescript block of cheap lodgings. Which made sense, because sometimes when I was working late I heard music through the office wall. Old music, rather lovely, very New York: jazz and swing tunes. There was an intercom with five empty name tags, an ancient indication of a Mr. Saunders in flat six, and a big red scrawl in magic marker pointing to flat four that said if I wanted a good time I should try Paris. Which I might, on another occasion, have found wry.

I tried every button. None of them answered. Not even Paris.

I tried them all again.

So I did the only sensible thing.

I kicked down the door.

Even with my DMs, it took a few hefty thumps. But honestly, it's not my fault that building standards in this part of the city are so lax. And I was positively looking forward to getting the Rep's enormous carpenters to pop by and make this place an actually better door, and pay for the materials, so don't look at me like that, okay?

I really must get round to doing that.

I realised, as I sprinted up the dingy stairwell, that, judging by the height, I was actually after one of the flats on the third floor. Or the second floor, or the fourth or something, if you're from this side of the Atlantic. So it was Mr. Saunders or one other.

I got to that landing, not even noticing how out of breath I was. I pounded on the door of the other flat, got no answer, then realised I was facing away from the theatre.

So. My problem was definitely being caused by Mr. Saunders. So I knew he had to be home. Progress!

I pounded on his door. And I may have screamed a little.

After a few moments, I heard movement inside. I stopped pounding. "Please!" I yelled. "Please, I need your help! I know you're an ace, and you're doing something terrible to me, I mean terribly inconveniencing, and you're doing it without knowing you're doing it, and I need your –!"

I realised there was a shadow and a sense of terrible movement behind me.

I turned round and saw –

Ten copies of the door to the apartment opposite, that I'd pounded on with my bare hands. Filling the landing. Lined up like dominoes.

Falling on me.

Something grabbed my arm and heaved.

And I was through the door and into the apartment and the many doors crashed against the door that had been quickly slammed on them.

And I was face to face with the most peculiar man.

Although I was relieved, at the time, and a little ashamed to be so relieved, that he was actually quite normal looking.

Well, better than normal, really.

He had old eyes in a very young face. Dark, curly hair, mussed up, stubble, a jittery look about him, like he wasn't sleeping too well. A hooded sweatshirt that looked like he lived in it. He had one hand on the door, and the other was still holding mine.

I grabbed it away from him. "Sorry –!"

"It's okay," he said. "I'm stopping the door from multiplying, and my own powers don't work on me, I mean, try touching yourself and you'll see – I don't mean *touching* yourself – Hey, look over there." He was pointing into his tiny bathroom. I looked over there, saw nothing, and looked back just as he closed the door onto his tiny bedroom, the room that was next to the theatre office –

Just quickly enough to see the enormous piles of identical DVDs that occupied every surface.

He grinned nervously at me, unsure whether I'd caught that or not, his eyes darting back and forth. "Oh, it was nothing. You're copying my power. I can see how that might inconvenience you, and you can't stop this because –?"

"I can't ever stop it! I pick up other aces' powers like... Wi-Fi! And I can't control them! But if you *are* in control of it, and you just think for a moment about how it works..." I put a hand on his face and let the information... sort of flood into me. He looked at me as I did it, as if he was assessing me with those ancient eyes. As if he were somehow understanding me. And somehow, just the tiniest part, asking for something. Without being vulnerable enough to ever ask for anything. The smell of his cologne was like some old military club, all deep seats and brandy and polish, and old wounds smiled at.

I had to find something else to look at before I took my hand away. Because I was suddenly feeling what the Americans call 'inappropriate' and we call nice work if you can get it. Very quickly, by my own standards, which previously have... actually there's not much to talk about there, and it's all rubbish. I am rather new at this, you know. People say I'm self-assured, and so they don't get –

Sorry. Anyhow –

Then that was done. Now I could control it. And switch it off if I wanted to. Which I did. No more randomly copying stuff.

But he was still looking at me.

"Mr. Saunders –" I began.

"Croyd Crenson," he said. Telling me his real name. Just like that.

"Abigail Baker."

And we didn't shake hands or anything.

"Lunch," he said. "I'm buying. To make up for your trouble."

And before I could tell him that I really needed the time to learn my lines, he was heading out of the door.

And, well, it would have been rude not to follow.

I have never seen anyone eat such an enormous lunch. Seriously, five sandwiches. And those are American sandwiches, so that's about twenty five on the UK sandwich scale. And soup. And a stacked salad bowl. And one of those malt things. While I had a mineral water and a chicken Caesar. He didn't eat like a pig, though, but with an old-fashioned decorum, dabbing at his mouth with his napkin, and making the sheer speed with which he got through that lot seem like the most natural thing in the world.

"My family first noticed it on a shopping expedition to London," I told him. "We passed this odd-looking man, and suddenly I was flying. Dad had to catch me by the ankle and walk me along like a balloon. It wore off after a day or so, and I fell onto a pile of carefully prepared cushions, just as my parents were about to crack and call the doctor. They hadn't wanted to, you see. Neither of them had any idea they carried the Wild Card gene. I had an auntie in Somerset who was supposed to be able to summon field mice, but that was it. Mum cried for days. They talked about taking me out of school, because I was a danger to people. It was only when I got older, and, you know, entered a rebellious phase, hence the tattoos, that I realised I wanted to be near people, to be in a big city, to actually... show who I was to people, get up in front of people. Which still feels a bit... wrong. Sorry. Anyway –" I looked up at those eyes again and realised I'd been going on and on. And that what my day was leading towards had made me tremendously vulnerable. And a bit gushy. "What it comes down to is this: I can't control it. I'm at the whim of whatever powers I get within twenty feet of. And today of all days –"

"So I can understand wanting to be in a big city, even though there are more aces. But why the hell pick Manhattan, ace central?"

"It has Broadway."

"You're into musical theatre?"

"I love the old show tunes. You know, it's funny, people do make assumptions, with the short hair and the tattoos, for a moment there I thought you were asking if I was gay –"

"Obviously not." His gaze danced over my face again, half a smile. "So you like the old tunes?"

I found I was smiling too. A bit too long. I looked at my watch. "I really can't take up any more of your time, I've got to get back to learning my lines. As for your secret, I mean your... business, well, I can't condone copying any artist's work, but since it was just that terrible new version of *Thirty Minutes Over Broadway* with Milla Jovovich – Hey, listen, perhaps I should get your phone number. Just in case..." I realised I didn't have an in case handy.

But it didn't matter. Because he was looking over my shoulder now, and his face had fallen.

I turned to look, and was surprised to see, striding into the diner, all of them rolling their arms like they were pretending to be little trains, all of them in white vests and tight red pants, all of them carrying heavy truncheons which they swung with deft musical precision...

No, it wasn't another duplication thing, as I had initially thought. It was not actually fifteen copies of Freddie Mercury (as he'd been two decades ago, not the whiskery knight of the musical profession he is now). It was fifteen gang members, all wearing a rubber mask of his face.

"Mr. Crenson!" enunciated their leader, like he was about to ask a stadium if it was ready to rock, "we are the Werewolves, and we are so pleased you have come out of hiding! Because you –" he slid the end of his stick under Croyd's jaw, "have been selling your DVDs in our territory, without the slightest little cut for us."

Croyd took another bite out of his sandwich, considering. "I heard this was Demon Princes territory," he whispered at last.

The Werewolves made a collective sharp intake of breath, all turning to look at their leader. Who tapped his stick rather forcefully under Croyd's jaw once again. "Don't say that, Mr. Crenson, that is very very bad of you, to bring up a subject of such personal displeasure." He pushed harder on the stick, forcing it up into Croyd's throat.

I realised that the staff and customers of the diner had melted away. Either out the doors or under the counter. I hoped someone was calling the police, but I doubted it.

But suddenly, the gang leader took a step back, surprised –

That he was holding, trying to hold, failing to hold –

A dozen sticks, all of which fell to the floor. Taking his dignity with them.

Croyd grabbed the coleslaw and threw it –

And a tsunami of cabbage and mayo threw the entire gang off their feet.

And suddenly he had my hand again and was hauling me towards the door.

We burst out onto the street, and I was certain we'd got away –

Until Croyd came to a skidding halt in the vast pool of mayo that was pouring out of the door, Werewolves skidding and falling over themselves, trying to get to their feet behind us. I spun round at the sound of gun... bits... being... well, whatever they are. Made ready to shoot. Which surprisingly sounded just like it does in the movies.

In the low autumn sunlight, silhouetted figures stepped forward. Their presence had made a crowd start to gather, jokers coming out of local businesses, watching warily. The newcomers wore black and silver, inverted crosses, serious boots and nice tats, frankly. They were carrying a range of automatic weaponry, and now the noise from the diner had changed too, as the Werewolves, obviously seeing them as well, had produced their own guns, and were taking up firing positions.

"We're the Demon Princes," growled the hairiest of the men. And now I could see that he not only had the one central head, but two tiny others, one on each shoulder.

"Tell it like it is, Ginger," said one of the heads, in rather a high pitched voice.

"Crenson," said the largest head, "you've been selling your DVDs in our territory, without giving us a cut."

I might have remarked that a man with three heads going by the nickname 'Ginger' showed either great sensitivity, a certain cunning or an enormous lack of imagination, but I did not, because I was busy being petrified. You don't get much in the way of gunplay in Dorset. All my Mum's worries about Jokertown were coming true.

Croyd looked stern at the gang. He took a step forward. "I heard," he said, "that this was Werewolves territory."

I really wished he would stop doing that.

I looked between the armed gang in front of us and the armed gang behind us, and made a decision. I looked at my watch again. "Well," I said, "this is all *very* interesting, but I'm in this play –"

"What play?" asked Ginger.

"Grey Hearts."

"Oh," the other small head squeaked, "how fabulous!" I was

charmed for a moment that while the central Ginger seemed to be of Polish stock, the heads were respectively Irish and Scots.

"It is, rather," I said, "and this particular production, at the Bowery Rep, I think you'd really like, because – "

"Right now," said Croyd, loudly interrupting, "I have the power to multiply things. I'm ready to multiply bullets. If you guys open fire, the guys behind me will open fire too. And I'll make it so that in the second the two of us die, so will all of you."

"But –" I said, 'I thought you could only do it if you were touching–?"

I was aware of everyone suddenly looking at me.

"Oh bollocks," I said.

Croyd looked reproachfully at me.

Ginger laughed and raised his gun to aim at Croyd's head.

Desperately, I did something I'd never done before. Something that it took immediate peril to make me do. Because I found it deeply embarrassing. Frightening, even. I took whatever mental muscle tension I felt about the possibility of picking up an ace's power –

And I reversed it. I relaxed it. I reached out.

And, from further away than a power that *randomly* affected me would be located...

There it was. Coming from that dull-looking shopkeeper over there with the swooshed-back hair. I held it in my head. I understood it. If I let this happen, I still wouldn't be able to control it. And that frightened me terribly.

But okay... needs must.

"Sorry," I said to Croyd. I grabbed his hand. And I let it happen.

The pavement suddenly became something like an ice rink. Immediately under our feet.

I grabbed Croyd's hand and let out one big breath over my shoulder, and –

We were off! Barrelling down the street, absolutely out of control. I think the man could make tiny surfaces absolutely frictionless. And no, I hadn't considered this plan one step further than our immediate getaway.

We sped over a crosswalk, narrowly missing a cab. It blared lazily at us.

We'd left the diner behind. We'd escaped.

Only now, coming up at us —

The bank building jutted further out into the street than the diner had. Beyond another street full of speeding cars going left and right, its huge grey wall was flying at us!

"Stop it!" yelled Croyd.

"I can't!" I screamed.

And then our feet hit sidewalk.

And we tumbled, head over heels.

And suddenly a fruit stall reared up out of nowhere and I was going to die —

Until I landed in an infinity of melons.

And exploded them with a great fruity burst of impact.

We lay there in the goo.

"We got out of range of the power," I whispered.

"I'm sorry I got you into this," said Croyd, quickly getting up. "I'll come to see your show tonight, okay? Don't look for me at the Saunders place, I'll tell you when I've got a new hideout." And he stuffed a big fold of bills into my hand. "Cab fare. Go learn your lines." And he was gone.

I slowly stood up. I shook melon from my clothing.

I realised that a joker shop owner, looking like a horrified Orca, had run out of the shop, and was yelling at me in something that sounded Eastern European. I started to leaf through the truly enormous sum of money Croyd had given me, wondering how much would satisfy him and leave me enough to get quickly back to the theatre —

And then I was looking into the trying to be stern faces of that twelve year old policeman and his fat sighing partner again.

"Oh come on," I said. "He must have ended up with more melons than he started with."

The boy cop took the money out of my hand and actually tutted at me.

"Destruction of property *and* counterfeiting," he said. "Are you going for some kind of a record?"

"I only want *one* thing," I said to the doll-like policewoman in charge of the cells. She paused for a moment at the door of my one.

"You've already turned down your phone call."

"A copy of *Grey Hearts*. Actor's edition, if poss. Please?"

She gave me a look and moved on.

"Is that so much to ask?" I yelled after her.

I'd been in there for nearly three hours. They'd be looking for me back at the Rep. Wondering if I'd done a runner. Maybe even starting to measure Kevin for that frock. I just hoped my mum would never hear of this. Here was I, in Jokertown, amongst jokers and aces, having been arrested on ace-related charges. I couldn't help but feel ashamed of how... acey everything was getting. Even though no part of me wanted to be.

Two figures appeared at the door of my cell. The first one, old and grumpy, was looking at me like he was deciding whether I was an irritation or an abomination. Beside him stood his younger, kinder-looking, partner. But I wasn't paying him much attention. Because the first cop had two enormous horns curling around his head. "So," he said, "how you feeling?"

"Rather sheepish," I said.

I think by the time they got me to the interview room, I'd managed to explain just how much I hadn't meant anything by that.

I didn't want to wait for a lawyer. I thought it was best to tell... well, almost the whole truth, from the top. I felt bad for Croyd, but really I'd only just met him. And he'd said he wasn't going back to the apartment. And somehow I knew he could get out of any trouble I might send in his direction.

"So," said the older Detective, who'd introduced himself as Storgman, "you got no family over here –"

"Right," I said, "I'm the only one without a safe, steady job. You could say I'm the black..." I saw his expression start to change, "... cat of the family! It's an expression. We have. In Britain."

The younger, nat cop, who was called Stevens, actually laughed. Which was a relief. But then his expression hardened. "I heard 'black'," he said, "and I so wondered where that was going."

I put a hand over my eyes. If this was good cop/bad cop, I'd managed to piss off the good cop too. "Sorry," I began. "I'm not in the least bit –"

"You should be quiet now."

"Yes, I promise I will be, apart from, you know, answering your –"

"*Now,*" said the older man.

And I was.

He gazed at me a moment. Then continued. "So tell me more about this guy you say 'zapped the cash into your hand'."

"The Sleeper," said Stevens. "That's what we call him. That's what cops have called him for a *long* time."

So I told them. I mentioned the warring gangs and the enormous meal. The latter seemed to make Storgman perk up. It was like he'd got a sudden idea in his head, and it was a lot more interesting than I was. Stevens looked questioningly at him, but Storgman waved him away. This was obviously something they weren't going to discuss in front of me. "And do you know where he is now?"

I gave them the address.

They paid no attention to my desperate pleas about having to learn my lines. I ended up back in the cells. With no indication of when this situation might change. Though I was told a public defender was on the way.

I waited another half hour.

And then I got to the end of my tether.

This lot might be a bit puzzled about how I came to encounter those melons at such velocity, but they still saw me as someone who happened to be around powers, maybe aiding and abetting 'the Sleeper' (why did they call him that?) and not as an ace myself.

I would return to face them tomorrow. Well, tomorrow night, after the matinee. And maybe I could fit in a press conference. But return I would. Afterwards.

Hesitantly, I did what I'd done earlier that day. I reached out. For only the second time in my life. And tried to feel what powers there were in the police station.

Aggh! Loads!

It felt like they were grabbing for me!

I managed to take a mental step back. Ye Gods. I'd never done this deliberately before. I'd always been kind of... *taken* by this stuff. Now it felt like I was deliberately... well, offering an *invitation* to an intimacy which seemed rather...

Phew, hell of a day all round, eh? Shall we just get on?

There were two powers that felt useful. I picked one of them... and teased it into coming away with me. Leaving its host none the wiser.

Just as well the owners of neither of these two powers had

wandered close to the cells earlier. They'd have given the game away. I'd been aware of the power of the doll-like officer affecting me, but thankfully hers was one of those powers that, even with it running wild in me, I'd need to be touching a person for it to do anything.

I concentrated on the new power until I understood it. I knew it would change me. I listened to hear if that Sergeant was coming back, then -

I let it. And suddenly –

I had a different shape! I was a lot smaller. I was furry. And it was dark. I was covered in fabrics. Fabrics that smelt fantastically interesting!

I got my head out into the light. I saw the gaps in the bars.

I leapt for one. Instinctively.

I squeezed my body through it.

I got about halfway. I heaved. I got my back feet down. I hauled my head forward –

And I was out! Trotting along the cell corridor. Bounding along the cell corridor.

Which made me feel suddenly very aware... of these two *vast* lumps that were bouncing back and forth between my legs. I slowed down. I tried to tiptoe. I couldn't.

I settled into the cat equivalent of a vaguely constipated saunter. I couldn't help but wonder if this was what it was like for human men. Because if it was, I really could forgive them *so* much.

As I was starting to become aware of these... objects, I also suddenly felt that... I really wanted to make *use* of –

Oh, this really did explain *such* a lot.

I harrumphed that sensation away, and, hoping I didn't encounter any female cats, and thus find myself in a situation the mere inkling of which would give my mum a seizure, I made my way through the station, moving between people's feet, getting, obviously, now I think about it, calls of greeting. I got a huge wave from some guy with enormous hands, who'd been tapping away with surprising dexterity at what to him must have seemed like a toy typewriter. And someone who looked like a whippet in a uniform bared her teeth at me, which I kind of hoped was in the way of friendly badinage, because at that point every single aspect of me agreed that I wanted to run.

I did not, however. I continued my blokeish saunter. And hoped that I wouldn't knock these enormous... things against anything on the way to the door.

I finally got to the street and bounded happily off in the direction of the theatre, trying not to be distracted by the sight of the sun reflected in puddles.

I made it about six blocks. So far that I started to worry about what was going to happen when I encountered Buffo. And kind of, well, fantasising about –

Sorry. Anyway -

All thoughts of potential feline sexual harassment were put out of my head as suddenly I was out of range... and big and human and standing up suddenly and... naked in the street... again.

If this had been Dorset, I could have expected cries of outrage. This being New York, what I got was some offhand stand up comedy, a handful of compliments and a lot of laid-back staring. But it could only be minutes before –

There was a shout from over my shoulder. Okay, make that seconds.

A patrol car had swung to a halt on the pavement beside me, and a short young female police officer with curly black hair was leaping out of it. "Have found suspect –!" she was yelling into her radio.

I wanted to yell about how unfair this was.

Instead of which, I threw my hands up in the air and ran. Pursued by the police. And several onlookers who wanted to keep being onlookers. Like something out of Benny Hill.

I swiftly decided to stop worrying about the naked bit and just sprint. But not straight for the theatre. That was too obvious. I ran into side streets, up alleys, always expecting to run into one of those high mesh fence things that for some reason people put up in alleys in movies.

The sounds behind me kept up with me. Thankfully, the onlookers kept shouting as they ran. I thought I was being clever, doubling back, ducking behind a pile of rubbish bags and letting them go past, but always, within seconds, the sounds followed me.

Not so surprising, I guess, that I was so noticeable. But then I realised –

Everywhere I went, there were dogs looking at me. Looking at me with hopeful, oh I'll get a treat for this, expressions on their faces. And

I could feel a power connected with them, something egging them on, asking questions of them.

That bloody copper. Honestly, you couldn't tell.

Ahead of me, a whole pack of strays suddenly rushed out into the middle of an alley. They growled and lowered their heads at me, all the different mangy breeds.

But I had two advantages. I could nick this power, and I was the children of country folk.

I raised a finger commandingly. As if I was in Mum's kitchen, and her eight dogs were acting up with a squeaky toy. "Sit!" I bellowed. With all the force of my purloined power behind it.

They did.

I told them they were very good dogs, and had served an entirely new pack by helping me, and if they told their old pack leader I hadn't been this way, there'd be –

I visualised my mum's yard, full of lovely muck and rats.

And they just about swooned and let me on my way.

Now, that was a power that I'd love to have on a regular basis.

I turned right and left, and realised that I was standing outside a church of some kind. The sign outside said it was Our Lady Of Perpetual Misery. The noises of pursuit had thinned out around the area instead of being right on my, erm, tail, but it wouldn't be long before they came through here. The most urgent thing I needed was clothes. Such as might be kept in a place like this and given to the poor.

I was considering stealing from the homeless.

Damn right I was, this was my opening night! And okay, so I was now losing track of all the things I had to pay back, but I'd get there.

I saw a side door was open and ran inside.

I failed to find any office or storehouse or anywhere with clothes. So I kept making my way deeper and deeper into the building. The beauty and rather pointedly joker character of the architecture stopped me when I entered the church itself. But I didn't have time to feel awed or less than welcome. Towards the altar, a figure in a purple hooded cassock was sweeping up, humming to himself.

Okay, I was desperate. I was going to have to appeal to a man of the cloth, and hope he'd do this my way instead of asking me to give myself up.

I hid most of me behind a pew, and called out. "Excuse me? Reverend?"

He turned and pushed back the hood of his cassock.

I'm not proud of what happened next, okay?

Father Squid was, in the end, very kind about me screaming like that. "You're obviously in a very vulnerable position," he said, as he found me a sweater and an enormous pair of jeans.

"Obviously," I said, still hiding behind the pew.

"It strikes me," he said, handing me said items, "that you may well feel recompense has to be made. Above and beyond you paying for the things you have to pay for, and returning to the police after you have completed this quest on which you have embarked."

"I do," I said, dressing. And, oddly, I did.

"I think the nature of that recompense might have to do with the uncertainty and fear you feel around jokers, around everything that is beyond your previous experience."

I frowned. I heaved on the belt to get the jeans around my waist, and found I could loop it around twice.

"The annual Christmas pageant at this church could do with some help from those in the theatrical profession," he continued. "Lights, costumes... and actors. Especially someone who is about to become a *cause celebre*, such as yourself."

"I'll bring these clothes back," I said.

He looked at me as seriously as his voice was deep.

"And I'll help out with your Christmas pageant," I said.

"Very good," he said. And he put some money in my hand. "Cab fare back to the theatre. Break a leg, as they say."

I closed my eyes for a moment, thankful that he'd anticipated my next problem. "I do want to make it better," I said. "I mean... everything."

"Good."

"The way I've had to lean on everybody, it makes me feel so... shellfish. I mean, selfish!"

I got out of there rather too fast. Apologising all the way.

I think he might have been amused by that. Either that or horrified beyond description. I couldn't read his expression well enough to tell.

"I've been arrested by mistake," I told Mr. Dutton, striding into his office at the theatre. Actually, *bursting* in would probably be a better way to put it. I was lucky: he keeps one of his many offices at the Rep, and he happened to be there. He's not the most un-spooky of jokers, in that he wears a black cloak and a death's head mask all the time. But I'd got used to that. So there was no screaming. This time. (He really shouldn't step out suddenly backstage like that. Especially not near a trapdoor. Especially not just after I'd been to see that musical.)

"I'm already aware," he muttered, not looking up from whatever he was signing. "The police have been in touch, and I've been told to alert them immediately should you arrive." He seemed to enjoy my discomfort for a moment. "So much for that. I've told everyone who knows to remain silent about your presence. We'll get one performance out of you, and no matinee tomorrow, but oh, the headlines."

I thanked him profusely. And wondered whether to question his decision concerning the matinee, but finally decided against and left.

On the way out, I noticed Buffo, now in the singular and looking slightly disappointed at this change in her circumstances. "You don't know what you missed, sweetheart," I told her, and with only a few hours left, raced to my dressing room.

Vita yelled at me for precisely one minute, then said she'd heard what had happened, and if I could at least make an attempt at learning the script she'd appreciate it. Klaus would be ready with idiot boards, and most of my lines were indeed going to be secreted around the set.

I'd just sat down with a cup of tea and the text when there was a knock on the door. And before I could yell at whoever it was to sod off –

In came Croyd. "Hey," he said. And he already sounded *fond* of me. In such a calm and certain way. Which made me feel like it was a good thing he was here.

"You shouldn't be here –"

"Relax. I took the very pretty way in. There are cops watching the doors."

"So how –?"

"If I can touch a fire escape, I can make *more* fire escape. And the, ah, owner here seems to have got the staff locked down. Nobody's talking. I told you I'd come see your performance."

"I need to learn my lines –"

"Here," he said, "let me help." And he picked up a copy of the play.

It turned out he knew it inside out. He read my cues to me, not acting them, but like a director. He gave me all kinds of *aide memoires* about where we were in the play, what everyone wanted, where my character was going.

"I've always loved *Grey Hearts*," he said, when we took a break for coffee. Which he took insanely strong. Just this once, I did too. "It's personal for me."

"Really?" I said. And I confess, my mind went swiftly to what exactly that might mean, *vis a vis* human anatomy and thoraxes, mandibles, etc.

He heard the sound in my voice, and laughed. "I mean," he said, "that I might wake up as... anything." And he told me about how his own powers worked. About how he slept and awoke with randomness in his life, a new power every time. About why they called him The Sleeper. "I could wake up *looking like* anything." And his face had that questioning look on it again.

"That's okay," I said, automatically. And then I thought about me screaming at Father Squid and what he'd said afterwards. About what I'd said to Storgman. About all my nervy reactions. And my distaste for my own power, that certain distance I had from it, that I'd never quite gotten over. "Actually," I said, "listen. I grew up somewhere where there were no jokers or aces. So I still... get it wrong a lot. I still blunder into doing terrible things. When these days, in this city, that rather means you're doing them deliberately, meaning to hurt people's feelings. But I don't. I want to get it right. I promise that when you go to sleep, I mean, when you wake up, I mean, if I'm... if I'm there, or if I happen to see you, after... I mean, after you've changed... for some reason..."

He grinned, and thankfully interrupted me. "Maybe you should have played Anabeth from the start."

"Oh, thanks!"

"I didn't mean –" He saw I was laughing and stopped. "I meant that seriously, because you're thinking about this stuff, and it's in you, but you're new to it." His gaze was dancing all over my face, as if I was some part of nature that he was newly appreciating. And that was a great look, actually. It felt like something I'd been missing for the longest time, without knowing it. "I look forward to seeing you handle it all. 'Cause you're going to. But there is... one thing I've got to say."

And then he told me how old he was.

"Oh," I said. "Right."

And he looked wonderfully worried about how I might react.

I couldn't find any modest way of saying that was okay. That that was fine by me. That I'd suddenly realised how much I liked older men. Much older men.

It would have been assuming so much to do so.

Because what had happened here, really? We'd had lunch and chatted. And seemed to be making grand decisions about each other. Which could be entirely mistaken.

Then Vita popped her head round the door and precisely yelled at me again, and hustled Croyd out of there.

"I'll be out there," he said.

And then it was time for make-up. And this half a romance and half a classic nightmare of extraordinary New York was actually going to happen.

I'm tempted to say that if I'd known about who was going to be coming along that night, I wouldn't have gone through with it. But that's not the case. I don't regret any of it really. Hideous, hideous hoo hah that it turned out to be.

Vita stayed with me through make-up and costuming. She didn't fuss. She led me through my cues, and was pleased by how far I'd got. "Everyone knows the circumstances," she said. "Just look them in the eye, and go straight for a prompt if you need one. As long as you're honest up there, they'll love you."

"What if the police arrive?"

"Mr. Dutton says he can hold them off until the end of the performance. And hey, you'll have a very receptive audience out there tonight."

"How do you mean?"

"The Miami Classics have booked the first three rows. They're in the city to see the sights and take in a show. They're a social club for, you know, mature guys who are also aces."

I suddenly found that my mouth had gone very dry.

"Problem?"

I managed to shake my head. And perhaps make some sort of squeaking noise.

Anabeth is the first onstage. In this production, she's there, wandering about, as the house fills, before the stage lights go on. Vita had told me to ignore anyone in the audience who tried to communicate with me, to stay in the part. And I did, pacing, nervous, waiting in what was meant to be a big empty park for the man I'd just met.

And so I was looking out at the audience and saw the man I'd just met take his seat. He made quick eye contact, and smiled at me, in a way which somehow said he knew I couldn't smile back and that was okay.

So that was good.

What was bad was the row of uniformed police that took their places right behind him. And they weren't so careful with the meaningful eye contact. I got the feeling Mr. Dutton had struck a deal that lasted only until the end of the show. But at least they seemed to be looking right past Croyd. He was sunk kind of low in his seat.

What was worse still were the Miami Classics. They came in laughing and joking, and calling out things to me like "hey, your boyfriend's a bug!" until their organisers imposed some order. They were kindly-looking silver-haired guys in leisurewear, some of them with wives, some of them displaying ace signifiers like glowing eyes.

The front row of them were sitting just far enough away so that if I really concentrated, if I wasn't taken by surprise by it...

Or if I stayed at the rear of the stage...

I might just be able to fend their powers off.

But the worse thing of all was what was going on at the back of the theatre, moments before the lights were due to go down. The Bowery Rep has always had a 'gangs welcome' policy, which has kept it out of trouble. But tonight, marching in down different aisles, looking quickly round to see if they could find a certain someone in the audience...

There came the Werewolves and the Demon Princes. Many Freddies and much leather, with Ginger leading the latter pack. They'd obviously reached some sort of agreement that allowed them to do this together.

Thankfully, in the few seconds before everything went dark, they didn't spot Croyd.

And then they had to quickly get into their seats. It seemed they'd all bought tickets. It's amazing what the sheer ritual of theatre can do.

Tonight, it was going to have to perform miracles.

"Hi," whispered Klaus from the prompt box, stage left.

"Hi," I mouthed to him, thinking that this was a bit daring of him.

He looked reproachfully at me. And I realised.

I looked quickly to stage right, where James Clark Brotherton was waiting for his cue, with much the same expression on his face.

"Hi!" I called to him, waving.

And we were off.

It's a surprisingly happy play to start with. The sense of new romance, of Spring, of the lovers remarking on the buzzing of fateful, ironic, bees. It's meant to remind the audience of a sort of innocence that's meant to have existed before Wild Cards Day. That's how this version was costumed, so what happens to our tragic hero seems to come out of nowhere. I've heard that for survivors of that day, the play can be either a very intense or very depressing experience. Which was one reason, considering the guys in the first three rows, that I was determined to keep it serious. I found myself locating the lines, either in my head, or on the picnic basket, and I think I managed to stay in character, and I was damn well doing it for them. The reviews, up to this point, offer wildly differing verdicts on just how I *was* doing, by the way. I did find myself improvising a bit, because it felt so easy, because what I was playing so far was... how I was feeling that evening. And, weirdly, representing it onstage made it seem even more real.

But I soon realised that both Klaus and James Clark Brotherton got that look on their faces again whenever I wandered off piste. I grabbed a paper plate and read out that there was a chill in the air, and perhaps we could go for a drink... someplace warmer?

The lights went down, and we exited.

Scene two involved the hero's sister and her own spouse, who know about our hero's circumstances, and fret for rather too long I personally think about whether or not to tell Anabeth.

James took me aside in the wings, and for a moment I thought he was going to slap me, but instead he took my hands in his. "Well done," he said. "We'll get through this. Just follow my lead."

I nodded, rather than saying that actually I'd been doing fine without, or anything like that.

"Do you know who's out there?" he said.

"Yeah, I saw!"

"Lucas Tate, the Editor-in-Chief of the *Jokertown Cry!* He didn't just send his theatre critic, he came down as well! Abigail, we have to show that great man something *extraordinary.*"

I could only manage a thin smile. I was rather hoping for the opposite.

It's act two where *Grey Hearts* really gets going. Anabeth starts to suspect her husband isn't telling her everything, and she tries to figure out what the nature of his secret is, suspecting everything but the truth. There's a scene where the two of them are caught in flashbulbs, just happening to be on the spot when Fortunato's about to exit a club, and Anabeth sees, standing in the shadows around the stage, lit up only by the strobes (and hence there was a big warning on the posters about epilepsy, fainting and the distant possibility of interdimensional travel for certain aces), all the different things her husband could be: gay; cheating on her; a criminal.

I just had to throw my hands up and strike poses, so I had a moment to see what was happening in the audience.

My gaze found Croyd.

And I saw that he was crying.

I guess he'd want me to say that it was in a very manly way. But it was what I wanted to see at that point. Because I'd been thinking, as we got into the scene... I knew so little about him. Except that he was a criminal. And an ace. A very *variable* ace. And so, after this was over, and I'd been... well, *arrested...* maybe I'd have to wait until I'd calmed down from this hyper-excited state I was in before embarking on any romance, especially with someone who my Mum would regard as –

But then the tears. That moment of him being illuminated. The experience on his face.

There was a man used to being misunderstood. And somehow, stupid me with all my phobias and hurdles, I'd got straight to the real him.

But emotional epiphanies apart, and, heaven knows, this play was becoming a bit of a rollercoaster on that front, it was going rather well so far. The audience were watching an actual play rather than a media spectacle. And judging from their applause, they seemed to be enjoying it. The gangs were keeping quiet, even. Maybe because, like with everything the Rep did, this was very much about them. When James made his big speeches, in a Jokertown accent that was period-specific, he got calls of support from the gang rows, and, when they heard that was okay, from the elderly aces in the front rows too. I thought that just added to the atmosphere.

Most of all: in my state of teeth-grinding concentration, I was actually managing to keep all those powers out there at bay. The first time I'd had to do that for any length of time. And dealing with that stuff didn't feel at all... tarty... but just like doing away with the sort of shyness an actor naturally has to shed to go onstage. So this was actually turning out to be an incredibly pivotal evening in my life, in all sorts of ways.

Which, I think was the thought in my head, that I was living in a tremendous moment... when actually I should have been thinking ahead.

We'd got to the point when James' character, discovered in all his beelike glory, rips open his shirt to reveal a rather impressionistic version of a striped, furry, thorax. Lost in the part, James shoved me as hard as he was used to shoving his regular leading lady, with whom he'd choreographed the move. Despite Vita telling him to take all the physical stuff down a couple of notches tonight.

He shoved me towards the front of the stage.

I staggered on the edge, my arms wheeling in mid-air, making the audience gasp, rather wonderfully actually, with that sensation of is it real or is an act?

And I realised, horrified, a second before it happened –

"You don't understand anything about what it's like to be me!" he yelled.

At which point, overcome by one of the powers in the front row –

I burst into flame.

The audience gasped.

Then wildly applauded.

I heard, weeks later, that Lucas Tate, who, doubtless succumbing to long hours fighting for the rights of jokers, had fallen excusably asleep, woke up at the sound of my inflammation.

"Abigail Baker is on fire!" his theatre critic gasped to him as, behind his ceramic white cat mask, he blinked his eyes open.

"That good, eh?" he replied.

"Fire!" yelled someone at the back of the crowded theatre.

Nobody moved.

I was *that* good.

At being convincingly on fire in a theatrical, as opposed to a realistic, way.

I flapped my flaming arms violently, terrified, trying to somehow roll my centre of gravity back onto the stage.

I failed. And plummeted, I thought, homicidally, into the front three rows.

But by then the Miami Classics had had time to get their act together. I found myself caught and held up by a giant rubbery (and I presume fireproof) hand.

I was held there long enough to illuminate the audience.

Long enough, I learned afterwards, for the Werewolves, cops and Demon Princes to look across the theatre and see Croyd.

My flame cut out a second later.

The ace that had caught me heaved me upright.

I fell forwards, all rubbery now, bounced back upright off my rubber nose, and pitched back helplessly into the audience again.

Where I was caught this time by a burst of warm (and rather stale) air.

Which again, pitched me forward.

With air bursting from every orifice.

I bounced across the stage on my face. I slammed into James, fell at his feet, and started levitating slowly away on my back like an air hockey puck.

I realised that I was glowing a bright, sparkly pink. I looked into the audience again and saw that the gangs and Croyd were all doing the same. And that a hefty policeman was waving his nightstick around his head as if it was a magic wand, throwing off the pink sparkles in waves, like he was the enforcement division of fairyland.

At least I remembered my line. I bellowed it at James. "I

understand pretty well now!"

Which brought the house down.

Which was hardly the desired effect, and I believe a first for the play in question.

I grabbed the curtain at the back, and managed to scramble to my feet, slipping on the air under me, trying to see what was happening in the auditorium.

Silhouettes were climbing over seats. Pink glows were converging. People had started to shout and cry out as feet landed in faces, and scuffles began.

The gangs had used the confusion to leap up and go find Croyd. The cops had leapt after.

I wantonly grabbed hold of the pink glow power, and switched it off from where he was. Which caused a pleasingly sudden yell of exasperation from somewhere nearby.

Vita was yelling from stage left for us all to get off the stage, to get the safety curtain down.

"No," I yelled. "The show must go –!"

James narrowly missed me as he sprinted off.

And looking out at the theatre, I could see his point. The Werewolves and Demon Princes were fighting their way towards the middle rows, where I now couldn't see Croyd. The police had waded in. And some of the more game Miami Classics had joined in, throwing ice bolts and doing rubbery-handed kung fu against the gang members with a kind of square-jawed glee. Where else but in this town can you see three Freddie Mercuries trying to escape an old man who's throwing handfuls of explosive dandruff at them? Lucas Tate was standing up, his mask reflecting the pink glow, seemingly dictating an on the spot account to his frantically scribbling theatre critic, who looked like he was considering alternative employment. Ginger was busy thumping a Werewolf as the two gangs contested over getting to Croyd, but one of his heads was looking over to me onstage. "Bravo!" it squeaked Scottishly. "I'll be back for the next show!'

I sincerely hoped the other two heads agreed.

The violence, thank goodness, was very much one on one. Nobody had started to rip up the seating.

As I may have already indicated, none of this was my fault. So how was I feeling, as the air gradually drained out from under me, and I watched the Miami Classics move further back into the auditorium, and thankfully out of range?

Complicated.

I looked at my hands. They were covered with the remains of ignition products, and still felt a bit rubbery. I thought about what my Mum would say, about me having got so thoroughly involved with so many aspects of aces and jokers, in so many different ways, in such a short space of time.

To just start to be properly involved. To look at a riot in a theatre and feel bad that these were... *my people*. That I owed things to, and had responsibilities to, and was caught up with.

I felt a sort of triumph that had nothing to do with the production.

But this had been going to be my big debut, and I was going to be so blamed, and I felt selfish for even thinking about how it was going to look like I'd ruined something while just trying to do my best –

The safety curtain came hurtling downwards and the house lights came up. And in the second I had to see the audience clearly before my view was blocked –

I still couldn't see him.

At the sound of heavy boots, I looked to stage left. And saw a new group of uniformed policemen running at me. The twelve year old was leading them. I looked to stage right, and there came another bunch of them, led by his fat partner.

They definitely seemed to have got the idea that I was somehow responsible for this.

Entirely wrongly. Look, can I take it as read that you get that now?

Sorry. Anyway –

I was about to start arguing my case, and rather hoping the cop who could turn into a cat wasn't among them, when suddenly I was falling –

Through a trapdoor that had opened underneath me.

Into the arms of Croyd Crenson.

Who had to hold me down to stop me bouncing right back up again with residual rubberiness.

"Hey," he said. "You were great." And he slammed down a lever to close the trapdoor, just as the cops above leapt for it. "But I've got another role in mind for you."

I hear that Leo Storgman was mightily pleased to get the two of us back into custody. That he'd spent the rest of that day going over lines about 'separating the sheep from the goats' and us not being able to 'pull the wool over his eyes'. I got a lot of this from Lucas Tate, who took up our cause, rather, after he'd worked out what had been going on while he was asleep.

The riot at the theatre came to a halt mostly because of the arrival of a truly huge number of uniformed police officers, who carted off everyone involved, including some of the Miami Classics, who'd got rather carried away, but were just as gleeful to be in the back of police vans, and still mixing it up. So it's good to know their night out wasn't ruined, and they had, as they'd been seeking, an emotional time which reminded them of the good old days. But a contributing factor to the violence winding down was the appearance in one of the theatre boxes of Croyd Crenson, with me beside him. Bows were taken, to even some applause from those in the fighting audience still minded to appreciate such gestures. Ginger's little left head even shouted for an encore. Which I thought was pushing it, rather. Croyd called upon the police to arrest him, which would settle the matter for the gangs, and the police, affronted that they hadn't already managed to do that without his permission, arrived moments later to do so.

I heard that Leo Storgman took great pleasure in marching up and down in front of the separate jail cells, his two new prisoners put on different corridors so they couldn't talk to each other. He interrogated Croyd about many matters entirely separate from anything to do with counterfeiting, about a murder case he was working on. He tried to discover from his female prisoner if she had powers herself, or if this was all something Crenson was doing, and how much she knew about The Sleeper, and whether or not she was willing to give him up in return for the charges being dropped over her 'fleecing' that shopkeeper.

She simply told him that the powers were hers, that she was an ace.

He realised, after a while, that neither prisoner was stalling, exactly, or playing dumb. That their relative simplicity and dull straightforwardness extended to the way they talked to their legal representatives also.

The truth of what was going on suddenly came to Storgman as he was about to go home the next day and heard from a fellow officer that an entire stack of seized pirate DVDS had gone. He raced back to the cells, and discovered that they were suddenly –

Empty.

The copies of the two of us having vanished.

By that time, the original versions, so to speak, had relocated to Croyd's new safehouse. On the way there, in the back of a cab, I'd read on my phone about all the arrests, and the first reports from people who'd said that the whole experience had summed something up for them, about how disparate and divided this community still was, that the riot had been, well, art. And amongst all that was Vita, saying that when the authorities had stopped harassing me she hoped I'd come back and play a lead, and Mr. Dutton, saying that the theatre would be open again for business the very next day, and that far from the incident putting people off, he was wondering how he'd be able to fit everyone in, considering the demand for tickets. And behind him in that news report, there was Shauna Montgomery, making an entrance on crutches, yelling that she was damned if she was going to let this grand old theatre go under.

And yes, that last bit did look slightly planned, rather.

I looked up from the display vastly relieved. My debut hadn't been a disaster after all.

Which was when I realised Croyd was looking seriously at me. "It'll work out for you," he said. "Dutton will get his lawyers on it. It'll end up being the first line in your autobiography."

"I hope so," I said. "I have a terrible feeling that Mum may already have read about this." I felt an angry text message in my hand, checked, and found that this was indeed so.

"Do you want me to drop you off somewhere?" he said.

"No," I said, and switched off the phone.

"When I wake up with some new power –"

"I'll have it too."

"So let's hope it's not the power to explode the thing nearest to you."

"Yes, let's."

"When I start needing sleep, when I start having to keep myself awake..." He sighed. "I'm pretty *variable*, Abigail."

"Well," I said, "aren't we all?"

And I saved him the trouble of worrying about whether or not he could kiss me.

'More' and 'The Elephant in the Room' are my two contributions (so far) to George R.R. Martin's Wild Cards universe. (They appeared in the mosaic novel Fort Freak (Tor, 2011) and at Tor.com (2013).) Wild Cards is a super hero universe that, unlike many of its cousins in the comics medium, has, since it started in 1987, maintained a real-time continuity. It's a great honour to be invited to take part. Wild Cards writers own the characters they create, and get a share in the proceeds of all publications in which they feature. It's always a pleasure to work for George (I went to his wedding, and survived!), and I was delighted to get to use Roger Zelazny's creation, Croyd Crenson, the Sleeper. Abigail Baker, my own character, reminds me in some ways of my Doctor Who companion creation Bernice Summerfield. She's the sound of terribly English domesticity encountering fantastic extremity, though Abigail is younger and less self-aware. Because, for the second of these stories, I needed an elephant, I brought in Elephant Girl, created by George's wife, Parris. Abigail's encounter with the Sleeper I now feel to be complete, but I'd love to look in on her again soon.

The Elephant in the Room

(Wild Cards)

"My dear," said my mother, "when your father told me you'd joined the circus and would be turning into an elephant, I had to come over immediately."

And I suppose that was true.

Mum, you see, on hearing about my biggest, though perhaps not my most prestigious, theatrical gig thus far, had decided, to my horror, to come to New York. Dad had stayed home, thank goodness. He was probably looking forward to enjoying his shed. But Mum, on being told that the New York School for the Performing Arts had placed me with the prestigious Big Apple Circus, had darted across the Atlantic like a salmon. Sorry, I should be more specific. I'm still, I suppose, not quite used to living amongst... I mean living *as part of*... a community who have special, you know, *powers*. So I should emphasise that that was a simile. My mother cannot turn into a salmon. (That is, I suppose, one of the little-talked-of features of living in a neighbourhood like New York's Jokertown, where someone of one's acquaintance might actually go green with envy or fall to pieces: one has to indicate where the line of metaphor is drawn.)

I'm making this all sound so very light-hearted, aren't I?

I met Mum at JFK in the company of Maxine, a Jokertown Yellow Cab driver of my acquaintance who really *drives* her vehicle. That is to say, she runs it off her own calorie intake. This, if one can do it, is, apparently, a good deal, economically. It means that Maxine is happy to be paid in junk food, which also makes economic sense for her passengers, and makes hers the hack that jokers and poor drama students head for after the show, with a bag of White Palace and fries for change. This ability came to her suddenly, when she was a child, when she was involved in a frightening car accident, and, in that extraordinary way which makes it very clear that our brains know our bodies better than we do, managed to turn the birthday meal she'd just eaten with her loving parents into a sudden burst of automotive power that saved their lives. Long term, however, it meant she lost her family.

Within the year, actually. Because that moment she used her, you know, *power* for the first time was also the moment she... changed. They couldn't deal. They put her up for adoption. Nobody took her. You get a lot of stories out of those children's homes that got packed with ace and joker kids back then. These days, they're the stuff of Young Adult novels, but I bet the truth of it was even more grim. People *understand*, to some degree, the original release of the Wild Card virus in September 1946. They *feel* for the first generation of those infected, be they powerful ace or differently-bodied joker. They feel the loss of those who 'drew the black queen' and died on the spot. They feel for the deformed and stillborn children of those infected. They're not quite as able to categorise their emotions for those of us unlucky enough to get infected in subsequent decades. The virus is still out there in the jetstream. It's been found on every continent. (At some point in my childhood it must have been drifting through rural Dorset.) Maxine, at the moment she expressed it, changed into, and now looks like... well, a pile of rubber tyres with a pair of googly eyes on top. Okay, yes, you know, like that advertising character. I've never said it out loud within earshot of her. That would be cruel. She makes reference to it every now and then, a nod out of the window when we pass a hoarding: "that's my dad". She says tourists who've come to gawk at the jokers sometimes go "no, really?"

My mother, however, rolled her luggage on wheels to the edge of the sidewalk in the airport pick up area, and when Maxine got out of the cab to help her with it, went way beyond any awkwardness and into the land of outright social horror. She saw Maxine and screamed.

I had to basically wrestle her into the cab, while looking desperately around to make sure there weren't any jokers about who might be offended. Maxine was silent all through the journey back, while Mum was a stream of "honestly, darling, you can't blame me, we don't *have* jokers in Dorset. I thought I was *dreaming*. I was prepared for your joker friends to be horrifyingly ugly monsters, not, I'm sure *charming*, if rather disconcerting, giant, blobby, vastly *flexible*, to fit in that seat up front, I mean you *must* be..." And this was all without the slightest forensic trace of guilt, as if we all yelled about this stuff all the time at the top of our voices in Jokertown.

"Maxine doesn't self-identify as a joker," I told her, my voice already a hiss. "She thinks of herself as an *ace*: someone with *useful* powers."

"Ah, of course, because jokers are your actual *monsters*," said Mum, "who can't do anything useful."

I stared at her, once again horrified by the prospect of taking this woman into my ghetto. "Except... sometimes they can, and very few of them self-identify as *monsters* –"

"So it's all a bit of a mess, classification-wise? How very American, not to have proper names for what things are. And what *is* this 'self-identify' business you keep on about?"

"It's about how they want to see themselves!"

"Darling," she said, "I'd like to see myself as Keira Knightley, but it's what the world sees that matters, isn't it? Hey, with your own, you know –"

"My *powers*."

"Yes, yes, well, you'll be picking up a bit of Maxine's *power*, won't you, how did you put it? 'Like hi fi'?"

"*Wi-fi.*"

"Yes, that! I mean you'll be sort of automatically catching on to what she's doing –"

"Unless I stop myself," I emphasised. "I can do that now."

"Well, well done darling, but don't stop yourself right now, because surely, if you're doing it too, you're contributing to keeping this car moving." She saw the look of befuddlement on my face and sighed, speaking as if to a toddler. "So you'll be contributing to the petrol money! I think we should negotiate a discount." She turned to start doing just that, but before she could I decided I had to put the possibility of being thrown out of the cab before my own comforts and make the ultimate sacrifice.

"Mum," I asked quickly, "how are my aunts?"

Which immediately distracted her onto her favourite subject, a conversation which was only dangerous to my nerves rather than to my health. My, you know, power, if you haven't read the reports of what happened, is that I pick up other peoples' powers (yes, like Wi-Fi) and start expressing them myself, utterly randomly. Well, until the last few weeks, when, as I said, I've managed to gain a level of control. But still, if I'm caught unaware, if, let's say, an ace passes me in the street, and their power is that they can turn into a pile of goo, well, there I suddenly am, a pile of goo with a sign saying 'golf sale' stuck in it. As happened that one time when I was, erm, between acting engagements. It took all my willpower then to literally pull myself together as the ace, unaware that it was all about proximity for me, and not noticing goo when it was other people, dawdled nearby, getting himself a coffee, passing the time of day. I ran the risk of being lapped up by a small dog, until I managed to rear up at it. And of course, once reintegrated, I was atop my clothes rather than in them. As happens to me rather too often for my taste. My taste in those matters would actually tend towards the not at all.

I'm distracting myself. Like I won't have to finish this if I do that. As if it won't have happened, then. Sorry. Anyway. I was able to just about ignore mother's usual drone about what the aunts were doing back in Dorset, all of which was, as usual, formidably dull. But she segued out of that into her equally doleful round up of cousins and distant relatives the provenance of which remained a mystery, while New York, bloody incredible New York, which she'd never seen before, sailed past the windows like an inflight movie. I had to lower my own window to get some early autumn air in my face to stay awake. Just as Mum started talking about the sleeping pills which had got her through that terrible flight. She was intending to use them to manage her awful jet lag. I was already feeling that, of Mum and I, only one of us was going to survive the next few days, and that it was going to be me, frankly, because I already wanted to murder her with a crowbar, just bash it across the back of her latest stupid hat, time after time after —

Sorry. I really need to calm down. Just thinking about the start of all this makes me so... well, there I am now. I'm angry. Which is better than sad, I suppose. But it's such an impotent anger. At how things worked out. At how things are. When I don't think they have to be. They really don't. No, let's not go there. Not yet, anyway. Not until I have to.

Sorry. As I think I already said. Many times, probably.

Hello. My name is Abigail Baker.

I am a serious actor.

Until just before the landing of my mother, I'd been having the summer of my life (apart from being arrested and accidentally publically naked quite a few times), working at the Bowery Repertory in Jokertown, the lovely Old Rep, on loan from the School, and making my debut as a stand in... but actually, you may well have read about that, as I said. It was all over the media, for all the wrong reasons. In the end Mr. Dutton, the theatre owner, got a team of lawyers involved, and I didn't even have to spend a single night behind bars, though I do now, technically, have a criminal record. And, erm, a suspended sentence. Well, several. Anyhow, now the Old Rep's autumn season was approaching, and with it the end of my placement there, and, having shown me off to the audience in a range of parts that frankly hadn't stretched my talent to its rawest extremes, Mr. Dutton had, rather too quickly to my mind, agreed to the Circus benefiting from my newfound notoriety when it came to my last role before the new School year began.

They actually asked for me. I don't know if my Mum ever got that, or if it just added to it for her.

Anyway, that was another reason why I wasn't entirely comfortable with her being in New York. I'd covered up all that unpleasantness with euphemism, made easier by the positive spin the joker-friendly elements of the media had given the incident. I'd sent her all the right press cuttings and crossed my fingers about whether or not the sort of newspapers my mother reads would take an interest. That was all I had to worry about. Mum doesn't do online media. She once, prompted by her favourite columnist, called me up to warn me that Facebook could literally kill me where I stood. As it turned out, she hadn't ever quite been aware of the me being arrested part. She does tend to mention these things if she hears about them. So that was fine. It joined the encyclopaedia of details concerning my life of which my mother was unaware. On the day of which I speak, for instance, I had concealed any of my tattoos that might be visible with several layers of foundation.

But there was one big thing I hadn't told her about. One big thing who, when Maxine angrily thumped Mum's luggage onto the sidewalk in front of my humble apartment building, was waiting inside. Because he'd insisted. Because he was strung out to the point of distraction and kept grabbing my hands and urging me that since we were together, he wanted my parents to know we were together, wanted them to see he was a good guy. I hadn't said to him that that wasn't exactly true. I'd have meant it as a good thing, but right now I didn't know how he'd take it. I didn't know how he'd take anything. I looked up at the building, wondering how this was going to go.

"So," said Mum, completely ignoring Maxine standing there staring at the packet of mints she'd offered her as a fare, "remind me, darling, when's your first public appearance as an elephant?"

"Tomorrow afternoon," I said, trying to indicate to Maxine with mere expression that, next time, I'd bring her at least a hamper. "At the matinee. And that's great, I thought you were going to say something about where I lived."

"Oh my dear, I wouldn't dream of hurting you like that. That's why I said something irrelevant to the moment, you see, to distract us both. But now you've spoiled that little act of grace on my part. You never were one for the social niceties." She glanced back to Maxine. "You know, your friend should come to the circus with you, she'd get straight on the bill. She'd do so well. Bouncy bouncy!" And with an engaging grin like this was the best idea ever, she actually made a motion like a trampoline.

My mother had told me that she liked circuses. And, she'd said on the phone, also elephants. I didn't wonder at the time that she'd never mentioned this before. She told me then that she and Dad had met at one. That they were there with their parents. I imagined at the time that, with the austerity of Britain in decades past, said Big Top probably consisted of three mice, a spoonful of jam and a man in an interesting hat. And that my Mum, even at such a young age, would have spent the evening telling my putative Dad at horrifying length about what her mother's sisters were up to. But now I wonder if that story was even true.

Anyway. Sorry. My expression to Maxine gained several extra dimensions, to the point where I hoped it intimated that next time I saw her I would provide her with nothing short of a feast. Finally, she just shrugged, her arms bouncing off her sides, and got sulkily back into her cab. Mother looked to me with an expression that said her words had once again fallen, inexplicably, on stony ground, and rolled her noisy luggage towards the front door of my block. Where, to my increasing worry, a greater class of horror awaited us.

His name, and I'm pretty sure it's his real one, is Croyd Crenson. He was infected by the Wild Cards virus in 1946, and since the events I mentioned that you might have already read about, with the being arrested and the nudity and everything, he'd been, erm, my boyfriend. He doesn't look his age. He just looks as if he has ten years or so on me. Okay, maybe twenty. All right, listen, if it was a thing on my part, it wasn't not that much of a thing, compared to being made of rubber or having the ability to reduce oneself to goo. That's something else I've realised about the people who live in Jokertown: their notion of what's socially acceptable for nats (sorry, I mean, non-infected people), extends quite a way beyond what's okay for those living elsewhere. It's all about what one is surrounded with, what one has as a background to compare oneself to. That, and the low rents, is what makes Jokertown such a vibrant, diverse, Bohemian environment. (That is to say, as Mum would translate it, there are a lot of gay and transsexual people here too. Actually, that's probably not how she'd translate it.)

But, sorry, I was talking about Croyd Crenson. As I probably will be for the rest of my life, now. Croyd has not always been on the right side of the law. And that was very much the situation that summer. The trouble we'd been in, as you may have read, had a lot to do with his then current ability to multiply objects (luckily for me given one particular escape from the police, people) with a touch of his hand. He had been using that for nefarious purposes involving DVDs.

I should have realised that something terrible was approaching (other than my mother) when, three weeks before her anticipated arrival, Croyd had appeared on my doorstep with flowers. They were beautiful, and he looked especially charming with his awkward, sad smile beside the blooms. Though his teeth were chattering even then. Croyd isn't one for grand romantic gestures. He's been alive long enough to know that it's the small things that matter: the way he understands a person, and wants to know about that person, and gives that person, if they're me, space to talk. And talk. He is, actually, rather the silent type, now I think of it, although maybe that was just because he was with me –

Oh dear. Oh, I'm crying now. Sorry. Sorry. So stupid.

Anyway. Where was I? Right. Right.

That night, he took me out to this back street Italian joker place. Its decor was a combination of Sicily and the kind of twisted outsider tattoo parlour chic that young jokers in New York had developed, that showed up in mainstream design in ways which made you wonder if said jokers were impressed or pissed off. Lady Gaga having the former effect, of course. Her concerts in Jokertown itself, with free admission for jokers, meant she could plaster her videos with orange and purple swirls if she liked. Croyd knew the owner, like he seemed to know everyone dodgy in New York City, so we got a table on our own, and had the food shown to us by the waiters as they sloped or skittered or flapped out to their customers.

Croyd put his hands on the tablecloth and visibly controlled their twitching. He didn't quite manage to make them stop. The speed of his breathing, in the last few days, had started to worry me. It was all the amphetamines he was taking. Looking back, I'd started to feel nervous around him, not to anticipate his visits with unbridled delight. I could feel him, whenever he put his arm in mine or his hand on my waist, treating me deliberately carefully, as if one day he might treat me otherwise. It had started to be like he took a deep breath before I opened my door. But on the flipside of that, the release of that, when I gave him licence, in intimate situations, to let all that energy loose... yes, well, I think you get the idea.

I suppose he made me feel a lot better about myself. Being with him kind of made one a lady, without anyone ever having to use the word. I hate to say this is true, but I suppose he really was something from the past that I'd tried to escape, that had reached out to me and said I was okay. And at the same time he was something from my new world of jokers and aces that had helped me to accept being one of that community, to stop standing quite so nervously apart from it. He listened to all my emo bollocks, because, unlike every other man I'd ever met, he seemed to soak up how people felt about each other, seemed to enjoy hearing about it, particularly when it was about me and him. Even when he started to get jittery and raging and paranoid, he still stopped and listened. He made himself do that for me. And he made his own rules but was nonetheless honourable, outside the law rather than against it, you know, the bad boy thing. But that so minimises what he was to me.

After dark, we would go for walks in Central Park. People say it's dangerous at night, but we never felt threatened there. We could always make more trees to hide behind or more stones to throw. Or I could reach out into the brilliant shining city above us and call over someone else's useful power. We never had to do any of that.

I often think New York feels like it does, natural and full of energy and about and for people, because it reminds us all of something from our evolution: we scurry about at the foot of what seem to be enormous trees, and we've got this clearing in the middle to rush out into and play and fight and change. You see so many jokers there, day and especially night, like that forest clearing is even there for this latest direction of evolution. And we were jokers too. We were part of the night, and so not threatened by it. We sat on benches, and we talked, or I suppose I did while he looked at me.

I see that look in my memory now. It's still a good thing.

And then we would go back to my apartment and shag like bunnies. And nobody ever says that at this point in stories, but they really should. They really should.

Oh dear. There I go again. Sorry.

He looked up from his hands, at that table in that restaurant that night. "The thing is, kid," he said (and I would hate it with a passion if anyone else called me that), "in this next couple of weeks, you don't know how extreme I'm going to get."

I watched his hands as I always did, as his fingertips went to absent-mindedly stroke the stem of his wine glass, well, not that absent-mindedly, or he'd have found himself with several wine glasses. And so would I have, except that I was managing to hold a place in my head back from his now very familiar, very intimate power. "You've told me," I said. "You need the speed to keep you awake –"

"– And I become a different person because of it. Irritable. Cranky. Sometimes... terrifying. That's a word people have used. You haven't seen that. I haven't let you see that. Not yet." I realised with a little jolt that he'd interrupted me. He never did that. 'But that's not what I wanted to talk to you about. You know that next time I go to sleep –"

"You'll wake with a new... you know..."

"Power, yeah." He hadn't been to sleep since I'd met him. I'd wake up in the night, and he'd be sitting up in bed beside me, reading these terrible 1950s crime novels. He once told me he was trying to catch up with all the books from his youth. "That's actually what my own power is. Sleeping. Every time I sleep, my DNA gets rewritten by the virus, and I wake up with a new power. But –" he held up a hand to stop me saying I knew all this. "What I haven't told you is, two other things might happen."

"You might wake up as a joker?" I guessed.

"Yeah. I might wake up with claws or no face or oozing sores, and you'd have to stop yourself getting those too. How you'd feel about that?"

I actually felt annoyed. I think I got that he was testing me. Although I don't know how conscious that ever was for him. But at the time I thought I knew everything that was on that table. "I'd still –" And then I quickly changed what I was going to say. Because neither of us had used that word. Yet. "I'd still feel the same way about you. How could you think I wouldn't? If I'm okay with our joker friends –!"

"Yeah, yeah, but –"

"And if it was that terrible for you, you could just go back to sleep and draw another card, right?"

He paused. He took a deep breath. "Okay, here's the thing. You might have wondered why I've stayed awake so long –"

"I thought you were just finding the duplication thing, you know, useful."

He laughed. And there was an edge to it. "I don't want to lose you, Abi. I don't want to lose you by turning into some horrible monster –"

"But I've said you won't! Don't say that word!"

"And I don't want to lose you by dying."

I stared at him.

"Every time I go to sleep, Abi, I risk drawing the black queen. It's like playing Russian roulette. One day I won't wake up. That's why I stay awake as long as I can before I start hating the speed makes me. That's why this time I've stayed awake... longer than ever."

"Because of me."

"Yeah." His expression searched my face.

I hoped I was looking back at him like he needed me to look. I took his hands in mine, and held one of them to my face. If I felt I could have gotten away with it in public, I'd have held it to my breast. "Listen," I said, "you could get hit by a bus. Or, this being New York, probably a cab. Thank you for telling me the risks. But this changes nothing."

He smiled. And yet there was something not quite satisfied about that smile. "You're young," he said. And then he looked up and realised we hadn't been served and let go my hand and started yelling for the waiter. We walked in the park that night, but, looking back, it was more like a march.

We didn't talk about it after that. We both knew where we stood. I found myself accepting the thought that I was a military girlfriend. That my love might vanish forever when he closed his eyes. Or I wonder if I did accept it. I wonder if I got there.

He would arrive at my doorstep with bruises and wave away what happened. "Just some stupid guy, you should see *him*."

He would get angry at some memory of the past, pacing and raging, "and then he said, this was in 1962, then he said –!" And then he'd realise I was standing there listening to him in silence, and he would make himself stop, panting.

The worse time was when he went to the window and said he thought he could hear police out there on the ledge. And then he looked at me as if he was using me to check on whether or not what he was saying was sane. And then he broke into a terrible false laugh, and clapped his hands at his own 'joke' and headed off, saying he needed a drink, and I didn't see him for two days and I thought he'd died.

I should have cancelled Mum's visit. If I could. She might have just shown up anyway. It was only because Croyd insisted so hard, insisted like it was a dying man's last request, that I didn't. He was trying so desperately to hang on to something. He so needed to be that decent, upright guy for me. I see that now.

Mother walked into the apartment and was confronted by the sight of Croyd, obviously at home here (though he actually wasn't, we were still in our separate messy apartments), finishing up washing the dishes. Thanks to Maxine's rage-fuelled, literally, driving, we were, I realised, a few minutes early. "Mrs. Baker," he said, drying his hands and then holding one out to her, keeping it steady through what I could see was sheer willpower. "Croyd Crenson. It's a pleasure to meet you."

Mother looked at him as if he was a burglar. At that time, Croyd didn't look anything other than nat, though maybe there was something a little too intense about those eyes. Even without the drugs. He was wearing vest and braces, like something glamorous from a 1940s movie, with his hair slicked back. Mum looked to me without taking his hand. "Who's he?"

I took a deep breath.

"Oh no," she said.

That sound of genuine anguish and despair in her voice may have been the most terrible thing I ever... no, actually, it wasn't. But at that moment, it was. I looked to Croyd, afraid that he'd be furious. But he'd kept that pleasant, fixed smile on his face.

"Croyd is my..." I had been going to say 'boyfriend'. But that suddenly seemed such a small, childish word. And the last thing I wanted to feel then was childish. But what? 'Lover?' 'Partner?'

Croyd didn't step in to help me. It wasn't that he was waiting to hear me describe him for the first time. It was, I think, that he realised that if he butted in, it would look like he'd provided the definition, that he had maybe coerced me into that way of seeing things. Holding on to his kindness, on that ledge above such a drop.

"We're... together," I finished.

Mother turned back to him and looked him up and down. "What are you?" she said, as if she was being shown round the zoo.

"Parched," said Croyd, "do you want a G&T as much as I do?"

"I mean –"

"I know what you mean." And that was still so jolly. "What are *you*?"

"Normal."

"Well, hey, me too."

"Oh," she visibly relaxed, as if she'd been told anything meaningful. "Well, *that's* a relief." And she actually took his hand.

I was about to bellow with righteous anger, but eye contact from Croyd stopped me.

"You'll have to forgive me," she said, "I'm just surprised that my daughter never mentioned you."

"She was worried that you might not approve."

She smiled *so* broadly. "I think, actually, I will have that G&T. Now, darling, where are your facilities?"

While she went to the bathroom, I followed Croyd into the alcove I laughingly called a kitchen. "You let her believe –!"

"I will explain the misunderstanding and tell her my true nature. Once she's got used to me. Okay?" And the tone in his voice, for the first time ever to me, sounded like he didn't want to hear any arguments.

The Big Apple Circus stands on 8th and 35th. It's not that huge a building, but that's kind of what makes the BAC authentic: it's a classic, one ring circus. As I'd discovered, from rehearsing with them for the last few weeks, the joy of actors at their comradeship and tradition, and especially about those situations where they find themselves in a rep company, is to be felt also in the troupe of a serious circus. Clowns aren't scary when they've devoted their life to their craft, and can project helplessness and pathos past their make-up to make kids squeal with laughter that's about a shared impotence. That fear of them that's arisen in the last few years: that's the product of a world which started accepting second rate clowns. The Big Apple's joker clowns are especially something to see, not concealing their differences, but using them as props. This isn't a freak show. It's about traditional joker skills, used as they've been used in circuses since the 1950s. On the morning of my debut, I got to the circus at seven, as usual, for my last rehearsal. Mum had departed for her hotel thankfully early the night before, popping a pill and succumbing to the jet lag I'd so desperately hoped for. Croyd had come to the end of his ability to listen to stories the protagonists of which he'd neither met nor heard of. But he'd remained resolutely charming, though I was proud he never nodded at her more ridiculous political assertions.

"Meet me for lunch tomorrow," she said to him on the way out to her taxi, "and then we can attend Abigail's debut performance together. I feel we should get to know each other." He'd agreed and feigned enthusiasm.

But after the door closed, and we'd heard the taxi drive off, he ran at the wall and kicked it, so hard I feared for his toes. "People like that –!" he yelled. "How is *she* your mother?"

I told him about how distant I felt from the ancient and immobile forces that mother represented. How she always tried to control what I did. I reassured him that we'd fooled her, that he'd done fine. And finally, his heart beating through his chest against my palm, he calmed.

I tried to sleep as he tried not to. He was listening on headphones to jazz that I couldn't help but hear seeping out, as if at some great distance. The man who never slept in the city that did likewise. The saxophone and the little lights way out there finally got into my head and I was unconscious. Which was just as well, because this hadn't been the greatest preparation for my first performance. But we'd both known it would be like this.

Next morning that taut look on his face was one notch more haunted. "Break a leg," he said when I was dressed and ready to go. I kissed him. I held him hard. "You too," I said.

Radha O'Reilly was waiting for me at the performers' entrance. She looks like a petite, incredibly fit fiftysomething (though I hear she's a lot older), with the sort of golden biceps that, to my eyes, demand a bit of ink. But that's not something I ever could say to her, because I'm a bit in awe of her. You'll appreciate the reasons why: she's been a famous ace for decades now, Elephant Girl, someone who walked out into the spotlight and declared who she was before there were the ace and joker communities and celebrities of today. She was the first person who turned into an elephant onstage and expected people to see it as entertainment rather than horror. Today I was to be the second.

"Okay this morning?" she said.

What she meant was, was I receiving her power, and was I able to control it? That was why she always met me outside, so we wouldn't be in a confined space for that moment. I'd been feeling her power from halfway down the street, in that way which I'd used to find so horribly intimate that the first few times I'd come to rehearse I'd been all kind of blushy when I got here. It was true that what we were going to do this afternoon, then tonight, then eight times a week was, if anything went wrong, vastly dangerous. But I'd never felt able to ask her if she felt I was the newbie, still likely to mess up, or an actor only trying to be a circus pro, or someone that had been foisted on her, because of my newfound bums on seats value, or even if I was any good. She had an utter calm about her that made one both desperately not want to flap around in front of her, and yet more likely to do so at any moment. There goes that language again: flapping around in front of her was exactly what I was there to do.

I told her I was fine, she finished her none blacker coffee and we went inside.

"My mother's going to be in the audience," I said, as we stood in the empty ring, me aching all over after the rehearsal.

Radha looked sidelong at me, taking this new factor on board. Realising, I think, that I was letting something out by saying it. "Does that add to the pressure?"

"I suppose."

"Only, I was wondering why you seemed distracted –"

What, distracted enough to dump me at the last moment and send the clown car out a second time? "No! No, there's... you know, stuff going on in my life. But when I'm up there, I'm completely focussed."

She rolled athletically onto her back, and lay there on the sawdust, looking up through the safety net that we knew would be totally inadequate for our own protection, this afternoon, but was entirely to make the audience feel that they were watching something only reasonably death-defying. "I do this for my mother, you know."

Feeling a little awkward, I sat stiffly down beside her. "In my case, it's kind of in spite of."

"My mother was on the *Queen Mary* in 1946. The death ship. She was transformed by the virus. She grew thick grey skin. People are still shocked by the pictures of her, but to me that's just Mum. I never heard her voice. I always wanted to. She'd never recorded herself when she was a nat. Dad stayed with her, while the rest of the world threw up their hands and backed away. They were taken in by this cult, back home in India. You'd see this awkward relationship between Dad and the priests. He loved Chandra, but they *worshipped* her. She took it, being seen as a kind of holy object, because, well, we needed a home, this was the only place we could live in peace. She had me seven months after the virus. She had a choice in that. Nobody was sure if she would survive the pregnancy. But they wanted me so much, they always told me that. My mother sacrificed so much, without being able to say a word."

It took me a moment to be able to speak. "That sounds like... the opposite of my mother. I think she'd find some... horrible words to describe yours."

"What, you're setting me up for meeting her today, all the while thinking of her like that?"

"Would you prefer it if I lied?"

"Well, she is your mother. Perhaps she deserves some falsehoods being told on her behalf. None of us can really judge our parents. I don't believe in karma, but..." She shook her head quickly and changed the subject. "I have to introduce you tonight. Have you chosen your ace name?"

"I sometimes think... The Understudy."

She considered it, flatteringly seriously. "I like the humility of that. But you'll need to know when to become the lead. You'll need to be strong enough to make that change and have people accept it."

I felt ridiculously close to tears. I shouldn't have got into such a serious conversation with everything that was hanging over my head. I needed to keep a distance. "I'm not ready yet. Nowhere near."

"Not after today?"

"Of course not."

She nodded, pleased again. "Have you told your mother your real name?"

I couldn't even shake my head.

"Before we go on," she said, "decide your name."

This next part of what happened is something that I can only tell you about second hand, from what Croyd told me when he called that afternoon. And yet it's the most important thing. So you'll have to accept my memories of his memories. He went over everything several times. The sound of his voice scared me from the moment I took the call. "I have to tell you," he said, "I have to tell you before you see her again tonight. She swore me to secrecy, and I said yes, I don't know why I said yes –!"

I was frightened that I was talking to someone who wasn't the man I knew any more. I also knew, instantly, that she'd done that to him. That the rocklike tradition of what she was had put a hole in him and he was sinking. I said don't tell me, let me come and see you, but he started yelling at me that my career was the most important thing, that I had to stay there and get ready, and he made me swear to keep that promise. Finally, I managed to get him to tell me what happened, and here it is, for you, through all the distortions.

He'd taken Mum out for lunch at an excellent diner he knew in Greenwich Village, one where the dodginess was a little more under the surface than usual, and which had, to use his words "a billion kinds of coffee, 'cause that always impresses you Brits."

"I'd just like to say," he said, holding her chair for her, "I'm charmed by how open-minded you've been about your daughter and me. I think she's a peach." He frowned at her reaction. "That's a good thing."

"You talk," she said, "like you're from my father's generation. Why is that?"

He'd shrugged. He didn't want to lie again to her, when he'd been going to tell the truth.

"What do you do for a living?"

"Recently I've been a DVD wholesaler. Before that, I was an importer. And I've been known to dabble in the security business." He coughed as the waiter brought them the coffee.

"The sort of thing a conman would say."

Again, he was forced to silence, cornered.

"Your daughter's got a delightful power –"

"Ah, I was wondering if she'd told you. Please don't use that as if it's a key to unlock the mysteries of my own approval. Abigail is *infected*. It's a medical condition, not a political cause. I mean, look at her, look what's become of her! I had to come over and see what she'd sunk to. Because I still care about her, you see."

He hadn't expected this. He'd just stared at her.

"Here she is, an exile from her home, because of what people there would say, living in a ghetto –"

"She came to New York for Broadway –!"

"An excuse, for when you've lost a life of comfort and ease, and have been reduced to scraping a living by performing as a *freak* in a *circus*."

"She is *not* a *freak*!"

"And neither are you."

"No!"

"And that's why you lied to me. When you told me you were normal."

And suddenly Croyd was trying, and failing, to hold a dozen full cups of coffee. Like a clown. It burst all over the table. It stained the cloth, it covered his clothes, it burnt him. It missed Mum completely.

"Tell me everything," she said. "I might be sympathetic to your plight."

That's all he told me of the conversation. It was only later I learned there was more to it. I stood there beside the ring with my phone in my hand, shaking. "I thought... she was proud of me," I said. I managed to swallow down the end of that sentence. And then I hated myself almost as much as I hated her. "Where is she now?"

"Shopping. We're still going to come to the show together. I don't know why I said yes. I kept thinking about you –"

I hate being angry. I hate rows. I hate people grandstanding like that. I hate disruption. I hate that my Mum drags me into all that. "I don't want her here. I don't want to *see* her –"

"Absolutely. You want it, I can get some of the guys to put her in the back of a cab and make sure she gets on a plane."

"Yes. Yes, that's great, do it!"

"Some of those guys I know. Who make sure of things. And you know she's not going to make it easy, she's going to push them. And then they might... reciprocate."

"Fine."

He gave up with that. He was just about yelling at me now. As if he was scared that neither of us could seem to find a way to stop the inevitability of all this. The inevitability. It only seems like that now. "And then, what, you're estranged from her? Cut off? You don't have a family no more?"

"I don't *now*!"

I went backstage for costume and make-up. Alice the make-up lady had to ask me to relax my face, because she wasn't going to be able to fill in the frown lines otherwise. I managed not to have her have to cope with tears. It was just basic stage make-up, and my costume was a deliberately ordinary frock and dark glasses. Covering up the tats hadn't just been for my mother's benefit.

Radha, in her colourful, loose fitting stage costume, was waiting for me outside. She looked at me, understood something, and took my hands in hers. "Breathe," she said.

I breathed.

"We're doing this for the audience. We owe them our best performance."

I managed to nod.

"Whatever this new crisis is, you have to put it behind you. For your own sake."

I managed to share a smile with her. I was already there, actually. Or I thought I was. Performing is my home, and I was deciding it was also going to be my family. It and Croyd.

"But most important of all, remember this: if you don't manage to put it out of your mind, and mess up up there, I will fucking *kill* you."

And that was said with such an enormous grin on her face, and such steely eyes, that I was right back to being overawed again. And that took something serious in my brain and fixed it there for the future. Because that was professionalism. There it was. "Understudy," I said, helplessly.

She shook her head. "No. Oh well. I'll just have to name you."

I couldn't find anything to say.

I hurried out towards the side door to join the queue.

That was the plan, you see, for me to head into the venue with the rest of the audience, anonymously. I'd been provided with a ticket that would place me in just the right seat. I hesitated on the corner, looking at the line, worried that I'd join it at just the point Croyd and mother did. But no, there they were, Croyd rolling his head to try and ease the tension, Mum looking pointedly at him and then all around, as if she were worried to be seen with him. As if the scales of right and wrong there were the other way round. Neither of them knew what the details of the act were going to be.

I joined the back of the queue and, desperately trying to put everything else out of mind, headed in with everyone else.

I took care to sense, as the four sides of bleachers around the ring filled up, if anyone else with, you know, powers, had entered. There were two, both deuces. That is, they had useless powers. One of them could turn her hands different colours, the other one had complete control over the style of his moustache. I relaxed, let my power harmlessly flirt with theirs. My palms ran through a range of hues, my top lip itched, but I didn't let it sprout. If one of the audience had turned out to have a major power that I couldn't deal with, I had a number ready to call on my mobile, and they'd have been led out, with gifts and a refund, before Radha's act. The circus authorities had obviously heard about my earliest experiences in professional theatre.

I sat through the clowns, who were a fast-moving bundle of acrobatic sight gags that made the children and a lot of the adults in the audience squeal with laughter. None from me. My gaze, in the moments when the lights were up, had found Croyd and my mother in the crowd. She was looking prim, her mouth a line, suggesting a smile but not being one. I sat through a joker high wire act, the Flying

Crustaceans, who used their pincers to snap from trapeze to trapeze. And I thought about me and, you know, love.

When I was in my teens, I'd been too focussed on getting away from Dorset and the weight of history there to have much in the way of romance. By which I mean there was, you know, stuff, of the usual kind, involving cider and boys who drove tractors. But I always had one hand reaching out ready to extricate myself. I'd fallen in with Croyd like it was going to be the obvious, central, relationship of my entire life; not, as these things seemed to be with some of my classmates at the School, a test drive, the first of maybe many. Maybe I was a bit old-fashioned like that. Made by my Mum. There was a terrible thought. I absolutely did not want to be. Had she been right that I'd run here not *to* something but *from* something? I thought about the times when my family had met other families from my parents' class, what their looks had meant, what the lack of party invitations had meant, why I'd ended up only with boys who drove tractors and never those who bought them.

Well. Maybe the bitch was right about some things.

The lights went up on the ring once more, revealing Radha standing there. "Ladies and gentlemen!" she called out. And the audience was silent. And she didn't need a mike. "You may have heard of me. You may think you know everything about me. You know I can do... this!" The lights flickered as the back-up generators kicked in, helping the grid handle the sudden demand for power. This was why the show had that sign outside saying no audience members with pacemakers allowed. The BAC had had to rent some serious mega wattage to avoid blacking out whole city blocks. With a dramatic gesture, Radha's body suddenly contorted and the space around her did too, as if reality had just done a magic trick with a folded handkerchief. Her garment burst from her in a moment which managed to be (and I'm told you can see it slowed down to individual frames on YouTube) both alluring and modest at the same time. She spun to a halt on the spot, taking up much of the ring, in her new form, that of a full-sized Asiatic Elephant.

"And," continued her voice, now a recording being played over the speakers, "you probably know I can do... this!" And with an impossibly graceful upward leap, and a single flap of her enormous ears, the elephant that was Radha took to the air. She soared straight up, to the top of the big top, then managed, the band striking up a boisterous tune with shrieking electric guitar as she did so, to turn that into an elegant spiral, flashing over the audience, heading down and down, faster and faster. They started to applaud wildly, because most of them, being tourists, although they had probably heard of Radha's power, wouldn't have seen it live before. I didn't applaud, though. Playing my part, I folded my arms over my chest, looking glum. This was not hard.

"But did you know," the recording continued, "that I can also do... this!" And as she swung her third turn down towards me, she tensed her trunk, raised it above her head, and then straightened it suddenly in my direction.

The blast of water hit me right in the face.

At that same moment I let down my guard and let her power take me.

We'd practiced this move for weeks, with dummies in the seats around me. (Which had, actually, each been moved an inch further away from mine.) I took the flight power a tiny instant before I took the transformation. My human feet sprang upwards a moment before my body above them burst into its new elephantine shape. My carefully weakened clothes sprang apart, to reveal nothing much in that nanosecond, I really hoped, because I didn't want that to become, you know, my signature move. To the audience, especially to those screaming in horror and glee nearby, it seemed that one of their number had suddenly exploded into being a flying elephant –

– who spiralled up to join, exactly as we'd rehearsed ten times a day, Radha, the two of us flying around the ring equidistantly. She was waving her trunk playfully, suggesting she could do it to many more of the audience too, and the clowns were running about putting up umbrellas over people. "No," cried out the recording, "you're quite safe. Ladies and gentlemen, may I present, Abigail Baker, The Actor!" And there was applause as, perhaps with some relief, the audience remembered that I was that girl they'd heard about and, oh yes, they'd wondered what I was going to be doing in the show.

And she'd named me in that instant. Like something out of *The Jungle Book*. In the recording she'd made just before we went on. But I only really paid attention to that later.

Because as I sped above them, I'd kept looking at Croyd and mother. Looking and looking. Round and round. Spiralling gradually downwards. He was applauding, yelling, bellowing, loving me. Though he'd never used that word.

She was nodding, sighing, acknowledging that this was the best I could do in these sad circumstances. I was such a disappointment to her.

I couldn't help it. I say that, but I know I could have. What was meant to happen now was that Radha and I were supposed to spiral in towards each other, clasp trunks, spin around until the moment it looked like we were going to fly up and hit the ceiling, then change back and fall, naked in the moment before the lights went out, into the net. Costumes would be thrown to us, and donned in the moment before we somersaulted out of the net and onto the sawdust to take our bows.

That's what should have happened.

I had got that expression of my mother's locked into my head, bigger and bigger, on every circuit of the room. All her condescension, and all my guilt and anger, always in my way, time after time. And here I was doing this incredible, beautiful thing, here I was, strong and famous and adult, and it was *never* going to be acknowledged, not from this woman whose acknowledgement would have meant everything. To her, all this was shameful. My love was shameful. And so in the end was I.

And I proved her right.

I swear, I just wanted to knock that stupid hat off her head.

I swung deliberately an inch lower. I extended one of my enormous elephant feet as I saw her turning to look up towards me as I approached, looking perhaps a little bored now. Croyd realised a second before she did. He started to yell no.

Him looking scared in that second... him starting to cry out in horror, the sudden expression of the fear that had been hanging over us, the things we weren't talking about... I think I must have instinctively reached out to him in that second, mentally. I think I must have connected us. For the last time. Because what his power really is, like he said... it's sleeping.

I suddenly found a terrible shuddering fatigue grabbing my body. I realised, as the audience before me became a screaming dreamscape of surreal clowns, that I was somehow –

Falling asleep.

With my last conscious thought, I managed to use the power of flight that was about to leave me to throw myself sideways.

I could feel myself spinning as time slowed down to a crawl. It was half a dream, half adrenalin trying desperately to keep me awake as I spun towards those hard bleachers and the flesh and bone of anyone I might connect with in a high speed crash.

Something grabbed me from behind. And threw me with the strength of an elephant.

And there was Croyd throwing himself forward out of the seats, heaving clowns out of the way and diving for the safety net. For so much more safety net. Than there had been. In a different place. And he was right underneath me now! If I was still an elephant when I landed –!

I woke up in hospital. I scrambled up, shouting, demanding to know if everyone was all right –! And standing there at the end of my bed wasn't Croyd or my mother... just Radha.

"Nobody got hurt," she said. "You included."

After a moment I was able to talk again. "That was sheer luck," I said finally. "It was all my fault."

"Yes," she said.

"Understudy," I said, starting to cry. Because it hadn't been Croyd that had nearly hurt someone in a careless rage.

"Yes," she said. And it turned out that had been all she'd been there to say. Because she headed for the door. A moment later, Croyd and Mum entered. Like she'd told them I'd said it was okay. They both looked horribly caring and fearful at me. I felt like I was twelve or something.

"My darling," said Mum, and meant it. "My darling, thank God."

The look on Croyd's face said he hadn't told her what I'd been trying to do. He looked more tired than I'd ever seen him.

They let me go home that same day. I was clearly not in shock, having been asleep at the moment when, thankfully as a human being, I'd been caught in Croyd's arms. Mother stayed beside me, occasionally looking at me as if to ask if it was all right she was there. I wondered if she'd somehow intuited that Croyd had told me what she'd said. She looked so frail, suddenly. She looked lost in a foreign country. She wasn't proud of me, but she was afraid for me. It weirdly seemed now like even that much must be difficult for such a small woman to manage. She and Croyd were careful with each other. We went back to my place in the same taxi. We didn't talk.

I found a message on my answerphone from the owner of the circus, asking me to call as soon as I felt able to, to talk about my 'employment options'.

I went into the kitchen space with Croyd, wondering what Mum would make of the tea we had over here. Croyd held me. He was quaking. I heard a noise from the other room. It sounded like a sob. And then the door opened.

I ran out into the stairwell, but Mum was already on her way down, as fast as her heels could take her. "I can't, darling," she called, before I could shout, "I'll come and see you tomorrow." And then she was gone.

Croyd sat on the sofa just staring at me. He looked desperately sick. "I thought... I thought..." He didn't look as if he could think anything. He looked like he was about to have a heart attack. Saving me had taken all the strength he had left. His eyes were half in a dream.

I decided.

I went to the kitchen and made him another cup of very strong coffee. In it, I dropped the sleeping pill I'd taken from my mother's purse.

He took a few sips of it, then as soon as he could, threw back the whole mug. He could hardly talk. He was desperately holding on. I put my arms around him, and rested his head on my shoulder, and hoped that I hadn't just committed murder. To go alongside all my other guilt that day. He tried to fight the feeling, tried to fight me, but finally, with an exhalation, his head slumped against mine and he was asleep.

I put him to bed. I piled food beside it, ready for when and if he woke: boxes of Hostess Twinkies. I lay beside him, trying not to think about the evening performance that was taking place amongst all those lights out there, without me. I wondered if I'd finished off my life here alongside his. I kept checking to see that he was breathing. Sometime in the early hours I fell asleep myself.

I woke and he was in the exact same position, still asleep, still breathing. I put a little water in his mouth. I checked my phone and found a message from Mum. She sounded calm, lost. She'd meet me at the same place she'd met Croyd. She said one o'clock, as if leaving it up to me to arrive or not, or controlling me still. One or the other.

I looked at Croyd and decided that he would either wake or he wouldn't. It might be days. I had to see her. I wasn't exactly sure what for.

We sat in the low angled sunlight of the coffee shop. She looked momentarily pleased to see me. Then she locked that expression away. "How is he?" she asked.

"Asleep."

"Yes. I thought it would be soon."

"He told you about his power?"

"Yes. Did he tell you what I said?"

"Yes."

She closed her eyes. "When I'd heard everything, I told him he reminded me of the wide boys my father used to hang around with. He was of that generation, and of that type. I asked him how he could ever be sure that he wouldn't hurt you in a drug-induced rage. My father, after all, gave my mother a black eye occasionally. And so that is something I would never allow, for myself or for you. I asked him that simple question, and he flung the table aside, bellowed at me, threw cups and plates at me, until I was quivering." She looked suddenly ashen at me. "Oh. He didn't tell you that part."

I was furious with her all over again. But I held it in. "I believe you," I said. "But he would never have hurt you."

"I understood that at the time, I think. And I became convinced of that when I saw him risk his life to save you. The elephant almost crushed him, you know –"

"You mean I did."

"I told him he was too old for you. That you could never keep up with him. That you still needed to grow. That he would get frustrated at that, and there would come a time for the black eye. He stopped yelling. He finally started listening to me."

I knew my apartment was empty before I entered. I found mucous and scales and what might have been feathers on the bed. I fell back against the wall.

He was alive.

But he had not stayed. He had not gone out to find a pizza or anything story book like that.

He wasn't coming back.

I was sure he had done it for me. But perhaps it was apt punishment also. I had, after all, controlled the most important decision he made. Perhaps, that day, we had saved each other's lives and parted because of it. Or perhaps we were just victims of the way the world is still made. I haven't decided yet.

I tried to stop myself, but I gave in. I tried to find him. But I'd left it too long. And he's good at not being found. I might have seen him, amongst the jokers passing me. I kept looking, for a while. I didn't know what he looked like.

Mum and I spent the next few days together. I told her Croyd had gone. She nodded. We didn't talk about what had happened. Or anything else meaningful. We talked about the weather, which was getting colder. We talked about New York, which she'd started to gaze at, from out of the window.

Finally, it was time for her to go home. She asked me when I had to return to school. I told her I still had two weeks. I thought she was about to offer me money, but she thought better of it. She kissed me on the cheek and I smelt the same perfume that I associated with what I'd fled, and felt the age of her skin on mine. I gave her some of the many boxes of Hostess Twinkies I still had lying around, which I was sure she'd give all of to Maxine. I was sure for many reasons.

The media coverage was minor to non-existent, an accident to an increasingly minor celebrity. A run of shows cancelled, understandably. I rejoined the School much as I'd left it.

I've talked to mother on the phone twice since then. She's more like her old self. Which is either normal, or evil, or scared, depending on the background she's seen against. The weather over there is much as it is here, getting colder. The aunts are fine. Thanks for asking.

As the snows came to New York, I realised that I'd stopped looking for Croyd in every crowd of jokers. That I'm sure I will see him again. I call myself The Understudy in ace circles now, and will until I feel justified doing otherwise. I don't know how that could happen. But I know it might.

I've finished crying, anyway. Telling this story cleared something away for me. I don't know if I entirely wanted it cleared. But it has been.

There's no justice to any of this. One day I may end up taking care of my mother. She will never apologise for anything. I'm not sure I could ever be sure enough to insist she should. The battles of our adolescence can never be won.

A New Arrival at the House of Love

The house of love was, in the beginning, an individual theme; stuff created by All Metal, and not from any of the basics, either, but from nothing. He'd made it at the highest point of a side he'd created as he ran upwards for joy, looping gravity under him so that the house, when he made it, bloomed out from under the top of the curve, and hung underneath a wave that would never break.

"Der, der de der, der de der, de der, de der der der de dum!" he had hummed, making one of his favourite heads to mosh as his new feet for the occasion had hammered out the basics of the house, blurring in shared vision. "Guitar!" he had shouted and, in an act he gazed inward later was probably accidental, kicked the house right over the top of the curve, so it landed – slam! – on top of the new cliff.

Oh!

He had hung there in mid-air, then, suddenly realising –

Suddenly, for All Metal, was less suddenly, by many sad moments, than for almost anyone else. But realising, for All Metal, everyone else then realised, before him, as they gazed at him, was somehow greater for him at that lovely moment than everyone else, because –

He'd knocked the house right out of everything ever!

Maybe it was what he'd done with the gravity that had caused it.

Everyone gazed inward to find out how he'd done it. But they couldn't work it out. So they started to applaud.

As on no previous occasions, All Metal had made something new. And this was extraordinarily new. It was a lovely sign that we continue!

Instead of falling, which might have been fun on any other occasion, he spun and shone and wrapped light about him. Then he took himself out of shared vision. And left everyone talking.

He went up to find out. He peeped over the edge of the thing he'd made, at the house he'd put there. Wherever *there* was.

It seemed safe up here. It seemed just like everything ever.

131

But it was clearly not quite. It was weird up here. It was where everything ever met everything else. Nobody had known there was an everything else.

And he'd built a house here! Brilliant!

He took an initial step forward into the house. And it was okay. Right, then! He immediately brought in loads of textures beloved to him, and filled the place with them, packed them in until the walls... whispered. Were they supposed to do that? He'd never heard that in shared vision before.

Oh well.

He decided on three of his favourite styles of architecture, without gazing inward, just by remembering from the textures. Yeah, he had favourite styles of architecture, but he didn't even know what they were called! That was him being him. He continued.

He gazed inward about colours, and decided on three of those too, ready for when there would be shared vision in the house. He added the colours to the textures, and the textures celebrated and remembered all sorts of extra stuff for him that filled up every bit of the house, like black holes or flowers blooming out of each other, pow pow pow!

He boggled in wonder! He would invite everyone ever over!

Just as soon as he'd done a bit of final editing.

All Metal's first guest, before he invited anyone, annoyingly, was Tom8967. All Metal found Tom being near the house, in the place where everything ever met everything else. He was gazing and gazing. One of the things Tom had before been was a dancer in the video for 'Can't Take My Eyes Off Of You' by the Boys Town Gang. Which always made All Metal curious about the things he couldn't find gazing inwards because he himself hadn't before been. Not in the way the words meant, that he'd been individual, like his favourite textures had been parts of.

All Metal didn't have to do anything, any more than anyone else did, but it pleased him to invite Tom8967 in. And Tom8967 brought shared vision with him. Which All Metal hadn't actually considered, but now he'd done that... well, that was all right, All Metal supposed.

Tom8967 gasped pleasingly at the sight of the interior of the house of love and did back flips. "You did something new!" he said. "I knew you could!"

"I knew I could too," said All Metal.

"But I knew it first."

"Well –" began All Metal.

But Tom had taken three random textures from the walls and was listening to them.

"Hey –" said All Metal.

"These textures are in their own everything ever, created by a long road trip." He sounded not just fascinated, as All Metal was himself by the textures he'd so carefully picked up in everything ever, but as if he was suffering from nostalgia, which All Metal gazed inward was one of those things that probably approximated to the genre rot he experienced whenever he ran into Nu Metal. "You can hear that up here! You can hear what they were part of! You don't have to swallow them!" He seemed surprised again. "Oh, they're reacting to me feeling that. They're having an alien abduction. Oh, I should have realised." He quickly put the textures back.

All Metal swept one great booted foot around the room and rather sulkily kicked some new textures from gazing inward up into his walls. *He* wanted to be the one who took things from gazing inward and put them in remembering! *He* wanted to be the one who found out more new things that could happen! This was *his* new house! "Why did you come here?" he asked.

"To find out what this house means!"

"It'll mean what I want it to mean."

"Oh, please, don't leave it at *that!*"

Before All Metal could gaze inward whether or not to be angry, Emma appeared. All Metal had gazed inward to invite her to come and visit the house he had named for her. It was to have been a 'surprise' tribute. But no. All his plans were being pre-empted. Perhaps, he gazed inward, he should swallow some of those textures and find if any of them could make him faster. But then he heard the textures screaming at having heard that off him. Which made Tom gaze at him with a gaze that said *that* confirmed the significant discovery *he* had made earlier.

Emma had brought with her Elinor Dashwood and Spurs. Which was also annoying. "Diddly dah," greeted Emma.

"Diddly dah," sighed All Metal in return.

"We continue."

"We continue, Emma."

"What exactly have you done?"

"Amazingly!"

"That's how, not what. And it is a rather lovely how. But I repeat: what have you done?"

"All that you allow," All Metal recited, "which is everything."

"Yes, yes, have a biscuit." She threw him one, which he swallowed with a gulp. It made him glow with increased pride, now faltering at 87, which was actually quite low for him. "But what... specifically?"

"Dunno," said All Metal. "Fun?"

"Fun. Hmm." Emma gazed to Spurs, who lit up as her gaze actualised him. "You're a different sort of thing. What can you gaze?"

Spurs gazed around and past the house. "Game of two halves," he said. He nodded towards All Metal. "Good servant to his club. But he always tries to go route one. Bit weak at the back."

"He means," translated Emma, "that you are indeed a delightful chap, but by being rather too, shall we say, direct in your methods, you may have created something rather worrying. Elinor?"

Miss Dashwood had marched into the middle of the house, gazing around like something was making her itch with close approximation. She was the same sort of thing as Emma was, but, of course, Emma could be any sort of thing. "I cannot say I like it," she said. "In fact I should say I dislike it, for dislike is at the root of all I survey. And that is a sensation both distinct and terrible. I feel it may be... it may be the doom of us all."

"Doom?" echoed Emma, one finely-sculpted eyebrow raised a precise distance, her voice, as ever, suggesting layers of mockery, self-mockery, irony and affection that filled all around her with delicious bonuses at every layered lovely moment.

"DOOM!"

And that had been an enormous voice from everything else. Which had shaken the house and all of them inside it. They were all silent for a sad moment, gazing in all directions, because it had come from all directions.

"Oh," said All Metal, very quietly, "sorry."

"Conference," said Emma, and snapped her fingers.

They were immediately standing amongst everyone in everything ever. "Diddly dah," Emma greeted them.

"Diddly dah!" the throng called back, making All Metal jump. That had nearly been as loud as the voice from everything else had been. He gazed behind him, and gazed how everyone ever stretched to, and then formed, the horizon in all directions. Emma had obviously, in the lovely moment she'd moved them here, put away the side he'd made, into safe keeping, perhaps in her own gazing inward.

"We continue."

"We continue!" All Metal had been prepared for it that time.

"There is, it seems, everything else."

The throng gasped.

"I didn't know, but there it is. All Metal here discovered it."

All Metal could feel everyone gazing at him. His scores rippled up and down until his gazing inward said enough of that and flashed back in a lovely moment to only Emma actualising him, and that made him feel a lot better.

"Now, there are shapes that suggest a course of action when someone does this. I could, for example, banish All Metal and close the gates of everything ever behind him –"

All Metal was speechless with horror.

"– But I think that would be terribly dull of me."

"Diddly dee!" swore All Metal, relieved.

"Is everything else the doom of us all?" asked the balloon. All Metal had always considered the balloon lucky to be here. It was, as far as anyone could tell, a balloon with a face drawn on it. It seemed to only say things others had said immediately before. It wasn't really anything more than a texture, and depending on what was inside it, perhaps a lot less. The balloon did, however, change colour. Perhaps that had made the difference when Emma had done the choosing. Or perhaps it was just that she'd erred hugely on the side of caution. Everyone ever followed those colour changes and gossiped about them, as if they might signify something. Unknown signifiers were all everyone ever ever gossiped about.

The balloon's colour at the sad moment was an alarming shade of red.

"I doubt it," said Emma.

"You don't *know?*" asked a horrified massive near the front of the crowd. "Double you tee eff?"

"I can't know," sighed Emma, breaking the massive's

communication options with a twirl of her finger, "about what's outside everything ever. By definition, in fact. But I intend to find out what this new thing is. I'm appointing an expedition. And putting my top people on it. And All Metal, because he found it, and the taking of responsibility is a joy to the score, and so forth."

"I –" began All Metal, raising his hand. But before he could compose a sentence Emma had healed the massive's communication options with another finger twirl and they'd all moved on and he was standing with Emma and her expedition. He lowered his hand again, annoyed, as ever, by how he was. And this had all begun with him being other than how he was, faster and more clever than how he was! "Grump," he said.

The expedition comprised another massive, who was already manifesting an enormous axe of sorting stuff, a bignome, who had a window to gaze at stuff in two ways, and, to All Metal's surprise, the balloon. "Grump," it agreed, wistfully.

"And I gaze inward I should include my opposite number," said Emma. "John? You're needed."

John appeared, smiling sidelong, as if, and All Metal knew this was impossible, she'd caught him by surprise. All he'd brought were his usual accessories: an umbrella and a bowler hat. "You called and I am at your side," he said, "like a genie from a bottle."

"I'm hoping," replied Emma, "you'll grant me at least three wishes."

"Three? You got through *those* a long time ago."

They shared a knowing smile.

All Metal closed his eyes. They could do this sort of thing forever, he knew, and had been.

When he opened his eyes again, a lovely moment later, the expedition was on its way. They were all peeping over the edge of everything ever, now once again an edge, into the boundary with everything else, now freed back into everything ever.

"Doom, eh?" said John. And he gazed in all directions, as if expecting a booming reply.

The bignome gazed at her window. "It seems like everything ever," she said, "but a different..." she put a finger to her window, then licked it, "flavour."

"Massive, if I may call you massive, would you be so kind –?" John gestured towards the house.

The massive gazed awkwardly at him.

"Oh, I do beg your pardon." John grabbed his umbrella by the shaft and used the handle to pull aside the massive's communications options. "Would you be so kind as to go first? Thanks awfully." And he adjusted the communications options back again.

The massive seemed to gaze inward for a sad moment, as if gazing inward that all in all too many liberties were being taken with massives' communications options lately. But finally it lifted the axe of sorting stuff into an attack posture, made itself into the shape of itself striding forward, and did so.

All Metal gazed up at the house. It was made, now he gazed inward about how he'd done it, entirely of textures. A large portion of his collection. He'd... well, gazing inward wasn't the way to talk about it, he'd just made in a lovely moment without gazing inward a place out of all that stuff. He'd hefted it with gravity, because he did gravity. Most didn't. When he'd first become himself here in everything ever, at the base of his gazing inward, he'd been given it by Emma, because, as with everything, the shape had suited him. Or that was what she'd said when he'd asked her once.

It was all about what suited what. He'd put the house here because it suited being here. Probably. It wasn't that great, now he gazed at it, three architectural styles: gothic; Edwardian and Tudor, on top of each other, with the textures murmuring scarily up and down the whole thing, and the colours sitting on top of it in shared vision, making the whole thing gaze like a side work of art. But still, he'd have liked to have had Emma enter it and love it.

The massive, whose back words said it was called Mmorg, had entered the house now. Suddenly, it shaped itself in one of its familiar ways, ready for combat.

"Ready for combat!" squeaked the balloon.

"DOOM!" bellowed the voice from everything else. Mmorg shaped himself into his defending posture, shared vision rippling around him. Pieces of him flew away, the textures thus dislodged slapping themselves onto the walls of the house in every direction. All Metal had gazed at massives in conflicts like this before. He knew Mmorg could lose a lot of textures before sad approximating.

The sound of the voice echoed away, finally, and Mmorg still stood there. He shaped himself into a ready posture.

The bignome gazed up from her window. "That was louder," she said. "As if closer."

"Closer?" asked the balloon, incredulous.

All Metal knew what the balloon meant. If it meant anything. How could there be further or closer in everything else? What sort of stuff *was* everything else?

"Come on," said John, "perhaps it takes a while to reload. And if it doesn't, Mmorg here can always shelter us." And he led them into the house.

All Metal was pleased that they took a few lovely moments to gaze around. It was taking basics now to keep his pride even at fifty. In fact, now he gazed inward, it would normally be way over fifty, so this whole texture was, on average, bringing him down. "Do you like it?" he asked, hopefully.

"Delightful, delightful!" cried John, his smile as sad moment deep as the outside shared vision of the house had been. "Such... variety."

"Variety," underlined the balloon.

"Why is the balloon with us?" asked All Metal.

"Because that is what Emma decided," said John, running his umbrella tip along the textures on the walls, making them once again voice all they were being as a result. "Not that, uniquely, I'm always obliged to abide by her wishes. I would continue if she did not."

All Metal had always gazed inward that this was probably the case, but was surprised to hear him say it. It seemed to have been not for his benefit, but directed at the textures. And indeed, they seemed to be reacting differently now, hushed, waiting.

"You know that my shape is to always find a different side," John continued. "I work on the lower slopes, but I do what she could not, should not, and will not." He suddenly spun his umbrella and speared one of the textures that the attack on Mmorg had sent splattering onto the wall. It gave up a joyous sensation of fun and play. John flipped it expertly off the end of the umbrella, and snapped it out of the air with his mouth. He chewed for a sad moment, looking inward. "Hmm," he said finally, "not the finest vintage. But I'm intrigued by its presumption. And it's told me a lot more about what's going on here."

138

He marched towards the stairs. "If you'll excuse me," he said, "I'm just going for a delve in the attic."

All Metal waited a sad moment or two. But he didn't want to wait. He especially didn't want to wait here, when the voice might come back again. He couldn't shed textures like Mmorg did. If shaken to approximation, he might give birth to Grindcore or Nwobhm, stuff he liked to have as part of him, and didn't want to meet awkwardly from time to time, like he did with Nu Metal. The shape of John's words, but not the letter of them, had told him to stay downstairs. But John was no Emma; he was, indeed, all about not following, and so All Metal found himself... following him.

He stopped for a few sad moments on the second floor to gaze at the style he'd thrown here. The textures were already adapting to it, muttering about living in Edwardian times, or going back to Edwardian times, or gazing at Edwardians, whatever they were. All Metal gazed inward that actually that added something to the house, that maybe creating on the edge of everything else might not be a bad idea if not for that horrible voice.

The others had not followed him. They had not gazed inward to. This was what had got him into trouble in the first place. He did new things. But it took him a few sad moments to get there.

He stopped at the bottom of the stairs to the third floor. He could hear John's voice, smooth and full of overlapping textures as always, withholding as many points as it gave, from the floor above. But who could he be talking to?

"You see, old chap, you couldn't swallow us all in one go. You need what we call an intermediary, someone who speaks the natives' lingo..."

All Metal put one huge foot on the bottom stair, and then, as slowly as only he could, he put another on the stair above, and hauled himself up so slowly that he gazed at between the lovely moments and the sad moments of shared vision, and suffered as all who did who didn't keep up to stay past that, with genre rot and epiphany rot and degrading, tending towards approximation, even. He allowed it. He was still himself. He could find shapes in him, shapes he wasn't even aware of, that supported him against that anciently, that echoed of before being, even if All Metal hadn't before been himself. He continued.

He finally got to a place where he could just peep over the edge onto the topmost floor. He could gaze where John was talking to... no, All Metal couldn't gaze that, he couldn't gaze anything about what John was talking to. It was... it was nothing. It was out of shared vision. All Metal checked gazing inward and it wasn't there either, thank Emma. It was like one of those things from between sad moments. He could only gaze at where it must be because it stopped other things being in shared vision. But that shape made no gazing inward either. John was gazing straight at it, but he might be pretending. Pretending was one of his most useful shapes.

"And speaking of native tongues," he was saying, "it's about time you learned all of ours, old sport. Here –" He took the carnation from his lapel, and with a very particular flick of his wrist cast it into the space where no stuff was. All Metal realised he must have included shared language in it.

"WHY ARE YOU DOING THIS?" said the nothing, immediately. But now its words didn't smash into All Metal or John or any of the textures. That must have been something John had included with the shared language.

"What are we," John said, his voice full of shapes, "if not the sum of our natures? My nature, my central shape, is that of a snake. If you cut me open, you would see it written through me like I was a particularly slippery stick of rock: not to be trusted and especially not to be swallowed. If I am given a side to be on, why, I shall almost immediately find a way to play for the other team. Which explains a lot about my school days."

All Metal found his gazing inward was hurting. He had gazed inward all this about John, always, but, always, John's shape made people's gazing inward spit that out and not swallow it. Did that even apply to Emma? Could she be *unaware* of this?

"YOU WANT MY TIME STOP EXPANSION POINT TO ENGULF YOURS?"

"Old man, I positively demand it! For everyone else, anyway. You already know you couldn't swallow me, and I see how that's causing you pause. Look around this place. This is what it's like all over: styles you won't be able to make head nor tail of; textures that must strike a chord with you, being as you're able to communicate shared ideas at all; a continuous slide of easy access for you and your kind, assuming, that is, you have a kind? Or is it just you?" He didn't give the nothing a lovely moment to answer. "We could do, in short, with a change of ownership, a change of scene – Oh, I beg your pardon, were you trying to say something?"

"*IT IS JUST ME. THIS LANGUAGE TASTES FUNNY. I CAN'T LIE IN IT.*"

"Lie?" John's voice got more shaped than ever, to the point where All Metal could hear shared vision slipping past it, making hushed shadows ricochet off the corners of the room. "What is this thing you call 'lie'?"

All Metal couldn't gaze inward at that. John must be lying, but he just said he couldn't.

"Why don't you step right inside and explain it to me at greater length, old chap? You must be catching your death of cold, lurking on the threshold like that."

The nothing seemed to gaze inward for a sad moment, if it had an inward. Finally, it moved forward, into the room. And now All Metal could gaze at what it had passed through: a number of textures that John must have taken from the walls and placed together at that point.

He realised that he should do something, that he couldn't go back to Emma and tell her that he'd just watched this sad thing happening. But he should go back to her and tell her about this –

Before he could start to move, John addressed some words to him, and only him, and they landed on his shoulder, as if John had always known he was watching. "All Metal," the words said, "you got here at exactly the speed you were meant to. Now be a good chap and fetch the others."

All Metal did. Mmorg didn't quite fit up the stairs, so shed textures into a fine spray. All Metal breathed in their horror and delight and nausea and kept them gazing inward. The balloon floated up above that. And the bignome just sniffed.

"Ah, just the stuff I was gazing for," said John when he gazed at the balloon. "You know, sometimes an inward gazing of something's like the thing itself. Don't know what chap said that, perhaps I just made it up." He hooked the string that dangled from the balloon with the handle of his umbrella. "When is a Time Stop Expansion Point not a Time Stop Expansion Point? Possibly never, if everyone involved agrees it is. But what if everyone is just the one?" And with a twirl of his hands that All Metal couldn't follow, but which filled them all for a lovely moment with points, John flipped the balloon inside out. All Metal lovely suddenly felt the force of whatever had been inside the balloon, sucking at him and everything else. He was pleased to have found out there was something inside after all, even if it was sucking at him. What had been inside the balloon turned out to be like nothing else in everything ever. It was a bit like the nothing, in fact. It flew suddenly from John's hands, bounced off Mmorg's locked communications options as something from outside everything ever of course would do, bounced off the bignome's window as not being able to be gazed at –

– And flew straight at the nothing in the room.

The nothing started to gather its breath, if it had breath, perhaps to try to shout *DOOM* again –

But then whatever had been in the balloon hit it, and their breaths and words and stuff became one, and that one hit the far wall where those textures had been placed by John, and the whole thing flew back at John -

And he caught it in the balloon. Then he swiftly knotted the end. And that knotting was bliss in scores, and gave everyone such pleasure with the flash of it. And it was done.

"Mood!" said the balloon. And it sounded calm. And then. "I have a mood. I'm a person. Oh. Where am I?"

"In everything ever," said John. He went over to the wall and nodded to All Metal. "Which now once more lives up to its name. Once you've tidied up, that is."

All Metal quickly kicked the textures off the wall and found -

Just a side beyond them. And that feeling had gone, that had made the textures murmur. The house felt like just a house again.

Emma appeared. "Charming place you have here," she said. "I love it. I look forward to visiting often." And with a snap of her fingers All Metal was filled with points and pleasure and knew that he was exactly as slow as he had to be.

John handed her the balloon and she grinned at it.

"Hi," said the balloon. "I really do have a lot of questions." It had turned a charming shade of blue.

"And I now once again have all the time in the world for answers," said Emma, "and will be delighted to give them."

"What are we going to name it?" said John, indicating the balloon.

"We?" said Emma, one eyebrow raised.

"One day I will manage to trick you into letting me name something. Until then, I try my best."

"Your best is, as always, very good indeed. In the baddest way. Now," she looked to All Metal again, "is there any tea?"

And of course, as soon as she said it, there was.

I've always been interested in the human urge to see character in a face drawn on a balloon, in the slightest indication of three circles on a bigger one. I think that architecture in our brains may form part of the structure of everything from alien abductions to religion to the relative success of cartoon characters. I also enjoy post-Singularity SF, stories set after some cataclysmic alteration of reality. (Though I think the idea of 'the Singularity' is ridiculous, another artefact of how our consciousnesses are constructed, a longing for punctuation in the face of an inability to emotionally process how big and complicated history is.) So when I set out to write a story for Ian Whates' Solaris Rising 1.5 eBook project (2012), which bridged the gap between two anthologies of that name, I made an attempt to deal in pure, simple, character, with only the slightest SFnal hints of background. Who are these beings, living genres, corporations, fictional characters, minds? Where are they? I hope you'll find it doesn't matter.

The Ghosts of Christmas

It was because of a row. The row was about nothing. So it all came from nothing. Or, perhaps more accurately, it came from the interaction between two people. I remember how Ben's voice suddenly became gentle and he said, as if decanting the whole unconscious reason for the row:

"Why don't we try for a baby?"

This was mid-March. My memory of that moment is of hearing birds outside. I always loved that time of year, that sense of nature becoming stronger all around. But I always owned the decisions I made, I didn't blame them on what was around me, or my hormones. I am what's around me, I am my hormones, that's what I always said to myself. I don't know if Ben ever felt the same way. That's how I think of him now: always excusing himself. I don't know how that squares with how the world is now. Perhaps it suits him down to the ground. I'm sure I spent years looking out for him excusing himself. I'm sure me doing that was why, in the end, he did.

I listened to the birds. "Yes," I said.

We got lucky almost immediately. I called my mother and told her the news.

"Oh no," she said.

When the first trimester had passed, and everything was still fine, I told my boss and then my colleagues at the Project, and arranged for maternity leave. "I know you lot are going to go over the threshold the day after I leave," I told my team. "You're going to call me up at home and you'll be all 'oh, hey, Lindsey is currently inhabiting her own brain at age three! She's about to try to warn the authorities about some terrorist outrage or other. But pregnancy must be *such* a joy'."

"Again with this," said Alfred. "We have no reason to believe the subjects would be able to do anything other than listen in to what's going on in the heads of their younger selves –"

"Except," said Lindsey, stepping back into this old argument as if I

145

hadn't even mentioned, *hello*, *baby*, "the maths rules out even the possibility –"

"Free will –"

"No. It's becoming clearer with every advance we make back into what was: what's written is written."

Our due date was Christmas Day.

People shown around the Project were always surprised at how small the communication unit was. It had to be; most of the time it was attached to the skull of a sedated Rhesus monkey. "It's just a string of lights," someone once said. And we all looked appalled, to the point where Ramsay quickly led the guest away.

They were like Christmas lights, each link changing colour to show how a different area of the monkey's brain was responding to the data coming back from the other mind, probably its own mind, that it was connected to, somewhen in the past. Or, we thought only in our wildest imaginings then, in the future.

Christmas lights. Coincidence and association thread through this, so much, when such things can only be illusions. Or artifice. Cartoons in the margin.

How can one have coincidence, when everything is written?

I always thought my father was too old to be a dad. It often seemed to me that Mum was somehow too old to have me too, but that wasn't the case, biologically. It was just that she came from another time, a different world, of austerity, of shying away from rock and roll. She got even older after Dad died. Ironically, I became pregnant at the same age she had been.

We went to see her: me; Ben and the bump. She didn't refer to it. For the first hour. She kept talking about her new porch. Ben started looking between us, as if waiting to see who would crack first. Until he had to say it, over tea. "So, the baby! You must be looking forward to being a grandmother!"

Mum looked wry at him. "Not at my age."

"Sorry?"

"That's all right. You two can do what you want. I'll be gone soon."

We stayed for an hour or two more, talking about other things, about that bloody porch, and then we waved goodbye and drove off and I parked the car as soon as we were out of sight of the house. "Let's kill her," I said.

"Absolutely."

"I shouldn't say that. I so shouldn't say that. She *will* be gone soon. It's selfish of me to want to talk about the baby –"

"When we could be talking about that really very lovely porch. You could have led with how your potentially Nobel-prize-winning discovery of time travel is going."

"She didn't mention that either."

"She *is* proud of you, I'm sure. Did something –? I mean, did anything ever... happen, between you, back then?"

I shook my head. There was not one particular moment. I was not an abused child. This isn't a story about abuse.

I closed my eyes. I listened to the endless rhythm of the cars going past.

The Project was created to investigate something that I'd found in the case histories of schizophrenics. Sufferers often describe a tremendous sensation of *now*, the terrifying hugeness of the current moment. They often find voices talking to them, other people inside their own heads seemingly communicating with them. I started using the new brain mapping technology to look into the relationship between the schizoid mind and time. Theory often follows technology, and in this case it was a detailed image of particle trails within the mind of David, a schizophrenic, that handed the whole theory to me in a single moment. It was written that I saw that image and made those decisions. Now when I look back to that moment, it's almost like I didn't do anything. Except that what happened in my head in that moment has meant so much to me.

I saw many knotted trails in that image, characteristic of asymmetric entanglement. That, unlike in the healthy minds we'd seen, where there are only a couple of those trails at any given moment (and who knows what those are, even today?) this mind was connected, utterly, to... other things that were very similar to itself. I realised instantly what I was looking at: what could those other things that were influencing all those particle trails be but other minds? And where were those other minds very like this one –?

And then I had a vision of the trails in my own mind, like Christmas lights, and that led me to the next moment when I knew consciously what I had actually understood an instant before, as if I had divined it from the interaction of all things -

The trails led to other versions of this person's own mind, elsewhen in time.

I remember that David was eager to cooperate. He wanted to understand his condition. He'd been a journalist before admitting himself to the psychiatric hospital.

"I need to tear, hair, fear, ear, see... yes, see, what's in here!" he shouted, tapping the front of his head with his middle fingers. "Hah, funny, the rhymes, crimes, alibis, keep trying to break out of those, and it works, that works, works. Hello!" He sat suddenly and firmly down and took a very steady-handed sip from his plastic cup of water. "You asked me to stay off the drugs," he said, "so it's difficult. And I would like to go back on them. I would very much like to. After."

I had started, ironically, to see him as a slice across a lot of different versions of himself, separated by time. I saw him as all his minds, in different phases, interfering with each other. Turn that polarised view the other way, and you'd have a series of healthy people. That's what I thought. And I wrote that down offhandedly somewhere, in some report. His other selves weren't the 'voices in his head'. That's a common fallacy about the history of our work. Those voices were the protective action that distances a schizophrenic from those other selves. They were characters formed around the incursion, a little bit of interior fiction. We're now told that 'a schizophrenic' was someone who had to deal with such random interference for long stretches of time.

"Absolutely, as soon as we've finished our interviews today. We don't want to do anything to set back your treatment."

"How do you experience time?" is a baffling question to ask anyone. The obvious answer would be "like you do, probably". So we'd narrowed it down to:

How do you feel when you remember an event from your childhood?
How do you feel about your last birthday?
How do you feel about the Norman Conquest?

"Not the same," David insisted. "Not the same."

I found myself not sleeping. Expectant mothers do. But while not sleeping, I stared and listened for birds, and thought the same thought, over and over.

It's been proven that certain traits formed by a child's environment do get passed down to its own children. It is genuinely harder for the child of someone who was denied books to learn to read.

I'm going to be a terrible parent.

"Will you play with me?" I remember how much that sound in my voice seemed to hurt. Not that I was feeling anything bad at the time; it was as if I was just hearing something bad. I said it too much. I said it too much in exactly the same way.

"Later," said Dad, sitting in his chair that smelled of him, watching the football. "You start, and I'll join in later."

I'd left my bedroom and gone back into the lounge. I could hear them talking in the kitchen, getting ready for bed, and in a moment they'd be bound to notice me, but I'd seen it in the paper and it sounded incredible: *The Outer Limits.* The outer limits of what? Right at the end of the television programmes for the day. So after that I'd see television stop. And now I was seeing it and it was terrible, because there was a monster, and this was too old for me. I was crying. But they'd be bound to hear, and in a moment they would come and yell at me and switch the set off and carry me off to bed, and it'd be safe for me to turn round.

But they went to bed without looking in the lounge. I listened to them close the door and talk for a while, and then switch the light off, and then silence, and so it was just me sitting there, watching the greys flicker.

With the monster.

I was standing in a lay-by, watching the cars go past, wondering if Mummy and Daddy were going to come back for me this time. They'd said that if I didn't stop going on about the ice cream I'd dropped on the beach, they'd make me get out and walk. And then Dad had said "right!" and he'd stopped the car and yanked open the door and grabbed me out of my seat and left me there and driven off.

I was looking down the road, waiting to see the car come back.

I had no way of even starting to think about another life. I was six years old.

Those are just memories. They're not from Christmas Day. They're kept like that in the connections between neurons within my brain. I have a sense of telling them to myself. Every cell of my body has been replaced many times since I was that age. I am an oral tradition. But it's been proved that a butterfly remembers what a caterpillar has learned, despite its entire neurological structure being literally liquidised in-between. So perhaps there's a component of memory that lies outside of ourselves as well, somewhere in those loose threads of particle trails. I have some hope that this is true. Because that would put a different background behind all of my experiences.

I draw a line now between such memories and the other memories I now have of my childhood. But that line will grow fainter in time.

I don't want to neglect it.
I'm going to neglect it.
I don't want to hurt it.
I'm going to hurt it.
They made me this way. I'm going to blame them for what I do. I'm going to end up being worse.

I grew numb with fear as autumn turned to winter. I grew huge. I didn't talk to Ben or anyone about how I felt. I didn't want to hear myself say the words.

In mid-December, a couple of weeks before the due date, I got an email from Lindsey. It was marked 'confidential':

Just thought I should tell you, that, well, you predicted it, didn't you? The monkey trials have been a complete success, the subjects seem fine, mentally and physically. We're now in a position to actually connect minds across time. So we're going to get into the business of finding human volunteer test subjects. Ramsay wants 'some expendable student' to be the first, but, you know, over our dead bodies! This isn't like lab rats, this is first astronaut stuff. Anyway, the Project is closing down on bloody Christmas Eve, so we're going to be forced to go and ponder that at home.

Enclosed are the latest revisions of the tech specs, so that you can get excited too. But of course, you'll be utterly blasé about this, because it is nothing compared to the miracle of birth, about which you must be so excited, etc.

I looked at the specs and felt proud.

And then a terrible thought came to me. Or crystallised in me. Formed out of all the things I was. Was already written in me.

I found myself staggered by it. And hopeful. And fearful that I was hopeful. I felt I could save myself. That's ironic too.

My fingers fumbling, I wrote Lindsey a congratulatory email and then re-wrote it three times before sending so that it was a model of everything at my end being normal.

I knew what I was going to be doing on Christmas Day.

Due dates are not an exact science. We'd had a couple of false alarms, but when Christmas Eve arrived, everything was stable. "I think it's going to be a few more days," I told Ben.

I woke without needing an alarm, the next morning, to the strange quiet of Christmas Day. I left Ben sleeping, showered and dressed in the clothes I'd left ready the night before. Creeping about amongst the silence made me think of Father Christmas. I looked back in on Ben and felt fondly about him. That would have been the last time for that.

I drove through streets that were Christmas empty. My security card worked fine on a door that didn't know what day it was.

And then I was into the absolute silence of these familiar spaces, walking swiftly down the corridors, like a ghost.

The lab had been tidied away for the holidays. I had to unlock a few storage areas and remember a few combinations. I reached into the main safe and drew out the crown of lights.

I paused as I sat in Lindsay's chair, the crown connected to a power source, the control systems linked up to a keyboard and screen in my lap. I considered for a moment, or pretended to, before putting it on my head.

Could what I was about to do to my brain harm the foetus?

Not according to what had happened with the monkeys. They were all fine, physically. I could only harm myself. We'd theorised that too long a connection between minds, more than a few minutes, would result in an extreme form of what the schizophrenics dealt with, perhaps a complete brain shutdown. Death. I would have to feel that coming and get out, or would have to unconsciously see it approaching on the screen, or just count the seconds.

Or I would fail my child completely.

I nearly put it all away again, locked up, walked out.

Nearly.

I put the crown on my head, I connected the power source, I took the keyboard in my hands and I watched the particle trails in my own mind begin to resolve on the screen. I concentrated on them, in the way we'd always talked about, and I started typing before I could think again. I hit activate.

The minds of the monkeys seemed to select their own targets. The imaging for those experiments showed two sets of trails reacting to each other, symmetrical, beautiful. That seemed to suggest not the chaotic accident of schizophrenia, but something more tranquil, perhaps something like a religious experience, we'd said. But of course we had nothing objective to go on. I had theorised that since we evolved with every moment of ourselves just a stray particle away, the human trait of seeing patterns in chaos, of always assuming there was a hidden supernatural world, was actually selected for. We'd devised a feedback monitor that would allow a human subject to watch and, with a bit of training alter, the particle tracks in one's own head, via the keyboard and screen. I had hypothesised that, because the schizophrenic state can be diagnosed, that is, it wasn't just interference like white noise, but a pattern of interference, there must be some rule limiting which past states were being accessed, something that let in only a finite number. It had been Lindsay who'd said that perhaps this was only about time and not about space, that perhaps one had to be relatively near the minds doing the interfering, and thus, perhaps, the range was limited by where the Earth was in its orbit.

That is to say, you only heard from your previous states of mind on the same calendar date.

Which turns out to have been what you might call a saving grace.

It was like being knocked out.

I'd never been knocked out. Not then.

I woke... and... Well, I must have been about three months old.

My vision is the wrong shape. It's similar to being in an enormous cinema with an oddly-shaped screen. Everything in the background is a blur. I hear what I'm sure are words, but... I haven't brought my understanding with me. It's as if that part of me can't fit in a baby's mind. This is terrifying, to hear the shapes of words but not know what they mean. I start yelling.

The baby that I'm part of starts yelling in exactly the same way! And then... and then...

The big comfort shape moves into view. Such joy comes with it. Hello, big comfort shape! It's me! It's me! Here I am!

Big comfort shape puts its arms around me, and this is the greatest feeling of my life. An addict's feeling. I cry out again, me, I did that, to make it happen again, more! Even while it's happening to me I want more. I yell and yell for more. And the comfort shape gives me more.

Up to a point.

I pulled the crown off my head.

I rubbed the tears from my face.

If I'd stayed a moment longer I might have wanted to stay forever, and thus harmed the mind I was in, all because I wasn't used to asking for and getting such divine attention.

Up to a point.

What was that point? Why had I felt that? I didn't know if I had, really. How was it possible to feel such a sense of love and presence, but also that miniscule seed of the opposite, that feeling of it not being enough or entire? Hadn't I added that, hadn't I dreamt it?

I quickly put the crown back on my head. I had a fix now, I could see where particular patterns took me, I could get to –

Oh. Much clearer now. I must be about two years old. I'm walking around an empty room, marching, raising my knees and then lowering them, as if that's important.

Oh, I can think that. There's room for that thought in my head. I'm able to internally comment on my own condition. As an adult. As a toddler.

Can I control...? I lower my foot. I stand there, inhabiting my toddler body, aware of it, the smallness of everything. But my fingers feel huge. And awkward. Like wearing oven gloves. I don't want to touch anything. I know I'd break it.

And that would be terrible.

I turn my head. I put my foot forward. It's not like learning to drive, I already know how all this is done, it's just slightly different, like driving in America. I can hear...

Words I understand. "Merry Christmas!" From through the door. Oh, the door. The vase with a crack in it. The picture of a Spanish Lady that Dad cut off the side of a crate of oranges and put in a frame. The smell of the carpet, close up. Oh, reactions to the smell, lots of memories, associations, piling in.

No! No! I can't take that! I can't understand that! I haven't built those memories yet!

Is this why I've always felt such enormous meaningless meaning about those objects and smells? I put all these things out of my mind, and try to just be. And it's okay. It's okay.

The Christmas tree is enormous. With opened presents at the bottom, and I'm not too interested in those presents, which is weird, they've been left there, amongst the wrapping. The wrapping is better. This mind doesn't have signifiers for wrapping and tree yet, this is just a lot of weird stuff that happens, like all the other weird stuff that happens.

I head through the doorway. Step, step, step.

Into the hall. All sorts of differences from now, all sorts of objects with associations, but no, never mind the fondness and horror around you.

I step carefully into the kitchen.

And I'm looking up at the enormous figure of my mother, who is talking to... Who is that? A woman in a headscarf. Auntie someone... oh, she died. I know she died! And I forgot her completely! Because she died!

I can't stop this little body from starting to shake. I'm going to cry. But I mustn't!

"Oh, there she goes again," says Mum, a sigh in her voice. "It's Christmas, you mustn't cry at Christmas."

"She wants to know where her daddy is," says the dead auntie. "He's down the pub."

154

"Don't tell her that!" That sudden fear in her voice. And the wryness that always went along with that fear. As if she was mocking herself for her weakness.

"She can't understand yet. Oh, look at that. Is she meant to be walking like that?" And oh no, Mum's looking scared at me too. Am I walking like I don't know how, or like an adult?

Mummy grabs me up into her arms and looks and looks at me, and I try to be a child in response to the fear in her face... but I have a terrible feeling that I look right into those eyes as me. I'm scaring her, like a child possessed!

I took the crown off more slowly that time. And then immediately put it on again. And now I knew I was picking at a scab. Now I knew and I didn't care. I wanted to know what everything in my mother's face at that moment meant.

I'm seven and I'm staring at nothing under the tree. I'm up early and I'm waiting. Something must soon appear under the tree. There was nothing in the stocking at the end of my bed, but they/Father Christmas/they/Father Christmas/they might not have known I'd put out a stocking.

I hear the door to my parents' bedroom opening. I tense up. So much that it hurts. My dad enters the room and sighs to see me there. I bounce on my heels expectantly. I do a little dance that the connections between my muscles and my memory tell me now was programmed into me by a children's TV show.

He looks at me as if I'm some terrible demand. "You're too old for this now," he says. And I remember. I remember this from my own memory. I'd forgotten this. I hadn't forgotten. "I'm off down the shops to get you some presents. If I can find any shops that are open. If you'd stayed asleep until you were supposed to, they'd have been waiting for you. Don't look at me like that. You knew there wasn't any such thing as Father Christmas."

He takes his car keys from the table and goes outside in his dressing gown, and drives off in the car, in his dressing gown.

I'm eight, and I'm staring at a huge pile of presents under the tree, things I wanted but have been carefully not saying anything about, things that are far too expensive. Mum and Dad are standing there, and as I walk into the room, eight year old walk, trying, no idea how, looking at my Mum's face, which is again scared, just turned scared in the second she saw me... but Dad starts clapping, actually applauding, and then Mum does too.

"I told you I'd make it up to you," says Dad. I don't remember him telling me. "I told you." This is too much. This is too much. I don't know how I'm supposed to react. I don't know how in this mind or outside of it.

I sit down beside the presents. I lower my head to the ground. And I stay there, to the point where I'm urging this body to get up, to show some bloody gratitude! But it stays there. I'm just a doll, and I stay there. And I can't make younger me move and look. I don't want to.

I'm nine, and I'm sitting at the dinner table, with Christmas dinner in front of me. Mum is saying grace, which is scary, because she only does it at Christmas, and it's a whole weird thing, and oh, I'm thinking, I'm feeling weird again, I'm feeling weird like I always feel on Christmas Day. Is this because of her doing that?

I don't think I'm going to be able to leave any knowledge about what's actually going on in the mind I'm visiting. The transmission of information is only one way. I'm a voice that can suggest muscle movement, but I'm a very quiet one.

I'm fifteen. Oh. This is the Christmas after Dad died. And I'm... drunk. No, I wasn't. I'm not. It just feels as if I am. What's inside my head is... huge. I *hate* having it in here with me. Right now. I feel like I'm... possessed. And I think it was like that in here before I arrived to join in. The shape of what I'm in is different. It feels... wounded. Oh God, did I hurt it already? No. I'm still me here and now. I wouldn't be if I'd hurt my young brain back then. No, I, I, sort of remember. This is just what it was like being fifteen. My mind feels... like it's shaped awkwardly, not that it's wounded. All this... fury. I can *feel* the weight of the world limiting me. I can feel a terrible force towards action. Do something, now! Why aren't all these idiots around me doing something, when I know so well what they should do? And God, God, I am horny even during this, which is, which is... terrible.

I'm bellowing at Mum, who's trying to raise her voice to shout over me, at the door of my room. "Don't look at me like that!" I'm shouting. "We never have a good Christmas because of you! Dad would always try to make it a good Christmas, but he had to deal with you! Stop being afraid!"

I know as I yell this that it isn't true. I know now and I know then.

She slams the door of my room against the wall and marches in, raising a shaking finger –

I grab her. I grab her and I feel the frailness of her as I do, and I use all my strength, and its lots, and I shove her reeling out of the door, and she crashes into the far wall and I run at her and I slam her into it again, so the back of her head hits the wall and I meant to do it and I don't, I so terribly don't. I'm beating up an old woman!

I manage to stop myself from doing that. Just. My new self and old self manage at the same time. I let go.

She bursts out crying. So do I.

"Stop doing that to me!" I yell.

"I worry about you," she manages to sob. "It's because I worry about you."

Is it just at Christmas she worries? I think hard about saying it, and this body says it. My voice sounds odd saying it. "Is it just at Christmas?"

She's silent, looking scared at how I sounded. Or, oh God, is she afraid of me now?

This is what did it, I realise. I make this mind go weird at Christmas, and they always noticed. It's great they noticed. What I grew up with, how I was brought up, is them reacting to that, expecting that, for the rest of the year. This makes sense, I've solved it! I've solved who I am! Who I am is my own fault! I'm a self-fulfilling prophecy!

Well, that's pretty obvious, isn't it? Should have known that. Everybody should realise that about themselves. Simple!

I realise that I'm smiling suddenly and Mum bursts into tears again. To her, it must seem like she's looking at a complete psycho.

I tore off the crown. I remembered doing that to her. Then I let myself forget it. But I never did. And that wasn't the only time. Lots of grabbing her. On the verge of hitting her. Is that a thing, being abused by one's child? It got lost in the layers of who she and I were, and there I was, in it, and suddenly it was the most important thing. And now it was again.

Because of Dad dying, I thought, because of that teenage brain, and then I thought no, that's letting myself off the hook.

Guilty.

But beyond that, my teenage-influenced self had been right: I'd found what I'd gone looking for. I'd messed up my own childhood by what I was doing here. That was a neat end to the story, wasn't it? Yes, my parents had been terribly lacking on occasion. But they'd had something beyond the norm to deal with. And I'd been... terrifying, horrible, beyond that poor frail woman's ability to deal with.

But that only let them off the hook... up to a point.

Hadn't that bit with there being no presents, that bit with the car, weren't those beyond normal? Had me being in that mind on just one day of the year really been such a big factor?

Would I end up doing anything like that? Would I be a good parent?

Perhaps I should have left it there.

But there was a way to *know*.

In *A Christmas Carol*, we hear from charity collectors visiting Scrooge's shop that when his partner Marley was alive they both always gave generously. And you think therefore that Scrooge was a happy, open person then. But Scrooge doesn't confirm that memory of theirs. When we meet Marley's ghost, he's weighed down by chains 'he forged in life'. He's warning Scrooge not to be like he was. So were the charity collectors lying or being too generous with their memory of Christmas past? Or is it just that they sometimes caught Scrooge and Marley on a good day? The latter doesn't seem the sort of thing that happens to characters in stories. I've been told that story isn't a good model for what happened to me. But perhaps, because of what's written in the margins, it is.

I sat there thinking, the crown in my hands. I'd been my own ghost of Christmas future. But I could be a ghost of Christmas past too.

Was I going to be a good parent?

I could find out.

I set the display to track the other side of the scale. To take me into the future, as we'd only speculated that someday might be possible.

And I put the crown back on before I could think twice.

Oh. Oh there she is. My baby is a she! I'm holding her in my arms. I love her more than I thought it was possible to love anything. The same way the big comfort thing loved me. And I didn't understand that until I put those moments side by side. This mind I'm in now has changed so much. It's hugely focussed on the little girl who's asleep right here. It's a warm feeling, but it's... it's hard too. Where did that come from? That worries me. She's so little. This can't be that far into the future. But I've changed so much. There's a feeling of... this mind I'm in wanting to prove something. She wants to tell me it's all going to be okay. That I have nothing but love inside me in this one year on future. And I do... up to a point.

Oh, there's a piece of paper with the year written on it sitting on the arm of the chair right in front of me. It's just next year. That's my handwriting.

The baby's name is Alice, the writing continues, *you don't need to go any further to hear that. Please make this your last trip.*

Alice. That's what we were planning to call her. Thank God. If it was something different, I'd now be wondering where that idea came from.

Oh, I can feel it now. This mind has made room for me. It knew I'd be coming. Of course it did. She remembers what she did with the crown last year. But what does this mean? Why does future me want me to stop doing this? I try to reach across the distance between her and me, but I can only feel what she's feeling, not hear her thoughts. And she had a year to prepare, that note must be all she wants to tell me. She wants me to feel that it's all going to be okay... but she's telling me it won't be.

Ben comes in. He doesn't look very different. Unshaven. He's smiling all over his face. He sits on the arm of the chair and looks down at his daughter, proud and utterly in love with her. The room is decorated. There are tiny presents under the tree, joint birthday and Christmas presents the little one is too small to understand. So, oh, he was born very near Christmas Day. We must make such a perfect image sitting together like this. I don't think I can have told Ben about what I know will be happening to me at this moment on Christmas Day. I wouldn't do that. I'd want to spare him.

159

But... what's this? I can feel my body move slightly away from him. It took me a second to realise it, because it's so brilliant, and a little scary, to be suddenly in a body that's not weighed down by the pregnancy, but... I'm bristling. I can feel a deep chemical anger. The teenager is in here again. But I look up at him and smile, and this mind lets me. And he's so clearly still my Ben, absolutely the same, the Dad I knew he'd be when he asked and I said yes. It's not like he's started to beat me, I can't feel that in this body, she's not flinching, it's like when I'm angry but I don't feel allowed to express it.

Is this, what, post-natal depression? Or the first sign of me doing unto others what was done to me? A pushed-down anger that might come spilling out?

I don't care what my one year older self wants me to do. She can't know that much more than me. I need to know what this is.

Alice is asleep in her cradle. She's so much bigger, so quickly, two years old! Again, that bursting of love into my head. That's reassuring. Another year on, I'm still feeling that.

But the room... the room feels very different. Empty. There's a tree, but it's a little one. I make this body walk quickly through the rest of the house. The bathroom is a bit different, the bedroom is a bit different. Baby stuff everywhere, of course, but what's missing? There's... there's nothing on that side of the room. I go back to the bathroom. There are no razors. No second toothbrush.

Where's Ben?

I start looking in drawers, checking my email... but the password's been changed. I can't find anything about what's happened. I search every inch of the house, desperate now, certain I'm going to find a funeral card or something. She knew this was going to happen to me, so wouldn't the bitch have left one out in plain sight? Why doesn't she want me to know? Oh please don't be dead, Ben, please –!

I end up meaninglessly, uselessly, looking in the last place, under the bed.

And there's a note, in my own handwriting.

I hate you.

She's deliberately stopping me from finding out. I can't let her.

Alice is looking straight at me, this time. "Presents," she says to me. "I have presents. And you have presents." And I can see behind her that it's true.

That rush of love again. That's constant. I try to feel what's natural and not be stiff and scary about it, and give her a big hug. "Does Daddy have presents?"

She looks aside, squirms; she doesn't know how to deal with that. Have I warned her about me? I don't want to press her for answers. I don't want to distress her.

I need to keep going and find out.

I'm facing in the same direction, so it's as if the decor and contents of the room suddenly shift, just a little. Alice, in front of me, four, is running in rings on the floor, obviously in the middle of, rather than anticipating something, so that's good.

Ben comes in. He's alive! Oh thank God.

I stand up at the sight of him. Has she told him about me? No, I never would. He looks so different. He's clean-shaven, smartly dressed. Did he go on a long journey somewhere? He hoists Alice into his arms and Alice laughs as he jumbles up her hair. "Happy Christmas birthday!"

Alice sings it back to him, like it's a thing they do together. So... everything's all right? Why didn't she want me to –?

A young woman I don't know comes in from the other room. She goes to Ben and puts a hand on his arm. Alice smiles at her.

"We have to be gee oh aye en gee soon," he says to me.

"Thanks for lunch," says the girl, "it was lovely."

The fury this time is my own. But it chimes with what's inside this mind. She's been holding it down. I take a step forwards. And the young woman sees something in my eyes and takes a step back. And that little movement –

No, it isn't the movement, it isn't what she does, this is all me –

I march towards her. I'm taking in every feature of her. Every beautiful feature of that slightly aristocratic, kind-looking, caring face. I'm making a sound I've never heard before, in the back of my throat. "Get away from him. Get your hands off him."

She's trying to put up her hands and move away. She's astonished. "I'm sorry –!"

"What the hell?" Ben is staring at us. Alice has started yelling.

Fearful monkey warning shouts.

Something gives inside me. I rush at her. She runs.

I catch her before she gets to the door. I grab her by both arms and throw her at the wall. I'm angry at her and at the mind I'm in too. Did she set me up for this? Did she invite them here to punish me? So she could let her anger out and not be responsible?

She hits the wall and bounces off it. She falls, grabbing her nose. She looks so capable and organised I know she could hit me hard, I know she could defend herself, but she just drops to the ground and puts her hands to her face. I will not make her fight. She can control herself and I can't.

Ben rushes in grabs me. I don't want him to touch me. I struggle.

"What are you doing?" He's shouting at me.

I can feel this mind burning up. If I stay much longer, I'll start damaging it. I half want to.

I ripped the crown from my head and threw it onto the ground. I burst into tears. I put my hands on my belly to comfort myself. But I found no comfort there.

But my pain wasn't important. It wasn't! The mistakes I'd made were what mattered. What happened to Alice, *that* was what was important.

I got up and walked around the room. If I stopped now, I was thinking, the rest of my life would be a tragedy, I would be forever anticipating what was written, or trying... hopelessly, yes, there was nothing in the research then that said I had any hope... to change it. I would be living without hope. I could do that. But the important thing was what that burden would do to Alice... if I was going to be allowed to keep Alice, after what I'd seen.

I could go to the airport now. I could leave Ben asleep, while he was still my Ben, and have the baby in France, and break history... no I couldn't. Something would get me back to what I'd seen. Maybe something cosmic and violent that wouldn't respect the human mind's need for narrative. That was what the maths said. Alice shouldn't have that in her life.   Alice shouldn't have me in her life.

But the me who wrote the first note wanted me not to try to visit the future again. When she knew I had. Did she think that was possible? Did I learn something in the next year that hinted that it might be? Why didn't I address that in future notes?

Because of anger? Because of fatalism? Because of a desire to hurt myself?

But... if there was even a chance it might be possible...

I slowly squatted and picked the crown up.

I've moved. I'm in a different house. Smaller. I walk quickly through the rooms, searching. I have to support myself against the wall in relief when I see Alice. There she is, in her own room, making a wall out of cardboard wrapping paper rolls. Still the love in me. I don't think that's ever going to go. It feels like... a condition. A good disease this mind lives with. But what's she doing alone in here? Did I make her flee here, exile her here?

She looks up at me and smiles. No. No, I didn't.

I find the note this time on the kitchen table. It's quite long, it's apologetic. It tells me straight away that Ben and... Jessica, the young woman's name is Jessica... understood, quite quickly after I left her mind and she started apologising. She apologises too for not doing anything to stop what happened. But she says she really wasn't setting me up for it. She says she's still working at the Project. She says she's still looking for a way to change time, but hasn't much hope of finding one.

I put down the letter feeling... hatred. For her. For her weakness. For her acceptance. That whole letter feels like... acting. Like she's saying something because she thinks she should.

From the other room comes the sound of Alice starting to cry. She's hurt herself somehow. I feel the urge from this mind to go immediately to her. But I... I actually hesitate. For the first time there is a distance. I'm a stranger from years ago. This isn't really my child. This is *her* child.

The next few visits were like an exhibition of time lapse photography about the disintegration of a mother and child relationship. Except calling it that suggests a distance, and I was amongst it, complicit in it.

You get so weird!' she's shouting at me. "It's like you get frightened every Christmas that I'll go away with Dad and Jessica and never come back! I want to! I want to go away!"

But the next Christmas she's still there.

"Will you just listen to me? You look at me sometimes like I'm not real, like I'm not human!" The mind of the future learned that from her memory of my experiences, I guess, learned that from her own experience of being a teenager with added context. Alice has had to fight for her mother to see her as an actual human being. I did that. I mean, I did that *to* her. I try now to reach out, but she sees how artificial it looks and shies away.

"Do I... neglect you?" I ask her.

She swears at me, and says yes. But then she would, wouldn't she?

And then the next year she's not there.

A note says the bitch arranged for her to stay with Ben and Jessica, and it all got too much in terms of anticipation, and she's sure she'll be back next time. She's certain of that. She's sorry, and she... hopes *I* am too?

I go to the wall in the hall. I've always used bloody walls to do my fighting. I stand close to it. And as hard as I can I butt my head against it. I love the roaring of the mind I'm in as the pain hits us both. Feel *that*, you bitch, do something about *that*! I do it again. And then my head starts to swim and I don't think I can do it again, and I get out just as the darkness hits.

That was why she 'hoped I was sorry too', because she knew that was coming.

I wonder how much I injured myself. She couldn't have known, when she wrote the note. She was so bloody weak she didn't even try to ask me not to do it.

I am such a bully.

But I'm only doing it to myself.

There's no sign of Alice for the next two Christmases. When the bitch was *certain* she'd be back next time. The liar. There are just some very needy letters. Which show no sign of brain damage, thank God.

Then there's Alice, sitting opposite me. She wears fashions designed to shock. "Christmas Day," she says, "time for you to go insane and hurt yourself, only today I'm trapped with you. What joy."

I discover that Ben and Jessica are on holiday abroad with their own... children... this year. And that the bitch has done... some sort of harm to herself on each of these days Alice wasn't here, obviously after I left. Is that just self-harm, am I actually capable of...? Well, I suppose I know I am. Or is she trying to offer some explanation for that one time, or to use it to try and hurt Alice emotionally?

"No insanity this year," I say, trying to make my voice sound calm. And it sounds weird. It sounds old. It sounds as if I've put inverted commas around 'insanity'. Like I'm trying to put distance on my own actions, wry about my own weakness... like Mum always is.

I try to have fun with her in the ten minutes I've got. She shuts herself in her room when I get too cloying. I try to enter. She slams herself against the door. I get angry, though the weak woman I'm in really doesn't want to, and try to muscle in. But she grabs me, she's stronger than me.

She slams me against the wall. And I burst into tears. And she steps back, shaking her head in mocking disbelief at... all I've done to her.

I slipped the crown from my head.

I was staring into space. And then my phone rang. The display said it was Mum. And I thought now of all the times, and then I thought no, I have a cover to maintain here, I don't want her calling Ben... I didn't want to go home to Ben...

I took a deep breath, and answered.

"Is there... news?" she asked. I heard that wry, anxious tone in her voice again. Did I ever think of that sound as anxious before? "You are due today, aren't you?"

I told her that I was, but it didn't feel that it was going to be today, and that I'd call her immediately when anything started to happen. I stopped then, realising that actually, I did know it was going to be today; Ben said "happy Christmas birthday" to Alice. But I couldn't tell her I knew that and I didn't want to tell her I felt something I didn't feel. "Merry Christmas," I said, remembering the pleasantries, which she hadn't.

She repeated that, an edge in her voice again. "I was hoping that I might see you today, but I suppose that's impossible, even though the baby isn't coming. You've got much more important things to do."

And the words hurt as much as they always did, but they weren't a dull ache now, but a bright pain. Because I heard them not as barbs to make me guilty, but as being exactly like the tone of the letters the bitch had left for me. Pained, pleading... weak. That was why I'd slammed her against the wall, all those years ago, because she was weak, because I could.

"I'm sorry," I said.

"Oh. I'm always sorry to hear you say that," she said.

I said I'd call her as soon as anything happened.

As soon as she was off the phone, I picked up the crown, and held it in my hands as if I was in a Shakespeare play. I was so poetically contemplating it. I felt like laughing at my own presumption at having opened up my womb and taken a good look at where Jacob Marley had come from.

I had hurt my own mother. I had never made that up to her. I never could. But I hadn't tried. I had hated her for what I had done. And I could not stop. And in the future, the reflection was as bad as the shadow. I had become my mother. And I had created a daughter that felt exactly the same way about me. And I had created a yearly hell for my future self, making sure she never forgot the lesson I had learned on this day.

I would release myself from it. That's what I decided.

I put the crown on for the last time.

I'm standing there with my daughter. She looks to be in her late twenties. Tidy now. A worried look on her face. She's back for a family Christmas, but she knows there'll be trouble as always. She's been waiting for it. She looks kinder. She looks guilty. The room is bare of decoration. Like the bitch... like my victim... has decided not to make the effort any more.

"Get away from me," I tell Alice, immediately, "get out of this house." Because I know what I'm going to do. I'm going to stay inside this mind. I'm going to break it. I'm going to give myself the release of knowing I'm going to go mad, at the age of... I look around and find a conveniently-placed calendar. Which was unbelievably accommodating of her, to know what I'm about to do and still do that. I will go mad at the age of fifty six. I have a finishing line. It's a relief. Perhaps she wants this too.

"Mum," says Alice, "Mum, please –!" And she sounds desperate and worried for herself as well as for me, and still not understanding what all this is about.

But then her expression... changes. It suddenly becomes determined and calm. "Mum, please don't do this. I know we only have minutes –"

"What? Did I tell you about –?"

"No, this is an older Alice. I'm working on the same technology now. I've come back to talk to you."

It takes me a moment to take that in. "You mean, you've found a way to change time?"

"No. What's written is written. Immediately after we have this conversation, and we've both left these bodies, you tell me everything about what you've been doing."

"Why... do I do that?" I can feel the sound of my mother's weakness in my voice.

"Because after you leave here, you go forward five years and see me again." She takes my hands in hers and looks into my eyes. I can't see the hurt there. The hurt I put there. And I can see a reflection too.

Can I believe her?

She sees me hesitate. And she grows determined. "I'll stay as long as you will," she says. "You might do this to yourself, but I know you'd never let your child suffer."

I think about it. I do myself the courtesy of that. I toy with the horror of doing that. And then I look again into her face, and I know I'm powerless in the face of love.

I'm looking into the face of someone I don't expect to see. It's David. Our experimental subject. The schizophrenic. Only now he's a lot older, and... Oh, his face... he's lost such tension about his jaw. Beside him stands Alice, five years older.

He reaches out a hand and touches my cheek.

I shy away from him. What?

"I'm sorry," he says, "I shouldn't have done that. We're... a couple, okay? We've been together for several years now. Hello you from the past. Thank you for the last four years of excellent family Christmases." He gestures to decorations and cards all around.

"Hello, Mum," says Alice. She reaches down and... oh, there's a crib there. She's picked up a baby. "This is my daughter, Cyala."

I walk slowly over. It feels as odd and as huge as walking as a child did. I look into the face of my grand-daughter.

David, taking care not to touch me, joins me beside them. "It's so interesting," he says, "seeing you from this new angle. Seeing a cross-section of you. You *look* younger!"

"Quickly," says Alice.

"Okay, okay." He looks back to me. And I can't help but examine his face, try and find the attraction I must later feel. And yes, it's there. I just never saw him in this way before. "Listen, this is what you told me to say to you, and I'm glad that, from what Alice has discovered, it seems I can't mess up my lines. It's true that you and Alice here fought, fought physically, like you say you and your Mum did. Though I once saw her deny that to your face, by the way. She sounded as if you were accusing *her* of something, and she kept on insisting it hadn't happened until you got angry and then finally she agreed, as if she was just going along with it. Oh God, this is so weird –" He picked up some sort of thin screen where I recognised something quite like my handwriting. "I was sure I added to what I was supposed to say there, but now it turns out it's written down here, and I'm not sure that it was... before. I guess your memory didn't quite get every detail of this correct. Or perhaps there's a certain... kindness, a mercy to time? Anyway!" He put down the screen again, certain he wouldn't need it. "But the important thing is, you only see one day. You don't see all the good stuff. There were long stretches of good stuff. You didn't create a monster, any more than your Mum created a monster in you. You both just made people." He dares to actually touch me, and now I let him. "What you did led to a cure for people like me. And it changed how people see themselves and the world, and that's been good and bad, it isn't a utopia outside these walls and it isn't a wasteland, she wanted me to emphasise that. It's just people doing stuff as usual. And these are all your words, not mine, but I agree with them... You are not Ebenezer Scrooge, to be changed from one thing into another. Neither was your mother. Even knowing all of this is fixed, even knowing everything that happened, even if you only know the bad, you'd do it all anyway."

And he kisses me. Which makes me feel guilty and hopeful at the same time.

And I let go.

I slowly put down the crown.

I stood up. I'd been there less than an hour. I went back to my car.

I remember the drive home through those still-empty streets. I remember how it all settled into my mind, how a different me was born in those moments. I knew what certain aspects of my life to come would be like. I had memories of the future. That weight would always be with me. I regretted having looked. I still do. Despite everything it led to, for me and science and the world. I tell people they don't want to look into their future selves. But they usually go ahead and do it. And then they have to come to the same sort of accommodation that a lot of people have, that human life will go on, and that it's bigger than them, and that they can only do what they can do. To some, that fatalism has proven to be a relief. But it's driven some to suicide. It has, I think, on average, started to make the world a less extreme place. There is only so much we can do. And we don't see the rest of the year. So we might as well be kind to each other.

There are those who say they've glimpsed a pattern in it all. That the whole thing, as seen from many different angles, is indeed like writing. That, I suppose, is the revelation, that we're not the writers, we're what's being written.

I write now from the perspective of the day after my younger self stopped visiting. I'm relieved to be free of that bitch. Though, of course, I knew everything she was going to do. The rest of my life now seems like a blessed release. I wrote every note as I remembered them, and sometimes that squared with how I was feeling at the time, and sometimes I was playing a part... for whose benefit, I don't know.

I remember walking back into my house and finding Ben just waking up. And he looked at me, at the doubtless strange expression on my face, and in that moment I recall thinking I saw his expression change too. By some infinitesimal amount. I have come to think that was when he started, somewhere deep inside, the chain reaction of particle trails that took him from potentially caring Dad to letting himself off the hook.

But that might equally just be the story I tell myself about that moment.

Each of us is but a line in a story that resonates with every other line. Who we are is distributed. In all sorts of ways. And we can't know them all.

And then I felt something give. There was actually a small sound in the quiet. Liquid splashed down my legs. And as I knew I was going to, I went into labour on Christmas Day.

Ben leaped out of bed and ran to me, and we headed out to the car. Outside, the birds were singing. Of course they were.

"You're going to be fine," he said. "You're going to be a great mother."

"Up to a point," I said.

'The Ghosts of Christmas' (Tor.com, 2012) is perhaps the story I'm most proud of. It reflects my own rather complicated relationship with family, through the medium of what's become this generation's emotional equivalent of the Victorian ghost story, the time paradox. I think more attention might have been paid to it if I hadn't presented it as a Christmas story, because we tend to associate those with slighter stuff. Christmas has always been for me, however, a time of deep emotion, those dark days in search of light when I wrote for the first time as a child. These days I deliberately exhaust myself with the 12 Blogs of Christmas feature on my website, sometimes in search of spiritual experience. Sometimes I find it. This story is the result of one of those times when I did.

Tom

You expect the platform to be stable. But actually it sways like a boat, gently, even though its legs are sunk into rock under the reef. That means if you come out on the launch just about keeping your nausea under control, you should get underwater as quickly as possible, let your inner ear sort itself. Having been an instructor here for five years, I'd stopped noticing that sway. But now I appreciate it again, because Tom appreciates it.

That feeling, looking at Tom's face, takes me back to a moment when the platform was swaying more violently. When the big guy showed up. I never got a name. Swav would never tell me. I don't know who that was meant to protect. Or maybe the males don't bother with names. I can see him even now, leaping, all blue muscle, with bright yellow stripes down his flanks, all the other colours on his skin that were at the edge of what we're able to see, that made strange rainbows through the spray. He hurled himself against the platform, time after time, making the tourists and the other scuba guides scream and fall around. He was the size of two or three Orca. I couldn't see any similarity between him and Swav. I couldn't see a face, even. If there were eyes they were hidden in the dark lines along what might have been his head. I couldn't imagine how they could ever be together. I was holding onto Swav, both of us getting soaked. All I was thinking was that, emotionally, I was fucked. I could hear him calling her name. He was booming it underwater, her name vibrating the platform as much as the waves did.

I looked into Swav's face, and there was an expression there I couldn't read at all. It was an arrangement of muscles on something very like a human face that wasn't akin to any expression I'd seen before. She broke from my arms, suddenly slippery, like I'd loved a mermaid. She ran for the rail. She leapt into the water as I was calling her name, my shout lost in his. She jumped into water that was suddenly full of him rising around her, an enormous mass that overwhelmed her. He twisted her round and slammed her against the side of the platform, so hard I was sure it had killed her. He held her there with slaps, battering her, left and right with his fins or wings or whatever they were. I'd run to the side, but there was nothing I could do but shout. She'd told me what she expected, but she'd never experienced it. Would she have dived in if she'd known what it would be like? She was pinned there, against the metal over the underwater dock, her fingers gripping the wire netting now, her knuckles, suddenly so human, white with the effort. I remember Annie, the biologist, came up behind me and grabbed me when I looked like I was going to jump in after her. I don't know if I really would have. We watched together as that huge white puppet snake of a penis rose out of the water, a flap like a flower jerking atop it, sucking air. Swav threw her head back and I could see something odd at her neck, kind of like a wound, and I screamed her name again because again I thought he'd killed her. And then the penis wrapped round her, impossibly fast, and the flap rose above her head like a snake about to strike. In that second, she turned and looked at me, and this time what I saw on her face I read as terror. Then the flap grabbed her around her head. He let himself fall from the platform and with an enormous splash took her with him into the depths.

I recall the water hitting us again. How we were swept aside. And then how we all found ourselves just sliding against the rails, the water draining off in seconds, as it was meant to, children screaming, guides yelling to grab onto the cables. But everyone was safe, it turned out. Except me. I felt as if I'd been beaten. I'd had something ripped out of me. Annie made me look her in the face, and I could see every detail of what she was feeling, such a contrast, like coming back to reality after a dream, just for a moment. "She'll come back to you," she said. "I'm pretty sure of it."

I was one of the first, I guess, to have that experience. My working on the Great Barrier Reef made it more likely. The Carviv always asked to visit reefs, and because they always asked to work, a lot of them in the first party ended up as tour guides, things like that. Their hosts tried to dissuade them, but the companies that took them on were delighted. Mate, we've got a guide who is herself a tourist attraction. The Carviv presence funded the regrowth initiative and the carbon sinks. It was so unthreatening, you know? They didn't want to see our armed forces, they wanted to be near our water. The females separated, integrated by not staying in groups at all, spreading out all round the Pacific rim. The males, we saw on television, lay on the ocean surface, somewhere off Hawaii, sleeping most of the time. Aussie blokes identified with that. That was a good first year, with the whole planet kind of sighing in relief. We'd met the aliens, and they turned out to be quite like us, really. None of the predictions of outrage and uprising came true. After a little while, nobody had that much of a problem. Humanity looked at itself in comparison with these guys, and decided we weren't that bad or that good, and stopped worrying so much about the end of the world. There was, after all, another one just over there, seventy light years away, and those guys didn't seem to think we were so bad. Looking back, I guess we started tidying the place up, now that the neighbours had come visiting. So much ecological repair in such a short time. The Carviv refused, even when asked, to express any negative opinions about the world they were visiting. But I think their love for the water contributed to us turning a corner, ecologically.

And the years after have continued to be good. But I still occasionally feel... well, just sometimes I don't know how I feel. Until I look at Tom.

Everyone turned out to welcome Swav when she arrived at the platform. She travelled on one of their boats, those slim white shells, their hulls shaped reassuringly like our own yachts, but with some sort of power source that made no sound, the sail only for braking, billowing out to do so as it approached us.

"Hi, everyone," she said as she stepped off the ladder onto the platform. Her accent already sounded Aussie. "Thanks for having me." She was sparkling white, a rounded head like a bowling pin, a diagonal sash that was decorated with dense designs as her only clothing, slim shoulders, big, three fingered hands like a cartoon character. She swept downwards to a tiny pair of feet, her whole body leaning to one side or the other with every step. There were no visible... well, it's weird to use a word like "genitalia" thinking back to that moment, but that's how biologists, how Annie, actually, would have been looking at her. Her chest was just... rounded, as if she was a clothed human. But it was her face that was the most extraordinary thing. Those enormous blue eyes; utterly like ours, but impossibly expressive. The ridges above them which danced like extraordinary eyebrows. The button nose with a single nostril. The wry squiggle of a mouth, never open enough so that you could see her teeth, but always in motion, saying so much even when she wasn't. She had a waterproof rucksack on her back that looked like she'd just bought it.

The others clustered around her, Helena, the boss, doing the air kissing which we'd been told delighted the Carviv. And it seemed, indeed, to do the business with Swav. That was when I heard that huge, honest, laugh for the first time. I was holding back for some reason, Annie, her arms folded, beside me. Swav glanced over and looked at me. And held my gaze, her laugh suddenly turning into what looked like quite a shy smile. I found myself smiling back.

Underwater, Swav was incredible. She swam in a blur of motion, her whole body vibrating, able to turn on a dime and talk to us in our scuba gear by directing individual yells right at our ears. Which must have been, as Annie put it, like shooting daisies from a rollercoaster. The fish, initially, hated her. Carl, our Bump-Headed Parrot Fish, who'd learned to come to the diving pit beside the platform twice a day for food and photo opportunities, actually left. Which made the crew feel kind of awkward: nobody knew how long swimming with Swav would be a tourist attraction, while Carl had served us well for a decade. There was one night at dinner when Swav became aware that there was something nobody was talking to her about. She made Helena tell her about Carl. And the sadness on her face when she heard, oh man! It was breaking my heart. She suddenly got up, and ran to the door, and stopped and made a gesture for nobody to follow her, that it would all be okay. And then she was gone and we heard a splash, and we all got to our feet, and went to see, but all there was in the moonlight was a trail of foam that already stretched out past the reef.

She was back for breakfast, hardly able to contain herself. "Guys, come and see!" she said. I jumped over the side with a couple of the others, and there was Carl, laid back as ever, but a notch hungrier, if his bumping against us was anything to go by. And behind him, as if intrigued by this food they'd heard about, was a shoal of Clownfish, our other major attraction, or they had been, when they'd been more common around here. "I found out what they were smelling about me," whispered Swav in my ear as she rocketed past, going round and round the platform in excitement. "I reversed it."

That night, in her honour, we got the grog out. There'd been a few who were a little awkward around Swav. Mostly I think they felt it was like being around, you know, someone who's very religious or a tranny or something; you get tense because you want to make sure you do everything right and don't offend them. But I had to admit, when I caught her in the corner of my eye, or ran into her without expecting to, I did react to her like she was a ghost. In a nanosecond, your brain realises you're not looking at what you thought you were, only she's enough like us that it slips gears a bit, and you find yourself jumping a moment *after* the conscious part of you has thought "oh, it's just Swav". She noticed, the second time it happened, and stopped me from making some sort of awkward apology. "It's okay," she said, "it happens to me too. You guys are kind of... large, you know?"

I laughed. "Not as large as your blokes! Oh, sorry –"

"Stop saying sorry! They're their sort of thing, not the sort of thing I expect to run into in a corridor."

"Are we ever going to get a visit from one of them?"

She laughed, like she was embarrassed. "Well, let's see how things work out." It was like I'd said something a little racy. Then she realised I was looking awkward again. "No, come on, I love them, honestly, but I like to get away, and... you know. Do stuff." Those huge eyes had been moving quickly, her attention resting briefly on every part of my face, as if she was taking me in. And enjoying it. She was waiting to see what I did next.

You hear blokes saying they fancy a cartoon character: Wilma Flintstone; Daphne from *Scooby Doo*; Mrs Incredible. But Swav kind of brought that feeling front and centre. Confronted you with it. I'd seen some of the other guys look at her, and then look away, awkward. Your eyes got halfway with it, and stayed on a curve or a motion, then they were lured into applying that feeling to something completely outside the lexicon of love. It felt kind of like fancying Carl. The women had started to make jokes about it. "And she walks about starkers," said Mia, another of the guides. "It's shameless." Swav looked puzzled when people said things like that, but now I think that was an affectation, to let everyone stay comfortable. Or maybe it was kind of like someone laughing along with a racist joke about them, I don't know.

"Is this...?" I wanted to ask her if she was coming on to me, but the thought seemed vastly weird and conceited and hey, potential diplomatic incident, plus all the guys laughing at me, forever. So I shut up again.

But she cocked her head on one side. "I guess. Maybe." While I was processing that, she took my hand in what felt very like a normal hand. "We've got a couple of hours. Let's have a cuppa."

She led me into her cabin. I didn't close the door, she did. I went to the kettle, but she came up behind me and put her hand on my chest. I started to turn around, and she very gently kissed me.

People always used to ask what it was like, before enough of them experienced it for themselves. I've got a bit fed up with describing it, honestly. It was great. It didn't feel very weird. I kept feeling that I wanted to close my eyes and then stopping myself because that might be insulting. What I was seeing might have been more complicated than I was used to, but it was still good. She didn't have breasts, but a curve that felt like them from behind. Her skin became softer and softer as I touched her. She laughed as she showed me all the incredibly complicated folds and openings and protrusions of her, and put my fingers where it would give her most pleasure, and I felt a huge sense of pride that I was arousing her so much, that I was seeing all this extra detail in what was normally a smooth surface. That she could even want me. She wanted to see me then, so I showed her, and what to do. She took to that! She told me not to worry about her teeth. I enjoyed that for a while, and then told her not to worry about mine. Although, you know, that was like my first time had been; I had no idea if I was doing it right, or even what I was aiming for. She smelt great, not like anything I'd ever smelt before, so there were no associations with it. It didn't take me back to any other time; there was just this enormous great now, this tremendous focus on this being just her and me. And even now, the smell of Tom takes me back only to her. I thought it was all going to be like teenagers playing around. While that was kind of frustrating, emotionally, for me, I assumed there couldn't be anything more. But then she told me that there wasn't really any equivalent of orgasm for her without penetration, that actually it was only the feeling of her partner coming that could set her off. She leaned over the bed, and moved her gorgeous roundness a little. "So, erm... how would you feel about...? I mean, I know it's a bit scary —"

It was, but no way was that enough to stop me. It had been

established pretty quickly that, having evolved in different biospheres, there wasn't any need to worry about humans and Carviv catching anything off... you know, I regret mentioning that now. "No possibility of biological interaction", that's what we thought back then. Well, I guess it's what a lot of people still think now. A lot of idiots. But that was nowhere in my head just then. I positioned myself behind her and let her reach for me and guide me into one of the many channels. "Push," she whispered, and I did. Something bigger than it needed to be suddenly contracted around me, until it was just the right size, so welcoming and tight that it felt like an invitation and a violation at the same time. Things were touching me that wouldn't normally be, let us say. Part of her slid urgently into place to cup me around my balls as I was inside her. She must have heard the noise I made and realised what that was about. She looked over my shoulder and grinned. "You all right there?"

I laughed. "God, you're beautiful. Is this the first time you've... you know, I mean with...?" I had visions in my head of one of those big guys lying in the ocean. I'd wondered about what she was used to, if you know what I mean.

"With anyone. My lot either."

"Oh –!" I suddenly felt like I should have acted a lot differently, somehow, but I wasn't sure exactly how.

She laughed again. "Mate, it's not such a big deal for us. There are plants that have evolved on my world to do basically what you're... and there's a lot of jokes about that amongst the shoal, you know, I'm just going to leave Mum and all the guys and go on to the land to have a walk among the pretty flowers. La la la! Your girl friends tell you about it and so then you kind of want a go, and your mum gets all emotional, and the guys all take turns saying surely you're not ready to go exploring on unsettled land yet, shit like that. Until Mum basically put me in the boat and said do what you like! That's how the plants pollinate, so you get these enormous forests of flowers on the islands. We look over to them every now and then and go, hey, we were pretty horny this year." Her voice became softer again, serious. "But I wanted to know what it was like with, you know, someone here. Someone cool. And you don't need to worry. I shrink. I clutch. You feel..." and she raised one of those things that looked a lot like eyebrows and now her voice dropped to a whisper, "pretty big, actually. So, you just go ahead and... let yourself go."

So I did.

We lay together afterwards. I watched, fascinated, as her bits sorted themselves out, retracted and relaxed until she looked smooth again. I was feeling pretty emotional. I mean, not that I wouldn't normally be, but... I felt I'd just gone through something intense, and I wasn't quite sure how I was meant to feel about it. Had we done something wrong? She must have realised that I wasn't feeling right. "It's okay," she said.

"Was it... all right?"

"It was brilliant. Mate, you're much better than a flower."

"I've never been told that before."

She looked suddenly serious. "Now you have to fight one of our males."

I looked at her shocked, and she burst out laughing. "Sucked in! You should have seen your face!" She wrapped her arms around me and I lay against her chest. "You needn't worry. I know I'm going home eventually."

"I wasn't going to say –!"

"It was fun. Lovely fun." She kissed me again, and I felt a kind of ache at what she'd just said. But she was right, it couldn't be more than that. Or so I thought then.

Over the next few weeks, the crew cottoned on to what we were getting up to. I got a lot of ribbing, but it was all good natured. The only person who seemed to have a problem was Annie, who looked away whenever I tried to make eye contact. I guess that was the start of the jealousy that would lead her to hurt me so much later on.

One night, Swav came to my cabin and held me back when I tried to kiss her. "I've had a message," she said, indicating a patch on her sash, "one of our males is on his way here. Now, you mustn't freak out..."

And she told me that he was coming to the platform in order to mate with her, that something had changed in the water temperature that made it feel like mating season back home, and so the males were all about to swim in various directions, meet up with the females and, well –

"It's not like you and me," she said. "I've seen it, and... you might want to go ashore rather than wait for –"

"What, and think about you and him? Do you *have* to do this? I mean, are you and he –?"

"It's not like anything you guys have. You shouldn't be jealous."

I asked loads more questions, none of which mattered, and she answered all of them, and, you know, I like to think I'm a guy who accepts different cultures, but still I was still left feeling pretty damn small.

I watched for any sign of mockery from the others. I knew Helena had told them about the forthcoming visit. They didn't say a word until the evening, when Ben clapped me round the shoulder. "What can I say, mate? You're about to be publically cuckolded by a fucking enormous whale."

"It's like the porn version of *Moby Dick*," added Mia.

"We can only hope," finished off Helena, "that he's not bi-curious."

I started to laugh. "You bastards." And we had a few drinks. They'd waited until Swav wasn't around, and they hadn't let it stay silent and terrible and I was grateful for that.

Everyone was shocked by how the male arrived. That he surged like a torpedo towards the platform, without any message to us, that it swiftly became clear that that day's tourists were going to be at the very least alarmed, and not, as expected, entertained by the spectacle of seeing one of the larger Carviv up close. Once we helped them to their feet, Helena elected to give them their money back and send them to dry land on the launch. The kids were already starting to ask awkward questions about the violence of what Swav had said would take place entirely underwater and out of sight. Maybe that had been the male's choice, and what she'd seen before had been different. Maybe the bastard had just been showing off.

I stayed by the rail, Annie beside me. "Why are you so sure she'll be back?" I asked.

She shook her head.

At that moment, Swav's head burst to the surface. We all helped her back on deck. She looked dazed, and she kept putting a hand to her neck. "It's sealed again," she said. "My... you know."

"I don't think I do," I said, and I couldn't keep the bitterness out of my voice.

She wrapped her arms around me and I let her, in front of everyone. The smell of her had changed. I realised I still liked it. Only that felt wrong now. Or for just a moment it did. "He's gone now," she said. "It's all going to be okay."

I helped her back to her cabin.

I had to ask how it had been. I had to. I don't know what I was expecting to hear. It was always going to be bad. "Just this enormous... natural experience," she said.

"Good?"

She looked pained for me, like she didn't want to lie to me. After that, she wouldn't say any more about it. It took us a few nights to get back to our old routine, but we did. I might have been kind of rough with her the first time, I don't know.

Swav apologised hugely to the crew for what the male's arrival had been like, even offered Helena her resignation. She hadn't known he'd make such a show of it, most didn't. Helena said her leaving was out of the question. Was there going to be a... happy event? Swav looked shocked for a moment at Helena's directness, then touched her neck and said she didn't know.

But in the next few weeks, it became obvious. The side of her neck and her lower back swelled, and you could see something shifting inside the translucent skin. She'd been spending a lot more time in the water, going deep under for hours at a stretch, for a long time now, even before there had been visible signs of her pregnancy. "And I'm going to have to be down there," she told me, "when it bursts." I spent as much time as I could down there with her. I didn't know how I felt about what she was carrying, but I wanted to be there for her, to help.

Of course, when it finally happened, I was on the platform, making dinner. I heard a weird cry from outside the galley, and rushed out, leaving the others, who hadn't heard it. Swav, who'd been deep underwater for most of that day, was bobbing on the surface, and in her arms was... Tom.

I looked at him, the little fella, small and blue and sleek, and I could see something about him, an expression in those eyes that were almost hidden in the folds of his face, an expression which just hadn't been there on that big male.

Swav smiled up at me, such an enormous smile of joy, and she didn't have to tell me what had happened. *How* it happened... Well, they're still debating that.

It was something chemical. The greatest rush of my life. I leapt into the water and took my boy into my arms.

In the next few weeks we took turns looking after Tom. Swav was going out to the edge of the reef on a regular basis to consult with a whole pack of males, yeah, including that one. They were talking, she said, about heading home soon.

"Do I get to come with?" I said.

"There's no way you could live on my world."

"But –"

"You want to be around Tom. I get that. So that's something else we've been talking about. How about you look after him for a bit? Then he comes back home with the second party, back to visit you again with the third?"

I was pleased at that. Though of course I'd miss Swav too. This arrangement would make it all feel much more grown up, and less like I'd feared, an adolescent melodrama, spurred on by my out of control hormones. I'd asked if her lot's scientists had come up with any ideas about how the two of us could have conceived, and she'd looked awkward. "Tom's not the only one," she said. "It's happened a lot."

And indeed, it was soon all over the news, proud fathers clutching human/Carviv kids. Though I've got to say, I didn't think any of them looked as much like them as Tom looked like me.

It was then that Annie made her feelings plain. I found her watching a clip of some nature show in the galley. She switched it off before I could see what it was, which made me ask if it was porn.

"Yeah," she said, "if you're a dunnock."

She didn't take much persuading to show it to me. It was a whole bunch of garden birds hopping about. "It's for this thesis I'm writing," she said. "The female dunnock mates with a number of males, each of which ends up thinking it's the father of her kids. So when the eggs are laid, all of them protect them."

"I thought you specialised in marine life?"

She paused, but I guess she couldn't help herself. "These days," she said, "I specialise in the Carviv."

It took me a moment to get what she meant. I think I was pretty harsh back to her. She deserved it. It was the last time we spoke.

Even after all these years, looking after Tom is still a joy. He swims like a torpedo. He's still only got a few words of English, but I've learned a lot of Carviv off him. He gets that just by listening to the sea. It sometimes makes me a little jealous about the guys who had Carviv daughters, the oldest of which are in school now, and charming the world. But no, I couldn't ask for more. There's this incredible bond between me and him, it just takes a while for others to see it. Every now and then I think about what Annie said, I mean, it comes up in some debate, but no... no, and anyway, even if it was true, so what?

Swav's been back once, and we took Tom over to Hawaii together, where the Carviv, having helped us sort out our climate issues, have started building an underwater holiday destination for their people. There are all these little islands covered in... Well, those flowers Swav told me about.

"Tempted?" I asked.

"Course not," she said, "I've got you."

I really wish that 'Tom' (Solaris Rising 2, 2013) didn't have that title, because it's also the name of my son, who didn't exist when I wrote this story about reproduction, but did by the time it appeared. (You may well ask what was going on in my mind.) I've dived from one of the platforms featured herein, where I experienced some of that openness to possibility that I associate with young Australasians. Here's another of my cartoon-faced beings, this time a creature whose life cycle is akin to that of some real-life birds. Whether the ending is heart-warming or something suitable for a horror story is a question I like to keep open, the answer, for me, changing depending on how optimistic I'm feeling.

Ramesses on the Frontier

Imagine Pharaoh Ramesses I, first of his dynasty, the father of imperial Egypt, being kept at the Niagara Museum and Daredevil Hall of Fame in Ontario, Canada. Ramesses himself can't. He lies in a stone casket, not his own. Only a rope strung between two sticks stops the casket from being interfered with. A sign nearby proclaims something in livid letters that he can't read. He's been put on display with several others. These include a man with two heads (one of them added post mortem, Ramesses has looked closely and seen the stitches), an unfortunate with some sort of skin disease that gives him webbing between his fingers, and something with a thick coating of fur, preserved under glass. To be arranged with them annoys Ramesses. One of these things is not like the others, that's what he wants to shout. These are dead bodies that have been defiled. He is... Well, he's not quite sure what he is right now, but he has the powers of awareness and motion, and these sorry bastards don't.

He keeps wondering if something went wrong with his funeral rites. He's sure his ka, which left his body at the moment of death, has been provided with excellent refreshment. And many spells had been written and placed to allow him to deal with the problems of the afterlife. He examined the lists himself, just days before he went to bed for what turned out to be his final sleep. There had been a great rush to get it all done. He'd only been Pharaoh for a few months before his illness, and they'd only made a small tomb as a result, but he'd been told that everything was ready. His son Seti had repeatedly assured him. But here he is, feeling like he's still in his body, but with his body being a... Well, Ramesses isn't really comfortable thinking about that.

His ka certainly left, because he remembers the moment of his death, him looking up at his beautiful son, and darkness moving swiftly in from the world all around his eyes. His ba, the record of his ethical efforts, is supposed to have stayed attached to his body until the correct ceremonies were performed, but there's no way to tell if they were, because he's as unaware of his ba now as he was in life.

If that new High Priest got that bit wrong, then perhaps that's why he's more like a corpse than an akh. This is definitely not what he was expecting. ⸌

He's sure that whatever's going on here, he won't be here forever. But time does seem to be stretching on, and nothing much seems to be happening. When he was High Priest, he put the correct religion back in its rightful place. The gods owe him. So what's the hold up?

It's not just himself he's worried for. It's his people. The nation of the river, the mirror of heaven, depends upon him completing this journey in order for others to follow. He is their ambassador. He changes the way as he passes through it. He makes it easier, like someone who stamps down reeds as they walk through a marsh. The rest of his folk who've died will be backed up by now for... well, who knows how long he's been here? The halls have certainly changed during that time, but they might change continually. He walks at night, but he doesn't know if that's every night. He only feels it is night because the mysterious lighting is kept so low, and he has a vague awareness of there being times when it's been brighter.

So that's his situation. He's awake again tonight. He's stuck. And he can't find a god to complain to.

As usual, he cautiously pulls back the lid of the casket, waits for a moment to check that there is only what passes here for silence, and climbs out. His feels the ache in his back. He sighs. He wonders if there is ever, actually, an end to pain. He sometimes thinks that's his punishment, but it's really not much of one, is it? And one should be aware of justice having been done to one, not just wake up in jail none the wiser. When he sent those sun worshippers running, he made damn sure they knew what was being done to them. Don't be such cowards, he bellowed at them, Ra will be back tomorrow, and it's the other gods you should worry about. The people applauded him and threw things at the sun worshippers as they ran from his soldiers. A great day.

Ramesses realises he's allowed himself to become lost in reverie. Again. This is no good. His mind is a little foggy. But maybe that's only to be expected, considering how far he is from his organs.

He goes for a wander.

He walks through the vast, quiet halls, looking up once more in undiminished awe at the crystal ceiling, the flowing images that are somehow pinned to the walls, put inside frames like important declarations. This building, so reminiscent of a tomb, must be the Duat, the underground world where spirits and gods come and go, which leads to final judgment. The images on the walls are one piece of evidence that points to this theory being correct. What he's seeing there are perhaps those caught on the way, because of his own predicament. He sees the same faces many times. They are mostly faces that are rather like those of Syrians, but paler, which is a bit weird. Perhaps that's just who were coming across when he got here, when the system seized up. It is a little surprising that these unknown races should be involved. That they should be depending on him. But pleasing, in a way. The true religion must be true wherever you go. His river people are ahead in that regard. At least, they are now he's got them back on track.

The pale people's clothes are bizarre. Ramesses assumes that their dream selves are being examined alongside their lives. There is no other explanation for the impossible wonders. Whoever these foreigners are, he's pretty sure that if they could, for instance, fly by the use of machines, they would have jealously come and taken the land of the river. He shivers at the thought of how many of them there are, and how strong. He's glad they're dead now, and not about to invade his beloved land. But still, he'll put in a good word for them. They seem fun.

Ramesses moves on.

At the end of the central chamber, there are a series of paintings, rendered to a high degree of detail, most of them oddly not in the colours of life but in blacks and silvers. Perhaps the artist only had those available. They show the great river that must be nearby, the sound of which Ramesses can sometimes hear when the halls are relatively quiet. In the pictures, souls are either in the river, or in containers placed in the river. These are very like the vases that, back in his grave, contain his own internal organs, assuming the new High Priest got that bit right. The pictures show people getting into these containers and being taken out of them. There are a few on display – just the remains of them, with no sign of the soul inside. All of them are pictured in the vicinity of a thing Ramesses has only heard of, but never previously seen: a great downward plunge of water, foam and rising mist.

He stands there staring up at the perplexing images. What *is* he supposed to do? What is he *missing*?

185

There are doors that obviously lead outside, but he has put his ear to them, and heard strange blarings and screamings every time he has done so, surely the wailings of those who haven't been allowed into the Duat. One is not supposed to arrive in the Duat and then simply leave. If he could find just one minor god, he could indicate to them that the Pharaoh is here, and they would surely realise that something has gone wrong and remember their obligations. He would be gracious. He would say hey, mistakes happen. They'd be tripping over themselves with an urgent need to put right this terrible *faux pas*.

He stops beside one of the upright walls of crystal and considers himself. He is not what he was. He looks as hollow as he feels, well, as hollow as actually, he is. His arms are used to resting across his chest now, so accustomed to the position that, whenever he gets up, he fears he will break one of them. His eyes have narrowed to slits, so he looks permanently to be holding in a laugh, which isn't how he feels at all. His nose, which used to be so fine, looks as if it's been broken in a fight. His neck is thin, like that of a strangled goose. At least his temples still remind him of himself. He still has wisps of hair, pushed back from his bald patch. He touches them sometimes. They remind him of touching the head of Seti, of smelling that scalp when the kid was newborn. His own head is that soft now. All that's left of his wrappings, so carefully prepared, are a few rags. They do not preserve his modesty. Not that he's got much to hide. His legs are so thin it's like walking on stilts. His hands are all knuckle. He holds one up and looks at his palm. It resembles papyrus. He is a scroll that has been filled with writing, and is now crisp out of its jar, and yet still he knows too little. No scroll knows the information it contains, he thinks. And all he wants is to be read.

No. He wants to see Seti again. He wants to touch his hair instead of his own.

There is a noise from behind him. He realises he has been so lost in his thoughts that he hasn't considered the possibility of him not being alone in the halls tonight. This has happened on a couple of previous occasions. The first time he saw the lamps he wanted to stop their owners and question them about where he was and what he could do to continue, but then he saw that those carrying the lamps were of the same people he'd seen on the walls, and realised that they must share his predicament, rather than be responsible for it, and not wishing to be weighed down by questions he could not answer, he'd avoided them. He's done so ever since.

But now the sound is so close that he's not sure he can avoid it. The light from the lamp is all around him.

He summons his regal bearing, highly aware that he is naked, and turns to see the newcomer.

Ramesses is relieved to see that this is not someone of an unknown race who is staring at him, but a Nubian woman. Finally! Here is someone who might understand how he came to be here. Perhaps they can share information, see if any new conclusions can be drawn. Ramesses raises his hands to call for silence, but then remembers, ridiculously, that he can't speak, that his tongue is still with his organs in their jar.

He attempts to speak anyway. He manages to summon a sound that vibrates like breath in his chest.

"Arrooooogghhhhhh!" he says.

The Nubian stares at him. She's playing that lamp in her hand up and down Ramesses' body as if what she's seeing might change any moment. He should tell her that in his condition that's pretty damn unlikely.

She finally says words that Ramesses doesn't understand. "You better come talk to my supervisor."

And then, bewilderingly, she turns around and starts to walk away. To turn her back on the Pharaoh! Ramesses can't quite take it in. In his working life he has seen comparatively few backs. He keeps his arms in the air, and repeats his opening statement, that takes such an effort of will to generate. "Arrooooogghhhhhh!"

The Nubian looks back over her shoulder and gestures to Ramesses with a crooked finger. He is, it seems, to follow.

Ramesses bridles for a moment, but then decides. He won't let pride get in the way of the first sign of progress since he got here. Putting stilt leg after stilt leg, trying to keep up with the Nubian, he follows.

They reach a small lighted enclosure, in an area that Ramesses has never explored, because it has always been full of foreigners. "Seth?" calls the Nubian, opening the door.

Inside the enclosure sits a Nubian man looking at unbound sheets of papyrus with the black and silver drawings on them. A greyhound sits at his feet. The dog is attached to his chair by a leather rein. It's looking imperiously at Ramesses, and now so does Seth. "Ah," says Seth, looking up and seeing Ramesses, "there you are. Finally."

Ramesses still doesn't understand a word of what's being said to him.

Seth reaches beside him, picks up a walking stick, and uses it to slowly get to his feet. Ramesses recognises the walking stick. It has a slim handle and a forked base. Ramesses smiles, opens his arms. Here he is! Finally! Seth goes to a cabinet, opens it and finds something. He hands it to Ramesses. The Pharaoh peers at it. It's a small, hard cake, with the image of a dog imprinted on it.

Apt. Ramesses wants to indicate that he has no tongue, but he assumes that the god Seth, bearer of a Was Staff, knows that. He puts the cake in his mouth and does his best, with so little water in him, to give it a good hard suck. As he does so, Seth starts talking, with little hand gestures that seem to say that it doesn't matter much what he's saying...

"... the god of foreigners, and so it's only apt that I'm in charge of – ah, okay, now you can understand me. Great."

Ramesses suddenly finds that, though he still has no tongue, he can talk properly too. "Have you been here all this time, Seth?" he says. "I consecrated my son to you, and still you didn't come to find me?"

"It was you who didn't come to find me."

Ramesses holds himself back. He's speaking, unlike at any other time in his life or afterlife, to an equal. So he must be diplomatic. And he knows Seth can be tricky, can be about storms and the chaos of the world, about what's over the border. That's why, while he was in the land of the living, he put in a word with him by naming his son that way. "Okay," he says, "well, putting that aside, maybe you could answer my questions now. How long have I been here?"

Seth looks at his watch. "Three thousand, three hundred years, give or take."

Ramesses frowns. It makes his brow hurt. "But... it doesn't feel like—"

"You've only been in this building for the last one hundred and thirty nine years. You were taken from your tomb by thieves. All part of the great design, but of course they can't know that, so the usual curses have been bestowed upon their families."

Ramesses wants to say that he's very much in favour of that, but he's been struck by what Seth said a moment earlier. "This... building?"

Seth sighs. He goes to another cabinet, and pulls out a rolled up piece of papyrus of a sort which is familiar to Ramesses. It's stored a bit offhandedly, but the Pharaoh stops himself from saying anything; the gods can keep things any way they like. Seth unrolls it onto the table.

The Nubian woman who led Ramesses here joins them to look down on it also. "I'm Mattie," she says. "If you're a good boy, you might be seeing me later."

Ramesses gets what she means. He nods his understanding.

The scroll turns out to be a map. Ramesses' gaze immediately seeks the river of his country and the green around it, but although he finds many rivers, none are the right shape. In fact, he doesn't recognise a single geographical feature. He can't even find the great waterfall that he's heard outside.

He looks up and sees that Seth is smiling at him. "You got separated from your coffin book," he says. "So I thought I'd show you our own *Book of the Dead*: a map of the United States, circa 1999." He puts a cook's relish into the pronunciation of each meaningless digit. "That's what the locals call the Duat and that's the year by their calendar. The Duat, you see, extends far beyond the walls of this building. In fact it only properly begins just south of here. We're in its hinterland, another country." His finger stabs down and down and down, faster than Ramesses can follow. "Over here's the White House, here's Disneyland, here's Canaveral, here's Graceland, here's Nashville." The finger spins. "In the air above it all, fear of the future, which is starting to crystallise as..." He spreads his palms wide to create a shadow with wiggling fingers on the map. "The Millennium Bug!" He laughs. It's not a nice laugh. "What the future actually holds for them... well, that's in the next drawer!"

Ramesses tries not to frown again. "You speak as though this is a real nation, with real subjects."

"They do think of it in that way, yes," he chuckles.

"So... if all this is the Duat..."

Seth nods. "You haven't started your journey yet."

"Why?"

"Because the Duat is the land of opportunity, a mirror of the mirror of heaven, and you've done nothing to take advantage of the opportunity you've been given. You were separated from your grave goods, which is where your ka goes back to during the day. And I've come back here night after night waiting for you to make your first move. In that time, I've seen so many other guys get to where they're going –"

"My people –"

"The ones who died after you did are in a holding pattern. They're fine. The ones born after you died went along after the next Pharaoh, your son."

"Seti has already –"

"He has indeed. And many others after him."

"What must I do?"

Seth gestures at the map. "I've let your ba go on ahead, as far as it can. Catch up to it, where it's waiting for you, at the Weighing of your Heart."

Ramesses leans closer, to where his thin eyes can see the words beside the geographical features, and he finally sees something he recognises. He finds he knows many of the inscriptions. They are familiar from the Books of the Dead he has seen prepared for others. So here are destinations. But they don't suggest a path. He is aware now of the shadow of the rest of his people, falling on him from behind. He is not even on this map yet. He doesn't know where he'll enter or how. He looks up at Seth again. "If I open the doors and go out there...?"

"You'll find your way. During your lifetime, you always had a map that led you along. But here, you'll be lucky if you can get a few pointers. It's all up to you. That's the way we made it. Go out into the world of the day. Go to America." And before Ramesses can take another look, he rolls up the map again, and puts it back in its cabinet. Then he looks back to the pharaoh. "You move on now."

And the dog even barks in warning.

It's winter here, he's told, so the day of these people's calendars will begin while it's still dark. Ramesses will be able to leave when the doors are opened, when he would normally be driven back to his bed by the noise.

So Ramesses waits, standing around the halls a little awkwardly. Then, when the big doors are opened, and these pale people, who live, unknowingly, right next to the Duat, and are coloured fittingly for a life in shadow, start to flood in, he boldly marches towards them. Some of them scream and point, but some of them laugh, or even, more suitably, applaud. The eyes of children are shielded from him, but he suspects that's not because of his magnificence, or his fearsomeness, but because of his tiny genitals.

He steps bravely out into this new world and winces. Oh, it's a bit cold out here. He sees that the screams he heard are mostly the sounds of unusual vehicles. But under that is a bigger sound.

He goes to see the waterfall. He stands there for quite a while, letting the spray moisten his face. He finds a smile cracking his lips. This is great. And he's full of hope, because he finally has a way.

A few passers-by actually ignore him when he asks which way America is. He's not so bothered by that, just pleased that he can make himself understood. Eventually there's one who points him in the right direction before hurrying away.

He spends several fruitless nights trying to get through customs. The guards at the gates turn him away and threaten him with arrest. He explains that he is the Pharaoh, that he is trying to save his people, but this does not impress them.

But he was not Pharaoh for nothing. He goes further away from the gates, into the streets and the buildings, and steals a coat. Then he tries the gates again, but is once more turned away. This is only to be expected. The journey through the Duat is all about getting past gates and those guarding them. During the days he sleeps in parks or in the gaps in the great stone palaces. Nobody bothers him. He wonders if this is part of his test.

He has an idea. He tries to find one of those urns he saw in the pictures. But those he sees are in strange contexts, unsuitable for his needs. Finally, he decides he can do without. That night, he steps over the low wall by the riverbank. He has never learned to swim, but it can't be as hard as all that, and will not be required for the hardest part of this.

He floats, initially quite slowly, downstream. He is aware of cries from the bank as people notice him. The roaring of the great falls gets ever closer. He speeds up. He paddles a bit to make it faster. There are flashing lights by the side of the river now, but it's too late, the spray is upon him!

He falls, laughing. He has passed the first gate!

He lands in the Duat in a deep pool. He waits. He does not need to breathe. He finally bobs to the surface a long way downstream, and is surprised to see the angry lights there too. He pushes at the water, and manages to head for where a group of trees stands beside the river, in some sort of park.

He struggles out of the river, and is away into the darkness before the guards can find him.

He is now in the Duat proper. The land of the souls that are free from their bodies. Not that they know it. He doesn't need very much. He doesn't get very much. He clothes himself by stealing, and drinks water from public fountains, merely to keep the power of speech. He expects the people here to be much more scared of him than they turn out to be. They can accept, it seems, almost anything. It helps that they will actually turn away from him rather than scare themselves by looking closely. It's just as well they're so hard to scare. But like animals that are hard to anger, Ramesses thinks, actually pushing them to that emotion might be a very bad idea.

He remembers a few things from the map. He knows where the challenges he must overcome can be found. And now he can look at other maps, and knows he is at the top, and presumably has to make his way to the bottom, as the country gets narrower and narrower. It is like being born again. And there was one name in particular that was meaningful to him on that first map, and so he must go there.

But there's something that worries him. "The world of the day" was how Seth described this place. That sounds worryingly like sun worshipper talk. And everything Ramesses sees of religion here suggests that is indeed the case. The false belief has flown here and taken root! And of course it suits the Duat, all these souls on the edge of hysteria, every moment seeking escape, angry with their lot without fully understanding their situation. He passes gigantic fields of worship, open to the sky, shining huge lights upwards at night in hope of the sun, from which he can hear the cry of "Ra! Ra! Ra!" He allows himself a painful frown.

Ramesses initially assumes it's his task here to once more drive the sun worshippers out, and so bursts into one of their temples and starts yelling, but he's repelled by sheer force of numbers, and threatened with the arrival of the guards, and worse still, invited to submit to the embrace of these heathen ways. They say they want to listen to him, but having heard him, finally decide they don't.

He falls onto a very finely cut lawn and is sprayed with water from something like a snake. He is gone before the guards arrive.

He's not here to learn that sun worship is true, is he? That'd be awful. But one thing he has discovered is that he's definitely not here to push the reeds down before him. Rather, it's like he's leading his people across a swamp. He must tread carefully and listen to local advice.

He makes his way down the country, night by night. He has to take many side-trips and excursions, dictated by the passage of the vehicles on rollers that he sneaks on board, or the wagons with drivers that he requests access to with a gesture. Those conversations are extraordinary. The drivers always assume he is something from their mythology, or something they can make money from. Because they have money here. When he tells them the true nature of their world, that's it all in the service of something else, they simply don't believe him.

He is not allowed access to the White House, where the guards tell him that instead of talking to the elected head of the peasants here, he should put his question in a net.

He asks around about that, and spends an evening with the god Thoth in a place that he is told is called Radio Shack. Thoth goes on a bit, but gives him a spell jar that is small enough to put in his pocket. He uses the spell jar to "download" and "update" all of the spells that are upon him, which he is pleased to see are still in place. One of them is a compass, which allows him to better navigate the Duat. Thoth's whole tone suggests that a moral conversation is beneath him, so this time Ramesses doesn't even try.

In Nashville, he wins a musical contest in front of an audience against a man in a wide-brimmed hat who, once backstage, identifies himself as the terrifying He Who Dances In Blood, a figure Ramesses is familiar with from many Books of the Dead. He tries to tell Dances that he's learned a moral lesson about humility, but Dances just looks at him oddly.

At Graceland he fights an army of warriors, all dressed alike, flinging them into each other, delighting in his martial grace, taking their songs for his own. "What did you stand for?" he asks the fallen. "What can I learn from you?" They all start to answer, but their answers are all different.

At Disneyland, he meets with He Who Lives On Snakes, who has a giant orange and white head, and a fierce tail, and keeps insisting that the most wonderful thing about him is his uniqueness, which is hardly the case. Every question Ramesses asks him about what his next test will be is met with a reply formed in cryptic poetry. Again, Ramesses tries to suggest that he's becoming a more moral character through these tests, but the answers he gets aren't receptive to that idea.

At Canaveral he is spun round and round by the goddess Nut, who every now and then allows those who live here to pierce her body, and tries to persuade them that they exist in a world which has no meaning, while everything else here says the opposite, thus torturing them with doubt, a nuance Ramesses can't help but think of as cruel. He tries to tell Nut he's learnt an important lesson, but all he does is vomit.

Finally, he makes his way to the lower left coast of the Duat, where the kidneys should be, and there finds the building with the title he recognises: "the SETI Institute". It must be named, he's sure, in honour of his son. It is unfortunate that he gets there as the sun is coming up, and so Ramesses falls asleep on a chair in the waiting room. When he wakes, he is in a room festooned with the instruments of torture, and he shakes until he realises that there is nobody here, that they have taken him as a corpse, that he interested them. He is sure this must be where he is intended to be, that this must be an important test on his journey, and so he waits until the peasants arrive once again, and then announces himself.

This time, they scream and run. Which is pleasing. But then they slowly come back, and remain interested. And that is even more pleasing.

He scares and interests them in equal measure, not too much of either. This, he thinks, might finally be the lesson he's meant to learn. He is only disappointed that his son isn't here.

This is how Ramesses ends up on Eater of His Own Excrement's chat show, carefully not quite explaining his mysterious origins, saying he's "from time as well as space" and wearing, after an intervention by an anxious wardrobe department, a clean, over-the-shoulder set of what the Pharaoh gathers are bandages.

Eater treats Ramesses as if he knows the answer to everything, which suits him down to the ground. "I see... the Millennium of your people will pass without an attack from this creature you call the Bug." This gets as much laughter as applause, which puzzles Ramesses, but he nods along, he'll take it. He's asked what his own beliefs are, and what he makes of the old time religion in the States. He lies enormously, saying he believes much as they do, and that all people should be free to worship as they wish. He manages to stretch out a gummy grin, which is really painful.

After the show, Eater shakes his hand and says that he'd be happy to send Ramesses on to his final destination by private helicopter. SETI will be angry, but with nothing but his own authority to go by, he's decided Ramesses is a person, not property. Ramesses feels elated and terrified at the same time. He runs to the helicopter pad, turning down autograph requests as he goes, waving to a crowd that's still screaming, but now not in fear.

And so he lands at the southernmost end of the country, in New Mexico, at the Acoma Pueblo, which, he is told, is "the town in the place that always was". A figure stands tall under the whip of the helicopter blades, and Ramesses is relieved to see that it's Anubis, actually wearing an appropriate head dress, dogs barking around his feet, and he's carrying a Was Staff too.

"This is where they keep what they think of as the truth," the god explains, leading him into a small pueblo hut. Ramesses looks around for a moment before he ducks inside, and sees the faces of the Acoma tribe, with all sorts of expressions suggesting interest and lack of it, involvement and lack of it, as real as life.

Inside the hut stands Osiris, green-skinned, his legs wrapped, holding his crook and flail in the posture of a Pharaoh. Ramesses relaxes. It really is time, and he's ready. "We've had your ba here for some time," says the god, unrolling a scroll and raising an eyebrow. "And when we heard you'd finally got around to gracing us with your presence, we sent ahead for your heart." And there it is, in his hand, a tiny shrivelled apple of a thing.

And now Ramesses is afraid again. For himself, and his people, and that he won't see his son. He can hear movement outside, a siren again; a shadow is cast through the door onto the wall. It's Ammit, the devourer, the end of the world, ready to take him.

Osiris produces the scales, and puts the heart on one of them. Ramesses gets out his spell jar, and switches it on, fingers fumbling with the tiny glyphs on the screen. Osiris makes a movement of his fingers, and produces a feather from the air, that is the goddess Maat, also represented by a glyph. It's good to see Mattie again. The green god puts the feather onto the other pan of the scale. The heart starts to grumble. Ramesses is fearful that it'll tell tales about the anger and cruelty of his life. So he quickly activates the spell he's been told will silence it. He lets out a long breath as the heart subsides. Osiris smiles at him. Well done.

The feather and the heart remain in balance. Osiris produces another scroll, and compares it to the ba. Then he asks the first of the forty-two questions. "Have you committed a sin?"

Ramesses makes sure the right spell is activated and quickly replies. "No."

The list includes having slain people, terrorised people or stolen the property of a god, all of which Ramesses knows he's done, but the spell lets his lies go unchallenged. One of the questions is whether or not he's felt remorse, which makes him feel particularly vindicated. He may not have changed the Duat, but it has not changed him.

Osiris reaches the end. The feather has remained in balance with the heart. He smiles again, and holds up his own spell jar to show Ramesses. On it is a communication from a Museum in Atlanta, who have bought him intending to set him free.

The transition finally happens on one of these people's flying machines, somewhere over the ocean. The context changes between the Duat and the mirror of heaven. Ramesses finds himself standing beside the crate containing his body, and here is Seti with him!

He laughs and cries, hugs his son to his breast. They are both themselves again. "The things the gods have put in place!" says Seti.

"I liked your Institute," says Ramesses.

"They do their best," says Seti, stroking his father's hair.

What on Earth do you do when asked for a mummy story? These days, the mummy is the least fancied of the Universal revenants, just a cartoon image, almost every facet of its original function lost or replaced. Maybe that's why Jared Shurin edited The Book of the Dead (Jurassic London, 2013), with many interesting answers to that question. In my case, I went gonzo and said it's all true, not just the horror bits. (The story of how Ramesses' body got to where he is at the start is true.)

Zeta Reticuli

Nn is watching for where it knows the faint star will rise. It hasn't lost its knowledge of the stars, despite the degradation. This star is special, of course. To Nn, if to nobody else. It's a puzzle to Nn that so many have become so obsessed with what was done near that star, with what they allege has come from that star, and yet they don't connect that to the star in the sky itself. They don't point at it and say there, that's where this fear is from. They don't know where it can be found.

Nn likes this time in main morning, before the pollution from the manufacturing burrows closes down the sky. On minor mornings, when only the small sun is up, Nn sometimes can't make itself leave its tiny gifted pod. It just stands there, thinking about finality. It does not have to work. Opting for gifted consensual degradation gave it that, at least, and a handful of plant at meal time. Nn remembers when there were three plants. They had three even on the expedition. It remembers itself and the rest of the crew eating the other two plants offhandedly, unaware that this would become a luxury. But of course the instruments with which they navigated were already a luxury, even the walls they were contained within. So much so that the pod had been taken apart and melted down soon after they'd returned, metal being much more important than history. History is now the rarest luxury of all. Instead, there is myth. It is Nn's fate to stand on the border between those two things.

Nn hopes that today, as it makes its way, as usual, in the day-long walk it takes for recreation and in the hope of finding plant leftovers, nobody will recognise it. Nn has sometimes been stopped by those with mental degradation, who want to hiss loudly in its face, but they are not the worst. The worst are the drones with theories about Nn's mission, usually that the grand burrow are hiding something about what happened, or, worse, that Nn must know all about the Barney and Betty, and what they are here to do, and is keeping a secret that Nn for some reason will suddenly reveal to them.

Nn is continually amazed that they are concerned about these things but not about the degradation all around them. The lifetime of a new drone is set shorter each year. Their worries about the expedition are artificial, have been constructed. Nn's own fears about it are grown inside it. Nn has come to think that the constructed fear is there to immunise these drones against real fear. Nn wakes from the first state of reality almost every night to find itself in the second, still in those memories. It then has to will itself into the third state, before it really wants to, to get on with the day before the day has come. Memories live in Nn like a parasite.

They were lost, that was the most terrible thing. They were the first of their kind to go out there, and they made their tunnels between the stars, and they placed beacons, as their people had always done when going on expeditions on the surface, of the world or of the universe, but they had lost the last beacon, and were despairing of ever getting home.

They had taken the pod in and out of the second state of reality, putting their heads into the soil and out again, as the metaphor went, afraid to be seen by the creatures of the world they had found, amazed and scared that those creatures were so like themselves: two arms; two legs; and the eyes –! Nn still felt that fear every time it thought of them: those small, inscrutable eyes with tunnels in the centre of them, like the thing was looking right into you, with a flap of skin so they could withdraw their attention, so that they were in control of who they admitted into their third state of reality. Nn had heard in the clickings along the tunnels, from experts, that it was now thought that biological material from that world where life was so ancient might have had time to drift as far as their own suns, might have seeded or bonded with the earliest life in the burrows. The creatures of that world they had visited, the only life the expedition had found, were the ancients, the creators. Nn thought the myth that had grown around them was about the feeling that the expedition had disturbed them, as a newly hatched drone disturbs the hatcher. Nn feared for the young picking out those clicks from the hiss of the nightly sharing. No wonder this myth preyed on so many of them, seemed to make them mad. There was the feeling in the air of the tunnels that they were being punished. Nn could remember from his own earliest days when that hadn't been so. Or at least when it hadn't felt as overwhelming. Or perhaps that was just how the newly hatched always felt. Perhaps the sense that reality was punishing the conscious was a universal thing.

The leader of the expedition – it was dead now, they were all dead but Nn and perhaps Ghh, Nn hadn't asked after it in the clicking – had decided they should set down in the third reality and interact with the creatures of the world they had found themselves falling into the burrow slope of. They might find out where they were, and how to get home. They had put on their uniforms, their luxurious caps and suits, all in the black of the night, the same they had been seen off in with glorious hisses and clicking that had vibrated around the whole world. Nn wondered if they had hoped to impress these huge beings, that this sign of their importance at home was meant to translate. As if one could ever impress that which hatched you.

The crew had waited by their pod, the lights on it wastefully full on, for one of the pods they had observed to approach along an artificial trail. Nn remembers those lights, white in the strange air of that world, that to their amazement they could breathe, unlike that of any other world they had found. The thought of the lights reminds Nn now of how quickly light information is degraded as it leaves a world, how what had been clickings sent on the electromagnetic spectrum became noise, almost before the final edge of the burrow slope of any drone worlds around a hatcher star. What their lights had been trying to say was that they were important, that their visit to that world was meaningful. Who knows if the Barney and Betty had got that message, or if they had heard something else? Who knows what their world had made of it? Every now and then, Nn wonders if the myth can somehow be true, if the Barney and Betty are really –? But then it stops that seed thought inside itself, feeling that there is the path to final degradation.

They had spaced themselves out across the trail, like young drones aiming to catch a beast, when there had been beasts. Nn remembers the taste of the air, so full of water and plant. There was too much of everything here. The head of the expedition had joked that they might annex this world, if they could only work out where it was, because it had so much that was needed back home. But none of them had thought that was possible. The thirteen of them were the most their world could manage to put out into the dark. They had found ways to many stars, but no matter what the plant at the end of the tunnel, they could not see how it would be possible to make more pods like this to follow them. Even then, they had known that. The expedition had been a way for the grand burrow to say they were big, and now here were Nn and his comrades, doing the same against the gods.

They had waited, across the track, trying to muster their authority. They had waited for something to arrive that they knew would be terrifying. But then they had not known just how terrifying it would be for their world.

Then there had been answering lights in the distance. Nn had waited, breathing only a little, trying to get information from those lights. The pod had appeared, and slowed, coming to a halt as the creatures inside it saw the lights that said something was across the track in front of them. Nn had joined with the others in clicking from his brain, making the electromagnetic messages that encouraged its own people to move from the third state into the first. The pod stopped, its lights went off. Nn and its comrades paused, clicked to each other to be brave, to approach. Nn remembers that it was the first to move, but that might be just the signal degradation of time. Nn got to the pod, and looked in through the transparent part of it... and saw them.

They were enormous, at least twice as tall as the tallest of Nn's comrades, and they were full citizens then, fed on three plants, who had eaten beast. The creatures wore luxuriously varied clothes, many different colours and textures. Their faces were big as beasts, their mouths and noses enormous, to eat all this world had, to breathe this big wet air. Their skin colours were both opposed to the beautiful varieties of grey that Nn's people were hatched in for their lives in tunnels, another startling luxury: one was much lighter, one much darker. Their bodies were different to each other too, varied in shape in multiple ways.

That was the first time, as they turned to look at Nn, with expressions that Nn could interpret, to some degree, as that of stunned beasts, and so it knew the clickings had been effective... that was the first time Nn had seen those eyes. They bored into it. They sought to make a connection, to impose their meaning on Nn, who couldn't close its own. It was as if they threw meaning imperiously around them, wasting it, splashing it. They seemed startled not to have done so in this moment, having done so all their lives. Nn forced down its fear and clicked to them to get out. They did, their shadows impossibly huge on the track. Nn reached up a hand, its own fingers so thin, and took the enormous hand of one of them in its own, and led her, because they were about to find, as with some of the extinct beasts, that this was a her, towards Nn's own pod.

They had taken the pod and their visitors and their pod out of the third state as soon as possible, in case another pod came along, and brought too many creatures to deal with. The creatures slowly asked questions, in their loud voices. Their language was expansive, so many sounds. The leader of the expedition clicked into them again, found that language, and then they at least had the sense of what was said. The leader spoke to them in their own tongue, its voice quiet and sibilant in comparison to how they said the same words, and it had to avoid some sounds it couldn't stretch its mouth to say. It asked questions about what they knew of astronomy, about whether a number of specific multiple star burrows could be seen from this world, about where the biggest electromagnetic source in the sky was. The creatures could hardly answer, had the same limited knowledge of what they did not need to know as any drone did. Nn remembers feeling angry at them: these were not all wise hatchers; they would be no help in getting home. That feeling has been lost as the myth was made into artifice by repetition. The crafters wanted to examine the creatures for their records, as was their duty, so what they would find out to be the male, what would later become known as the Barney, was led away by them, while the leader showed the female the map of burrows that the expedition had built up during their wanderings. It showed the eleven worlds they had burrowed to. She looked at it for a long time, but seemed bemused, her huge finger wandering just as lost across it, taking no message from it. Nn remembers wondering at the time if these two were degraded by their world, were, to whatever extent, victims of it, if the expedition had the bad luck to pick such as that. But it had put the thought from its mind quickly: they brought such luxury with them, would any who were hatched into such excess ever be degraded? This one was the Betty, or rather she was not the Betty yet, she was just Betty, as she had called herself, Betty Hill. Dee dee dee. Nn can still recall the leader's voice buzzing strangely as it repeated the expansive and formal name. The huge name of a god.

Nn took Betty into the other part of the pod, where the crafters were examining Barney. They had inserted a needle into his strange sexual organs. He was protesting, weakly, which had put the crafters on edge. They were worried that he might move back into the third state, and attack them, and then all would be lost. They drew out the needle, and projected what they had found onto the wall. Nn saw the horrid, scuttling shapes of how these creatures reproduced. The males threw this stuff out, and it could infect any female that got it inside them. The crafters told Nn that only one of these millions of cells would successfully mate with an egg. They had that from Barney's knowledge. It was, again, frighteningly expansive, an obscene waste. The crafters told Barney to lie face down on the table, and inserted a rectal probe. They sampled what he'd eaten. The screen revealed such variety, so many sources, so many flavours that seemed to have no point except pleasure.

Betty was looking on, with a huge expression on her face, her feelings so obvious, as if she was projecting herself on the wall. It was actually a little hard to look at her. She seemed to occupy so much more space than her physical body did. The crafters told Barney to get up, and started to soothe Betty into getting onto the examination bench. They did this carefully, fearfully, and finally, her expression changing into something between emotions that was a shout and yet at the same time nebulous, she did so. They examined her womb with the needle, and, to Nn's relief, she wasn't carrying a child inside her. Nn squirmed at the idea of these creatures doing that. It was so unsafe. As if they felt able to waste their children as well.

Now, Nn sees the star appearing over the mound of a burrow to the east. It should feel a chill because of it, but over the years the fear has become Nn's touchstone, its only certainty. This world, running down, its people and history draining away, hasn't got much mythology left. What it does comes from that place. Nn is pleased, almost, for a moment, that it found that for its people. But no, it's a burden, something that mocks them as they die. Nn wonders if the creatures near that star remember them. The expedition tried to click into Barney and Betty that they shouldn't. But how certain could they have been that such big brains would obey? Perhaps they should have treated them more gently. Would things be different if they had? Nn keeps trying to find reasons for the myth. But perhaps myths are built because of different processes than reason. Perhaps myths are from the second state of reality.

Nn watches its star rise for a while, until the light of great dawn is in the sky, then begins its usual round. Things are as they always are to the extent that, as usual, Nn finds itself spending much of the time in the second state, its body just doing what it usually does, head popping out of the burrow only when something unusual is sighted on the daytime trail. It is towards the end of the day when it sees something surprising ahead, and it takes a moment to realise what it is seeing.

Here is Ghh, another member of the expedition. It is alive after all. Ghh is from a distant burrow, but Nn has often thought that it could go and see it if it really wanted to. Not wanting to is from the first reality and wanting to from the third, and that border is also one Nn stands on. Still, here Ghh is. Nn raises a hand and Ghh looks surprised to see Nn, not displeased on the surface, but certainly shaken inside.

They talk, initially, about their lives now, but there isn't much to say. They talk about the expedition. Nn realises, with horror, that Ghh believes the myth. "We disturbed something," says Ghh. "Strength like that, has to be a beast, following what hurt it back to its home. What a waste of what it has otherwise. Think about it."

Nn argues that the creatures would have come in force. That there is no reason for them to behave as Ghh thinks they are doing. They have so little. Surely if they came, they would come to save. Or, if not, to conquer.

"That wouldn't punish us. They'd have to look after us then, to actually be hatchers. They punish and run."

By the end of the conversation, Nn is very tired. It asks Ghh how its degradation is going. Ghh says not long now. Nn wishes it well, leaves it knowing they will never see each other again. Nn leaves Ghh with no means of finding it, which makes sure of that, really. Nn returns to its burrow alone as the light is fading.

Nn fastens its burrow and stands in the darkness, listening to the clicks and the hiss from down the tunnels. It stays in the third state a long time. It wonders if there is a sort of signal that can also be a creature, that can take a culture repeatedly, continually, across the universe, that is so proud that it does not have to hide and burrow. If they are coming here, it thinks, it's good, in a way, because that means they must be striving to understand this place.

The seed has been planted. Nn lets itself drift off into the second state, and finds itself again back at that night. It moves into the first state and sees the universe, consciousness inside it, spreading out, thinning, being wasted, maintaining coherence only through the stupid will of those who can close their eyes.

Nn knows what's coming. It shifts back into the second state, then quickly into the first, at unexpected light.

They have entered through the wall. They stand there, imperious expressions filling the room, unknowable and yet insisting that they will be known. Here are Barney and Betty Hill. Nn doesn't try to run. It wants to know what they bring. It only hopes they bring something, even if only meaning.

They step forward and lay hands on Nn and lead it quickly over the border.

The UFO myth is the USA's fundamental, original body of lore, as American as jazz, exported successfully around the world, but manufactured in New Mexico. (Perhaps literally, as recent document releases reveal more about an intelligence culture that wanted people to see something in the sky other than spy planes.) It's always fascinated me, since I was a child leafing through 'true' UFO books, scared by what I might see on every page. It's hard to write tales about. How do you write a story about a true story that most people think is fiction? I have some time for the possible reality of one of the founding texts of this mythology, the narratives of Barney and Betty Hill, who might, might, have been the only people ever to have been abducted by aliens. Also/ or they were masters of the zeitgeist who created, out of nothing (don't believe what people tell you about an episode of The Outer Limits that has no resemblance to the abduction narrative and they almost certainly didn't see), a myth arc that persists to this day. So I had some fun thinking, as I have often had cause to in my career, about creatures of myth who also have to deal with the awkwardness of being real. This story appeared in Paradox (NewCon Press, 2014), an anthology about the Fermi Paradox, the idea that we really should have found extraterrestrial intelligence by now, that humans not having done so is worrying. I felt even more worry was needed.

Hamilton

The Jonathan Hamilton stories are one of a few ways I've found to try to talk about masculinity. The masculine construct is something I've always struggled with. I live inside it undercover. I pass pretty well. I don't know what thing it is that I really am, I only know my cover story. When I was in my twenties, even my thirties, I was a horrifying child of a man. I was allowed to be until, thankfully, I was caught and halted and put on a different path. I find Ian Fleming's James Bond novels to be extremely well-written products of a masculinity decades older than mine, attempts to deal with the same awkwardness that affect a direct, guileless manner. They're self-revelatory in a way critics sometimes feel the author wouldn't have wanted, but that, I think, is part and parcel of being a novelist. They're about a man who engages our sympathy by getting horribly, continually hurt, both physically, by Bulgarians, and psychologically, by the patriarchy, which he's lost in and can't even see the dimmest edges of. He dreams of alternatives, but loves his boss and having a place in the pack too much to explore them. We should, I feel, include this modern reading in any appreciation of Fleming's talent, because he put it there, no matter what part of his brain he used to do it, and he's expressing a reality. The Hamilton stories begin with a hint of pastiche, but I hope they swiftly go beyond that, though I do have shades of Bond, in terms of the movies as well as the books, slipping through scenes every now and then. They're a different set of answers to the questions Fleming poses. They're also me having fun with Hussar jackets and deep Britishness, a worrying amount of the cruelty and delight of which is real. I think SF readers seek cues to the nature of the world they're reading about like Mystery readers seek clues and red herrings. I like SF with a high cues-per-word ratio, and the Hamilton stories sometimes bombard the reader with them. The nature of the parallel universe Hamilton inhabits, where it diverged from our own and what the date is are puzzles the answers to which appear, slowly, in the stories.

The four stories here appeared in Fast Forward 2 (Pyr, 2008), The Solaris Book of New Science Fiction, Vol. 3 (2009), Isaac Asimov's Science Fiction Magazine (July 2011) and Rogues (Tor, 2014). 'One of Our Bastards is Missing' was nominated for the Hugo Award for Best Novelette in 2010, and 'The Copenhagen Interpretation' won the 2011 BSFA Award for Short Fiction.

Catherine Drewe

Hamilton could hear, from the noises outside the window, that the hunters had caught up with their prey. There was a particular noise that Derbyshire Man Hounds made seconds before impact. A catch in their cries that told of their excitement, the shift in breathing as they prepared to leap at the neck of the quarry the riders had run in for them. He appreciated that sound.

He looked back to where Turpin was sitting in a wing chair, the volume of Butriss he'd taken from Sanderton's library in the early stages of the hunt still open on his lap. The skin on Turpin's face was a patchwork of different shades, from fair new freckles that would have put an Irishman to shame to the richer tones of a Mulatto. This was common in the higher ranks of the military, a sign that parts of Turpin's body had been regrown and grafted back on many different occasions. Hamilton saw it as an affectation, though he would never have said so. He had asked for his own new right arm to match the rest of his body completely. He'd expected Turpin, or one of the other ranking officers who occasionally requested his services, to ask about it, but they never had.

The noise from outside reached a crescendo of cries and horns and the sudden high howl of one dog claiming the prey and then being denied more than a rip at it. Turpin opened his eyes. "Damn," he said. He managed a slight smile. "Still, five hours. They got their exercise."

Hamilton reflected the smile back at him, shifting his posture so that he mirrored Turpin's nonchalant air more exactly. "Yes, sir."

Turpin closed the book. "I thought they had me an hour ago, which is why I sent for you. How's your weekend been? Has Sanderton been keeping you in the style to which you're accustomed?" Turpin had arrived unannounced and unexpected, as he often did, late last night, sitting down at the end of the dinner table as the gentlemen were about to adjourn, and talking only about the forthcoming day's hunting, including asking his host for Hamilton to be excepted from it.

"It's been a most enjoyable house party, sir. Dinner was excellent."

"I heard you bagged your share of poultry."

Paul Cornell

Hamilton inclined his head. He was waiting for Turpin to get to the point, but it wouldn't be for a while yet. Indeed, Turpin spent the next twenty minutes and thirty three seconds asking after Hamilton's family, and going into some of the details of his genealogy. This happened a lot, Hamilton found. Every now and then it occurred to him that it was because he was Irish. The thought registered again now, but did not trouble him. He had considerable love for the man who had ordered him to return home from Constantinople when it became clear the only good he could do there was to remind the Kayser that every disturbance to the peace of Europe had consequences, that every action was paid for in blood. Hamilton would have done it, obviously, but it was one less weight to drag up the hill when he woke each morning.

"So." Turpin got up and replaced the book on the library shelf. "We've seen you're fit, and attended to your conversation, which rang like a bell with the white pudding crowd. We have a job for you, Major. Out of uniform."

Hamilton took that to be the Royal we. He found that a healthy smile had split his lips. "Yes, sir. Thank you, sir."

Turpin touched his finger to the surface of the table, where the imprint glowed with bacterial phosphorescence. Hamilton leaned over and made the same gesture, connecting the receptors in his skin with the package.

"Nobody else knows about this," said Turpin.

The information rolled into Hamilton. It exhilarated him. He felt his nostrils flare at the smells and pictures of a land he'd never been to. New territory. Low white newly grown wood buildings, less than a day old by the look of them, with the banners of imperial Russia fluttering gallant. That is, fluttering not entirely through the progression of an atmosphere past them. Near darkness. Was it dawn? Not unpleasant.

And there was the woman. She stood on a bluff, looking down into a dark grey canyon, looking at a prize. He couldn't see what she was looking at, the emotion came with the package, and Hamilton reacted to it, making himself hate her and her prize for a moment, so if anything like this moment came in the world, he would be in charge of it.

She wore her hair green, but bundled in the knots which suggested she rarely had to unfurl it and take the benefit. Her neck was bare in the manner which said she was ready for the guillotine, the black collar of her dress emphasising her defiance. Hamilton let himself admire that bravery, as he did the martial qualities of all those he met in his work. Her gown was something that had been put together in the narrow hell of the foundry streets of Kiev, tiny blue veins of enforcement and supply across Imperial white, with the most intricate parchment wrinkles. It looked as if she was wearing a map.

Her hands were clasped before her, and she was breathing hard, controlling her posture through an immense effort of will. She wanted to exult, to raise herself in triumph.

Hamilton found himself wishing she would turn around.

But the information froze there, and the rare data tumbled into his mind. He sent most of it into various compartments, for later examination, keeping only the index in the front of his attention.

"Catherine Drewe," said Turpin. "Ever meet her?"

Just because they were both Irish? Hamilton killed the thought. "No."

"Good. We got that emotional broadcast image by accident. From someone standing behind her, a bodyguard, we think. One of our satellites happened to be passing over the Valles Marineris at the right moment, three days ago."

Hamilton had already realised. "The Russians are on Mars."

Turpin nodded. "Terrifying, isn't it?"

"Is her army –?"

"Down there with her, because if so, we're acting with a criminal disregard for the safety of our allies in the Savoy court?"

Hamilton acknowledged Turpin's smile. "Thought you might be ahead of me, sir."

"We hope not. And we don't see how. So we're not getting Chiamberi involved as yet. She's probably down there on her own, either negotiating a rate to take the Russian side in whatever their long term plans against the House of Savoy might be, or already part of those plans, possibly as a consultant. Now, the mercenary armies alarm us all, but the good thing about them is that we've sometimes been able to use them as passive aggregators of intelligence, allowing them to serve a side to the point where they're trusted, and then buying them off, netting all they know in the process."

"Is that the mission, sir?"

"No. We've created and are ready to plant chaotic information of an unbreakable nature strongly suggesting that this has already happened, that we have paid Miss Drewe in advance for her dalliance with the bear. Your front cover will be as a serf, your inside cover as a deniable asset of the Okhranka. Your mission is to kill her and any associates in one move."

Hamilton felt himself take another deep breath. "So the world will think the Russians discovered her treachery and covertly executed her."

"And botched the cover, which the world will enjoy working out for itself. Miss Drewe's mercenaries are tremendously loyal to her. Many of them declare themselves to be in love with her. Doubtless, several of them are actually her lovers. They will not proceed with any contract should she die in this way. Moreover, they may feel obliged to expose the Russian presence on Mars –"

"Without us having been involved in exposing it."

"So the Czar's state visit at Christmas and the superconductor trade talks won't have any awkwardness hanging over them. Savoy won't ask and won't tell. They'll be able to bring pressure to bear before the Russians are anywhere near ready to tussle. There will be no shooting war, the balance will be preserved, and even better –"

"Miss Drewe's disaffected mercenaries may actually give us the information on Russian arms and intentions that we're alleging she did."

"And other such groups, irked at Russian gall, will be less disposed to aid them. It *is* rather beautiful, isn't it?" Turpin held out his hand, the ring finger crooked, and Hamilton touched fingertip to fingertip, officially taking on the orders and accepting them. "Very good. You leave in three days. Come in tomorrow for the covers and prep."

There was a knock on the door. Turpin called enter, and in marched a hearty group of hunters, led by Sanderton, the mud still on their boots. At the front of the pack came a small girl, Sanderton's daughter. She'd been blooded across the cheeks, and in her right hand she held, clutched by the hair, Turpin's deceased head. "Do you want to eat it, Uncle?" she asked.

Turpin went to her, ruffled her hair, and inspected the features of his clone. "Yes, I'll take my prion transmitters back, Augusta. Can't be spendthrift with them at my age."

Sanderton advised him that his chef was used to the situation, and would prepare the brain as a soup.

Hamilton caught the eye of the girl as she hefted the head on to a plate provided by a servant. She was laughing at the blood that was falling on to the carpet, trying to save it with her hand.

Hamilton found that he was sharing her smile.

Hamilton made his apologies to his host, and that night drove to Oxford in his motor carriage, a Morgan Sixty-Six. The purr of the electrical motor made him happy. Precision workings. Small mechanisms making the big ones tick over.

It was a clear run up St. Giles, but glancing at his watch, Hamilton knew he wasn't going to make it in time for the start of the service. He tore down the Banbury Road, and slowed down at the last moment to make the turn into Parks, enjoying the spectacle of the Pitt Rivers, lit up with moving displays for some special exhibition. The Porters, in all their multitudes, ran out of their lodge as he cut the engine and sailed into the quad, but the sight of the 4th Dragoons badge had them doffing their caps and applauding. After a few words of greeting had been exchanged, Loftus, the head porter, came out and swore at Hamilton in her usual friendly fashion, and had her people boost the carriage onto the gravel just beyond the lodge.

Hamilton walked across the quad in the cold darkness, noticing with brief pleasure that new blades had appeared in neon scrawl on the wall of his old staircase. The smells of cooking and the noise of broadcast theatric systems in students' rooms were both emphasised by the frost. The food and music belonged to Moslems and Hindus and the registered Brethren of the North American protectorates. Keble continued its cosmopolitan tradition.

He headed for the Chapel. As he passed the main doors, the bells that had been sounding from inside fell silent. He put his hand to the wood, then hesitated, and went to sit in the hallway outside the side door. He listened to the start of the service, and found his heart lifted by the words, and by the voice that was saying them. "Your world turns as the solar system turns as the universe turns, every power in balance, for every action an opposite, a rotation and equalisation that stands against war and defeats death, and the mystery of what may happen in any moment or in any space will continue..."

He waited an hour, until the service was over, enjoying the cold, listening to that voice through the wood of the door, intimate and distant.

As the congregation came out, Hamilton stepped through the mass of them, unnoticed, and past churchwardens putting out candles and gathering hymn books. There she was. She had her back to him. Annie. In the gleaming vault of the Chapel interior, dominated by the giant depiction of God with a sword for a tongue, reaching across time and space with his Word.

She turned as the sound of his footsteps. She was as lovely as he remembered. "Jonathan," she whispered, "why are you here?"

He took her hand and put it to his face and asked for a blessing.

The blessing only gave him an edge of 0.2 per cent. Annie checked again, in his head behind his eyes, and for a moment he thought how splendid it would be to show her all his old covers, to share. But no. He could not. Not until this part of his life was over.

"It's a very slight effect," she said. "Your prayers have hardly provoked the field. Are you contemplating murder?"

Hamilton laughed in a way that said of course not. But really his laugh was about the irony. It wasn't the first time the balance had stood against he who sought only to maintain it.

They went into the side chapel where *The Light of the World* by Holman Hunt was kept, the one on display to the Empire's gawkers in St. Paul's being a copy.

Places like this, to Hamilton, were where the sons of Empire returned to after they had done terrible things, the clockwork pivots about which their dangerous world turned, where better people could keep what they did those things for. Annie, his old tutors like Hartridge and Parrish, the architecture and custom, the very ground were why he went to work. On his way from here, he would look in on the Lamb and Flag and drink a half of beer with the hope that he would return to drink the other half. As had many before him, for all the centuries.

After the churchwardens had left, Annie did him a certain service behind the altar, and Hamilton returned the favour.

And then he left holy ground, and went out into the world that wasn't England, equipped only with a tiny and ironic blessing.

At the square, anonymous offices off Horse Guards Parade, they armed him and briefed him. He looked out from the secret part of his mind and saw that he was now Miquel Du Pasonade, a bonded serf of three generations. He let Miquel walk to the door and bid farewell, only leaning forward to take over during weapons familiarisation.

He let his cover take the overnight to Woomera, switching off completely, waking only as he was paying in Californian Rubles for a one-way ticket up the needle.

Hamilton always preferred to watch the continents drop below him as he ascended. He mentally picked out the shapes of the great European Empires, their smaller allies, colonies and protectorates. The greater solar system reflected those nations like a fairground mirror, adding phantom weight to some of the smaller states through their possessions out there in the dark, shaming others with how little they'd reached beyond the world.

Hamilton waited at Orbital for two days, letting his cover hang around the right inns, one of the starving peasantry. He let himself be drunk one night, and that was when they burst in, the unbreachable doors flapping behind them, solid men who looked as if they should be in uniform, but were conspicuously not.

His cover leapt up.

Hamilton allowed himself a moment of hidden pride as they grabbed his hair and put their fingers onto his face. And then that was that.

Hamilton woke up pressed into service, his fellows all around him celebrating their fate with their first good meal in weeks. They sat inside a hull of blue and white.

They were heading his cover didn't know where.

But Hamilton knew.

Normally on arriving at Mars, Hamilton would have booked into the Red Savoy Raffles, a tantalising distance from Mons, as the gauche advertising put it, and spent the evening arguing the toss of the wine list with Signor Harakita. Serfdom to the Bear offered a different prospect. The hull the serfs were kept in smelt of unaltered body. During the passage, they did the tasks which would have needed continual expensive replacements had mechanisms been assigned to them: maintaining the rocket motors, repairing the ship's life support infrastructure. There were two fatalities in the three weeks Hamilton was on board.

They didn't take the serfs on face value. All of them were run through an EM scan. Hamilton watched it register the first level of his cover, accepting it. The deeper cover would only be noticed once that print was sent, hopefully long after the fact, to the cracking centres in the hives of St. Petersburg. It had also, to more deadly effect, been registered in public with the authorities at Orbital, and would thus also be cracked by every Empire's mind men in every capital.

But that was not all that the EM scanner did. It suddenly went deeper. But not searching, Hamilton realised –

Cutting!

Hamilton winced at the distant sight of some of the higher functions of his cover's mind dissolving.

From that point on, it was like sitting on the shoulders of a drunkard, and Hamilton had to intervene a couple of times to stop his body getting into danger. That was all right. The serfs also smoked tobacco, and he declined that also. A cover couldn't look too perfect.

The serfs were strapped in as the Russian space carriage aerobraked around Mars' thin atmosphere, then started its angled descent towards the surface. This was the first surprise. The carriage was taking a completely conventional course: it would be visible from every lighthouse. This must, realised Hamilton, wishing for a window, be a scheduled flight. And by now they must be very close to whatever their destination was, the resorts of Tharsis, perhaps –

Then there came a roar, a sudden crash, and the giddy sensation of falling. Hamilton's stomach welcomed it. He knew himself to be more at home in freefall than the majority of those he encountered. It was the sea welcoming the shark.

He could feel the different momentum: they must have been jettisoned from the main carriage, at a very narrow angle, under the sensor shadow of some mountain range –

The realisation came to him like the moment when Isaac Newton had seen that tiny worm and started thinking about the very small.

Hamilton started to curl into the crash position –
Then with an effort of will he forced himself not to. Too perfect!
His seat broke from its fastenings and he flew at the ceiling.

The quality of the air felt strange. Not enough! It felt like hell. And the smell. For a moment Hamilton thought he was in a battle. So where were the noises -?

They pulled the darkness from around him. They were rough. There were bright lights, and a curt examination, his body being turned right and left. Hamilton had a sudden moment of fear for his body, not belonging to him now, carelessly damaged by the puppet he'd lent it to! He wanted to fight! To let his fists bite into their faces!

He held it in. Tried to breathe.

He struggled out of their grasp for a moment, only to look round.

A serf barracks, turned into a makeshift hospital. Bunks growing out of packed-down mud, providing their own sawdust. Bright Russian guard uniforms, blue and white with epaulettes gleaming, polished, ceremonial helmets off indoors. All wearing masks and oxygen supplies. All ceramics, no metal. Afraid of detectors. A Russian military medic, in his face again, flashing a torch into his eye. Masked too.

There was a rectangle of light shining in through the doorway. They were pushed from their beds, one by one, and sent stumbling towards it. Still couldn't breathe. That was where the smell of battle was coming from –

No, not battle. A mixture. Bodies from in here. From out there –

Gunpowder.

Soil with a high mineral content.

He moved into the light and put a hand up.

He felt his skin burning and yelled. He threw himself forward into a welcome sliver of dark, shielding his eyes from a glare that could have blinded him.

He lay in shadow on the gunpowder grey ground, with laughter from behind him, the sun refracting off angled rock, through a blurred sky, like a cold furnace.

He was in the Mariner Valley, the deepest gorge in the solar system, with the sun flaring low in the west, rebounding off the white buildings. There was hard UV in the sky. His lungs were hoiking on tiny breaths. Frost was already burning his fingers. And he wasn't wearing any kind of protective equipment.

They made the serfs march along the shaded side of the valley. At least they gave them gloves.

An enormous wind would suddenly blast across the column of men, like a blow to the ground, slewing them with rock dust, and then it would be gone again. It was a shock that breathing was even possible. Hamilton stole glances from the shade, as he struggled to adjust, looking upwards to the nearest escarpment. In the Valley proper, you wouldn't necessarily assume you were in a gorge, the vast depression stretched from horizon to horizon. So this must be one of the minor valleys that lay inside the great rift. They could be six miles deep here. Given the progress of terraforming on the rest of the Martian globe, the air pressure might just be enough.

He realised, at a shout from the overseer in the Russian uniform, that he had slowed down, letting his fellow serfs march past him. But his cover was pushing his body to move as fast as it could.

He realised: he was different to the others.

He was finding physical action more difficult than they were. Why?

He looked at the man next to him, and was met with a disinterested misty expression.

The mental examination! They hadn't ripped out the higher functions of the serfs purely in order to make them docile, they'd shut down brain processes that required oxygen!

Hamilton added his own mental weight to that of his cover, and made the body step up its march. He could feel his lungs burning. The serfs had perhaps a couple of months of life before this exposure caught up with them. It felt as if he had a week.

He considered, for a moment, the exit strategy. The personal launcher waiting in a gulley... he checked his internal map... sixteen miles away.

That was closer that it might have been. But it was still out of the question without the oxygen supply that previously had been standard for serfs working in such conditions. If he was going to get out of this, he would need to steal such equipment, the quicker the better, before his body weakened.

On the other hand, if he stayed and died, after having made his kills, the mission would be successfully completed. The cover would still be planted.

He decided. He would not leave quickly while there was still a chance of success.

He took care to think of Annie and the quad and the noise of the Morgan's engine. Then he did not think of those things again.

In the days that followed, Hamilton was put to work alongside the other serfs. He mentally rehearsed that Raffles wine list. He remembered the mouth feels and tastes. He considered a league table of his favourites. Although the details changed, it was headed every day by the 2003 Leoville Las Cases.

Meanwhile, his body was collapsing, blisters forming on his exposed, sunburnt and windburnt skin, deep aches and cramps nagging at his every muscle, headaches that brought blood from his nose. And the worse of it was he hadn't seen Catherine Drewe.

His work crew were using limited ceramic and wooden tools to install growing pit props into what was obviously a mine shaft. Other serfs were digging, fed off nutrient bath growths that had been thrown up the walls of the valley. There was a sense of urgency. The digging was being directed precisely, according to charts.

These were not fortifications that were being dug. Turpin's conclusions had been rational, but wrong. This was not a military offensive. The Russians gave the impression of sneak thieves, planning to smash and grab and run.

So what was this? Hamilton had only seen one mercenary uniform, bearing the coat of arms of Drewe's Army. The badge displayed the typically amateur and self-aggrandising heraldry of the mercenary bands. It claimed spurious (and now non-existent) Irish aristocracy, but had nods to all the major courts of Europe, nothing that would enflame the temper of even the most easily- offended monarch. The badge irked Hamilton. It was a bastard thing that revealed nothing and too much.

The emblem had been on the sleeve of some sort of bodyguard, a man with muscle structure that had been designed to keep going having taken some small arms fire. He moved awkwardly in the lower gravity. Hamilton felt a surge of odd fellow feeling, and knew this was the man from whom the emotional broadcast had originated.

He and his mistress would doubtless appear together at some point.

After three days, Hamilton's crew swapped tasks with the other group, and were put to dig at the rock face down the tunnel. Hamilton welcomed it: the air pressure was slightly greater here.

He had started to hallucinate. In his mind, he saw great rolling clockworks against a background of all the imperial flags. Armies advanced as lines across maps, and those lines broke into sprays of particles, every advance countered to keep the great system going. He himself walked one of the lines, firing at imaginary assailants. Women spun in their own orbits, the touch of their hands, the briefest of kisses before they were swept away maintaining the energy of the whole merry-go- round.

And at the centre of it all... He didn't know, he couldn't see. The difference of accident, the tiny percentage effect that changed the impossible into the everyday. He bowed his head amongst the infinite cogwheels and prayed for grace.

He was broken out of his stupor by the sudden noise in front of him. There had been a sudden fall of rocks. The whole working face in front of him had given way.

Something, maybe the pebbles beneath their feet, was making the serfs working with him sway and stumble. One beside him fell. The Russian overseer bent to check on the man's condition, then took out a gun, thought better of the expense, and instead used a ceramic knife to slit the serf's throat. The body was carried out to be bled over the nutrient baths, the overseer calling out orders as he walked with the man back towards the exit.

Hamilton put his face close to the rock wall that had been revealed. It felt different. It looked blacker. Iconic. Like a wall that was death ought to look. He thought he could hear something in there. That he was being called. Or was that the thought he wasn't allowing himself, the Chapel and Annie inside?

A voice broke that terrible despair that would have led him away. "There!"

Hamilton turned and smiled in relief to see her at last. Catherine Drewe. Face to face. Her hair was dark with dust, her face powdered around her oxygen mask in a way which looked almost cosmetic. Her eyes were certain and terrified. The other serfs were staring at her. Behind her came the bodyguard, his bulk filling the tunnel.

Hamilton's right hand twitched.

She pushed past him and put her ear to the rock.

He decided not to kill her yet.

"You," she said, turning to point at one of the serfs, "go and tell Sizlovski that we've hit a snag. The rest of you, get out of here, you're relieved."

The serfs, barely understanding, took a moment to down tools and start following the first towards the light.

Hamilton let his cover open his mouth in blank surprise and kept it there. He stayed put.

The bodyguard tapped her shoulder and Drewe turned to look at him, puzzled. "I said you're finished."

Hamilton detected something urgent in her voice, something he'd heard in the moments before other situations had got rough. This was no setback, no sighing pause.

He crumpled his cover into the darkness of his mind.

He slammed his palm against the wall beside her head.

The bodyguard moved –

But she put up a hand and he stopped.

He let out his Irish accent. "You've got a problem Miss Drewe," he said.

She considered that for a moment.

He smelt the edge of the ceramic knife as it split molecules an inch from his eye.

He flathanded the wrist of her knife hand into the wall, his other hand catching the gun she'd pulled at his stomach, his finger squashing hers into firing it point blank into the bodyguard. His face exploded and he fell and Hamilton ripped aside the weapon and threw it.

There was a shout from behind.

Hamilton grabbed the Webley Collapsar 2mm. handgun from the folded dimensions in his chest, spun into firing stance and blasted a miniature black hole into the skull of a Russian officer, sending the man's brains flying into another universe.

He spun back to catch Drewe pulling another device from her boot.

He grabbed her wrist.

He knew intuitively how to snap her neck from this posture.

In moments, the gunfire would bring many soldiers running. Killing the overseer had compromised Hamilton's mission but slightly. It was still something that a Russian assassin might do, to give his cover credibility. He had completed half his mission now.

But why had she pulled *that*, instead of something to kill him with?

He looked into her eyes.

"Do what you were going to do," said Hamilton.

He let go.

Drewe threw the device at the overseer's body, grabbed Hamilton and heaved him with her through the rock wall.

The thump of the explosion and the roar of the collapsing tunnel followed them into the chamber, but no dust or debris did. It was a vaulted cavern, sealed off, with something glowing -

Hamilton realised, as he didn't need to take a breath, that the air was thick in here. He started to cough, doubling up. Precious air! Thick air that he gulped down, that made his head swim.

When he straightened up, Drewe was pointing a gun at him. She looked shocked and furious. But that was contained. She was military all right.

He let his gun arm fall to his side. "Well?" he said.

"Who are you?"

Hamilton carefully pulled out his uniform swash identification.

"British. Very well. I assume you're here for that?" She nodded towards the glow.

He looked. Something was protruding from the rock in the centre of the chamber. A silver spar that shone in an un-natural way. It seemed to be connected to something that was lodged... no, that was in some way *part of* the rocks all around it. There were blazing rivulets threaded in and out of the mass. As if someone had thrown mercury onto pumice stone.

It was like something trapped. And yet it looked whole and obvious. Apt that it had formed a place where they could live, and a wall they could step through. It spoke of uneasy possibilities.

"What is it?"

She cocked her head to one side, surprised he didn't know. "A carriage."

"Some carriage."

"You don't know. That wasn't your mission."

"I was just having a poke around. I didn't expect a non-Russian here. You're Katherine Drewe, aren't you? What's *your* mission?"

She considered, until he was sure she wasn't going to tell him. But then: "I saw this thing. In my prayers. I spent a week in an isolation tank in Kyoto. You see, lately I've started to think there's something wrong with the balance –"

"Everyone always thinks that."

She swore at him. "You have no idea. Inside your Empires. You know what that is?"

"No."

"A new arrival."

"From –?"

"Another universe."

Hamilton looked back to the object. He was already on his way to the punchline.

"I followed its calling," Drewe continued, "via a steady and demonstrable provocation of the field. I proved the path led to Mars. I used my rather awe-inspiring political clout to whisper all this into Czar Richard's ear. By which I mean: his ear."

"Why choose the Russians?"

She ignored the question. "I dreamed before I set off that only two people would find it, that their motives would be different. I took Aaron into my confidence. He was motivated only by art, by beauty. But you killed him."

"How do you feel?"

She bared her teeth in a grim smile, her gaze darting all over his face, ready for any provocation. "I'm strongly inclined to return the compliment."

"But you won't." He slowly replaced his gun in its dimensional fold. "Destiny says two people."

She kept him waiting another moment. Then she slipped her own gun back into the folds of that dangerous gown.

They looked at each other for a moment. Then they stepped over to the glowing object together. "That glow worries me," she said. "Have you heard of nuclear power?"

Hamilton shook his head.

"Energy produced by the radioactive decay of minerals. An alternative technology that might have been developed if Newton hadn't had his moment of revelation. It's poisonous like hard UV. One of the outsider sciences something like this might bring in."

Hamilton consulted his internal register, holding in a shudder at the damage he'd already taken. He hadn't anything designed to log radioactivity, but he changed the spectrum on his UV register, and after a moment he was satisfied. "I'm not seeing *any* radiation. Not even..." He stopped. He wasn't even detecting that light he could see with his own eyes. But somehow he doubted that what he was seeing would allow him to come to harm.

Drewe put a hand on the apparently shining limb, deploying sensors of her own. "There's nobody in here, no passenger or driver. But... I'm getting requests for information. Pleas. Greetings. Quite... eccentric ones." She looked at him as if he was going to laugh at her.

In a civilian, Hamilton thought, it would have been endearing. He didn't laugh. "A mechanism intelligence? Not possible."

"By our physics. But this opened a door for us through solid rock. And let me know it had. And there's air in here."

Hamilton put his own hand on the object, realised his sensors weren't up to competing with that dress, and took it away in frustration. "All right. But this is beside the point."

"The point being —"

"This thing will tip the balance. You can't be the only one who's intuited it's here. Whoever gets it gains a decisive advantage. It'll be the end of the Great Game —"

"The start of a genuine war for the world, one not fought by proxies like you and me. All the great nations give lip service to the idea of the balance, but —"

"So how much are you going to ask? Couple of Italian Dukedoms?"

"Not this time. You asked why I used the Russians to get here —" She reached into the gown. She produced another explosive device. A much larger one. "Because they're the Empire I detest the most."

Hamilton licked his lips quickly.

"I don't think mere rocks can hold this being. I was called here because it got caught in... this mortal coil. It has to be freed. For its own sake, and for the sake of the balance."

Hamilton looked at the object again. Either of them could pull their gun and put down the other one in a moment. He wondered if he was talking to a zealot, a madwoman. He had pretty vague ideas about God and his pathway through the field, and the line that connected his holy ground to the valley of death. He'd never interrogated those ideas. And he wasn't about to start now.

But here were answers! Answers those better than him would delight in. That could protect the good people of his Empire better than he could!

There was a noise from outside. They'd started digging.

Drewe met his gaze once more.

"You say it can be reasoned with –"

"Not to get itself out of here. That's not what it wants."

Hamilton looked around the chamber, once and conclusively, with every sense at his disposal. No way out.

"You have to decide –"

Hamilton reached into the hidden depths of his heart once more. He produced his own explosives. "No I don't," he said. "Thank God."

Drewe had an exit strategy of her own. She had a launcher waiting, she said, lying under fractal covers in the broken territory of a landslide, two miles east of the Russian encampment.

It was again like walking through a door. As soon as they had both set the timers on their explosives to commit in that otherwise inescapable room, an act of faith as great as any Hamilton had experienced –

The room turned inside out, and they had taken that simple step, and found themselves on the surface again.

Hamilton gasped as the air went. His wounds caught up with him at once. He fell.

Drewe looked down at him.

Hamilton looked back up at her. There was auburn hair under the green.

She pulled her gun while his hand was still sailing slowly towards his chest. "I think God is done with you," she said. "We'll make a balance."

"Oh we must," said Hamilton, letting his accent slip into the Irish once more. He was counting in his head, doing the mathematics. And suddenly he had a feeling that he hadn't been the only one. "But your calculations are out."

Paul Cornell

The amusement in his voice made her hesitate. "How so?"

"By about… 0.2 per cent."

The force of the explosion took Drewe and she was falling sideways.

Hamilton rolled, got his feet on the ground.

A wall of dust and debris filled the canyon ahead of them –

And then was on them, racing over them, folding them into the surface until they were just two thin streaks of history, their mortal remains at the end of comet trails.

There was silence.

Hamilton burst out of his grave, and stumbled for where the launcher lay, bright in the dust, its covers burst from it.

He didn't look back. He limped with faith and no consideration. With an explosion that size there would be nothing left of the encampment. His mission had not succeeded. But he felt his own balance was intact.

He hit a codebreaker release code on his palm onto the craft's fuselage, and struggled into the cockpit. He was aware of his own silhouette against the dying light.

He looked back now. There she was. Only now staggering to her feet.

In this second and only this second, he could draw and shoot her down and with a little adjustment of leaks and revelations his mission would be done.

He thought about the grace that had been afforded him.

He hit the emergency toggle, the cockpit sealed, and he was slammed back in his seat as the launcher sailed up into the Martian sky. He thought of a half pint of beer. And then let himself be taken into darkness again.

One of our Bastards

is Missing

To get to Earth from the edge of the Solar System, depending on the time of year and the position of the planets, you need to pass through at least Poland, Prussia and Turkey, and you'd probably get stamps in your passport from a few of the other great powers. Then as you get closer to the world, you arrive at a point, in the continually shifting carriage space over the countries, where this complexity has to give way or fail. And so you arrive in the blissful lubrication of neutral orbital territory. From there it's especially clear that no country is whole unto itself. There are yearning gaps between parts of each state, as they stretch across the Solar System. There is no congruent territory. The countries continue in balance with each other like a fine but eccentric mechanism, pent up, all that political energy dealt with through eternal circular motion.

The maps that represent this can be displayed on a screen, but they're much more suited to mental contemplation. They're beautiful. They're made to be beautiful, doing their own small part to see that their beauty never ends.

If you looked down on that world of countries, onto the pink of glorious old Greater Britain, that land of green squares and dark forest and carriage contrails, and then you naturally avoided looking directly at the golden splendour of London, your gaze might fall on the Thames valley. On the country houses and mansions and hunting estates that letter the river banks with the names of the great. On one particular estate: an enormous winged square of a house with its own grouse shooting horizons and mazes and herb gardens and markers that indicate it also sprawls into folded interior expanses.

Today that estate, seen from such a height, would be adorned with informational banners that could be seen from orbit, and tall pleasure cruisers could be observed, docked beside military boats on the river, and carriages of all kinds would be cluttering the gravel of its circular drives and swarming in the sky overhead. A detachment of Horse Guards could be spotted, standing at ready at the perimeter.

Today, you'd need much more than a passport to get inside that maze of information and privilege.

Because today was a royal wedding.

That vision from the point of view of someone looking down upon him was what was at the back of Hamilton's mind.

But now he was watching the princess.

Her chestnut hair had been knotted high on her head, baring her neck, a fashion which Hamilton appreciated for its defiance of the French, and at an official function too, though that gesture wouldn't have been Liz's alone, but would have been calculated in the warrens of Whitehall. She wore white, which had made a smile come to Hamilton's lips when he'd first seen it in the Cathedral this morning. In this gigantic function room with its high arched ceiling, in which massed dignitaries and ambassadors and dress uniforms orbited from table to table, she was the sun about which everything turned. Even the King, in the far distance, at a table on a rise with old men from the rest of Europe, was no competition for his daughter this afternoon.

This was the reception, where Elizabeth, escorted by members of the Corps of Heralds, would carelessly and entirely precisely move from group to group, giving exactly the right amount of charm to every one of the great powers, briefed to keep the balance going as everyone like she and Hamilton did, every day.

Everyone like the two of them. That was a useless thought and he cuffed it aside.

Her gaze had settled on Hamilton's table precisely once. A little smile and then away again. As not approved by Whitehall. He'd tried to stop watching her after that. But his carefully random table, with diplomatic corps functionaries to his left and right, had left him cold. Hamilton had grown tired of pretending to be charming.

"It's a marriage of convenience," said a voice beside him.

It was Lord Carney. He was wearing open cuffs that bloomed from his silk sleeves, a big collar and no tie. His long hair was unfastened. He had retained his rings.

Hamilton considered his reply for a moment, then opted for silence. He met Carney's gaze with a suggestion in his heart that surely

His Lordship might find some other table to perch at, perhaps one where he had friends?

"What do you reckon?"

Hamilton stood, with the intention of walking away. But Carney stood too and stopped him just as they'd got out of earshot of the table. The man smelled like a Turkish sweetshop. He affected a mode of speech beneath his standing. "This is what I do. I probe, I provoke, I poke. And when I'm in the room, it's all too obvious when people are looking at someone else."

The broad grin stayed on his face.

Hamilton found a deserted table and sat down again, furious at himself.

Carney settled beside him, and gestured away from Princess Elizabeth, towards her new husband, with his neat beard and his row of medals on the breast of his Svenska Adelsfanan uniform. He was talking with the Papal ambassador, doubtless discussing getting Liz to Rome as soon as possible, for a great show to be made of this match between the Protestant and the Papist. If Prince Bertil was also pretending to be charming, Hamilton admitted that he was making a better job of it.

"Yeah, jammy fucker, my thoughts exactly. Still, I'm on a promise with a couple of members of his staff, so it's swings and roundabouts." Carney clicked his tongue and wagged his finger as a Swedish serving maid ran past, and she curtsied a quick smile at him. "I do understand, you know. All our relationships are informed by the balance. And the horror of it is that we all can conceive of a world where this isn't so."

Hamilton pursed his lips and chose his next words carefully. "Is that why you are how you are, Your Lordship?"

"'Course it is. Maids, lady companions, youngest sisters, it's a catalogue of incompleteness. I'm allowed to love only in ways which don't disrupt the balance. For me to commit myself, or, heaven forbid, to marry, would require such deep thought at the highest levels that by the time the Heralds had worked it through, well, I'd have tired of the lady. Story of us all, eh? Nowhere for the pressure to go. If only I could see an alternative."

Hamilton had decided that, having shown the corner of his cards, the man had taken care to move back to the fringes of treason once more. It was part of his role as an *agent provocateur*. And Hamilton knew it. But that didn't mean he had to take this. "Do you have any further point, Your Lordship?"

"Oh, I'm just getting –"

The room gasped.

Hamilton was up out of his seat and had taken a step towards Elizabeth, his gun hand had grabbed into the air to his right where his .66mm Webley Corsair sat in a knot of space and had swung it ready to fire –

At nothing.

There stood the Princess, looking about herself in shock. Dress uniforms, bearded men all around her.

Left right up down.

Hamilton couldn't see anything for her to be shocked at.

And nothing near her, nothing around her.

She was already stepping back, her hands in the air, gesturing at a gap –

What had been there? Everyone was looking there. What?

He looked to the others like him. Almost all of them were in the same sort of posture he was, balked at picking a target.

The Papal envoy stepped forward and cried out. "A man was standing there! And he has vanished!"

Havoc. Everybody was shouting. A weapon, a weapon! But there was no weapon that Hamilton knew of that could have done that, made a man, whoever it had been, blink out of existence. Groups of bodyguards in dress uniforms or diplomatic black tie leapt up encircling their charges. Ladies started screaming. A nightmare of the balance collapsing all around them. That hysteria when everyone was in the same place and things didn't go exactly as all these vast powers expected.

A Bavarian princeling bellowed he needed no such protection and made to rush to the Princess' side –

Hamilton stepped into his way and accidentally shouldered him to the floor as he put himself right up beside Elizabeth and her husband. "We're walking to that door," he said. "Now."

Bertil and Elizabeth nodded and marched with fixed smiles on their faces, Bertil turning and holding back with a gesture the Swedish forces that were moving in from all directions. Hamilton's fellows fell in all around them, and swept the party across the hall, through that door, and down a servants' corridor as Life Guards came bundling in to the room behind them, causing more noise and more reactions and damn it, Hamilton hoped he wouldn't suddenly hear the discharge of some hidden –

He did not. The door was closed and barred behind them. Another good chap doing the right thing.

Hamilton sometimes distantly wished for an organisation to guard those who needed it. But for that the world would have to be different in ways beyond even Carney's artificial speculations. He and his brother officers would have their independence cropped if that was so. And he lived through his independence. It was the root of the duty that meant he would place himself in harm's way for Elizabeth's husband. He had no more thoughts on the subject.

"I know very little," said Elizabeth as she walked, her voice careful as always, except when it hadn't been. "I think the man was with one of the groups of foreign dignitaries –"

"He looked Prussian," said Bertil, "we were talking to Prussians."

"He just vanished into thin air right in front of me."

"Into a fold?" said Bertil.

"It can't have been," she said. "The room will have been mapped and mapped."

She looked to Hamilton for confirmation. He nodded.

They got to the library. Hamilton marched in and secured it. They put the happy couple at the centre of it, locked it up, and called everything in to the embroidery.

The embroidery chaps were busy, swiftly prioritising, but no, nothing was happening in the great chamber they'd left, the panic had swelled and then subsided into shouts, exhibitionist faintings (because who these days wore a corset that didn't have hidden depths), glasses crashing, yelled demands. No one else had vanished. No Spanish infantrymen had materialised out of thin air.

Bertil walked to the shelves, folded his hands behind his back, and began bravely and ostentatiously browsing. Elizabeth sat down and fanned herself and smiled for all Hamilton's fellows, and finally, quickly for Hamilton himself.

They waited.

The embroidery told them they had a visitor coming.

A wall of books slid aside, and in walked a figure that made all of them turn and salute. The Queen Mother, still in mourning black, her train racing to catch up with her.

She came straight to Hamilton and the others all turned to listen, and from now on thanks to this obvious favour, they would regard Hamilton as the ranking officer. He was glad of it. "We will continue," she said. "We will not regard this as an embarrassment and therefore it will not be. The Ball Room was prepared for the dance, we are moving there early, Elizabeth, Bertil, off you go, you two gentlemen in front of them, the rest of you behind. You will be laughing as you enter the Ball Room as if this were the most enormous joke, a silly and typically English eccentric misunderstanding."

Elizabeth nodded, took Bertil by the arm.

The Queen Mother intercepted Hamilton as he moved to join them. "No. Major Hamilton, you will go and talk to technical, you will find another explanation for what happened."

"*Another* explanation, Your Royal Highness?"

"Indeed," she said. "It must not be what they are saying it is."

"Here we are, sir," Lieutenant Matthew Parkes was with the Technical Corps of Hamilton's own regiment, the 4th Dragoons. He and his men were, incongruously, in the dark of the buttery that had been set aside for their equipment, also in their dress uniforms. From here they were in charge of the sensor net that blanketed the house and grounds down to Newtonian units of space, reaching out for miles in every direction. Parkes' people had been the first to arrive here, days ago, and would be the last to leave. He was pointing at a screen, on which was frozen the intelligent image of a burly man in black tie, Princess Elizabeth almost entirely obscured behind him. "Know who he is?"

Hamilton had placed the guest list in his mental index and had checked it as each group had entered the hall. He was relieved to recognise the man. He was as down to earth as it was possible to be. "He was in the Prussian party, not announced, one of six diplomat placings on their list. Built as if his muscles have been grown for security and that's how he moved round the room. Didn't let anyone chat to him. He nods when his embroidery talks to him. Which'd mean he's new at this, only…" Only the man had a look about him that Hamilton recognised. "No. He's just very confident. Ostentatious, even. So you're sure he didn't walk into some sort of fold?"

"Here's the contour map." Parkes flipped up an overlay on the image that showed the tortured underpinnings of spacetime in the room. There were little sinks and bundles all over the place, where various Britons had weapons stowed, and various foreigners would have had them stowed had they wished to create a diplomatic incident. The corner where Elizabeth had been standing showed only the force of gravity under her dear feet. "We do take care you know, sir."

"I'm sure you do, Matty. Let's see it, then."

Parkes flipped back to the clear screen. He touched it and the image changed.

Hamilton watched as the man vanished. One moment he was there. Then he was not, and Elizabeth was reacting, a sudden jerk of her posture.

Hamilton often struggled with technical matters. "What's the frame rate on this thing?"

"There is none, sir. It's a continual taking of real image, right down to single Newton intervals of time. That's as far as physics goes. Sir, we've been listening in to what everyone's saying, all afternoon –"

"And what are they saying, Matty?"

"That what's happened is Gracefully Impossible."

Gracefully Impossible. The first thing that had come into Hamilton's mind when the Queen Mother had mentioned the possibility was the memory of a political cartoon. It was the Prime Minister from a few years ago, standing at the dispatch box, staring in shock at his empty hand, which should presumably have contained some papers. The caption had read:

Say what you like about Mr. *Patel,*
He carries himself correct for his *title.*
He's about to present just his *graceful* apologies,
For the *impossible* loss of all his policies.

Every child knew that Newton had coined the phrase 'gracefully impossible' after he'd spent the day in his garden observing the progress of a very small worm across the surface on an apple. It referred to what, according to the great man's thinking about the very small, could, and presumably did, sometimes happen: things popping in and out of existence, when God, for some unfathomable reason, started or stopped looking at them. Some Frenchman had insisted that it was actually about whether *people* were looking, but that was the French for you. Through the centuries, there had been a few documented cases which seemed to fit the bill. Hamilton had always been distantly entertained to read about such in the inside page of his newspaper plate. He'd always assumed it could happen. But here? Now? During a state occasion?

Hamilton went back into the great hall, now empty of all but a group of Life Guards and those like him, individuals taken from several different regiments, all of whom had responsibilities similar to his, and a few of whom he'd worked with in the field. He checked in with them. They had all noted the Prussian, indeed, with the ruthless air the man had had about him, and the bulk of his musculature, he had been at the forefront of many of their internal indices of threat.

Hamilton found the place where the vanishing had happened, moved aside a couple of boffins, and against their protestations, went to stand in the exact spot, which felt like anywhere else did, and which set off none of his internal alarms, real or intuitive. He looked to where Liz had been standing, in the corner behind the Prussian. His expression darkened. The man who'd vanished had effectively been shielding the Princess from the room. Between her and every line of sight. He'd been where a bodyguard would have been if he'd become aware of someone taking a shot.

But that was ridiculous. The Prussian hadn't rushed in to save her. He'd been standing there, looking around. And anyone in that hall with some strange new weapon concealed on their person wouldn't have taken the shot then, they'd have waited for him to move.

Hamilton shook his head, angry with himself. There was a gap here. Something that went beyond the obvious. He let the boffins get back to their work and headed for the Ball Room.

The band had started the music, and the vast chamber was packed with people, the dance floor a whirl of waltzing figures. They were deliberate in their courses. The only laughter was forced laughter. No matter that some half miracle might have occurred, dance cards had been circulated amongst the minds of the great powers, so those dances would be danced, and minor royalty matched, and whispers exchanged in precise confidentiality. Because everyone was brave and everyone was determined and would be seen to be so. And so the balance went on. But the tension had increased a notch. The weight of the balance could be felt in this room, on the surface now, on every brow. The Queen Mother sat at a high table with courtiers to her left and right, receiving visitors with a grand blessing smile on her face, daring everyone to regard the last hour as anything but a dream.

Hamilton walked the room, looking around as if he was looking at a battle, as if it was happening rather than perhaps waiting to happen, whatever it was. He watched his opposite numbers from all the great powers waltzing slowly around their own people, and spiralling off from time to time to orbit his own. The ratio of uniformed to the sort of embassy thug it was difficult to imagine fitting in the diplomatic bag was about three to one for all the nations bar two. The French had of course sent Commissars, who all dressed the same when outsiders were present, but followed a byzantine internal rank system. And the Vatican's people were all men and women of the cloth and their assistants.

As he made his way through that particular party, which was scattering, intercepting and colliding with all the other nationalities, as if in the explosion of a shaped charge, he started to hear it. The conversations were all about what had happened. The Vatican representatives were talking about a sacred presence. The details were already spiralling. There had been a light and a great voice, had nobody else heard? And people were agreeing.

Hamilton wasn't a diplomat, and he knew better than to take on trouble not in his own line. But he didn't like what he was hearing. The Catholics had only come to terms with Impossible Grace a couple of decades ago, when a Papal bull went out announcing that John XXVI thought that the concept had merit, but that further scientific study was required. But now they'd got behind it, as in all things, they were behind it. So what would this say to them, that the divine had looked down on this wedding, approved of it, and plucked someone away from it?

No, not just someone. Prussian military. A Protestant from a nation that had sometimes protested that various Swedish territories would be far better off within their own jurisdiction.

Hamilton stopped himself speculating. Guessing at such things would only make him hesitate if his guesses turned out to be untrue.

Hamilton had a vague but certain grasp of what his God was like. He thought it was possible that He might decide to give the nod to a marriage at court. But in a way which might upset the balance between nations that was divinely ordained, that was the centre of all good works?

No. Hamilton was certain now. The divine be damned. This wasn't the numinous at play. This was enemy action.

He circled the room until he found the Prussians. They were raging, an ambassador poking at British courtiers, demanding something, probably that an investigation be launched immediately. And beside that Prussian stood several more, diplomatic and military, all convincingly frightened and furious, certain this was a British plot.

But behind them there, in the social place were Hamilton habitually looked, there were some of the vanished man's fellow big lads. The other five from that diplomatic pouch. The Prussians, uniquely in Europe, kept up an actual organization for the sort of thing Hamilton and his ilk did on the never never. The Garde Du Corps had begun as a regiment similar to the Life Guards, but these days it was said they weren't even issued with uniforms. They wouldn't be on anyone's dance cards. They weren't stalking the room now, and all right, that was understandable, they were hanging back to protect their chaps. But they weren't doing much of that either. They didn't look angry, or worried for their comrade, or for their own skins –

Hamilton took a step back to let pretty noble couples desperately waltz between him and the Prussians, wanting to keep his position as a privileged observer.

They looked like they were *waiting*. On edge. They just wanted to get out of here. Was the Garde really that callous? They'd lost a man in mysterious circumstances, and they weren't themselves agitating to get back into that room and yell his name, but were just waiting to move on?

He looked for another moment, remembering the faces, then moved on himself. He found another table of Prussians. The good sort, not Order of the Black Eagle, but Hussars. They were in uniform, and had been drinking, and were furiously declaring in Hohenzollern

German that if they weren't allowed access to the records of what had happened, well then it must be – they didn't like to say what it must be!

Hamilton plucked a glass from a table and wandered over to join them, careful to take a wide and unsteady course around a lady whose train had developed some sort of fault and wasn't moving fast enough to keep pace with her feet.

He flopped down in a chair next to one of the Prussians, a Captain by his lapels, which were virtual in the way the Prussians liked, to implicitly suggest that they had been in combat more recently than the other great powers, and so had a swift turnover of brevet ranks, decided by merit. "Hullo!" he said.

The group fell silent and bristled at him.

Hamilton blinked at them. "Where's Humph?"

"Humph? Wassay th'gd Major?" the Hussar Captain spoke North Sea Pidgin, but with a clear accent: Hamilton would be able to understand him.

He didn't want to reveal that he spoke perfect German, albeit with a Bavarian accent. "Big chap. Big big chap. Say go." He carefully swore in Dutch, shaking his head, not understanding. "Which you settle fim?"

"Settle?" They looked amongst each other, and Hamilton could feel the affront. A couple of them even put their good hands to their waists, where the space was folded that no longer contained their pistols and thin swords. But the Captain glared at them and they relented. A burst of Hohenzollern German about this so-called mystery of their mate vanishing, and how, being in the Garde, he had obviously been abducted for his secrets.

Hamilton waved his hands. "Noswords! Good chap! No name. He won! Three times to me at behind the backshee." His raised his voice a notch. "Behind the backshee! Excellent chap! He *won!*" He stuck out his ring finger, offering the winnings in credit, to be passed from skin to skin. He mentally retracted the other options of what could be detailed there, and blanked it. He could always make a drunken show of trying to find it. "Seek to settle. For such a good chap."

They didn't believe him or trust him. Nobody reached out to touch his finger. But he learnt a great deal in their German conversation in the ten minutes that followed, while he loudly struggled to communicate with the increasingly annoyed Captain, who couldn't bring himself to directly insult a member of the British military by asking him to go away. The vanished man's name was Helmuth Sandels. The name suggested Swedish origins to his family. But that was typical continental back and forth. He might have been a good chap now he'd gone, but he hadn't been liked. Sandels had had a look in his eye when he'd walked past stout fellows who'd actually fought battles. He'd spoken up in anger when valiant Hussars had expressed the military's traditional views concerning those running the government, the country and the world. Hamilton found himself sharing the soldiers' expressions of distaste: this had been someone who assumed that loyalty was an *opinion*.

He raised a hand in pax, gave up trying with the Captain, and left the table.

Walking away, he heard the Hussars moving on with their conversation, starting to express some crude opinions about the Princess. He didn't break stride.

Into his mind, unbidden, came the memories. Of what had been a small miracle of a kind, but one that only he and she had been witness to.

Hamilton had been at home on leave, having been abroad for a few weeks, serving out of uniform. As always, at times like that, when he should have been at rest, he'd been fired up for no good reason, unable to sleep, miserable, prone to tears in secret when a favourite song had come on the theatricals in his muse flat. It always took three days for him, once he was home, to find out what direction he was meant to be pointing. Then he would set off that way, and pop back to barracks one night for half a pint, and then he'd be fine. He could enjoy day four and onwards, and was known to be something approximating human from there on in.

Three day leaves were hell. He tried not to use them as leaves, but would find himself some task, hopefully an official one if one of the handful of officers who brokered his services could be so entreated. Those officers were sensitive to such requests now.

But that leave, three years ago, had been two weeks off. He'd come home a day before. So he was no use to anyone. He'd taken a broom, and was pushing accumulated grey goo out of the carriage park alongside his apartment and into the drains.

She'd appeared in a sound of crashing and collapse, as her horse staggered sideways and hit the wall of the mews, then fell. Her two friends were galloping after her, their horses healthy, and someone built like Hamilton was running to help.

But none of them were going to be in time to catch her –

And he was.

It had turned out that the horse had missed an inoculation against miniscule poisoning. Its body was a terrible mess, random mechanisms developing out of its flanks and dying, with that terrifying smell, in the moments when Hamilton had held her in his arms, and had had to round on the man running in, and had imposed his authority with a look, and had not been thrown down and away.

Instead, she'd raised her hands and called that she was all right, and had insisted on looking to and at the horse, pulling off her glove and putting her hand to its neck and trying to fight the bloody things directly. But even with her command of information, it had been too late, and the horse had died in a mess.

She'd been bloody angry. And then at the emergency scene that had started to develop around Hamilton's front door, with police carriages swooping in and the sound of running boots –

Until she'd waved it all away and declared that it had been her favourite horse, a wonderful horse, her great friend since childhood, but it was just a bloody horse, and all she needed was a sit down and if this kind military gentleman would oblige –

And he had.

He'd obliged her again when they'd met in Denmark, and they'd danced at a ball held on an ice flow, a carpet of mechanism wood reacting every moment to the weight of their feet and the forces underlying them, and the aurora had shone in the sky.

It was all right in Denmark for Elizabeth to have one dance with a commoner.

Hamilton had got back to the table where his regiment were dining, and had silenced the laughter and the calls, and thus saved them for barracks. He had drunk too much. His batman at the time had prevented him from going to see Elizabeth as she was escorted from the floor at the end of her dance card by a boy who was somewhere in line for the Danish throne.

But she had seen Hamilton the next night, in private, a privacy that would have taken great effort on her part, and after they had talked for several hours and shared some more wine she had shown him great favour.

"So. Is God in the details?" Someone was walking beside Hamilton. It was a Jesuit. Mid-thirties. Dark hair, kept over her collar. She had a scar down one side of her face and an odd eye as a result. Miniscule blade, by the look. A member of the Society of Jesus would never allow her face to be restructured. That would be vanity. But she was beautiful.

Hamilton straightened up, giving this woman's musculature and bearing and all the history those things suggested the respect they deserved. "Or the devil."

"Yes, interesting the saying goes both ways, isn't it? My name is Mother Valentine. I'm part of the Society's campaign for Effective Love."

"Well," Hamilton raised an eyebrow, "I'm in favour of love being –"

"Don't waste our time. You know what I am."

"Yes, I do. And you know I'm the same. And I was waiting until we were out of earshot –"

"Which we now are –"

"To have this conversation."

They stopped together. Valentine moved her mouth close to Hamilton's ear. "I've just been told that the Holy Father is eager to declare what happened here to be a potential miracle. Certain parties are sure that our Black Eagle man will be found magically transplanted to distant parts, perhaps Berlin, as a sign against Prussian meddling."

"If he is, the Kaiser will have him gently shot and we'll never hear."

"You're probably right."

"What do you think happened?"

"I don't think miracles happen near our kind."

Hamilton realised he was looking absurdly hurt at her. And that she could see it. And was quietly absorbing that information for use in a couple of decades, if ever.

He was glad when a message came over the embroidery, asking him to attend to the Queen Mother in the buttery. And to bring his new friend.

The Queen Mother stood in the buttery, her not taking a chair having obviously made Parkes and his people even more nervous than they would have been.

She nodded to Valentine. "Monsignor. I must inform you, we've had an official approach from the Holy See. They regard the hall here as a possible site of miraculous apparition."

"Then my opinion on the subject is irrelevant. You should be addressing –"

"The ambassador. Indeed. But here you are. You are aware of what was asked of us?"

"I suspect the Cardinals will have sought a complete record of the moment of the apparition, or in this case, the vanishing. That would only be the work of a moment in the case of such an… observed… chamber."

"It would. But it's what happens next that concerns me."

"The procedure is that the chamber must then be sealed, and left unobserved until the Cardinals can see for themselves, to minimise any effect human observers may have on the process of divine revelation."

Hamilton frowned. "Are we likely to?"

"God is communicating using a physical method, so we may," said Valentine. "Depending on one's credulity concerning miniscule physics."

"Or one's credulity concerning international politics," said the Queen Mother. "Monsignor, it is always our first and most powerful inclination, when another nation asks us for something, to say no. All nations feel that way. All nations know the others do. But now here is a request, one that concerns matters right at the heart of the balance, that is, in the end, about deactivating security. It could be said to come not from another nation, but from God. It is therefore difficult to deny this request. We find ourselves distrusting that difficulty. It makes us want to deny it all the more."

"You speak for His Royal Highness?"

The Queen Mother gave a cough that might have been a laugh. "Just as you speak for Our Lord."

Valentine smiled and inclined her head. "I would have thought, Your Royal Highness, that it would be obvious to any of the great powers that, given the celebrations, it would take you a long time to gather the Prime Minister and those many other courtiers with whom you would want to consult on such a difficult matter."

"Correct. Good. It will take three hours. You may go."

Valentine walked out with Hamilton. "I'm going to go and mix with my own for a while," she said, "listen to who's saying what."

"I'm surprised you wear your hair long."

She looked sharply at him. "Why?"

"You enjoy putting your head on the block."

She giggled.

Which surprised Hamilton and for just a moment made him wish he was Lord Carney. But then there was a certain small darkness about another priest he knew.

"I'm just betting," she said in a whisper, "that by the end of the day this will all be over. And someone will be dead."

Hamilton went back into the Ball Room. He found he had a picture in his head now. Something had swum up from somewhere inside him, from a place he had learned to trust and never interrogate as to its reasons. That jerking motion Elizabeth had made at the moment Sandels had vanished. He had an emotional feeling about that image. What was it?

It had been like seeing her shot.

A motion that looked like it had come from beyond her muscles. Something Elizabeth had not been in control of. It wasn't like her to not be in control. It felt... dangerous.

Would anyone else see it that way? He doubted it.

So was he about to do the sudden terrible thing that his body was taking him in the direction of doing?

He killed the thought and just did it. He went to the Herald who carried the tablet with dance cards on it, and leaned on him with the Queen Mother's favour, which had popped up on his ring finger the moment he'd thought of it.

The Herald considered the sensation of the fingertip on the back of his hand for a moment, then handed Hamilton the tablet.

Hamilton realised that he had no clue of the havoc he was about to cause. So he glanced at the list of Elizabeth's forthcoming dances and struck off a random Frenchman.

He scrawled his own signature with a touch, then handed the plate back.

The Herald looked at him like the breath of death had passed under his nose.

Hamilton had to wait three dances before his name came up. A Balaclava, an Entrée Grave (that choice must have taken a while, unless some Herald had been waiting all his life for a chance at the French), a Hornpipe for the sailors, including Bertil, to much applause, and then, thank the deus, a straightforward Waltz.

Elizabeth had been waiting out those last three, so he met her at her table. Maidservants kept their expressions stoic. A couple of Liz's companions looked positively scared. Hamilton knew how they felt. He could feel every important eye looking in his direction.

Elizabeth took his arm and gave it a little squeeze. "What's grandma up to, Johnny?"

"It's what I'm up to."

She looked alarmed. They formed up with the other dancers.

Hamilton was very aware of her gloves. The mechanism fabric that covered her left hand held off the urgent demand of his hand, his own need to touch her. But no, that wouldn't tell him anything. That was just his certainty that to know her had been to know her. That was not where he would find the truth here.

The band started up. The dance began.

Hamilton didn't access any guidelines in his mind. He let his feet move where they would. He was outside orders, acting on a hunch. He was like a man dancing around the edge of a volcano.

"Do you remember the day we met?" he asked when he was certain they couldn't be heard, at least, not be the other dancers.

"Of course I do. My poor San Andreas, your flat in Hood Mews –"

"Do you remember what I said to you that day, when nobody else was with us? What you agreed to? Those passionate words that could bring this whole charade crashing down?" He kept his expression light, his tone so gentle and wry that Liz would always play along and fling a little stone back at him, knowing he meant nothing more than he could mean. That he was letting off steam through a joke.

All they had been was based on the certainty expressed in that.

It was an entirely British way to do things. It was, as Carney had said, about lives shaped entirely by the balance.

But this woman, with the room revolving around the two of them, was suddenly appalled, insulted, her face a picture of what she was absolutely certain she should feel. "I don't know what you mean! Or even if I did, I don't think –!"

Hamilton's nostrils flared. He was lost now, if he was wrong. He had one tiny ledge for Liz to grasp if he was, but he would fall.

For duty, then.

He took his hand from Princess Elizabeth's waist, and grabbed her chin, his fingers digging up into flesh.

The whole room cried out in horror.

He had a moment before they would shoot him.

Yes, he felt it! Or he thought he did! He thought he did enough –

He grabbed the flaw and ripped with all his might.

Princess Elizabeth's face burst off and landed on the floor.

Blood flew.

He drew his gun and pumped two shots into the mass of flesh and mechanism, as it twitched and blew a stream of defensive acid that discoloured the marble.

He spun back to find the woman without a face lunging at him, her eyes white in the mass of red muscle, mechanism pus billowing into the gaps. She was aiming a hair knife at his throat, doubtless with enough mechanism to bring instant death or something worse.

Hamilton thought of Liz as he broke her arm.

He enjoyed the scream.

He wanted to bellow for where the real Liz was as he slammed the imposter down onto the floor, and he was dragged from her in one motion as a dozen men grabbed them.

He caught a glimpse of Bertil, horrified, but not at Hamilton. It was a terror they shared. For her safety.

Hamilton suddenly felt like a traitor again.

He yelled out the words he'd had in mind since he'd put his name down for the dance. "They replaced her years ago! Years ago! At the mews!"

There were screams, cries that we were all undone.

There came the sound of two shots from the direction of the Vatican group, and Hamilton looked over to see Valentine standing over the corpse of a junior official.

Their gaze met. She understood why he'd shouted that.

Another man leapt up at a Vatican table behind her and turned to run and she turned and shot him twice in the chest, his body spinning backwards over a table.

Hamilton ran with the rout. He used the crowds of dignitaries and their retinues, all roaring and competing and stampeding for safety, to hide himself. He made himself look like a man lost, agony on his face, his eyes closed. He was ignoring all the urgent cries from the embroidery.

He covertly acknowledged something directly from the Queen Mother.

He stumbled through the door of the buttery.

Parkes looked round. "Thank God you're here, we've been trying to call, the Queen Mother's office are urgently asking you to come in –"

"Never mind that now, come with me, on Her Royal Highness' orders."

Parkes grabbed the pods from his ears and got up. "What on Earth –?"

Hamilton shot him through the right knee.

Parkes screamed and fell. Every technician in the room leapt up. Hamilton bellowed at them to sit down or they'd get the same.

He shoved his foot into the back of Parkes' injured leg. "Listen here, Matty. You know how hard it's going to get. You're not the sort to think your duty's worth it. How much did they pay you? For how long?"

He was still yelling at the man on the ground as the Life Guards burst in and put a gun to everyone's head, his own included.

The Queen Mother entered a minute later, and changed that situation to the extent of letting Hamilton go free. She looked carefully at Parkes, who was still screaming for pity, and aimed a precise little kick into his disintegrated kneecap.

Then she turned to the technicians. "Your minds will be stripped down and rebuilt, if you're lucky, to see who was in on it." She looked back to Hamilton as they started to be led from the room. "What you said in the Ball Room obviously isn't the case."

"No. When you take him apart," Hamilton nodded at Parkes, "you'll find he tampered with the contour map. They used Sandels as the cover for substituting Her Royal Highness. They knew she was going to move around the room in a pre-determined way. With Parkes' help, they set up an open-ended fold in that corner –"

"The expense is staggering. The energy required –"

"There'll be no Christmas tree for the Kaiser this year. Sandels deliberately stepped into the fold and vanished, in a very public way. And at that moment they made the switch, took Her Royal Highness into the fold too, covered by the visual disturbance of Sandels' progress. And by old-fashioned sleight of hand."

"Propped up by the Prussians' people in the Vatican. Instead of a British bride influencing the Swedish court, there'd be a cuckoo from Berlin. Well played, Wilhelm. Worth that Christmas tree."

"I'll wager the unit are still in the fold, not knowing anything about the outside world, waiting for the room to be sealed off with pious care, so they can climb out and extract themselves. They probably have supplies for several days."

"Do you think my grand-daughter is still alive?"

Hamilton pursed his lips. "There are Prussian yachts on the river. They're staying on for the season. I think they'd want the bonus of taking the Princess back for interrogation."

"That's the plan!" Parkes yelled. "Please –!"

"Get him some anaesthetic," said the Queen Mother. Then she turned back to Hamilton. "The balance will be kept. To give him his due, cousin Wilhelm was acting within it. There will be no diplomatic incident. The Prussians will be able to write off Sandels and any others as rogues. We will of course cooperate. The Black Eagle traditionally carry only that knowledge they need for their mission, and will order themselves to die before giving us orders of battle or any other strategic information. But the intelligence from Parkes and any others will give us some small power of potential shame over the Prussians in future months. The Vatican will be bending over backwards for us for some time to come." She took his hand, and he felt the favour on his ring finger impressed with some notes that probably flattered him. He'd read them later. "Major, we will have the fold opened. You will enter it. Save Elizabeth. Kill them all."

They got him a squad of fellow officers, four of them. They met in a trophy room, and sorted out how they'd go and what the rules of engagement would be once they got there. Substitutes for Parkes and his crew had been found from the few sappers present. Parkes had told them that those inside the fold had left a miniscule aerial trailing, but that messages were only to be passed down it in emergencies. No such communications had been sent. They were not aware of the world outside their bolt hole.

Hamilton felt nothing but disgust for a bought man, but he knew that such men told the truth under pressure, especially when they knew the fine detail of what could be done to them.

The false Liz had begun to be picked apart. Her real name would take a long time to discover. She had a maze of intersecting selves inside her head. She must have been as big an investment as the fold. The court physicians who had examined her had been as horrified by what had been done to her as by what she was.

That baffled Hamilton. People like the duplicate had power, to be who they liked. But that power was bought at the cost of damage to the balance of their own souls. What were nations, after all, but a lot of souls who knew who they were and how they liked to live? To be as uncertain as the substitute Liz was to be lost and to endanger others. It went beyond treachery. It was living mixed metaphor. It was as if she had insinuated herself into the cogs of the balance, her puppet strings wrapping around the arteries which supplied hearts and minds.

They gathered in the empty dining room in their dress uniforms. The dinner things had not been cleared away. Nothing had been done. The party had been well and truly crashed. The representatives of the great powers would have vanished back to their embassies and yachts. Mother Valentine would be rooting out the details of who had been paid what inside her party. Excommunications *post mortem* would be issued, and those traitors would burn in hell.

He thought of Liz, and took his gun from the air beside him.

One of the sappers put a device in the floor, and set a timer, saluted and withdrew.

"Up the Green Jackets," said one of the men behind him, and a couple of the others mentioned their own regiments.

Hamilton felt a swell of fear and emotion.

The counter clicked to zero and the hole in the world opened in front of them, and they ran in to it.

There was nobody immediately inside. A floor and curved ceiling of universal boundary material. It wrapped light around it in rainbows that

Paul Cornell

always gave tunnels like this a slightly pantomime feel. It was like the entrance to Saint Nicholas' cave. Or, of course, the vortex sighted upon death, the ladder to the hereafter. Hamilton got that familiar taste in his mouth, a pure adrenal jolt of fear, not the restlessness of combat deferred, but that sensation one got in other universes, of being too far from home, cut off from the godhead.

There was gravity. The Prussians certainly had spent some money.

The party made their way forward. They stepped gently on the edge of the universe. From around the corner of the short tunnel there were sounds.

The other four looked to Hamilton. He took a couple of gentle steps forward, grateful for the softness of his dress uniform shoes. He could hear Elizabeth's voice. Not her words, not from here. She was angry, but engaged. Not defiant in the face of torture. Reasoning with them. A smile passed his lips for a moment. They'd have had a lot of that.

It told him there was no alert, not yet. It was almost impossible to set sensors close to the edge of a fold. This lot must have stood on guard for a couple of hours, heard no alarm from their friends outside, and then had relaxed. They'd have been on the clock, waiting for the time when they would poke their heads out. Hamilton bet there was a man meant to be on guard, but that Liz had pulled him into the conversation too. He could imagine her face, just round that corner, one eye always toward the exit, maybe a couple of buttons undone, claiming it was the heat and excitement. She had a hair knife too, but it would do her no good to use it on just one of them.

He estimated the distance. He counted the other voices, three... four, there was a deeper tone, in German, not the pidgin the other three had been speaking. That would be him. Sandels. He didn't sound like he was part of that conversation. He was angry, ordering, perhaps just back from sleep, wondering what the hell –!

Hamilton stopped all thoughts of Liz. He looked to the others, and they understood they were going to go and go now, trip the alarms and use the emergency against the enemy.

He nodded.

They leapt around the corner, ready for targets.

They expected the blaring horn. They rode it, finding their targets surprised, bodies reacting, reaching for weapons that were in a couple

248

of cases a reach away amongst a kitchen, crates, tinned foods –

Hamilton had made himself know he was going to see Liz, so he didn't react to her, he looked past her –

He ducked, cried out, as an automatic set off by the alarm chopped up the man who had been running beside him, the Green Jacket, gone in a burst of red. Meat all over the cave.

Hamilton reeled, stayed up, tried to pin a target. To left and right ahead, men were falling, flying, two shots in each body, and he was moving too slowly, stumbling, vulnerable –

One man got off a shot, into the ceiling, and then fell, pinned twice, exploding -

Every one of the Prussians gone but –

He found his target.

Sandels. With Elizabeth right in front of him. Covering every bit of his body. He had a gun pushed into her neck. He wasn't looking at his three dead comrades.

The three men who were with Hamilton moved forward, slowly, their gun hands visible, their weapons pointing down.

They were looking to Hamilton again.

He hadn't lowered his gun. He had his target. He was aiming right at Sandels and the Princess.

There was silence.

Liz made eye contact. She had indeed undone those two buttons. She was calm. "Well," she began, "this is very –"

Sandels muttered something and she was quiet again.

Silence.

Sandels laughed, not unpleasantly. Soulful eyes were looking at them from that square face of his, a smile turning the corner of his mouth. He shared the irony that Hamilton had often found in people of their profession.

This was not the awkward absurdity that the soldiers had described. Hamilton realised that he was looking at an alternative. This man was a professional at the same things Hamilton did in the margins of his life. It was the strangeness of the alternative that had alienated the military men. Hamilton was fascinated by him.

"I don't know why I did this," said Sandels, indicating Elizabeth with a sway of the head. "Reflex."

Hamilton nodded to him. They each knew all the other did.

"Perhaps you needed a moment."

"She's a very pretty girl to be wasted on a Swede."

Hamilton could feel Liz not looking at him. "It's not a waste," he said gently. "And you'll refer to Her Royal Highness by her title."

"No offence meant."

"And none taken. But we're in the presence, not in barracks."

"I wish we were."

"I think we all agree there."

"I won't lay down my weapon."

Hamilton didn't do his fellows the dis-service of looking to them for confirmation. "This isn't an execution."

Sandels looked satisfied. "Seal this tunnel afterwards, that should be all we require for passage."

"Not to Berlin, I presume."

"No," said Sandels, "to entirely the opposite."

Hamilton nodded.

"Well, then." Sandels stepped aside from Elizabeth.

Hamilton lowered his weapon and the others readied theirs. It wouldn't be done to aim straight at Sandels. He had his own weapon at hip height. He would bring it up and they would cut him down as he moved.

But Elizabeth hadn't moved. She was pushing back her hair, as if wanting to say something to him before leaving, but lost for the right words.

Hamilton, suddenly aware of how unlikely that was, started to say something.

But Liz had put a hand to Sandels' cheek.

Hamilton saw the fine silver between her fingers.

Sandels fell to the ground thrashing, hoarsely yelling as he deliberately and precisely, as his nervous system was ordering him to, bit off his own tongue. Then the mechanism from the hair knife let him die.

The Princess looked at Hamilton. "It's not a waste," she said.

They sealed the fold as Sandels had asked them to, after the sappers had made an inspection.

Hamilton left them to it. He regarded his duty as done. And no message came to him to say otherwise.

Recklessly, he tried to find Mother Valentine. But she was gone with the rest of the Vatican party, and there weren't even bloodstains left to mark where her feet had trod this evening.

He sat at a table, and tried to pour himself some champagne. He found that the bottle was empty.

His glass was filled by Lord Carney, who sat down next to him. Together, they watched as Elizabeth was joyfully reunited with Bertil. They swung each other round and round, oblivious to all around them. Elizabeth's grandmother smiled at them and looked nowhere else.

"We are watching," said Carney, "the balance incarnate. Or perhaps they'll incarnate it tonight. As I said: if only there were an alternative."

Hamilton drained his glass. "If only," he said, "there *weren't.*"

And he left before Carney could say anything more.

The Copenhagen Interpretation

The best time to see Kastellet is in the evening, when the ancient fortifications are alight with glow worms, a landmark for anyone gazing down on the city as they arrive by carriage. Here stands one of Copenhagen's great parks, its defence complexes, including the home of the Forsvarets Efterretningstjeneste, and a single windmill, decorative rather than functional. The wind comes in hard over the Langeline, and after the sun goes down, the skeleton of the whale that's been grown into the ground resonates in sympathy and gives out a howl that can be heard in Sweden.

Hamilton had arrived on the diplomatic carriage, without papers, and, as etiquette demanded, without weapons or folds, thoroughly out of uniform. He watched the carriage heave itself up into the darkening sky above the park, and bank off to the south west, swaying in the wind, sliding up the fold it made under its running boards. He was certain every detail was being registered by the FLV. You don't look into the diplomatic bag, but you damn well know where the bag goes. He left the park through the healed bronze gates and headed down a flight of steps towards the diplomatic quarter, thinking of nothing. He did that when there were urgent questions he couldn't answer, rather than run them round and round in his head and let them wear away at him.

The streets of Copenhagen. Ladies and gentlemen stepping from carriages, the occasional tricolour of feathers on a hat or, worse, once, tartan over a shoulder. Hamilton found himself reacting, furious. But then he saw it was Campbell. The wearer, a youth in evening wear, was the sort of fool who heard an accent in a bar and took up anything apparently forbidden, in impotent protest against the world. And thus got fleeced by Scotsmen.

He was annoyed at his anger. He had failed to contain himself.

He walked past the façade of the British embassy, with the

Hanoverian regiment on guard, turned a corner and waited in one of those convenient dark streets that form the second map of diplomatic quarters everywhere in the world. After a moment, a door with no external fittings swung open and someone ushered him inside and took his coat.

"The girl arrived at the front door, in some distress. She spoke to one of our Hanoverians, Private Glassman, and became agitated when he couldn't understand her. Then she seems to have decided that none of us should understand her. We tried to put her through the observer inside the hallway, but she wouldn't hear of it." The Ambassador was Bayoumi, a Musselman with grey in his beard. Hamilton had met him once before, at a ball held in a palace balanced on a single wave, grown out of the ocean and held there to mark the presence of royalty from three of the great powers. He had been exactly gracious, as he had to be, making his duty appear weightless. In this place, perhaps that was what he took it to be.

"So she could be armed?" Hamilton had made himself sit down, now he was focusing on the swirls of lacquered gunwood on the surface of the Ambassador's desk.

"She *could* be folded like origami."

"You're sure of the identification?"

"Well…" Hamilton recognized that moment when the diplomatic skills of a continental ambassador unfolded themselves. At least they were present. "Major, if we can, I'd like to get through this without compromising the girl's dignity –"

Hamilton cut him off. "Your people trusted nothing to the courier except a name and *assume* the EM out of here's compromised." Which was shoddy to the point of terrifying. *"What?"*

The ambassador let out a sigh. "I make it a point," he said, "never to ask a lady her age."

They had kept her in the entrance hallway and closed the embassy to all other business that day. Eventually, they had extended the embassy's security bunker to the hallway, created a doorway into it by drilling out the wall, and set up a small room for her inside it. She was separated from the rest of the embassy by a fold, which had light pushed through it, so Hamilton could watch her on an intelligent projection that took up much of a wall in one of the building's many unused office spaces.

Hamilton saw her face, and found he was holding his breath. "Let me in there."

"But if –"

"If she kills me nobody will care. Which is why she won't."

He walked into the room made of space, with a white sheen on the walls for the visual comfort of those inside. He closed the door behind him.

She looked at him. Perhaps she started to recognise him. She wavered with uncertainty.

He sat down opposite her.

She reacted as his gaze took her in, aware that he wasn't looking at her as a stranger should look at a lady. Perhaps that was tipping her towards recognition. Not that that would necessarily be a sign of anything.

The body was definitely that of Lustre Saint Clair: bobbed hair; full mouth; the affectation of spectacles; those warm, hurt eyes.

But she couldn't be more than eighteen. The notes in his eyes confirmed it, beyond all cosmetic possibility.

This was the Lustre Saint Clair he'd known. The Lustre Saint Clair from *fifteen years ago*.

"Is it you?" she said. In Enochian. In Lustre's voice.

He had been fourteen, having left Cork for the first time, indentured in the 4th Dragoons because of his father's debt, proud to finally be able to pay it through his service. He'd had the corners knocked off him and had yet to gain new ones at Keble. Billeted in Warminster, he had been every inch the Gentleman Cadet, forced to find a common society with the other ranks, who tended to laugh at the aristocracy of his Irish accent. They were always asking how many Tories he'd killed, and he'd never found an answer. Years later, he'd come to think he should have told the truth and said two and seen if that would shock them. He'd been acutely conscious of his virginity.

Lustre had been one of the young ladies it was acceptable for him to be seen with in town. Her being older then he was had appealed to Hamilton very much. Especially since she was reticent, shy, unable to overawe him. That had allowed him to be bold. Too bold, on occasion.

They were always seeing and then not seeing each other. She was on his arm at dances, with no need of a card on three occasions, and then supposedly with some other cadet. But Hamilton had always annoyed Lustre by not taking those other suitors seriously, and she had always come back to him. The whole idiocy had taken less than three months, his internal calendar now said, incredibly. But it was years written in stone.

He had never been sure if she was even slightly fond of him until the moment she had initiated him into the mysteries. And they had even fought that night. But they had at least been together after that, for a while, awkward and fearful as that had been.

Lustre was a secretary for Lord Surtees, but she had told Hamilton, during that night of greater intimacy, that this was basically a lie, that she was also a courier, that in her head was the seed for a diplomatic language, that sometimes she would be asked to speak the words that made it grow into her, and then she would know no other language, and be foreign to all countries apart from the dozen people in court and government with whom she could converse. In the event of capture, she would say other words, or her package would force them on her, and she would be left with a language, in thought and memory as well as in speech, spoken by no other, which any other would be unable to learn, and she would be like that unto death, which, cut off from the sum of mankind that made the balance as she would be, would presumably and hopefully soon follow.

She'd said this to him as if she was making an observation about the weather. Not with the detachment that Hamilton had come to admire in his soldiers, but with a fatalism that made him feel sick that night and afraid. He hadn't known whether to believe her. It had been her seeming certainty of how she would end, that night, that had made him react, raise his voice, drag them back into one of their endless grindings of not yet shaped person on person. But in the weeks that followed, he had come to half appreciate those confidences, shrugging aside the terrible burden she put on him, and her weakness in doing so, if it all was true, because of the wonder of her.

He had done many more foolish and terrible things while he was a Cadet. Every now and then he supposed he should have regrets. But what was the point? And yet here was the one thing he hadn't done. He hadn't left that little room above the inn and gone straight back to barracks and asked for an interview with Lieutenant Rashid and told him that this supposed lady had felt able to share the secret of her status. He hadn't done it in all the weeks after.

The one thing he hadn't done, and, like some Greek fate or the recoil from a prayer too few, here it was back for him.

Six months later, Lustre Saint Clair, after she'd followed His Lordship back to London and stopped returning Hamilton's letters, had vanished.

He'd only heard of it because he'd recognised a friend of hers at some ball, had distracted the lady on his arm and gone to pay his respects, and had heard of tears and horrors and none of the girls in Surtees' employ knowing what had become of her.

He'd hidden his reaction then. And ever after. He'd made what inquiries he could. Almost none. He'd found the journals for that day on his plate, and located something about a diplomatic incident between the Court of Saint James' and the Danes, both blaming the other for a 'misunderstanding' that the writer of the piece was duty bound not to go into in any more detail, but was surely the fault of typical Dansk whimsy. Reading between the lines, it was clear that something had been lost, possibly a diplomatic bag. Presumably that bag had contained or been Lustre. And then his regiment had suddenly mustered and he'd been dragged away from it all.

For months, years, it had made him feel sick, starting with a great and sudden fear there at his desk. It had stayed his burden and only gradually declined. But nothing had come of it. As he had risen in the ranks, and started to do out of uniform work, he had quieted his conscience by assuring himself that he had had no concrete detail to impart to his superiors. She had been loose-lipped and awkward with the world. This is not evidence, these are feelings.

That had been the whole of it until that morning. When he had heard her name again, out of Turpin's mouth, when Hamilton had been standing in his office off Horse Guards Parade.

That name, and her seeming return after fifteen years of being assumed dead.

Hamilton had concealed the enormity of his reaction. He was good at that now. His Irish blood was kept in an English jar.

At last he had heard the details he had carefully never asked about since he'd started doing out of uniform work. All those years ago,

Lustre had been sent to Copenhagen on a routine information exchange, intelligence deemed too sensitive to be trusted to the embroidery or anything else that was subject to the whims of man and God. Turpin hadn't told him what the information was, only that it had been marked For Their Majesties, meaning that only the crowned heads of specific great powers and their chosen advisors could hear it. Lustre had been set down in one of the parks, met by members of the Politiets Efterretningstjeneste, and walked to Amalienborg Palace. Presumably. Because she and they never got there. They had simply not arrived, and after an hour of Dansk *laissez faire*, in which time it was presumably thought they might have gone to the pub or had a spot of lunch, the alarms had begun. Nothing had ever been found. There were no witnesses. It had been a perfect abduction, if that was what it was.

The great powers had panicked, Turpin had said. They'd expected the balance to collapse, for war to follow shortly. Armies across the continent and solar system had been dispatched to ports and carriage posts. Hamilton remembered that sudden muster, that his regiment had been sent to kick the mud off their boots in Portsmouth. Which soon had turned into just another exercise. Turpin's predecessor had lost his job as a result of the affair, and shortly after that his life, in a hunting accident which was more of the former than the latter.

Hamilton had known better, this morning, than to say that whatever was in Lustre's head must have extraordinary value, for it to mean the end of the sacred trust of all those in public life, the end of everything. The thought of it had made him feel sick again, tugging on a thread that connected the import of what she'd carried to her willingness to talk.

"Is this matter," he'd asked, "still as sensitive?"

Turpin had nodded. "That's why I'm sending you. And why you're going to be briefed with Enochian. We presume that'll be all she's able to speak, or that's what we hope, and you're going to need to hear what she has to say and act on it there and then. The alternative would be to send a force to get her out of there, and, as of this hour, we're not quite ready to invade Denmark."

His tone had suggested no irony. It was said mad old King Frederik was amused by the idea of his state bringing trouble to the great powers. That he has aspirations to acquisitions in the Solar System beyond the few small rocks that currently had Dansk written through them like bacon.

The warmth of Turpin's trust had supported Hamilton against his old weakness. He'd taken on the language and got into the carriage to cross stormy waters, feeling not prayed for enough, yet unwilling to ask for it, fated and ready to die.

And so here she was. Or was she?

Was she a grown homunculus, with enough passing memory to recognise him? And speak Enochian too? No, surely that was beyond what could be stuffed into such a foul little brain. And assigning such personhood to such an object was beneath even the depths to which the Heeresnachrichtenamt would sink. Was she a real person with grown features to suggest young Lustre? That was entirely possible. But what was the point, when she'd be suspected immediately? Why not make her look the age she was supposed to be?

"Yes," he said in Enochian. "It's me."

"Then... it's true, God's-seen-it. What's been obvious since I... since I got back."

"Back from where?"

"They said someone with authority was coming to see me. Is that you?"

"Yes."

She looked as if she could hardly believe it. "I need protection. Once we're back in Britain –"

"Not until I know –"

"You know as well as I do that this room, this building –!"

"On the way in, when this was a hallway, why didn't you let yourself be observed?"

She took a breath and her mouth formed into a thin line. And suddenly they were back fighting again. Fools. Still. With so much at stake.

He should have told them. They should have sent someone else.

"Listen," she said, "how long has it been since you last saw me?"

"Decade and a half, give or take."

He saw the shock on her face again. It was like she kept getting hurt by the same thing. By the echoes of it. "I saw the dates when I got out. I couldn't believe it. For me it's been... four years... or... no time at all, really."

Hamilton was certain there was nothing that could do this. He shook his head, putting the mystery aside for a moment. "Is the package safe?"

"Typical you, to gallop round. Yes! That's why I didn't take the observer machine! Those things have a reputation, particularly one here. It might have set me babbling."

But that was also what a homunculus or a cover would say. He found he was scowling at her. "Tell me what happened. Everything."

But then a small sound came from beside them. Where a sound couldn't be. It was like a heavy item of furniture being thumped against the wall.

Lustre startled, turned to look –

Hamilton leapt at her.

He felt the sudden fire flare behind him.

And then he was falling upwards, sideways, back down again!

He landed and threw himself sidelong to grab Lustre as she was falling up out of her chair, as it was crashing away from her. The room was battering at his eyes, milky fire, arcing rainbows! Two impact holes, half the chamber billowing from each. An explosion was rushing around the walls towards them!

A shaped charge, Hamilton thought in the part of his mind that was fitted to take apart such things and turn them round, with a fold in the cone to demolish artificially curved space.

Whoever they were, they wanted Lustre or both of them alive.

Hamilton grabbed her round the shoulders and threw her at the door.

She burst it open and stumbled into the sudden gravity of the corridor beyond. He kicked his heels on the spinning chair, and dived through after her.

He fell onto the ground, hard on his shoulder, rolled to his feet, and jumped to slam the door behind them. It did its duty and completed the fold seconds before the explosion rolled straight at it.

There was nobody waiting for them in the hallway.

So they'd been about to enter the fold through the holes they'd blown? They might have found their corpses. It was a mistake, and Hamilton didn't like to feel that his enemy made mistakes. He'd rather assume he was missing something.

He had no gun.

Alarms started up in distant parts of the building. The corridor, he realised, was filling with smoke from above.

There came the sound of running feet, coming down the stairs from above them.

Friend or foe? No way to tell.

The attack had come from outside, but there might have been inside help, might now be combatants pouring in. The front door had held, but then it had been folded to distraction. If they knew enough to use that charge, they might not have even tried it.

Lustre was looking at the only door they could reach before the running feet reached them. It had a sign on it which Hamilton's Danish notations read as 'cellar'.

He threw himself back at the wall, then charged it with his foot. Non-grown wood burst around the lock. He kicked it out. The damage would be seen. He was betting on it not mattering. He swung open the door and found steps beyond. Lustre ran inside, and he closed the door behind them.

He tried a couple of shadowy objects and found something he could lift and put against the door. A tool box. They were in a room of ancient boilers, presumably a backup if the fuel cells failed.

"They'll find –!" Lustre began. But she immediately quieted herself.

He quickly found what he had suspected might be down here, a communications station on the wall. Sometimes when he was out of uniform he carried a small link to the embroidery, usually disguised as a watch to stop anyone from wondering what sort of person would have something like that. But he would never be allowed to bring such kit into a supposedly friendly country. The link on the wall was an internal system. He could only hope it connected to the link on the roof. He could and should have called the FLV. But he couldn't afford to trust the locals now. He couldn't have their systems register an honest call to Buckingham Palace or the building off Horseguards Parade. That would be a sin against the balance. So there was now only one person he could call. If she wasn't in her boudoir, he was dead and Lustre was back in the bag.

He tapped on the connector and blew the right notes into the receiver, hopefully letting the intelligent sound he was connecting to push past any listening ears.

To his relief, Cushion McKenzie came straight on the line,

sounding urgent. Someone in the Palace might have tipped her off as to where he was tonight. "Johnny, what can I do for you?" Her voice came from the roof, the direction reserved for officers.

"Social call for Papa." He could hear the running feet coming along the corridor towards the door. Would they miss the damage in the gathering smoke?

"Extract, package or kill?"

Kill meant him, a stroke that would take his life and erase what he knew, painlessly, he was assured. It was the only way an out of uniform officer could choose to die, self-murder being an option denied to the kit stowed in their heads. Cushion represented herself on the wider shores of the public embroidery as a salonist, but she was also thoroughly job. She'd once walked Hamilton out of Lisbon and into a public carriage with an armed driver, keeping up a stream of chatter that had kept him awake despite the sucking wound in his chest. He'd wanted to send her flowers afterwards, but he couldn't find anything in the *Language of Blooms* volume provided by his regiment that both described how he felt and kept the precious distance of the connection between them.

"Extract," he said.

"Right. Looking."

She was silent for a moment that bore hard on Hamilton's nerves. Whoever was seeking them was now fumbling around like amateurs in front of that door. Perhaps that was why they'd botched the explosives. Hamilton feared amateurs most of all. Amateurs killed you against orders.

"You're in an infested rat hole, Major. You should see what's rolling out on my coffee table. Decades of boltholes and overfolding, hidden and forgotten weapons. None near you, worse luck. If a point time stop opens there and collapses Copenhagen —"

"If we punch out here, will it?"

"Possibly. Never was my favourite city. Preparing."

Something went bump against the door. Then started to push at it. Lustre stepped carefully back from where the bullets would come, and Hamilton realised that, thanks to the length of the comms chord, he had no option but to stand in their way.

He thought of moments with Annie, giving his mind nothing else to do.

The thumping on the door was concerted now. Deliberate.

"Ready," said Cushion.

Hamilton beckoned and then grabbed Lustre to him.

"And in my ear... Colonel Turpin sends his complements."

"I return the Colonel's complements," said Hamilton. "Go."

The hole opened under them with a blaze that might be the city collapsing. Hamilton and Lustre fell into it and down the flashing corridor at the speed of a hurricane. Bullets burst from the splintering door in the distance and tore down the silver butterfly tunnel around them, ricocheting ridiculously past them –

Hamilton wished he had something to shoot back into their bastard faces.

And then they were out, into the blessed air of the night, thrown to the ground by an impossible hole above them –

– that immediately and diplomatically vanished.

Hamilton leapt to his feet, looking round. They were in a side street. Freezing. Darkness. No witnesses. Cushion had managed even that. That was all she was going to be able to do tonight, for him or for any of his brothers and sisters anywhere in the solar system. Turpin had allowed that for him. No, he checked himself, for what was inside Lustre.

He helped Lustre up, and they stared at the end of the street, where passers-by were running to and fro. He could hear the bells of Saint Mary's tolling ten o'clock. In the distance, the embassy was ablaze, and carriages with red lights and bells were flashing through the sky, into the smoke, starting to pump water from their ocean folds into it. Those might well come under fire. And they were the only branch of public life here that was almost certainly innocent of what had just happened. The smell of smoke washed down the street. It would be enough to make Frederik close the airways too. Turpin and Her Majesty the Queen Mother were being asked, in this moment, to consider whether or not the knowledge Lustre had was worth open warfare between Greater Britain and a Dansk court who might well know nothing of all this, who already *knew* those secrets. But rather than let a British carriage in to collect the two of them, they'd spend hours asserting that their own services, riddled with rot as they might be, could handle it.

Across the street was a little inn with grown beef hanging from the roofline, pols music coming from the windows. The crowds would be heading to see the blaze and offer help in the useless way that gentlemen and those who wished to be gentlemen did.

Hamilton grabbed Lustre's hand and ran for the door.

He ordered in Dutch he called up from some regional variation in the back of his head, some of the real beef, potatoes and a bottle of wine, which he had no intention of drinking, but which served as an excuse as to why they wanted a discrete booth to themselves. Lustre looked demure at the landlord, avoiding his glance, a maid led astray. A maid, it suddenly occurred to Hamilton, in clothes that would raise eyebrows in London, being fifteen years out of the fashion. But they had no choice. And besides, this was Denmark.

They vanished into the darkness of their snug. They had a few minutes before the food arrived. They both started talking at once, quietly, so that the landlord wouldn't hear the strange tongue.

She held up a hand and he was silent.

"I'll tell you the whole bit," she said. "Fast as I can. Have you heard of the three quarters of an ounce theory?"

Hamilton shook his head.

"It's folk science, *Golden Book* stuff, the kind of infra religious thing you hear in servant pools. This chap weighed all these dying people, and found, they say, that three quarters of an ounce leaves you at death. That being the weight of the soul."

"Is this really the time for dollymop theology?"

She didn't rise to it. "Now I'm going to tell you something secret, For Their Majesties secret —"

"No —!"

"And if I die and not you, what happens then?" she snapped. "Because just killing me will *not* save the balance!" She'd added an epithet to the word, shocking him at the sound of it in her mouth. "Oh yes, I want to make sure you know that, in case push comes to shove." She didn't give him time to formulate a reply and that was probably a blessing. "What kind of out of uniform man have you become, if you can't live with secrets? I don't care what you're cleared for, it's just *us* at the moment!"

Hamilton finally nodded.

"All right, then. You probably haven't heard either, your reading still presumably not extending beyond the hunting pages, about the astronomical problems concerning galaxies, the distribution of mass therein?"

"What? What is this –?"

"No, of course you haven't. What it comes down to is: galaxies seem to have more mass than they should, loads of it. Nobody knew what it was. It's not visible. By just plotting what it influences, astronomers have made maps of where it all is. For a few years that was the entire business of Herstmonceux. Which I thought odd when I read about it, but now I know why."

The dinner came and they were forced to silence for a moment, just looking at each other. This new determination suited her, Hamilton found himself thinking. As did the harsh language. He felt an old, obscure pain and killed it. The landlord departed with a look of voyeuristic pleasure. "Go on."

"Don't you see? If the three quarter ounce theory is true, there's weight in the world that comes and goes, as if in and out of a fold, up God's sleeve as it were. Put loads of that together –"

Hamilton understood, and the distant enormity of it made him close his eyes. "That's the extra mass in those galaxies."

"And we have a map of it –"

"Which shows where there are minds, actual foreigners from other worlds, out there –!"

"And perhaps nearby."

Hamilton's mind reeled at the horror of it. The potential threat to the balance! Any of the great powers, damn it, any *nation*, could gain immeasurable advantage over its fellows by trading intelligence with foreigners. "And this is what's in your head. The greatest secret of the great powers. But this is old news, they must have found a way to deal with it –"

"Yes. Because, after all, any of them could put together enough telescope time to work it out. As near as I can figure, they shared the info. Every great court knows it at the highest level, so the balance is intact. Just about. I suppose they must have all made a secret agreement not to try to contact these foreigners. Pretty easy to check up on that, given how they all watch each other's embroidery."

Hamilton relaxed. So these were indeed old terrors, already dealt with by wiser heads. "And of course communication is all we're talking about. The distances involved –"

She looked at him like he was an erring child.

"Has one of the powers *broken* the agreement?"

She pursed her lips. "This isn't the work of the great powers."

Hamilton wasn't sure he could take much more of this. "Then who?"

"Have you heard of the heavenly twins?"

"The Ransoms?"

"Yes, Castor and Pollux."

Hamilton's mind was racing. The twins were arms dealers, who sold, it had been revealed a few years ago, to the shock of the great powers, not just to the nation to which they owed allegiance (which, them being from the northern part of the Columbian colonies, would be Britain or France), or even to one they'd later adopted, but to anyone. Once the great powers had found that out and closed ranks, dealing with the twins as they dealt with any threat to the balance, their representatives had vanished overnight from their offices in the world's capitals, and started to sell away from any counter, to rebels, mercenaries, colonies. Whoring out their services. The twins themselves had never shown their faces in public. It was said they had accumulated enough wealth to actually begin to develop new weapons of their own. Every other month some new speculation arose that one of the powers was secretly once more buying from them. Not something Britain would ever do, of course, but the Dutch, the Spaniards? "How are they involved?"

"When I was halfway across this city, on my original mission, a rabbit hole similar to the one we just fell down opened up under me and my honour guard."

"They can do that?"

"Compared to what else they're doing, that's nothing. They had their own soldiers on hand, soldiers in uniform –"

Hamilton could hear the disgust in her voice, and matched it with his own. Tonight was starting to feel like some sort of nightmare, with every certainty collapsing. He felt like he was falling from moment to moment as terrible new possibilities sprang up before his eyes.

"They cut down my party, taking a few losses themselves. They took the bodies with them."

"They must have mopped the place up afterwards too."

"I was dragged before them. I don't know if we were still in this city. I was ready to say the words and cut myself off, but they were ready for that. They injected me with some sort of instant glossolalia. I thought for a second that I'd done it myself, but then I realised that I couldn't stop talking, that I was saying all sorts of nonsense, from anywhere in my mind, ridiculous stuff, shameful stuff." She paused for breath. "You *were* mentioned."

"I wasn't going to ask."

"I didn't talk about what I was carrying. Sheer luck. I wrenched clear of their thugees and tried to bash my brains out against the wall."

He had put his hand on hers. Without even thinking about it.

She let it stay. "I wouldn't recommend it, probably not possible, but they only gave me two cracks at it before they grabbed me again. They were planning to keep injecting me with the stuff until I'd spilled the words that'd let them use an observer to see the map. They locked me up in a room and recorded me all night. That got quite dull quite swiftly."

Listening to her, Hamilton felt himself calm. He was looking forward, with honest glee, to the possibility that he might be soon in a position to harm some of these men.

"I gambled that after it got late enough and I still hadn't said anything *politically* interesting they'd stop watching and just record it. I waited as long as I could with my sanity intact, then had at one of the walls. I found main power and shoved my fingers in. Wish I could tell you more about that, but I don't remember anything from then on until I woke up in what turned out to be a truly enormous void carriage. I came to in the infirmary, connected to all sorts of drugs. My internal clock said it was... four years later... which I took to be an error. I checked the package in my head, but the seals were all intact. I could smell smoke. So I took the drug lines out best I could, hopped out of bed. There were a few others in there, but they were all dead or out of it. Odd looking wounds, like their flesh had been sucked off them. I found more dead bodies in the corridor outside. Staff in that uniform of theirs. There was still somebody driving the thing, because when I checked the internal embroidery, there were three seats taken. I think they were running the absolute minimum staff, just trying to get the thing home, three survivors of whatever had happened. The carriage was throwing up all sorts of false flags and passport deals as we approached Earth orbit from high up above the plane. I went and hid near the bulwark door, and when the carriage arrived at one of the Danish high stations I waited until the rescue party dashed on. Then I wandered out." Her voice took on a pleading edge, as if she was asking if she was still in a dream. "I... took a descent bus and I remember thinking what classy transportation it was, very bells and whistles, especially for the Danes. When I listened in to the embroidery, and checked the log against what I was hearing, I realised... and it took some realising, I can tell you, it took me checking many times..."

Her hand had grasped his, demanding belief.

"It had been four years unconscious for me... but..." She had to take a deep breath, her eyes appealing once again at the astonishing unfairness of it.

"Fifteen years for us," he said. Looking at her now, at how this older woman who had started to teach him about himself had stayed a girl of an age he could never now be seen with in public... the change had been lessened for him because it was how he'd kept her in his memory, but now he saw the size of it. The difference between them now was an index of all he'd done. He shook his head to clear it, to take those dismayed eyes off him. "What does it mean?"

She was about to answer him. But he suddenly realised the music had got louder. He knocked his steak knife from the table to the seat and into his pocket.

Lustre looked shocked at him.

But now a man looking like a typical patron of an inn had looked in at their booth. "Excuse me," he said, in Dutch with an accent Hamilton's eye notes couldn't place, 'do you know where the landlord's gone? I'm meant to have a reservation –"

A little something about the man's expression.

He was getting away with it.

He wasn't.

Hamilton jerked sidelong rather than stand up, sending the knife up into the man's groin. He twisted it out as he grabbed for the belt, throwing him forward as blood burst over the table cloth and he was up and out into the main bar just as the man started screaming –

There was another man, who'd been looking into the kitchen, suddenly angry at a landlord who, expecting the *usual* sort of trouble, had turned up the piped band. He turned now, his hand slapping for a gun at his waist –

Amateurs!

Hamilton threw the bloody knife at his face. In that moment, the man took it to be a throwing knife, and threw up a hand as it glanced off him, but Hamilton had closed the gap between the two of them, and now he swung his shoulder and slammed his fist into the man's neck. The man gurgled and fell, Hamilton grabbed him before he did and beat his hands to the gun.

He didn't use it. The man was desperately clutching at his own throat. Hamilton let him fall.

He swung back to the booth, and saw the other twitching body slide to the floor. Lustre was already squatting to gather that gun too.

He turned to the landlord coming out of the kitchen and pointed the gun at him. "More?"

"No! I'll do anything –!"

"I mean, are there more of *them?*"

"I don't know!" He was telling the truth.

Professionals would have kept everything normal and set up a pheasant shoot when Hamilton had answered a call of nature. So, amateurs, so possibly many of them, possibly searching many inns, possibly not guarding the exits to this one.

It was their only hope.

"All right." He nodded to Lustre. "We're leaving."

He got the landlord to make a noise at the back door, to throw around pots and pans, to slam himself against a cupboard. Gunfire might cut him down at any moment, and he knew it, but damn one Dane in the face of all this.

Hamilton sent Lustre to stand near the front door, then took his gun off covering the landlord and ran at it.

He burst out into the narrow street, into the freezing air, seeking a target –

He fired at the light that was suddenly in his eyes.

But then they were on him. Many of them. He hurt some of them. Possibly fatally. He didn't get off a shot.

He heard no shots from Lustre.

They forced something into his face and at last he had to take a breath of darkness.

Hamilton woke with a start. And the knowledge that he was a fool and a traitor because he was a fool. He wanted to bask in that misery, that he'd failed everyone he cared about. He wanted to lose to it, to let it halt his hopeless trying in favour of certainty.

He must not.

He sought his clock, and found that it was a few hours, not years, later. He'd kept his eyes closed because of the lights. But the light coming at him from all around was diffuse, comfortable.

Whatever situation he found himself in, his options were going to be limited. If there was no escape, if they were indeed in the hands of the enemy, his job now was to kill Lustre and then himself.

He considered that for a moment and was calm about it.

He allowed himself to open his eyes.

He was in what looked like the best room at an inn. Sunlike light shone through what looked like a projection rather than a window. He was dressed in the clothes he'd been wearing on the street. A few serious bruises. He was lying on the bed. He was alone. Nobody had bothered to tuck him in.

The door opened. Hamilton sat up.

It was a waiter, pulling a service trolley into the room. He saw that Hamilton was awake and nodded to him.

Hamilton inclined his head in return.

The waiter took the cover off the trolley, revealing dinner: what looked like real steak and eggs. He placed cutlery appropriately, bowed, and left once more. There was no sound of the door being locked.

Hamilton went to the trolley and looked at the cutlery. He ran his finger on the sharp, serrated edge of the steak knife. There was a message.

He sat down on the bed and ate.

He couldn't help the thoughts that swept through him. He felt them rather than discern them as memories or ideas. He was made from them, after all. They all were, those who kept the balance, those who made sure that the great powers shared the solar system carefully between them, and didn't spin off wildly into a war which everyone knew would be the last. That end of the world would free them all from responsibility, and join them with the kingdom which existed around the universe and inside every miniscule Newton Length. The balance, having collapsed, would crest as a wave again, eventually, and stay there, finally including all who had lived, brought entirely into God. That much rough physics Keble had drummed into him. He'd never found himself wanting the final collapse. It was not to be wished for by mortals, after all. It was the shape of the very existence around them, not something they could choose the moment of. He enjoyed his duty, even enjoyed suffering for it, in a way. That was *meaning*. But concussions like this, explosions against the sides of what he understood, and so many of them, so quickly... No, he wouldn't become fascinated with the way the world around him seemed to be shaking on its foundations. This was just a new aspect to the balance, a new threat to it. It had many manifestations, many configurations. That was a line from some hymn he barely remembered. He would be who he was and do what had to be done.

That thought he heard as words, as the part of himself that had motive and will. He smiled at this restoration of strength and finished his steak.

The moment he'd finished eating, someone came for him.

This one was dressed in the uniform that Lustre had mentioned. Hamilton contained his reaction. To his eyes, it looked halfway to something from a carnival. Bright colours that nevertheless had never seen a battlefield, with no history to be read therein. The man wearing it looked like he'd been trained in a real army, he walked, Hamilton behind him, as if he'd known a parade ground. A former officer, even. One who'd bought himself out or deserted. He ignored Hamilton's attempts to start a conversation. Not questions, because he was already preparing himself for the forthcoming interrogation, and pointless questions were a hole in the dam. Instead Hamilton asked only about the weather, and received just a wry look in return. A wry look from this bastard who'd sold his comrades for a bright coat.

Hamilton gave him a smile, and imagined what he'd do to him, given the chance.

He'd left the knife beside his plate.

The corridors were bright and smooth, made of space, cast with colours and textures for the comfort of those who lived here. Hamilton followed the man to the door of what looked like an office and waited as he knocked on it and was called to enter. The door slid open on its own, as if servants were in short supply.

The chamber they stepped into was enormous. It was a dome, with a projected ceiling, on which could be seen...

Above them was a world. For a moment, Hamilton thought this must be Jupiter, on its night side. But no. He reeled again, without letting his face show it. This was a world he hadn't seen before. Which was impossible. But the notes in his eyes told him the projection was hallmarked as real space, not as an imagined piece of art. The sphere was dark and enormous. Its inky clouds glowed dully like the coals of hell.

"Hey," said a voice from across the room, in a breezy North Columbian accent, "good evening, Major Hamilton. Delighted you could join us."

Hamilton tore his gaze away from the thing above them.

Across the chamber stood two men, one to each side of an enormous fireplace, above which was carved, and Hamilton was sure it had actually been carved, a coat of arms. Normally, the out of uniform man would have recoiled, but he was now in a world of shock, and this latest effrontery couldn't add to it. The arms weren't anything the International Brotherhood of Heralds would have approved of, but something... *personal*... the sort of thing a schoolboy would doodle in his rough book and then crumple before his peers saw it. Arms of one's own! The sheer *presumption*.

The two men were smiling at him, and if he hadn't been before, now Hamilton was ready to hate them. They were smiling as if the coat of arms and the unknown world they claimed was real were a joke. Like their pantomime guards were to Hamilton, though he wondered if these two saw *them* like that.

"Am I addressing the two... Mr. Ransoms?" He looked between them. And found a mystery had been repeated.

The men were both tall, nearly seven footers. They both had thinning hair, the furrowed brows of an academic, and had decided to wear glasses. More ostentation. They were dressed not like gentlemen, but in the sort of thing one of the husbands who came home to those little boxes in Kent might have worn for an evening at the golf club. They were similar in build, but...

One had at least a decade on the other.

And yet –

"These are Castor and Pollux Ransom, yes," said Lustre, from where she stood on the other side of the room. She had a glass of brandy in her hands, which were shaking. "The twins."

Hamilton looked between them. Everything about them was indeed exactly the same, apart from their ages. This must have the same cause as Lustre's situation, but what?

The younger man, Pollux, if Hamilton recalled correctly, separated himself from the fireplace and came to regard him with that same mocking gaze. "I assume that was Enochian for the obvious answer. It's true, Major. We were born, in a place that had the Iroquois name of 'Toronto', but which people like *you* call Fort York, on the same day in 1958."

Hamilton raised an eyebrow. "What's the difference, then? Clean living?"

"Far from it," laughed the older twin. "In either case."

"I guess you'd like some answers," said Pollux. "I'll do my best. You certainly left chaos in your wake. At 9.59pm, the Court of Saint James officially declared Denmark a 'protectorate of His Majesty', and dispatched forces 'in support of King Frederik', whom they allege –"

"They declare," corrected Hamilton.

Pollux laughed. "Oh, let's get the manners right, and never mind the horrors they describe! All right. They *declare* that the mad old bastard has been the victim of some sort of coup, and intend to return him to his throne. A coup very much in the eye of the beholder, I should think. A lie more than a declaration, I'd call it. I wonder if Frederik will survive?"

Hamilton gave no reply. He was pleased to hear it. But this only underlined how important the contents of Lustre's head were.

Pollux continued his explanations with a gesture around him. "We're in a mansion, a perfectly normal one, in lunar orbit." He gestured upwards. "That's an intelligent projection from another of our properties, one considerably beyond the political boundaries of the solar system. We've named that object 'Nemesis'. Because *we* discovered it. It's the sun's twin, much less bright." He shared a smile with Castor. "No metaphor intended." He looked back to Hamilton. "Travelling at the speed of light, it'd take around a year to get there."

"You speak of a property there –" Hamilton wondered if they'd sent some automatic carriage out to the place and were calling it by a lofty name.

"We've got several properties there," said Castor, stepping forward to join his brother. "But I think Pollux was referring to the star itself."

Hamilton knew they were goading him. So he gave them nothing.

"Do you remember the story of Newton and the worm, Major?" asked Pollux, as if they were all sharing the big joke together. But the man wasn't attempting courtesy, his tone of voice scathing, as if addressing a wayward child. "It's part of the balance nursery curriculum in Britain, right? You know, old Isaac's in his garden, an apple falls on his head, he picks it up and sees this tiny worm crawling across its surface, and so he starts thinking about the very small. *Unaligned* historians have sunk almost every detail of that old tale, by the way, but never mind that. Isaac realised that space needs an observer, God, to make reality keep happening when there's none of us around. You know, he's the guy in the forest when the tree falls, and because of him it makes a noise. He's part of the fabric of creation, part of and the motive behind the 'decreed and holy' balance. And the stars and the galaxies and the tremendous distances between them are as they are just because that's how he set up the stage, and that's all there is to it. The balance in our solar system is the diamond at the centre of an ornate setting, the further universe. But it is just a setting. Or at least that's the attitude that great powers academia has always encouraged. It keeps everything fixed. Held down."

"But you know, we're not much for academia, we like to get our hands dirty," said Castor, who sounded a little more affable. "The two of us have our feet planted in the muddy battlefields of mother Earth, where we've made our money, but we've always looked at the stars. Part of our fortune has gone towards the very expensive hobby of first class astronomy. We have telescopes better than any the great powers can boast, placed at various locations around the solar system. We also make engines. A carriage that slides down a fold, altering gravity under itself at every moment, is capable, in the void, of only a certain acceleration. The record keeps inching up, but it's a matter of gaining a few miles an hour because of some technical adjustment. And once you've reached any great acceleration inside the solar system, you're going to need to start decelerating in a few days, because you'll need to slow down at your destination. It wouldn't be out of the question to send an automatic carriage out into the wilds beyond the comet cloud, but somehow nobody's gotten around to doing it."

"That always puzzled us."

"Until we heard whispers about the great secret. Because people talk to us, we sell weapons and buy information. It became clear that for a nation to send such a carriage, to even prepare a vehicle that greatly exceeded records, would be to have every other nation suspect they'd found something out there, and become suddenly aggressive toward them, in a desperate attempt to keep the balance."

Hamilton kept his silence.

"When we stumbled on Nemesis in a photographic survey, we realised that we had found something we had always sought, along with so many other disenfranchised inhabitants of Earth –"

"Land," said Hamilton.

They laughed and applauded like this was a party game. "Exactly," said Castor.

"We tossed a coin," said Pollux, "I was the one who went. With a small staff. I took a carriage with a fold full of supplies, and set it accelerating, using an engine of our own, one limited by *physical* rather than *political* principles. I struck out for a new world. I opened up a new frontier. For *us*, this time. For all the people shut out when the great powers closed down the world –" He noticed that his brother was frowning at him, and visibly reined himself in. "The carriage accelerated until after a year or so we were approaching the speed of light. We discovered, to our shock, that as we did so, the demands on the fold became extraordinary. It seems, incredibly, that there is a speed limit on the universe!"

Hamilton tried to keep his expression even, but knew he was failing. He didn't know how much of this he could believe.

"By my own internal clock, the round trip took four years –"

"But I remained here as fifteen years passed," said Castor. "Because when you approach the speed of light, time slows down. Just for you. Yeah, I know how mad it sounds! It's like God starts looking at you *differently!*"

"And you should see the beauty of it, Major, the rainbows and the darkness and the feeling that one is... finally close to the centre of understanding."

Hamilton licked his dry lips. "Why does all this happen?"

"We don't know, exactly," admitted Castor. "We've approached this as engineers, not theorists. 'God does not flay space', that's what Newton is supposed to have said. He theorised that God provides a frame of reference for all things, relative to Him. But these spooky changes in mass and time depending on speed... That seems to say there's a bit more going on than Newton's miniscule gravitation and miniscule causality!"

Hamilton nodded in the direction of Lustre. "I gather she wasn't on that first trip?"

"No," said Pollux. "That's what I'm coming to. When the carriage started decelerating towards Nemesis, we began to see signs of what we initially took to be a solar system surrounding the star. Only as we got closer did we realise that what we had taken to be small worlds were actually carriages. Ones the size of which human beings have not dreamt. The carriages of foreigners."

Hamilton's mouth set in a line. That these had been the first representatives of humanity! And the foreigners were so close! If any of this could be true. He didn't let his gaze move upwards as if to see them. He could almost feel the balance juddering. It was as if something dear to him was sliding swiftly away, into the void, and only destruction could follow. "So," he said, "you drew alongside and shook hands."

"No," laughed Pollux. "Unfortunately. We could see immediately that there were enormous symbols on the carriages, all the same design, though we couldn't make anything of them. They were kind of... like red birds, but deformed, unfocussed. You needed to see two to realise they were a symbol at all. We approached with all hulloos and flags, and suddenly our embroidery was flooded with what might have been voices, but sounded like low booming sounds. We yelled back and forth, uselessly, for about an hour. We were preparing a diagram to throw into the void in a canister, stick figures handing each other things—"

"I'll bet," said Hamilton.

"— when they switched on lights that just illuminated their insignia. Off, then again. Over and over. It was like they were demanding for us to show ours."

Hamilton pointed at the monstrosity over the fireplace. "Didn't you have that handy?"

"That's a later invention," said Castor, "in response to this very problem."

"When we didn't have any insignia of our own to display," said Pollux, "they started firing at us. Or we assume it was firing. I decided to get out of there, and we resumed acceleration, rounded the star, and headed home."

Hamilton couldn't conceal a smile.

"Before the next expedition," continued Castor, "we built the biggest carriage we could and had the coats of arms painted all over it. But we needed one more thing: something to barter with." He gestured towards Lustre. "The contents of her head, the locations of the missing mass, the weight of all those living minds, a trading map of the heavens. Depending on where the foreigners came from, we might have information they didn't. Or at least we could demonstrate we were in the game. And if one group of foreigners didn't like us, we could go find another."

"But she proved to be made of strong stuff," said Hamilton.

"After she'd tried to shock herself into either death or deadlock, we kept her on ice," said Castor. "We sent her with the staff on the main carriage, in the hope they could find a way to breach her along the way, or maybe offer her to the foreigners as sealed goods." Hamilton was certain the twin was enjoying trying Lustre's modesty with his words. "But their response this time was, if anything, more aggressive. Our people left a number of orbiting automatics, and a number of houses ready for occupation, but barely escaped with their lives."

"It seems they don't like you any more than we do," said Hamilton. "I can understand why you'd want her back. But why am I still alive?"

The twins looked at each other as if they'd come to an unpleasant duty sooner than they would have liked. Castor nodded to the air, the doors opened by themselves, and a number of the pantomime guards strode into the room.

Hamilton controlled his breathing.

"Chain him to the fireplace," said Pollux.

They pulled the shackles from the same folds where Hamilton had been certain they'd kept weapons trained on him. His kind retired, if they did, to simple places, and didn't take kindly to parties in great houses. A room was never a room when you'd worked out of uniform.

They fixed his wrists and ankles to the top of the fireplace, and stripped him. Hamilton wanted to tell Lustre to look away, but he was also determined to not ask for anything he couldn't have. He was going to have to die now, and take a long time about it. "You know your duty," he said.

She looked horribly uncertain back at him.

Pollux nodded again, and a control pedal appeared out of the floor, light flooding with it. He placed his foot on it. "Let's get the formalities out of the way," he said. "We'd give you a staggering amount of money, in carbon, for your cooperation."

Hamilton swore lightly at him.

"And *that's* the problem with the world. All right, I tried. What I'm going to do now is to open a very small fold in front of your genitals. I'll then increase the gravity, until Miss Saint Clair elects to stop using Enochian and says the words that will allow us to observe the package in her mind. Should she cut herself off from the world with her own language, I'll start by pulling off your genitalia, and then move on to various other parts of your body, using folds to staunch the blood flow, killing you slowly while she's forced to watch. Then I'll do the same to her." He looked quickly to Lustre, and for a moment it looked to Hamilton like he was even afraid. "Don't make me do this."

Lustre stood straight and didn't answer.

"Say what you have to say to cut yourself off," said Hamilton. "Say it now."

But, to his fury and horror she maintained the same expression, and just looked quickly between them.

"For God's sake –!" he cried out.

Pollux pressed gently with his foot, and Hamilton tensed at the feel of the fold grabbing his body. It made him recall, horribly, moments with Lustre, and, even worse, moments with Annie. He didn't want that association, so he killed it in his mind. There could be no thoughts of her as he died. It would be like dragging a part of her through this with him. There was no pain, not yet. He reserved his shouts for when there would be. He would use his training, go cursing them, as loud as he could, thus controlling the only thing he could. He was proud to have the chance to manage his death and die for king, country and balance.

Pollux looked again at Lustre, then pressed slightly more. Now there was pain. Hamilton drew in a breath to begin telling this classless bastard what he thought of him –

– when suddenly there came a sound.

Something had crunched against something, far away.

The twins both looked suddenly in the same direction, startled.

Hamilton let out a choked laugh. Whatever this was –

And that had been an explosion!

A projection of a uniformed man flew up onto the wall. "Somehow there are three carriages –!"

"The church bells!" said Hamilton, realising.

Castor ran for the door, joining a great outflowing of guards as they grabbed arms from the walls, but Pollux stayed where he was, a dangerous expression on his face, his foot poised on the pedal. One guard had stayed beside Lustre also, his rifle covering her. "What?"

"The bells of Saint Mary's in Copenhagen. Ten o'clock." He was panting at the pain and the pressure. "You said the city became a British possession at 9.59. While we were falling." He swore at the man who was about to maim him, triumphant. "They must have put a fold in me with a tracker inside, as we fell! Didn't harm the balance if we landed in Britain!"

Pollux snarled and slammed his foot down on the pedal.

Hamilton didn't see what happened in the next few seconds. His vision distorted with the pain, which reached up into his jaw and to the roots of his teeth.

But the next thing he knew, Lustre had slammed a palm against the wall, and his shackles had disappeared. There was a shout of astonishment. The pressure cut off and the pain receded. He was aware of a guard somewhere over there in a pool of blood. Reflexively, he grabbed the rifle Lustre held. She tried to hold onto it, as if uncertain he could use it better than she could. They each scrabbled at it, they only had seconds –!

He was aware of regimental cries converging on the room, bursting through the doors.

He saw, as if down a tunnel, that Pollux was desperately stamping at the pedal, and light had suddenly blazed across his foot again.

Pollux raised his foot, about to slam it down, to use the fold in the centre of the room, opened to its fullest extent, to rip apart Hamilton and everyone else!

Hamilton shoved Lustre aside and in one motion fired.

The top of Pollux's head vanished. His foot spasmed downwards.

It seemed to be moving slowly, to Hamilton's pain dulled eyes.

The sole of the man's shoe connected with the control.

For a moment it looked as if it had done so with enough force that Pollux Ransom would not die alone.

But it must have landed too softly. By some miniscule amount.

The corpse fell aside. Its tormented soul had, a moment before, vanished from the universe.

"That'll be a weight off his mind," said Hamilton.

And then he passed out.

Six weeks later, following some forced healing and forced leave, Hamilton stood once again in front of Turpin. He had been called straight in, rather than return to his regiment. He hadn't seen Lustre since the assault on the mansion. He'd been told that she had been interviewed at length and then returned to the bosom of the diplomatic corps. He assumed that she'd told Turpin's people everything, and that, thus, at the very least, he was out of a job. At the worst, he could find himself at the end of the traitor's noose, struggling in the air above Parliament Square.

He found he couldn't square himself to that. He was full of concerns and impertinent queries. The lack of official reaction so far had been trying his nerves.

But as Turpin ran down what had happened to the various individuals in the mansion, how Castor was now in the cells far beneath this building, and what the origins and fates of the toy soldiers had been, how various out of uniform officers were busy unravelling the threads of the twins' conceits, all over the world, Hamilton gradually began to hope. Surely the blow would have landed before now? King Frederik had been found, hiding or pretending to hide, and had been delighted, once the situation had been starkly explained to him, to have the British return him to his throne. Denmark remained a British protectorate while His Majesty's forces rooted out the last of the conspirators in the pay of the Ransoms. And, since a faction in that court had been found and encouraged that sought to intermarry and unify the kingdoms, perhaps this would remain the case for some considerable while.

"Of course," said Turpin, "they weren't really twins."

Hamilton allowed the surprise to show on his face. "Sir?"

"We've found family trees that suggest they're actually cousins, similar in appearance, with a decade or so between them. We've got carriages on the way to what we're going to call George's Star, and people examining that projection. We don't expect to find anything beyond a single automatic in orbit."

"So... the girl –" He took a chance on referring to her as if he didn't know her, hoping desperately that she'd kept the secret of what he hadn't reported, all those years ago.

"We kept an eye on her after the interviews. She told us she'd learned the access codes for Ransom's embroidery from when she was on that enormous carriage she mentioned. Another thing we tellingly haven't found, by the way, along with any high performance carriages in the Ransom garages. But she hadn't quite got enough detail on the earliest years of Lustre Saint Clair's life. A brilliant cover, a brilliant grown flesh job, but not quite good enough. She faltered a little when we put it to her that, struggling over that gun with you, she was actually trying to save Pollux Ransom's life. We decided to let her out of the coop and see where she led us. As we expected, she realised we were on to her and vanished. Almost certainly into the Russian embassy. Certainly enough that we may find ourselves able to threaten the Czar with some embarrassment. You must have wondered yourself, considering the ease of your escape from the embassy, her reluctance to take the observer machine..." He raised an eyebrow at Hamilton. "Didn't you?"

Hamilton felt dizzy, as if the walls of his world had once more vibrated under an impact. "What were they after?"

"Easy enough to imagine. The Russians would love to see us move forces out of the inner solar system in order to secure an otherwise meaningless territory in the hope that these fictitious foreigners might return. And just in the week or so while we were interviewing her, you should have seen the havoc this story caused at court. The hawks who want to 'win the balance' were all for sending the fleet out there immediately. The doves were at their throats. The Queen Mother had to order everyone to stop discussing it. But fortunately, we soon had an answer for them, confirmed by what we got out of Castor. An elegant fable, wasn't it? The sort of thing Stichen would put together out of the

White Court. I'll bet it was one of his. You know, the strange-looking wounds, red birds, booming sounds, fine fly detail like that. If we hadn't planted that tracker on you, the girl would have had to find some way to signal us herself. Or, less wasteful, you'd have been allowed to escape. Of course, the Ransoms' worldwide network isn't quite the size they made it out to be, not when you subtract all the rubles that are vanishing back to Moscow. But even so, clearing all that out makes the balance a bit safer tonight."

Hamilton didn't know what to say. He stood there on the grown polished wood timbers and looked down at the whorls within whorls. An odd thought struck him. A connection back to the last certainty he recalled feeling. When his world had been set on sturdier foundations. "Ambassador Bayoumi," he said. "Did he make it out?"

"I've no idea. Why do you ask?"

Hamilton found he had no reason in his head, just a great blankness that felt half merciful and half something lost. "I don't know," he said finally. "He seemed kind."

Turpin made a small grunt of a laugh, and looked back to his papers. Hamilton realised that he'd been dismissed. And that the burdens he'd brought with him into the room would not be ended by a noose or a pardon.

As he made his way to the door, Turpin seemed to realise that he hadn't been particularly polite. He looked up again. "I heard the record of what you said to him," he said. "You said nobody would care if she killed you. It's not true, you know."

Hamilton stopped, and tried to read the scarred and stitched face of the man.

"You're greatly valued, Jonathan," said Turpin. "If you weren't, you wouldn't still be here."

A year or so later, Hamilton was woken in the early hours by an urgent tug on the embroidery, a voice that seemed familiar, trying to tell him something, sobbing and yelling in the few seconds before it was cut off.

But he couldn't understand a word it said.

The next morning, there was no record of the exchange.

In the end, Hamilton decided that it must have been a dream.

A Better Way to Die

Cliveden is one of the great houses of Greater Britain. It stands beside the Thames in Buckinghamshire, at the end of the sort of grand avenue that such places kept and made carriages fly up, when carriages were the done thing. In the extensive forests, a Grand Charles tree from the Columbian colonies has been grown into the shape of a guest house. The yew tree walk leads down to a boathouse that has, painted on its ramp, dated, descending notches of where the water once rose, taken at the flood. The ramp has twice now been extended to reach the river. From the house itself, one can look out over the parterre to a one hundred and eighty degree horizon of what were once flood meadows, now seamless farmland. The view of the other half of the world is that which one would expect of a hunting estate. There is a smooth, plunging hill, kept clear to present targets on the horizon, with trees either side, towards which the game can break. There are hides for beaters. There is a balcony that looks down on the yard, from which favours can be thrown and bloods scored. At certain times of the year you will hear the reports of guns, the calling of the hounds and the sohos of those on the chase, unimpeded by fence or ditch. The gutters of the forecourt are there to catch the blood.

Hamilton often worked out of uniform, so he knew the great estates. They were where royalty risked a social life outside of their palaces, still requiring careful eyes beside them. They were where were hauled those individuals who had lost so much of their souls in the great game that they had actually changed sides. Houses like this were where such wretched people would be allowed to unburden themselves, their words helping to reset the balance that their actions had set swinging. Houses like this were also where officers like himself were interviewed following injury or failure. And finally, always finally, they were places from where such as he sometimes did not return. They were the index that ran alongside the London and abroad half of an out of uniform man's life, the margin in which damning notes were made. Such buildings were the physical manifestation of how these things had always been done, the plans of them a noble motto across the English countryside. Those words could be read even if your face was in the mud. Especially then. In the circumstances in which Hamilton now found himself, that thought reassured him. But still, he could not make himself ready to die.

He'd found the invitation on his breakfast table: the name of the estate and a date which was that same day. The handwriting was in the new style, which meant that no hand had been near it, that it had been spoken onto the card as if by God. He could not decide anything based upon it. Except that the confidence of this gesture indicated that, despite everything, those who had power over him still did not doubt who they were and what they could do.

He had picked it up with none of the anticipation he might once have felt, just a dull, resigned dread. This was the answer to a question he hadn't put into words. He had started to feel a deeper anger, nameless, useless, than any he had felt before. He knew what he was owed, but had become increasingly sure he wouldn't receive his due. The fact of him being owed would be seen now as an impertinent gesture on his part, a burden on those who had invested elsewhere. He had one request now, he'd decided, looking at the card in his numb fingers: he would ask to be sent to contribute to some hopeless cause. But perhaps those were only to be found in the blockade now, and if they didn't want him, they especially wouldn't want him there. Still, he'd held onto that thought through dressing appropriately and packing for the country. But then even that hope had started to feel like treachery and cowardice. The condemned man must not have anything to ask of the executioner. That was the beginning of pleading.

And yet hope stayed with him. It played on him. His own balance ate at him as he prepared. A fool, he told himself, would assume he was on his way to Cliveden to be given what he was owed. To at least be thanked for all these years and given a fond farewell. He made sure he was not hoping for that.

Now he watched from the carriage as it swung down towards the avenue that led to Cliveden. He saw nobody in the grounds, not a single worker on the fields. That was extraordinary. Normally, they would be out there in numbers, waving to any carriage from their enormous harvesters and beaters and propulsion horses. Hamilton had no idea how many servants were required to maintain an estate like Cliveden, but it must be numbered in the hundreds. There would traditionally be too many, in fact, "a job for every man and several of those jobs are lounging about just in case" as some wag had put it. On the two occasions when he'd seen an officer die in such places, it had been done (in one case like an accident, in another, and that was a scene he'd take to his grave, like a suicide) in the grounds, away from the eyes of the help. You didn't need to clear them all out. But no, he stopped himself: surely this was just the larger version of what he'd seen at Keble? He was making new horrors for himself with no new evidence.

The carriage settled onto the end of the drive, and Hamilton stepped down onto the gravel. His knee spasmed and he nearly fell. Getting old. He wondered if they were watching this, and killed a thought that he didn't care. He did. He must. It had been an affectation to take a carriage, he realised, when, in moments, these days, he could have walked down a tunnel from his rooms in London. And he'd brought a valise, as if he was unwilling, should he need to dress for dinner, to return there in the same way to do so. He was silently making statements with these actions. Stubborn statements. Like he'd made, as if with the intention of ending his service, that night at Keble. This new realisation angered him more than anything else had. Only fools and criminals didn't know why they did things. It seemed that he was no longer strong enough to hold that fate at bay. To arrive here as someone who bowed to the command of those other voices within one, to pain or desire or selfishness, to have allowed those threats to the balance to have grown within oneself, and to only realise it on this threshold... it was an invitation to the powers in this house to strike him down. And they would be right to do so.

He allowed himself to smile at the relief of that thought. *They would be right to do so.* If he could accept that, all would be well. He had brought the valise. He would not baulk and desperately fly to return it, like a panicked undergraduate. If he suddenly did, or said, or hinted at anything not of his own volition, but that had come out of the other half of him that should be under his control, then the balance could still be restored at the cost of his life. He didn't have to worry about that.

But the thought still came to him: those with his life in their hands didn't seem to value the balance so much these days, did they?

That thought was like a far greater death that lay in wait.

If the world was tempting him into plucking at his own house of cards, it was because that was all everyone seemed to be doing now. He was hesitating on this drive, actually hesitating. He had seen his life as a house of cards.

Perhaps the world was dying too.

Perhaps everyone his age felt that.

But surely nobody had ever felt it in circumstances like these?

The carriage finally moved off. He made himself step forward, looking down at the valise now inescapably in his hand.

He found he had orders in his eyes. He wasn't to go into the house, but into the forest.

He made his way down a winding path to the edge of the woods. It was overcast, but the shadows from inside the forest were slanting at impossible angles, as if somewhere in there someone was lighting a stage.

He walked into the forest.

The path took him past fallen trees, not long ago cut down, by a logger who was now absent. He stopped to listen. The sounds of nature. But no sawing, no distant echo of metal on wood, no great machines. Strange that the effect could be so complete.

He came to the edge of a clearing. Here was where the strange light was coming from. It seemed to be summer here, because the light was from overhead. The air was warmer. Hamilton kept his expression steady. He walked slowly into the centre, and saw the trees that shouldn't be here. He wanted to follow etiquette, but that was difficult when those one was addressing had abandoned propriety. It was as if they had grabbed the ribbon of his duty and then leapt down a well. He felt like bellowing at them. He felt awful that he felt like bellowing at them.

He addressed the tallest of the trees. "You wanted to see me, sir?"

It had been just a few weeks ago that he'd been invited to meet Turpin at Keble. His commanding officer had been a guest of the Warden, and had asked Hamilton to join him at High Table. This had seemed at the time the most natural thing in the world, Keble being where Hamilton himself had been an undergraduate. He'd driven down to Oxford as always, had the Porters fuss over the Morgan as always. He'd stopped for a moment outside the chapel, thinking about Annie; the terrible lack of her. But he could still look at the chapel and take pleasure in it. He'd been satisfied with his composure, then. At that time he'd already been on leave for several weeks. He should have realised that had been suspiciously long. And before that he'd been used for penny ante jobs, sent on them by junior officers, not even allowed to return to the Dragoons, who were themselves on endless exercises in Scotland. He really should have understood, before it had been revealed to him, that he was being kept away from something.

It had been in the Warden's rooms at Keble that Turpin had first appeared in his life, all those years ago, had first asked him about working out of uniform. To some people, he'd said, the balance, the necessary moment by moment weighing and shifting of everything from military strength to personal ethics that kept war from erupting between the great nations and their colonies right across the solar system, was something felt, something in the body. This had been a couple of years before the medical theologians had got to work on how the balance actually was present in the mind. Hamilton had recognised that in himself. Turpin had already been then as Hamilton had always known him, his face a patchwork of grown skin, from where he'd had the corners knocked off him in the side streets of Kiev and the muck-filled trenches of Zimbabwe.

But on entering the Warden's rooms on this later occasion, after decades of service, Hamilton had found himself saluting a different Turpin. His features were smooth, all trace of his experience removed. Hamilton had carefully not reacted. Turpin hadn't offered any comment. "Interesting crowd this evening, Major," he'd said, nodding to indicate those assembled under the Warden's roof. Hamilton had looked. And that had been, now he looked back to it, the moment his own balance had started to slide dangerously towards collapse.

Standing beside the dress uniforms and the evening suits and the clerical collars had been a small deer.

It was not some sort of extraordinary pet. Its gaze had been following the movements of a conversation, and then it was taking part in it, its mouth forming words in a horribly human way. Hamilton had looked quickly over to where a swirl of translucent drapery had been chatting with the Chaplain. Nearby, a circling pillar of... they had actually been continuously falling birds, or not quite birds, but the faux heraldic devices often displayed by the Foreigners whose forces were now encircling the solar system. He'd guessed that the falling was the point, rather than the... He'd wanted to call it a dress... being a celebration of the idea that the Foreigners might flock together and make their plans in great wheeling masses. The pillar held a glass of wine, supported somehow by all those shapes dropping past it. These creatures were all ladies, Hamilton had assumed. Or rather, hoped.

"It's all the rage at the Palace," said Turpin. "It's all relative this, and relative that."

Hamilton hadn't found it in him to make any sensible comment. He'd heard about such things, obviously. Enough to disdain them and move on to some other subject. That the new King had allowed, even encouraged this sort of thing, presumably to the continuing shame of Elizabeth... he'd stopped himself. He was thinking of the Queen, and he could not allow himself to feel so intimate with what she might or might not think of her husband.

"Not your sort of thing?" asked Turpin.

"No, sir."

Turpin paused a moment, considering, and offered a new tack. "The Bodlean is, I believe, now infinite."

"Good for it."

Turpin had nodded towards the corner. "So. What about him?"

He was indicating a young man, talking to a beautiful woman. Hamilton's first thought had been that he was familiar. Then he had realised. And had first found the anger that hadn't left him since. This was what downed Foreigner vessels had brought here. Of course it wouldn't all be used for frippery. Or perhaps now frippery had invaded war.

It had been like looking at the son he'd never had, at his own face without everything time had written on it. There was for a moment a ghost of a thought that they'd taken away from him that moment of seeing a son. That had been the first of the many ghosts.

The hair was darker. The body was thinner, more hips than shoulders. The boy had worn not uniform, but black tie, so they hadn't managed, or perhaps even wished, to get him into the regiment. The young woman the boy was talking to had nudged him, and he had looked towards Hamilton. It was the shock of running into a mirror.

The eyes were the same. He hadn't known what his own expression had been in that instant, but the younger version of him had worn a smile as he made eye contact. It hadn't been in the slightest bit deferential. It wasn't attractive, either. But Hamilton had recognised it. He contained his anger, knowing that this boy would be able to read him like a book. Hamilton had had no idea that such things were now possible. This must be a very secure gathering, for the two of them to be seen together. The boy had expected this. He had been allowed that.

He had turned back to his superior officer with a raised eyebrow. "Who's the girl?"

Turpin had paused for a moment, pleasingly, taken aback by Hamilton's lack of comment about the boy. "Her name is Precious Nothing."

"Parents who like a challenge?"

"Perhaps it was a *memento mori*. She's –"

"With the College of Heralds, yes." Hamilton had seen the colours on her silk scarf, which was one hell of a place to put them.

"Well, only just about, these days. She's a senior Herald, but she's been put on probation."

"Because of him." Hamilton found the idea of a Herald being linked to such a peculiar creature as the boy utterly startling. Heralds decided what breeding was, what families and nations were. The College held the records of every family line, decided upon the details of coats of arms, were the authority on every matter of grand ceremony and inheritance. Of course, every other week now one heard rumours that the College was on the verge of dissolution or denunciation, as they tried and failed to find some new way to protest at the new manners. They seemed continually astonished that His Majesty was being advised this badly. Some of this conflict had even reached the morning plates. But it had always gone by the evening editions. To Hamilton, the idea of parts of the body public fighting each other was like the idea of a man punching himself in the face. It was a physical blasphemy that suited this era as an index of how far it had all gone.

"You really haven't another word to say about him?" Turpin had asked, interrupting his woolgathering.

Hamilton had feigned a moment's thought. "How is he on the range?"

"Reasonable. You were only ever reasonable." He hadn't

emphasised the *you*.

Then the Warden had clinked his glass with a spoon, and the ladies and the gentlemen and the *trompe-l'oeil* and the small deer had gone in to dinner.

Hamilton had been relieved to find that the younger version of himself had gone to the far end of the dining table that stood on a rise at the end of the hall. In any other circumstances, it would have been comforting to be back in this place, with the smell of polish and the candlelight, but as he looked out at the tables of undergraduates, he realised that something was missing. There would normally be numerous servants moving between the rows, delivering plates of food and refilling glasses. Suddenly, he saw just such a meal appearing beside one chattering youth, something which caused the lad no surprise whatsoever. Hamilton had been seated opposite Turpin, and now he looked back to him.

"Hidden service," the senior man said. "Happens in a lot of places now. The servants move through an infinite fold, in effect an empty optional world, beside the real one. One more use for the new engines. And neater, you must admit."

Hamilton didn't feel the need to agree with such young opinions from his old mentor. He was now wondering if the man's new smoothness of face was because this was also a younger version. But no, surely not, here was still the experience, the tone of voice he was used to. Turpin had seen that look. "One of the out of uniform men found it for me," he said, as if he was talking about a carriage. "As soon as the great powers recognised that various of the engines that had fallen into our hands gave us access to optional worlds, outside the balance, the Palace felt it was our lot's duty to start mapping them, to find out where all these open fold tunnels lead. Our regimental hunting parties have been going all over."

Hamilton thought he understood now why he hadn't been included in that effort. "Including another one of you?"

"Several. The original owner of this was only a Newton or so different to the original. Well, in physical terms. Where he came from, a lot of our conflicts didn't happen, hence the smoothness of face. Our lads put him in the bag, and when they got back, connected his mind to an infinite tunnel. Like using a terrier to root out a fox. Once he was out, I moved in, using the same method. Should keep me going for a bit longer."

Hamilton had found himself wondering at that statement. His balance had been thrown by the boy, and so he'd allowed himself the seditious thought, because it had felt not so dangerous then, that Turpin was seeking not, as he said, an extension of his service, but actually tactical advantage at Court. He was now more like those he served were. And never mind the distance that took him from his officers. "What if optional worlds start raiding us in the same way?"

"First thing we thought of. We seem to be unique, at least in all those options nearby. We're the only ones who've encountered the Foreigners. Or they may even only exist in this world. If they do start popping over, we may have to start making treaties with optional Britains rather than raiding them."

"And extending the balance into them?"

Turpin had raised his hands. Perhaps he felt this was beyond his duty or understanding.

"How can there be younger versions of people? How is there an optional world where... I'm... his age?"

"These worlds form in waves, I'm told."

"Like the waves that interfere with each other in this world to create the heights and depths of the balance?"

"Presumably." There had been that impatience with the matter of the balance once more. "Some waves are a bit behind us in time, some a bit forward."

"And there are some options where there are chatty deer and pillars of birds? Or are those just fashions anticipating such stuff?"

"A little bit of both. There's a rather large selection box, all told." Turpin had leaned forward, as if wishing Hamilton would get to the meat of it. And Hamilton had been pleased that it hadn't been him that had taken them there. "Listen, that younger you, he's the first of his kind to be brought over. He's got nobody's mind but his own. He's a whole chap, a volunteer from a world so like ours that there wasn't an iota of difference."

"Except no Foreigners?"

"Exactly."

"And no balance?"

"Yes, yes!"

Hamilton had wondered if Turpin was planning on putting his mind in the boy's skull. But he'd hardly have invited them both to a social occasion first. "If we can do all this now, and I didn't know we could –"

"I'm telling you now under a seal. You'll find, if you look, that your covers have already reacted to my tone of voice. You won't be able to tell anyone any of this." He looked suddenly chagrined at Hamilton's startled look. "Not that you *would*, of course!"

Turpin's manners seemed to have changed with his new body. That had been shocking too, a shock like one felt sometimes at things one had heard were said and done at Court. "If we can do all this now we've got their engines, why can't the Foreigners open a tunnel at the blockade, pop up in Whitehall and have at us?"

"Good question. The great powers have been pondering that. Together." Enough had been made public for Hamilton to understand that there was now a significantly greater degree of cooperation between the courts of the great powers of Europe. The arrival of the Foreigners had forced that, when the haphazard capture of the new engines in various parts of the solar system might otherwise have set the balance rocking. There, he suspected, was the hand of the deity in this. If it was anywhere. "The leading theory at the moment is that, for some reason, the Foreigners forbid, among themselves, the use of optional worlds. That it's a principle of whatever mistaken religion they practice. Optionalism is perhaps just a side effect of what they use as propulsion, but so far we've only made sense of the side effect, and none at all of the propulsion."

"Can we use it to surprise *them*?"

"Working on just that."

This was far more the sort of conversation Hamilton had been used to with his commanding officer. He had found himself regretting his earlier reactions, understanding them, regaining control of himself. Tonight, whatever else it was, was surely planned as a test of his character, and so far he had just about stumbled through. What he *felt* about anything was as beside the point now as it had always been.

Turpin had spent the rest of dinner sounding him out about the myriad aspects of the shared defence strategies being adopted by the 'grand alliance' of great powers. There was some new addition to their ranks every day. Savoy, most recently. There were even rumours the

Turks were going to join. Hamilton had wanted to ask where the balance was in all this. What was going to happen to it if every nation was on the same side? Was the arrival of the Foreigners and their engines, at the same time, the fatal shock, the final moment when the balance would collapse and resolve into some new social or actual reality, as experts in the matter had often hypothesised? Was that what was happening all around them now? He had always conceived of that moment as being grand, somehow, and not a matter of finding wild animals in the Warden's rooms. Or was this just some particularly ferocious swinging of the pendulum, which would resolve itself, as it always had, into a gentler motion?

But Turpin, true to his new form, hadn't mentioned the balance at all, apart from when he'd joined in the grace before the meal. Hamilton had half hoped one of the divines would strike up a debate on the subject. He had known, through the gossip of his maid, Alexandria, that all was not well amongst the clergy, that the next synod at York was going to be rough on His Majesty and his terrifying commonwealth of nations, but there was no sign of that here. These particular clerics were as content to swim amongst this stuff as that Herald had been.

All through the conversation, Hamilton had kept his gaze on his superior. He hadn't wanted to be seen craning his neck to get a look at the younger version of himself. He had continued to affect nonchalance. And hoped he was not projecting affectation. The bell had rung, the students had started to exit, and the Warden had invited his guests back to his rooms for brandy. Turpin had announced that he wanted to talk to someone, and gone ahead.

As Hamilton had entered, the younger man had stepped straight to intercept him. Precious was with him. She had had an interested look on her face. Turpin had already got to the other side of the room, thank God, so there had been nobody to attempt some sort of crass introduction. But Hamilton had known his superior officer's gaze would be upon him now. He still hadn't known what was expected of him. But if this was a game, he was going to win it.

"Major," said the youth. "I can't tell you how much I've been looking forward to this moment."

"I wish I could say the same." That had come out like an insult. So he had kept his jaw firm and damn well let it stand. "Where did they find you?"

The youth had seemed unperturbed. "Oh, in some dusty corridor of what one might still call reality."

"This year's model." Hamilton couldn't help but look at Precious rather than at his younger self. She was looking back at him too. He wondered in how many ways she was comparing them.

"Most people would be full of questions," said the youth.

"It's the nature of innocence to question, the nature of duty to accept."

"And it's the nature of age to be too sure of itself." The boy had been ready to get angry if he felt he had to. He seemed very conscious of his honour. Sure he was being looked at too. Which was why Hamilton had poked him on the nose just then, to see his control, or lack of it. That rationalisation, horribly, had come to Hamilton only after the fact.

Perhaps that was the point of this, to see which of them displayed the most grace? Had the boy been told what fate might await him, if he failed whatever test this was? Could it be that Hamilton was, after all, being allowed to inspect his new... vehicle? Or was this his replacement? He couldn't let himself dwell on that possibility. Hamilton had instead turned politely to Precious. She was petite, with long red hair set off by a green evening dress that... yes, the influence of the optional was here too, the dress had been, or still was, a sunlit meadow. To be in her presence wasn't so much to see it as to be in the presence of it. She was used to being looked at, and sought it. Her freckles didn't look girlish on her, but somehow added to the passionate seriousness of those eyes, which held an expression of tremendous interest, a challenge to the world that equalled that of her dress. She had a welcoming mouth. "So," he'd said, "where did you meet me?"

She'd smiled, but she hadn't laughed. "We were introduced at the College of Heralds. Colonel Turpin brought him to visit. But I note that *we* haven't been."

"You'll have to forgive me. I assumed we had already shared... a degree... of intimacy."

He'd wondered if she would bristle at that. But she had smiled instead of being offended. Still, it had been a forced smile. She wasn't quite on board for the anything goes of the new manners, then. Still a Herald at heart. Hamilton had found something he liked in her. Which should have come, he supposed, as no surprise.

"Why do you think," the boy asked, "that Turpin wanted us to meet?"

"Perhaps he's deciding on a suit, and wants to see both tried on." He had looked back to Precious, as if suggesting she might be doing the same thing. She'd just inclined a fine eyebrow.

The boy had stepped between them then. He had decided on both a need to bring this intangible contest into the physical world, and a way to do it. "Tell me, Major," he said, "do you play cards?"

The Warden, no doubt encouraged by Turpin, had quickly warmed to the notion of a game. The select crowd, who had doubtless now realised what they were looking at when they looked between Hamilton and his younger self, had been intrigued, had talked at the top of their voices about it. He supposed, as the cards were prepared and he'd looked again at the throng, that there were clusters of people like this across Greater Britain now, in the most fashionable salons, changing their shapes and their ages and their appearances and the balance be hanged, and from now on they would all be grabbing at the novel and the extreme like they were bloody Icelandic. Perhaps the blockade had done this. Perhaps they were all starting to dance as the ship went down.

The game, someone had decided, should be clock seconds. Neither he nor the boy knew it. Which again, Hamilton supposed, was no accident. They had each taken a hand of ten from a new deck, one of a series being placed on the table. Hamilton took a glass of comfort while he was at it, a Knappogue Castle, from the Tullamore distillery, a pure pot still whiskey. Nothing served here or at High Table would be the kind of thing that the covers in his head could shrug off. That was the whole point of evenings like this. To get at the reality, that had been the thought, he supposed, back when those invited here had been interested in that. So now he was accepting a disadvantage. The boy, of course, had had to do the same, and, despite Precious' warning glance, had taken the same measure.

The idea was to form tricks of differing value by discarding cards and picking new ones from another pack. But the nature of what constituted a legal trick changed depending on the time, each ten minute arc on the Warden's gilt bronze clock deciding the rules at that given moment. There was also a time limit of a few seconds on how long they could take to play a hand, so one couldn't just sit there waiting until the terrain became favourable. So, Hamilton had realised as they waited for nine o'clock to chime on the chapel bell, one could either hold on to cards for long term advantage, or keep burning one's fuel steadily, playing the averages instead of waiting for some huge coup. Time and meaning in this game were freakishly interconnected. A somewhat garish intelligent projection of the rules was thrown onto the wall behind them, startling the deer. The projection had all the washes of colour and blurred lines that suggested a courtier who was paying too much attention to His Majesty's aesthetic tastes. It was said that the look of the ballroom at Hampton Court now changed depending on where you were in it, often just a blur of movement, as if it was seen from a carriage. Several ladies had already fallen as a result during one of the new dances, which had all struck Hamilton as being graceless gallops where the tempo was continually changing, people might collide at any moment, and it would be hard to tell where anyone was. They had been quick to blame their own shortcomings rather than question he whose perspective made all this. And well they should, of course that was the way they had to behave, what was Hamilton thinking? He had chided himself again.

They had taken up their initial hands. The boy had made eye contact with him again. No smile now. The obvious thing would be for Hamilton to underestimate him. He would not do that. That would be to lie about himself. He had let his eyes move upwards from his seated opponent, and linger, for a moment, where they should not.

"What are you looking at?" asked the boy, without turning to look.

"Nothing," Hamilton had said, and had glanced back to his cards with a precisely calculated raise of his eyebrow.

In the first ten minute round, Hamilton had surged ahead, his opponent failing to score while he put down some obvious, simple tricks. The boy seemed to always be waiting for something that was just one card away. Hamilton had recognised that in himself. That had been something that the service had beaten out of him.

A cheer and the Warden chiming spoon on glass had marked the end of the round, and the boy had immediately thrown down what he'd had but couldn't previously score from, putting him in the lead, and generating another cheer with the flourish of it. Hamilton had wondered if there were any in this crowd who were favouring him, or if to those who came to a party dressed as a mirage, the older version of an individual would be automatically the less interesting. He'd looked again to Precious, and thought he caught something in her expression. Why did he feel she wasn't quite of that opinion? She was biting her bottom lip, her eyes large with the excitement of the game. He'd turned back to the boy. "You know your fables?" he said, to conceal something that was brewing in his cards. "Slow and steady wins the race."

"Yes, the Greeks would be keen on this game." And he'd thrown down the first of a series of quick payoffs, building up a steady lead, trying to force Hamilton to bet on something that might never happen. "It's full of transformations."

"Yet hardly classical."

"What's seen as classical changes with time, just like anything else."

So he seemed to share the opinions that had made his arrival here possible. Or to be willing to join in the chorus, at least. But surely he might feel as if he were still a slave, a chattel taken by a raiding party from an invaded province? There was, after all, something of that in Hamilton himself. Hamilton had risked a glance at Turpin and decided to raise the temperature. "Shall we make it interesting?" Having heard how finely cut the boy's accent was, he had let a little Irish back into his own.

"How much?"

Hamilton had tried to remember what would have broken his bank in his twenties. Not that much less than what would now. Or was that his memory distorting time again? He didn't want to quote something that the boy would consider a trifle. Still, the value of money hadn't changed much over the years, just his concept of what sufficed. "A thousand guineas?" The onlookers made shocked noises. Hamilton had realised his mistake immediately. It looked like he was bullying the boy. Precious was shaking her head at the young man, urging him to throw in his cards. "Or, no, perhaps not, let's say –"

"A thousand guineas." The boy had been roused by that. Of course he had. Hamilton had baited him in front of his girl.

He'd have done the same at that age if Annie were here, might have done the same now. He wouldn't humiliate his younger self by backtracking now. "All right, then."

The next three rounds seemed to go by in a flash. Hamilton and the boy had barely looked up as they drew, considered, threw in, the Warden calling the scores as they did so. Aces were high or low. The order of the court cards, to gasps from a few of those assembled who under pressure revealed a more traditional turn of mind, changed too. And the Ambassador, the Horse and the Devil could sometimes raise or lower the values of the numerals in Cups, Swords, Staves and Coins.

With eleven minutes to go, everyone had surrounded the table where Hamilton and the boy were sweating, looking to their hands and then to each other, grabbing and throwing down, faster and faster. Hamilton was considering how hard it would be for him to take a loss of a thousand. It would mean selling something, perhaps the Morgan. He could deal with that pressure because of his experience, his training. The boy would have the surety and indestructibility of youth, but he had more to lose. His life, even, if he couldn't pay, or if whatever he had here instead of a family or a regiment decided his existence wasn't worth the expenditure. Perhaps his life, at least as a mind in his own body, was dependent, even, on the larger game they were playing tonight, whatever it might be. Hamilton had put aside a twinge of conscience. That was why he'd done this, wasn't it? Not to harm the boy, but to put him off his game. Or *was* that the whole of it? Then he cursed himself for losing his concentration in that second, as he saw, as he threw his hand down, that he could have kept some of those cards a moment more for much greater reward. The crowd cheered at the arrival of the last round and the last rule change. The boy was ahead, marginally. He was barely considering each hand before he threw it in, and now he didn't have to think about what might be round the corner. They had turned the last bend and were sprinting for the finishing line. Hamilton decided that the only way to go was to match him for speed, glimpsing the best hand, throwing in, hoping for better, hoping to push the boy that way too. The Warden shouted the score more and more swiftly. Fumbling fingers on cards became an issue. Hamilton drew level, and had found that all he had in the final seconds was luck. It wouldn't be the first time he'd thrown himself on her mercy. He saw that he had tens of each suit, not the best hand and not the worst, and threw it down with just a moment left to play. The boy had looked at his own hand... and seemed to freeze. Hamilton could see his fingers trembling. Was he waiting, deliberately prolonging the misery? He himself had often been cruel, when a job had given him licence to. The clock hand had thumped round the final three seconds... two... Hamilton was just a point ahead, surely the boy must have something – ? The boy fumbled with the cards and threw down his whole hand with a shout and the chimes of the chapel bell rang out across the room and the Warden rang his glass in unison and everyone had immediately leaned forward to see –

The boy had had nothing. He could have made nothing. And now he was staring at Hamilton, and Precious had stepped forward to defend him, her face furious, never mind that all tradition called for her to move in the opposite direction. And now, like a father, Hamilton had suddenly found he agreed.

"I'm satisfied," Hamilton had begun, "I'll just take one good bottle of –"

"Don't you dare!" bellowed the boy. "Don't you *dare!* I will pay what I owe!" And his voice had been fully Irish now, the sound which Hamilton heard often in his own thoughts and rarely in his speech. And with that the lad had leapt to his feet and had marched out, without properly taking his leave or thanking his host. Precious had stared after him, outraged with the world. But she had not had the indecency in her to follow.

There had been only a brief silence before chatter had filled it.

Hamilton had looked over to the Warden, who was awkwardly closing the plate he'd used to keep the score. He didn't meet Hamilton's gaze. There didn't seem to be much joy in the room at what had happened. It wasn't that this crowd had been on the younger man's side, as such. But there was a sense of something broken. It was as if these people had suddenly discovered, upon being shaken, that a lot had changed, within them and without, and they didn't know what to cheer for any more.

Hamilton had got to his feet and taken a last sip from his glass. He had been pleased, despite everything, to find, a moment later, that Precious had joined him.

"He didn't deserve that," she said.

"No, he didn't. But *deserve* is very rarely in it."

Around them, the party had been breaking up. Farewells were being said. And now Turpin had chosen his moment to wander over. He had placed his hand on Hamilton's shoulder. Hamilton wasn't sure if he remembered his superior officer ever touching him before. Precious had stepped quickly away.

"Bad show," Turpin had said, very quietly.

"I'm sorry, sir. I assumed this was a contest."

"You didn't have to force him into a choice between bankruptcy and disgrace. I was hoping our young Herald here might be led, through her closeness to the lad, to begin a new trend in her College, to bring more of them towards His Majesty's point of view. Win or lose, she'd have felt more taken with him, having seen him prove his mettle. But now she'll be unable to see him and retain her position." Turpin had looked over to where Precious stood, her face, now she thought she was unobserved, betraying a sort of calculation, as if she was working out propriety against length of time waited before she made after the boy. Then he had looked again to Hamilton, shook his head, and gone to take leave of his host.

And, until that card on his breakfast table, that was the last Hamilton had heard from him. Hamilton had said goodnight to his host, had left the Warden's rooms and had gone to the door of the Chapel. And he had found, in the despair that was already sinking into his stomach, that that building was now a horror to him after all.

And now he was here at Cliveden, addressing what he only knew were his superior officer, and an Equerry of the Court of Saint James', and the Crown Secretary of Powers, because the orders in his eyes told him so. They were presumably still back in London, in Turpin's office off Horseguards Parade, or at least part of them was. They were wearing the trees, far across their nation, with no more thought than one might wear a coat.

"Good afternoon, Major." Turpin's voice came from the air around him. "I'm sorry to say... we have a job for you."

The sheer relief made Hamilton unable to speak for a moment. "A... job, sir?"

"You seem, during your encounter with him, to have fathomed the character of your younger self. Just as His Majesty wished you to." That was the Equerry. There would have been a time when the former Queen Mother would have seen to such matters herself, but now she never left her wing of the Palace, and was rumoured to be... Hamilton found himself letting the thought breathe in his mind, his relief giving him licence... people said she was mad now.

"I didn't realise I was acting on His Majesty's service, sir." He hoped his tone didn't convey the knowledge he was sure they both shared, that His Majesty had known as much about it as he had.

"That was of course as he wished. And he wishes to convey that you did well."

"The younger man," Turpin added, "should have dealt better with the pressure you put him under. It was the first sign of what was later revealed." He had a sound in his voice that Hamilton hadn't heard before. He was cornered, apologetic.

"The Palace offered to cover his debt to you," said the tree that was the Crown Secretary, "but, in his pride, the boy refused. We took this as a noble gesture and tried again, made it clear the offer was serious." Hamilton could imagine that whatever pressure he himself had subjected the youth to would be as nothing compared to the Palace 'making something clear'.

"Then," continued Turpin, "he suddenly declared he had the funds. I asked him where he had got them. He told me he'd won at cards. But he was clearly lying. Shortly afterwards I had the pleasure of receiving a surprise visit at my office from His Grace the Earl Marischal, the Duke of Norfolk, on official business as officer of arms at the College of Heralds. He told me that a thousand guineas had gone missing from the College's account at Cuits."

He had taken exactly the right amount of money. Hamilton felt perversely annoyed at the association between the boy's amateurishness and himself. "Did Precious do that for him?" The Herald hadn't seemed capable of such foolishness. Was his younger self really that alluring? It was too tempting a thought to be true.

"Perhaps it was done with information from her, but without her knowledge," said Turpin. "His grace also informed me that the Herald herself had gone missing. Our people inspected her rooms and found signs of a struggle, and a rather shoddy attempt to conceal those signs. The boy himself did not report when instructed."

By now Hamilton had gone beyond feeling impugned by association, and was finding it difficult to conceal his satisfaction. So their golden boy had gone rogue. "Needless to say," he said, "he hasn't paid me."

"I daresay Precious caught him with his hand in the till. An infinite fold had been opened up in her rooms some hours before our people arrived. We found traces of it. We're able to some degree to keep track of where such tunnels end up. Our quarry has fled here, to Cliveden."

"Why?"

"There is... a newly-laid complex of fold tunnels on this estate," said the Equerry, sounding almost apologetic about his Court's fashions. "His Majesty was... is still... planning to summer here, among the optional worlds of his choosing. The College is... still... privy to such sensitive information. Your younger self, Major, is hiding in some optional version of these woods."

The Crown Secretary cleared his throat and there was silence. "His Majesty," he said, "remains intrigued by the concept of bringing optionals into our service. He is minded to wonder if their numbers might serve against the blockade. He would need good reasons to turn aside from this policy. But he is alive to the possibility that such good reasons might be provided."

Hamilton inclined his head. He had been told all outcomes were still allowed. That if he was to bring an astonished youth out of the bushes, protesting a misunderstanding, the boy would be listened to, though possibly that conversation would take place in Cliveden's cellars. Well, then. He had a job to do. He put down his valise and opened it, then wormed his hand quickly through the multiple folds to find his Webley Collapsar and shoulder holster.

"We're keeping a watch on the boundaries," said Turpin. "We've narrowed the realities around him so he can't get out." The quality of light in the clearing changed, and Hamilton was aware that something had been done to the covers in his eyes. "We were trying these out on the boy, soon to be standard issue. It'll enable you to see all the optional worlds around you and move between them, just as he can."

Hamilton finished strapping on his holster, slipped the gun into it, and replaced his jacket. He felt what he had to do to use the new covers and did so. Suddenly, there were people in the clearing, right beside him. He went back to the previous setting, and they vanished again. He'd seen some of the labourers and farm hands, those who kept the estate going. They were, presumably, the least entertaining option for His Majesty and his friends to explore.

"Enter the folds here," said Turpin, "bring back the boy and the Herald, alive if you can." And those last three words had been delivered in a tone that privately suggested to his covers that, as far as Turpin was concerned, all Hamilton's options did indeed remain open. He hadn't seen fit to replace Hamilton's sidearm with any less deadly weapon, after all. These courtiers might not have the military knowledge to be aware of such a decision made through omission. Hamilton looked at the trees giving him orders. The question of what was owed to him because of his service had collapsed into the simplicity of that service continuing. They had all assumed, after all, that he would do his duty. His thoughts of death at their hands had become something from an optional world. He turned and headed into the forest.

"Godspeed, Major," said the Equerry.

Hamilton didn't look back. After a moment, he began to run.

He looked at the map of the estate in his head. He jogged from tree to tree, changed his eyes for a moment, was suddenly lost again. He made himself keep checking the options. He couldn't afford to let the boy take him by surprise.

Had his younger self done this dishonourable thing because the balance wasn't an idea that had been discovered in the optional worlds? That must be what His Majesty was considering, the idea that there was no army to be raised there because his putative subjects from those worlds wouldn't have the required ethical fibre. Perhaps in those worlds the balance simply didn't exist, an indication that those places were less real than this world. Or perhaps the balance spread out somehow across all the worlds, perhaps that was how it endured so many shocks. Perhaps it was simply ambient and hard to fathom in his younger self's existence. He wondered what the boy, therefore, had judged himself against, in his formative years. Did this lack excuse him? It was hard to say whether or not the same rules should apply. If everything was real, if value itself was relative, what did it mean here and now to be an arms dealer, to wear a tartan, to abuse the flag, if those doing so could easily go somewhere else, where different rules applied? That might have been the boy's feeling on being made that miraculous offer of advancement, honour, the interest of a pretty woman, from somewhere aside from his own world. He had, presumably, been dragged from it in the night and had his new horizons made clear to him, over weeks, perhaps months. And if this new world included this strange custom, this desperate ideal about the preservation of order in the face of collapse, well, when in Rome...

But Turpin had said the boy's world was alike to ours in almost every detail, if set a few years back along the wave. And yet they didn't have the balance. The idea that they could get along without it, that their great powers had, presumably through mere accident, in his world still preserved the status quo enough for consciousness and society... well, there was a subversive tidbit. No wonder Turpin felt a little vulnerable at having opened that door. No wonder he himself seemed to be leaning less and less on the balance.

Hamilton chided himself. These musings were not appropriate when in the field. He found his bearings in the forest as it stood, if anything could be said to stand on its own now. He quartered it, and moving as silently as he could, explored the territory down to the river, all the angles of the estate. He found nobody.

He used the covers in his eyes to move to the next nearest option after the servants' world. This would be one of those chosen for His Majesty's sport.

The house was much the same, with a few minor architectural differences. A flag with some sort of meaningless symbol flew over it. Hamilton didn't want to know what it meant. He quartered the ground again, and found only some old men in a uniform he didn't recognise and some young women in entertainingly little. Presumably that situation would get more extraordinary as the season arrived. He wondered if ladies would be brought here, or if they would be offered their own options of tea and mazes.

He changed his eyes again, and this time when he searched he found Columbians walking the paths, that quaint accent that reminded him of watching Shakespeare. These people, as he crouched nearby and listened to them pass, spoke with a horrid lack of care, as if there was nobody to judge them, no enemy opposing them. Some of them would know of the interest of a King in their world, some would surely not. For His Majesty to venture into any of even these carefully chosen worlds should be for him to go on safari, into territory that was not his own. And yet the choice was everything, wasn't it? These worlds must be utterly safe. Unless one of them had the boy in it.

He searched through several worlds. He kept all their meanings at bay. He considered where he would go if he was in the boy's shoes, and in so considering realised there must be something he was missing...

because he couldn't imagine coming here at all. He finally found, among the dozen or so options, somewhere empty. There was no house visible through the trees, the river was in a different place, the height of where he stood above sea level was different, and yet, according to the bare information about where he was on the globe that his covers insisted upon, he was in the same place. He looked slowly around, made sure he was hidden from all angles. Not only was the house gone, there were no houses on the plain, as far as he could see. And there was something... something extraordinary about -

"So they did send you." The voice was his own. It came from up the hillside.

Hamilton couldn't see its source. He stepped to put the trunk of a tree between it and himself. He took the Webley Collapsar from its holster.

"Where's the Herald?" he called.

"You won't find her –"

That told Hamilton she wasn't right there beside him. He dropped to his knee as he swung out from the tree, his left hand on his pistol wrist, and fired at the voice. The report and the whump of the round going off made one sound. And then there was another, a crash of branches as the boy broke cover. Hamilton leapt out and fired twice more at the sound, foliage and undergrowth compacting in instants, momentary pulses of gravity sucking at his clothes, newly focussed light dazzling him like a line of new stars blossoming and then gone in a moment.

Without looking for a result, he swung back behind the tree. Then he listened.

The movement had stopped. Of course it had. He wouldn't have kept moving. He'd have laid there for a few moments, then laid there a bit longer.

He heard small movements from up the hill. With these rounds, it was likely that if the boy was still alive, he was also unwounded. He began to slowly make his way through the trees, making sure he also wasn't going to be where the boy had last placed him. As he walked, he started to wonder about his surroundings. There was indeed something very strange about this empty world. He'd sometimes heard, at parties, at Court, back when he'd been invited, the sort of people who had nothing better to do talking about the glories of nature, about some mysterious poetic energy that looking at the simplicity of it could inspire in them. Hamilton thought, and had once ill-advisedly said, that nature wasn't simple at all, that the billions of edges and details and angled surfaces in any view of it were the essence of complexity, much more so than any of the artefacts of civilisation. To him, nature was cover, and all the better for its detail. Liz... her Royal Highness... had made some joke on that occasion to cover the fact that he'd just bluntly contradicted the French ambassador.

But here was some strange feeling of glory. The trees all around him, the undergrowth he was paying such attention to as he stepped through it, it all seemed to be shouting at him. The colours seemed too bright. Was this some flaw in his covers? No. This was too complete. But it wasn't about simplicity. The objects he saw nearby, even the river glimpsed down there, they were all... there was more detail than he was used to. He recalled a time when he'd injured one of his corneas, the fuzziness of view in one eye, until they'd grown and fitted a new one. It was like he'd suffered from something like that all his life, and now he could see better. God, it would be good to be able to stay here. Such relief and rest would be his.

No. These were dangerous thoughts.

There was a noise ahead of him and he brought the gun up. But he swiftly saw what it was. A fox was staring at him from between two bushes. Of course, he'd been downwind of it, and it had turned to face him in that instant. Better luck than he'd ever had on the hunt. But the eyes on this thing, the sheen of its fur, the intensity of every strand, that he could see from here ...

The fox broke the instant and ran.

Something in the world broke with it and Hamilton hit the ground hard, realising in that moment that his eardrums were resounding and being glad they were resounding because that meant he was still alive, and he threw himself aside as the soil and leaves still fell around him and were sucked suddenly sideways, and he was rolling down the hill, crashing into cover and grabbing the soil to stop himself before the noise had died.

The boy had nearly had him. The boy had the same gun. Of course he had.

He lay there, panting. Then he lay there some more. The boy couldn't be sure he was here or he'd have fired by now. He wondered, ridiculously, for a moment, about the life of the fox. He killed the thought and started to push himself forward on his elbows. He realised, as he did so, that he wasn't injured. This might come down to a lucky shot. It was a contest of blunderbusses and balloons.

He felt, oddly, that it was apt his life should come to this. Then he killed that thought too. It would be more bloody apt if his life came to this then continued after the death of the other fellow.

"You could just stay here." That was the boy again, hard to trace where it was coming from beyond the general direction. He'd placed himself somewhere where the sound was broken, some trees close together, a rock wall.

Hamilton kept looking. "Why do you say that?"

"Don't you know where you are?"

"An optional Britain."

"Hardly, old man." The affectations he'd lost along the way. "It's not a country at all if there's nobody in it."

"I presume His Majesty has been in it. And probably found good hunting."

"As well he might. In heaven."

Hamilton grinned at the oddness of that. "How do you make that out?" It felt as if the boy wanted to debate with his father. Wanted to test the bars of his cage. Perhaps he'd felt like that, at that age, but his own father's failure had meant he never felt able to, or perhaps had never felt the need. A place where there was no identity for him and no reason to do anything? More like the hell with no balance that the boy came from.

"It's more... real... than where either of us are from. And I say it's obviously heaven, because nobody got here."

Hamilton had heard the smile in his voice. "Except us. Are you sure it's not the other place?" A curious thought came to him. "Is that why you want me to stay?"

"I mean that if I went back, they wouldn't search in here. You could wait a few days, go anywhere you want."

Hamilton grimaced at that lack of meaning in the boy's life. "You think I'd abandon my duty?" He had a vision for a moment of being replaced in his life by the younger man. It felt like an invasion of himself. But also there was the frightening feel of temptation to it.

"I wouldn't dream of suggesting that, old man." He meant it, too.

"I mean you could take advantage of this game. They need one of us to die, so..."

Where had he got that idea? Turpin would have liked to see the boy hauled back as a trophy, but the Palace was decidedly lukewarm on the matter, and Hamilton couldn't see any way in which any of the interested parties would be satisfied with the boy, rather than himself, emerging from the forest. "Who told you that?"

A pause. "Are you trying to lie to me?"

"I wouldn't dream of it... old man. I'm just here to bring you back." The boy might assume that Hamilton had been given covers he had not, lies that could fool ears that could detect lies. Or he might know that whatever he had in his head was in advance of anything Hamilton had as standard issue. But they knew each other's voices too well.

There was a sound from a direction Hamilton didn't expect. He turned, but he made himself do it with his gun lowered. There stood the boy. He had his gun lowered too. Hamilton stepped towards him. He allowed himself to make the first honest eye contact he'd had with his younger self. To see that face looking open to him was truly extraordinary, a joy that needed to be held down, a kindness worth crossing the waves that held worlds apart. He took a deep breath of an air that was indeed better than any he'd tasted. Whether or not this was heaven, he could imagine His Majesty walking in it and it giving him ideas of what should belong to him, of hunting endlessly here, with new youth for himself whenever he wished, and younger versions of every courtier and courtesan at his command. There would be, thanks to this boy, if some sort of misunderstanding could be proved, new manners forever. But that was hardly the boy's fault. And in that moment, Hamilton decided to lead him back to the clearing, and to another thing often denied to their kind: explanations.

"I was told," began the boy, "that I could only secure my place in society, in your world, by killing you. That that was why we had been brought together in... different contests."

Hamilton realised that this was exactly what he had once himself imagined. "Who –?"

A shot exactly like his or the boy's rang out across the absolute clarity of the sky. The boy's face bloated, in a moment, his body deformed by the impact, blood and the elements of a name bursting from his mouth. The collapsar shell sucked in again and the body dropped to the ground, emptied.

She stepped forward, lowering her gun. At least she had the grace to look sad. "Miss Nothing," she said.

She was still wearing that bloody dress. She slipped her gun back inside it, hiding it again. She and Hamilton stood looking at each other for a while, until Hamilton understood that if he wanted to shoot her she was going to let him, and angrily holstered his gun.

She immediately started back towards the house. He considered the idea of burying the boy. The absurdity of it made something catch in his throat. He marched after her and caught up. "Damn you. Damn both of us for not seeing you coming." He grabbed her by the arm to stop her. "I take it you were never truly out of favour with the College?"

She looked calmly at him. "We don't mind the idea of raiding optional worlds. We don't mind stealing new bodies for old minds. Up to a point. But we draw the line at *them* replacing *us*. We're the bloody College of Heralds, Major. Without family trees, we'd be out of business."

"And by setting up the boy to look as if he was capable of theft, kidnapping and treachery, to the point of even being a threat to His Majesty –"

"We've proven such replacements to be unreliable. They never had the balance, you see."

"And you're telling me this because –?"

She looked truly sad for him in that moment. She understood him. "Because you're going to let me get away with it."

They emerged into the clearing. As they did so, Precious immediately became the model of a trembling, rescued victim. "He was a monster!" she cried out, supporting herself on Hamilton's arm.

"Was?" asked the voice of Turpin from the trees.

Hamilton kept his expression calm. "The boy is dead now," he said.

About the Author

Paul Cornell is a writer of science fiction and fantasy in prose, comics and television. He's written Doctor Who for the BBC, Batman & Robin for DC, and Wolverine for Marvel. He's won the BSFA Award for his short fiction, the Eagle Award for his comics and shares in a Writer's Guild Award for television. He's one of only two people to be Hugo Award nominated for all three media. His Shadow Police urban fantasy series is out now from Tor and This Damned Band, from Dark Horse, is his latest creator-owned comic.

He can be found online at: http://www.paulcornell.com/
And on Twitter as @paul_cornell

Paradox

Stories inspired by
the Fermi Paradox

Paradox
Edited By Ian Whates

With introduction by astronomer Marek Kukula and Rob Edwards of Royal Observatory Greenwich, and original stories from:

Pat Cadigan, Adam Roberts, Paul Cornell, Mike Resnick, Robert Reed, Tricia Sullivan, Paul di Filippo, Adrian Tchaikovsky, Eric Brown, Keith Brooke, Stephanie Saulter, Mercurio D Rivera, Rachel Armstrong, and more…

The Fermi Paradox is the apparent contradiction between the high probability of extraterrestrial civilizations' existence and the lack of contact with such civilizations.

In Paradox, a selection of the world's leading science fiction authors are joined by physicists and other scientists in writing exciting and original stories inspired by Fermi's famous paradox, daring to ask…

Where Is Everybody?

"*Paradox* lives up to the usual high standards we have come to expect from Newcon Press…. most of the stories here are very good. Four or five are outstanding." – *Amazing Stories*

"Whates has assembled a splendidly diverse collection of stories, ranging from coolly cerebral thought experiments to unashamedly pulpy twist-in-the-tail romps. His real coup, though, is commissioning tales from scientists – space technologist Gerry Webb and biology innovator Rachel Armstrong among them – alongside SF stalwarts."
– *The Financial Times*

IMMANION PRESS
Speculative Fiction

A Different City by Tanith Lee

Night is falling, and shadows are gathering in crowds across the city, bronze and sable, flickering, or still as stone. There is always an audience here, for anything – human, beast or object – that comes close to tell its story, or betray its deadly secret... What now? Heartless unkindness – lust for riches – suppressed hatred and rage honed to a razor–? Or some epic sorrow passed into a silver scream. Above everything, the drifting and unavoidable webs of the spinning City gods. So, will you listen in the shadows, or become yourself a story-teller in the bronze half-light? Or do you have another mission here, in Marcheval?

A new triumphant trio of dark fantasy stories, in the same vein as Tanith Lee's previous imaginary city novels of Paradys and Venus.
ISBN: 978-1-907737-65-7 £10.99, $16.99

Ghosteria 2: The Novel: Zircons May be Mistaken by Tanith Lee

Sometimes when people die, it comes as a great shock. Even to them... A group of the dead linger here, in the yellow dwelling on the hill – once a castle, then a stately home, now falling into ruin. These ghosts drift and mingle, and brood on their lost lives. Death can be caused by so many things – war, pandemics, ordinary murder – even suicide or accident. Even time. But after death, surely, one could hope for peace? Not any more. For with 2020 the New Apocalypse began. Civilisation crashed, and outside this ancient building things terrible, predatory, mindless and unkillable roam and bellow. Now all the lights have gone out for good –Where do you turn?
ISBN: 978-1-907737-63-3 £9.99 $18.99

Also Available: **Ghosteria 1: The Stories** by Tanith Lee
ISBN: 978-1-907737-61-9 £10.99 $19.99
Plus Tanith Lee's cross genre **Colouring Book** series. See our web site for more details.

Immanion Press
http://www.immanion-press.com
info@immanion-press.com

Lightning Source UK Ltd.
Milton Keynes UK
UKOW04f1909070915

258235UK00003B/215/P